PRAISE FOR
JEANETTE BAKER'S
SENSATIONAL ROMANCES

CATRIONA

"Jeanette Baker is rapidly proving herself one of the shining talents of the paranormal genre. *Catriona* is an outstanding blend of past and present that makes for inspiring and irresistible reading!"

—Jill M. Smith, *Romantic Times*

"Catriona . . . comes alive with the paranormal, burning sensuality, and a notable plot of outstanding quality that will have readers eagerly awaiting Ms. Baker's next book. Readers of all genres will cherish this prize."

—*Rendezvous*

"Jeanette Baker has joined the ranks of such award-winning authors as Kristin Hannah, Christina Skye, and Barbara Erskine, who have all striven to create unique stories that blend the reality of history and time so that love will triumph. Baker's *Catriona* and *Legacy* are classics."

—Jody Allen, CompuServe Romance Reviews

LEGACY

"[FOUR STARS]. . . . A fascinating time-travel yarn. Jeanette Baker has woven history and fantasy into a tale about the Murray clan, and about four women of the clan connected through the centuries by a curse first uttered in 1298. . . ."

—Helen Holtzer, *Atlantic Journal*

"Fans of rich and unusual novels are in for a treat and should not miss this truly unique and mesmerizing tale. . . . A marvelous book that is as riveting as it is haunting."

—Jill M. Smith, *Romantic Times*

"Tantalizing. . . . Ms. Baker is a talented writer. . . . [She kept] me intrigued and enthralled. . . . A thought-provoking novel not to be missed."

—*Rendezvous*

"Jeanette Baker's love of Scottish history shines through. . . ."

—*Heartland Critiques*

Books by Jeanette Baker

Irish Lady
Catriona
Legacy

Published by POCKET BOOKS

Jeanette Baker

Irish Lady

POCKET BOOKS

New York London Toronto Sydney Tokyo Singapore

This book is a work of fiction. Names, characters, places and
incidents are products of the author's imagination or are used
fictitiously. Any resemblance to actual events or locales or persons,
living or dead, is entirely coincidental.

An *Original* Publication of POCKET BOOKS

POCKET BOOKS, a division of Simon & Schuster Inc.
1230 Avenue of the Americas, New York, NY 10020

Copyright © 1998 by Jeanette Baker

ISBN: 0-671-01734-9

First Pocket Books printing March 1998

10 9 8 7 6 5 4 3 2 1

POCKET and colophon are registered trademarks of
Simon & Schuster Inc.

Cover art by Peter Fiore

Printed in the U.S.A.

To
Seán O'Faolain, Kevin Toolis, Gerry Adams,
Eamon Collins, John Conroy, Tim Pat Coogan,
Jonathon Stevenson and Seamus Heaney,
without whose works I could not have come to
an understanding of Irish politics.

A very special thank you to Patricia Perry and Jean Stewart, who continue to provide valuable insight and support and who greet every one of my new projects with the same enthusiasm and energy as the first one.

Thanks to:

Kate Collins, my editor, for envisioning this wonderful cover, and to Peter Fiore for creating it.

Loretta Barrett, my agent, whose words of wisdom go above and beyond the call of duty, and to Karen for her immediate response to everything I ask her to do.

Leslie and Lena McCalmont from Whitehead, County Antrim, who, over Irish coffee, put the Northern Irish conflict into perspective and later offered the hospitality of their home to my daughter.

the young man from Derry who, after learning that I was an American, excused himself and decided not to hijack my rented automobile after all.

the RUC officer at the checkpoint at Newry who didn't confiscate my film and didn't ticket me for not wearing my seat belt.

the two men from the Republic who were rating the quality of railroad stations. Without them I may still have been stranded in Rosslare.

Marguerite O'Conor Nash and her daughter Barbara, who made our stay at Clonalis House one of the highlights of my visit.

Mícheál, a history graduate of Trinity University, who on his guided tour of Dublin brought new meaning to the word *storyteller*.

IRISH LADY

Prologue

❦

Nuala, Belfast, Ireland, 1968

Four centuries had passed and yet I had not forgotten the smell of charred wood nor the searing heat of a fire bent on destruction. I opened my eyes and saw the leap of flame against shadow, gutted dwellings, the silhouette of a church steeple outlined against an orange sky—an entire world engulfed in fire.

Painful memories, long repressed, struggled for release. Deliberately I willed them back. I had not come through the shadowy portals of time to relive my past. I came for Meghann, poor lost child that she was, and Michael, too, but mostly Meghann. Michael knew who he was and what he must do. It was Meghann who needed my guidance to find her strength.

Gingerly, I stretched my arms and worked at placing one foot in front of the other. Every muscle ached with fatigue. How strange to feel my body again. I never realized how restricting human form could be, and how heavy, even for a small woman.

I didn't know yet where to find her. That would come later, after my thoughts became hers and hers mine, after we had stepped into each other's minds and traveled there, after she learned to face down the demons that kept her afraid.

She was still very young, and our journey together would be a long one. I admit that I was curious to know her. My own daughter had grown to womanhood without me. Like everyone, I assumed that I would live a long life, but it was not to be. Through Meghann, fate had given me another chance at mothering. It wasn't until I first saw her that I understood why.

When she was grown she would be tall. Centuries and the mixing of bloodlines had muted her coloring. Her hair would not be as red nor her eyes as green as mine. But the bones of her cheeks, the shape of her nose and mouth and the pure, poreless texture of her skin could only have come from me.

She would never replace Chiara, my daughter and Rory's, our child of light and laughter. Meghann was herself, born into this world because of me, a distant ancestor, and that was close enough. From the moment I held out my arms in the burned-out rubble that was her home, and she ran into them, I loved her.

1

London, England, 1994

His Honorable Lord Justice, James Fitzwilliam, watched in fascinated awe as Meghann McCarthy trailed her fingers across the mahogany bar separating the jury box from the rest of the courtroom. Nearly three weeks had passed since she first stood before him proclaiming herself council for the defense. He knew her, of course. Everyone in London's exclusive legal community knew her. But it was the first time she had tried a case in his courtroom.

Meghann Anne McCarthy was something of a legend in British legal circles. An obscure civics student, of the Irish Catholic persuasion, she had made the nearly impossible climb from Queen's University in Belfast to the hallowed halls of Oxford University, where she shocked her professors and fellow students, mostly male, wealthy and titled, by graduating first in her law school class.

Upon commencement she was recruited by the exalted firm of Thorndike and Sutton. Within a year she married the elderly Lord David Sutton and vanished from the judicial world. Five years later, after the death of her husband, she claimed his share of the partnership, redecorated his office, soothed his more conventional clients and established her own reputation. Now she was regarded as one of the finest legal minds in all of England.

All of which Lord Justice Fitzwilliam was quite aware of before the woman stepped into his courtroom. What he hadn't known, what he couldn't have known, what he would never have believed without seeing firsthand, was the way Miss McCarthy manipulated an entire courtroom, himself included.

It wasn't that the woman was strident or domineering, nor was she abrasive or even dramatic. On the contrary, she was gracious and compellingly civil, combining an unschooled elegance of movement, an understated attractiveness with a voice so perfectly pitched, so filled with expressive understanding and compassion that it seemed as if the courtroom had been transported back to another time, a time before radio and television, a time when legend told of a siren's song and the men who fell helpless under her spell.

Good God! Fitzwilliam pressed his eyelids with his thumb and third finger. He hadn't heard a word in ten minutes. Even the prosecution had neglected to voice a single objection. Fitzwilliam didn't blame them, not when the senses of every man in the room were filled with the image of Meghann McCarthy. It was enough to just look at her even when she wore the required masculine wig and black robes of a barrister practicing in the Old Bailey. She couldn't be more than thirty-five. Where, for Christ's sake, had she acquired such technique?

Suddenly, Fitzwilliam was aware of his courtroom. Moments had passed. The silence stretched out, embarrassingly long. Faces looked at him expectantly. Was there a question? His face paled. Good Lord, was he supposed to do something?

As if she could read his mind, Meghann seemed to

understand. Smiling conspiratorially, she called forth that compelling politeness for which she was renowned and repeated her statement. "This rests our case, my lord."

Relieved, Fitzwilliam pounded his gavel. "Very well, then. Defense rests. The jury will begin deliberations immediately."

"Brilliantly done, Meghann, brilliantly done." Cecil Thorndike, junior partner at Thorndike and Sutton, lifted the Sèvres china teacup to his lips and beamed at his companion. "You were inspired today, truly inspired."

Meghann smiled politely and looked out the bay window of the Saint James Hotel. The rain depressed her, as did the gray London streets and the man who insisted on plaguing her with conversation when all she wanted was an anonymous spot to drink her tea in peace.

Deliberately, she closed her mind against Cecil's endless prattle. It wouldn't matter. He always repeated himself. She would get it the second time if she missed it the first. Normally his harmless quirk didn't bother her, but today it grated on nerves already sensitive from the case she had won.

Loman Willard was a killer. Meghann knew it, the judge knew it, the prosecution knew it, even the jurors knew it. Yet, for all that, he would walk free, suffering nothing more than a minimal fine and probation, simply because he was an expatriate Orangeman from Derry and his victim had been Catholic, a despised minority in a majority of Protestants determined to maintain their advantage in the status quo. There was a special place reserved in hell for men like Loman Willard. Most likely there was also a place for their lawyers. Cupar Street had never seemed so far away.

Unconsciously, Meghann rubbed the tips of her fingers across her lips, smoothing the lines into fullness, worrying off the last vestiges of coral lipstick. The haze around her head lifted and she heard Cecil's words. "You're tired. Why not take a holiday? I'll handle your load at the firm."

Meghann stared at him in disbelief. When the day ever came that she needed Cecil Thorndike for anything, she would retire to her house in Surrey and take up breeding hounds.

Cecil occupied a spot on the payroll, nothing more. He was the only son of Theodore Thorndike, original owner and creator of the firm, Thorndike and Sutton. Meghann often marveled at how a genius like Theodore could have produced a son like Cecil. But then she remembered Elizabeth. The late Elizabeth Thorndike, Cecil's mother, had passed her unfortunate genes down to her only living child. How Cecil had ever passed his third levels remained a mystery. The man had the mind of an artichoke, plodding, perennial, mushy, tunnel-visioned and completely devoid of insight. Still, he meant only kindness. Because he was inherently warmhearted and had loyally visited her husband's bedside during that long and painful year before David died, Meghann cared for him deeply.

Because of that, and because of the good manners instinctive to one born in the Six Counties, she smiled graciously and said she would think about it. Years later, looking back at the quiet comfort of that drizzly afternoon, Meghann mentally thanked Cecil Thorndike over and over again from the bottom of her heart, realizing that his sympathetic offer, his plodding mind and the tenacious nature of his personality had made all the difference during those terrifying weeks after Michael's escape from Long Kesh Prison.

Frowning into her bathroom mirror later that evening, Meghann remembered looking critically at the color of her hair. The telltale copper, proclaiming her heritage, was beginning to appear in strands around her temples and forehead again. If she didn't make a salon appointment quickly, her natural color would take over and the dark, burnished elegance of her coiffure would disappear, turning her into a different person, a person she had worked for thirteen years to eradicate, a person who remembered that the civilized, refined people with whom she surrounded herself were capable of acts so horrific, so inhuman, so hate-inspired, so filled with prejudice, that names like Auschwitz and Buchenwald flitted through her mind more than occasionally.

Securing the auburn-tinted cloud on top of her head with a clip, Meghann slipped off her robe and stepped down into the recessed marble tub. Scented water lapped against her knees, closing over her breasts and shoulders as she stretched out full-length in the soothing warmth. Deliberately, with the discipline acquired during weary nights of study in the dimly lit, damp-infested quarters she'd rented while studying for her exams, Meghann closed her mind against the smirking countenance of Loman Willard. She was Meghann McCarthy, Lady Sutton, wealthy widow, respected barrister and major shareholder of the law firm of Thorndike and Sutton. The past was of no consequence. Her two living sisters had emigrated to America, married and become citizens. There was no one left, no one who could possibly matter.

Despite his acquittal, Loman Willard would rot in hell. Meghann knew it with the same pure faith she had known twenty-seven years before when she lifted the white mesh of her First Communion veil and accepted the flat, tasteless wafer of the Body of Christ on her tongue.

It had been almost that long since she had stepped inside a church. Even so, Meghann had great confidence in the wrath of God. Occasionally He exacted his vengeance immediately, mercifully, with a minimum of pain. More often He would wait, allowing the sinner his flush of glory, the rosy, hedonistic glow of premature success. Then, without warning, He would strike as flawlessly and systematically as only a master archer bent on destruction can strike. Either way, justice would be served. Meghann would soak in her bouquet-scented water and leave Loman Willard to God.

The faint ring of the telephone penetrated her thoughts. She tensed, waiting for the shrill second half of the double ring. It came, followed by the professional tones of her housekeeper. Mrs. Hartwell was on until nine, a luxury David had instituted upon their marriage and Meghann continued to allow herself after his death.

A soft knock sounded on the bathroom door. Meghann frowned. Mrs. Hartwell never interrupted her in the bath. "Yes?" she asked with a hint of subtle disapproval in her voice.

"I'm sorry to disturb you, ma'am. But the woman said it was an emergency. She said you would take the call. Her name is Annie Devlin."

Meghann froze, the sponge clutched in her right hand, the bath gel in her left. *Annie Devlin? Good God! Annie Devlin.* The blood left her extremities and her arms sank lifelessly down into the bathwater.

"Lady Sutton?" The housekeeper knocked again. "Will you take the call? Shall I tell her to ring again?"

Words formed inside Meghann's throat but no sound came out. She tried again. The words were hoarse, rasping.

"Lady Sutton? Are you ill?"

Meghann's heart resumed its beating, and the blood pulsed against her throat and wrists. She looked at the wall clock over the towel rack. "Take down her number, please. Tell her I'll call back at half past the hour."

Solid footsteps marched down the hall, stopping at

the phone. Again, Mrs. Hartwell's comforting voice penetrated through the bathroom door. Not until she heard the comforting click of the receiver and the diminishing tap of the housekeeper's soles against the wooden floor did Meghann rouse herself, pulling the purple terry robe from its hook on the door, dropping it in a crumpled heap near the floor mat.

She began reciting the mantra that calmed her nerves and reduced the emotions roiling within her. *"Je suis, tu es, il est, nous sommes, vous êtes, ils sont."* Again and again she conjugated the French verb. *"Je suis, tu es, il est, nous sommes, vous êtes, ils sont."* To feel deeply was dangerous. *"Je suis, tu es, il est, nous sommes, vous êtes, ils sont."* Caring threatened one's sanity. She'd cared for her parents and Michael and David. *"Je suis, tu es, il est, nous sommes, vous êtes, ils sont."* David was different. He was ill. She'd had time to prepare for his death. David had saved her. He had been her sanity.

Again she looked at the clock. Twenty minutes. She had twenty minutes to compose herself, dismiss Mrs. Hartwell for the night, punch in the numbers on the phone pad and hear the voice that would bring it all back, the person she had buried and the life she had left behind, the guns and guard towers, the barbed wire of the Peace Wall that had nothing to do with peace, the internment of Catholics, the late-night searches and the dreadful, inevitable singsong whine of a police car forcing young men to the side of the road to search for weapons, bombs and Irish Republican Army sympathies.

Automatically, Meghann stood and reached for a towel, wrapping the generous length of it around her body before reaching for another to systematically wipe dry her legs, her feet, her arms, the back of her neck and her shoulders. There had never been enough towels at Annie's. Plumbing wasn't reliable in the Falls. Washing was a horrendous chore, and two towels for one person was an act of selfishness not even contemplated by the residents of Clonard.

That person, the person who would no more use a second towel than she would spit on the curbside, the Meggie McCarthy buried beneath a cultured accent, expensive clothing and buffed fingernails, first made her appearance thirty-five years ago. She was the youngest child of a large, unemployed Roman Catholic family living in West Belfast's public housing, one more member of the despised forty-six percent of the population destined to be forever on the dole of the British welfare roles.

Even worse was the Republican inclination of her family. Her grandfather, James Connelly, one of the original thirteen Bloody Sunday martyrs, had been executed for proclaiming Ireland a republic, free and separate from Britain. Her father, Padraic McCarthy, remained a loyal Fenian and member of Sinn Fein during the apathetic years of the fifties and sixties, and all three of her brothers, self-proclaimed IRA members, had done their time in Long Kesh and the H-Blocks, formerly "the Maze," a prison located outside of Belfast on the scenic road that led to the Glens of Antrim.

Armed with cakes and chocolate biscuits, two of her sisters had made monthly pilgrimages to the jail cells to visit their husbands, all political prisoners, all IRA members, all indivisibly harboring a rabid hatred of everything British.

They were dead now, her father, her mother, her brothers, all victims of plastic bullets, those six-inch-long, three-inch-wide missiles condemned by Parliament and the Human Rights Commission for use in the London riots but accepted as commonplace against the Irish Catholic population of Ulster. Lance Cavendish, liberal reporter for the London *Times,* reported that the lethal missiles were projected with deadly force from the guns of Ulster's finest, the

Royal Constabulary, the same pro-union force who shot men in the backs if they crossed into the Shankill at night and who bashed the heads of children carrying rosary beads in the Falls.

They had died, all together on one shattering night, and Annie had taken her in. Gentle, warmhearted Annie, her godmother, the mother of her heart, the woman in whose ample lap she had rocked, at whose table she had worked on her lessons, drunk her tea, consumed a thousand salty, grease-soaked fries, the table where slowly, painfully, over years of unconditional love, the empty hole in her heart had filled and she had smiled and teased and laughed and loved as if the ugly, hate-filled, rampaging crowd had never broken through the Cupar Street barrier and destroyed everything and everyone that was hers.

She had nearly come to terms with the random ugliness of her past when Michael, Annie's son and the light of Meghann's life, didn't come home for three days. And when finally he did, he came with four broad-shouldered, tight-jawed young men dressed in black ski jackets, with telltale bulges in the hip pockets of their denim trousers.

When nineteen-year-old Michael Devlin joined the IRA, Meghann made her decision to leave Belfast. Blessed with a sharp intelligence, she knew, even at fifteen, that there was no future for a Catholic in the Six Counties. Even the name of her school, St. Mary's Hall, condemned her. She resolved to go on to university, first to Queen's and then to England, where no one cared whether one was Catholic or Protestant.

Applying herself, Meghann earned a full scholarship to the Catholic preparatory school and from there, another to Queen's University in Belfast. Her American brother-in-law had provided the supplement that financed her living expenses at Oxford. After Queen's there had been little communication with the Devlins, and after Meghann's marriage, by tacit agreement, the two women lost touch. Not once, during all the years she had lived in Annie's house, had the older woman reminded Meghann of her obligation. Now, it appeared that she was calling in the debt.

Because it was Annie who said, "Please come," she did not hesitate. No matter what had occurred between Michael and Meghann in those long-ago days in the Falls, no matter that she would pull out her pepper spray and run to the other side of the street if he came her way, no matter that the words *terrorist* and *murderer* were badges he proudly wore in the name of a united Ireland, no matter that his words were deleted on national television and that he had spent nearly half his life in jail as a political prisoner, she would come. The idea of living in a world of which Michael was no longer a part brought the swift, driving pain of a loss she could no more dwell on than she could come to terms with.

Two hours later, after personally making all the necessary arrangements, Meghann packed her last pair of socks and zipped up her suitcase. She would take a taxi to Heathrow, fly into Shannon, rent a car under her married name and drive to Belfast, where she would meet with Annie and find out the details of her puzzling summons. Even if she was discovered by British authorities, it wouldn't be difficult to enter the city as Lady Sutton.

Lodging was another matter. Her first inclination had been to stay in the inexpensive Ash-Rowan Town House on Lisburn Road near the university. Upon closer reflection, she decided against it, choosing instead the elegant Culloden Hotel, five miles east of the city in County Down. No one would question her for vacationing in its luxurious surroundings.

Her call to Cecil had been easier than expected. He had been delighted with her decision, agreeing to oversee her clients and postpone any hearings until her return. Now, all there was left to do was write a note to Mrs. Hartwell and wait until eight the next morning, when her taxi would arrive to take her to the airport.

The flight and the drive north were too short. The breath-stealing beauty of dark turf, marsh grass, and boiling clouds stained pink with sunlight, churning and twisting their way across a soft spring sky, filled her senses. Unable to bear the all-consuming beauty of her homeland, Meghann pulled off the road to catch her breath. It was all so achingly familiar, the long-haired sheep blocking the roads, the golden igloo-shaped haystacks, the green hills and jutting peaks of the Cliffs of Mourne, the white Queen Anne's lace, the blood-colored fuchsia bells, the purple foxglove and the golden wild mustard. Fifteen years. Fifteen years since she had seen an Irish spring. Meghann leaned her head against the steering wheel and watched as a single curlew rested momentarily on an updraft, its wings splayed and turned down to follow the wind current. Ireland.

She turned the key and the engine zoomed to life. Maneuvering the finely tuned compact back onto the left side of the road, Meghann turned on the radio. It was early, not even ten. Reaching for the radio dial, she found the news station she wanted. Nigel Wentworth was as straightforward as he was factual. No editorializing for this morning anchor. Meghann preferred her news that way. She resented people who tried to sway her opinion using inconclusive evidence.

At first the words did nothing more than soothe her battered nerves, until a single name jarred her into acute, undivided attention. *"James Killingsworth. James Killingsworth,"* the anchor repeated, *"was murdered last night while entering a taxi after a Labour Party fund-raising event at West Belfast's Europa Hotel. With him were his wife, Pamela, and their ten-year-old daughter, Susan. Susan remains in critical condition at Royal Victoria Hospital."*

Good Lord. James Killingsworth, rising star of the Labour Party and most likely to have been England's next prime minister. Meghann admired him. He was a charismatic and popular liberal who cut through the red tape of politics, disregarded tradition, and did what needed to be done. Against the wishes of his wife, who came from a staunch Unionist family, James had agreed to speak with Sinn Fein's Gerry Adams on the subject of the Nationalist Party's participation in the Irish Peace Initiative. Who would have wanted him dead?

Wentworth's voice carried a thread of excitement, most unusual for the stoic reporter. *"Evidence suggests that the attack was perpetrated in the name of the Irish Republican Army. Michael Devlin of Andersonstown is being held for interrogation at the headquarters of the Royal Ulster Constabulary in Belfast."*

Blood pounded in Meghann's temples and her hands tightened on the wheel until the knuckles showed bone-white through her stretched skin. Somehow she managed to avoid the car coming toward her from the opposite direction. Slowing to a crawl, she forced herself to concentrate on the curves in the road, the construction ahead, the cramp in the arch of her foot resting against the gas pedal, anything but the words spewing from the speaker on the rental car radio.

Years later, when she stopped to recollect this moment, she would wonder why she didn't turn off the radio or pull over and listen until the broadcast was finished. Everything was always so logical in retrospect, when the mind is settled and the heart calm, but when it happens, at the crucial moment, it is all one can do to hold on and pray for an end. And so it was with Meghann. Holding on to the wheel, maneuvering the car through the twisting roads, forcing the panic from her pounding head and trembling hands down through her feet and out of her body was the most she could manage.

Michael Devlin, arrested for the murder of James Killingsworth. The words repeated themselves over and over in her head. Meghann coaxed her multi-taxed mind into the logic for which she earned a staggering salary. Michael was IRA. Michael was Sinn Fein. Michael had killed in defense. No.

Meghann shook her head, disciplined her mind and started over. Michael was IRA. Michael was Sinn Fein. Michael's words were censored from every television screen in Britain. Michael believed in killing for an end to British occupation. Michael had killed for his cause. Dear God. Would he kill James Killingsworth? No.

Again, she forced herself to maintain objectivity. James Killingsworth's politics were liberal. He had campaigned for the removal of British troops from Irish soil. Just two weeks before, he had spoken in Parliament against the enormous expense of housing and feeding a hostile government presence in the North.

Whatever Michael Devlin was, stupid he was not. Without James Killingsworth's influence, Sinn Fein hadn't a prayer of participating in the peace talks. Meghann would speak with Annie and find out why Michael was being held for questioning. All at once, she felt better. It was possible that Michael wasn't involved at all, that his detention was merely a formality because of who he was and who he had been.

Three hours later, after settling into her room at the Culloden, Meghann placed a call to Annie. Her fingers shook as she punched in the numbers that would connect her to Falls Road, to Andersonstown, to Clonard, to her past, a world she had hoped to exorcise forever.

2

Belfast, Northern Ireland, 1994

The beating must be over because Michael no longer felt the blows. He sat tied to a chair, his arms handcuffed behind him. Blood poured from a gash in his forehead. His groin throbbed and his testicles felt swollen bigger than footballs. He could barely see the man standing before him, but he could hear well enough, and what he heard caused the corner of his mouth to turn up in a painful but humorous twitch.

"Enough, Robby." A voice came out of the corner. "They won't recognize him tomorrow. He's not talkin'."

"Bloody Taig," his interrogator growled. "He'll talk when I'm through with him."

"Don't count on it," Michael rasped and was rewarded by a blow to the mouth that knocked several teeth loose and filled his mouth with the familiar, metallic taste of fresh blood. He tried to lift his head, but the effort was too much. After a final unsuccessful attempt, his chin sagged against his chest.

"For Christ sake, Robby," the voice protested.

"Don't kill the man. He's got a lawyer comin' tomorrow. Besides, we'll get nothin' from a corpse."

Michael recognized the frightened tones of the boy who'd arrested him. He was a child, no more than eighteen, but then that was two years above the age when a youth was conscripted into the Republican cause. Childhood was short in the Six Counties, and no one knew it better than the men and women who watched their children sport the colors, regurgitate the jargon and lay down their lives before British tanks and loyalist guns.

His mind faded in and out, depending on the level of pain in his head. It would be too much to hope for a doctor. Men charged with the murder of popular English politicians could hope for nothing more than a cold grave dug in the back of a farmer's bog. Still, he was Michael Devlin and that name stood for something in the world of Irish nationalists.

They said he had a lawyer coming tomorrow. At least he would be kept alive until then. What poor sap would Ulster's finest hire to defend him? Probably an earnest young graduate of Queen's University, eager to try his first case and see justice done. He would be eaten alive by the prosecution. It didn't matter. He wouldn't accept a lawyer. He was a soldier, not a criminal. He needed no defense and didn't recognize the jurisdiction of any English judge in Ireland.

Michael grimaced and moved his right leg. Shooting pains, like the jabbing of a thousand needles, signaled the return of circulation. The peelers' voices, deep in conversation, sounded far away. Michael sighed. He hadn't seen the inside of Castlereagh Interrogation Center or the H-Blocks for nearly three years.

The H-Blocks, those square cells built to house political prisoners just off the M1 motorway, ten miles from Belfast near the town of Lisburn, had never seen a single moment of its twenty years without a member of his family interned there. First there had been his father, then Dominic and Liam, Sean and Niall, Bernadette, Connor, Davie and young Cormack. Every male Devlin in the Six Counties and all, without exception, sentenced by a Diplock Court, those travesties of justice headed by a biased judge who sentenced prisoners without benefit of trial whether or not they had been convicted of a crime.

Either he'd grown soft during his three years of freedom or the peelers had improved their methods of torture. The pain in his side was unbearable and his body refused to cooperate. He should have been unconscious long ago. A wave of vomit rose from his stomach, so violent and all-consuming that his feeble attempts at control were brushed aside like a twig in the eddy of a mighty current. Muscles, tight and angry from abuse, revolted, spewing yellow bile in a four-foot projectile from his mouth to his jailors' feet, coating their shoes and trousers with liquid filth.

"Mick," a soft voice murmured into his ear. "Mick, it's your ma. Can you hear me?"

Michael opened one eye and quickly closed it again. The light was too bright. He tried his voice. It was raspy and thick, but intelligible. "Where am I?"

"In hospital." Annie Devlin patted his hand. "They ruptured your spleen in the beatin'. Lucky for you they're afraid to kill you."

Michael laughed, felt the draw in his cheek and abdomen, decided it was worth it, and laughed again. "How long have I been here?"

"Nearly a week. Y' look much better than y' did in the beginnin'. Meghann would never have recognized you."

Both eyes opened into tiny slits as he focused on his mother's face. Her features floated in a fuzzy blur, but he could make out the brilliant blue of her eyes as they stared down at him.

"Y' haven't mentioned Meghann's name in ten years. Why now?"

"How would you know when I speak of Meggie?" his mother retorted. "Yer never home."

Michael reached out and gripped his mother's wrist. "What have y' done, Ma?"

"They've accused y' of murdering James Killingsworth, Michael. I had no choice. I sent for Meggie."

He released her arm and swore fluently. Annie watched him, saying nothing, allowing his barrage of anger to rise, sweep through him, peak and dissipate. Michael had always been this way, quick-tempered, passionate, argumentative, intuitive, fiercely loyal. He was also forgiving, courageous, charismatic, a leader of men, a believer in miracles—"all heart," her late husband used to say.

Michael *was* all heart, or at least he had been until that day, twelve years ago, when Meghann McCarthy's picture had appeared in the London *Times* as the bride of Lord David Sutton. At first, Annie hadn't realized what Meggie's marriage had done to Michael. It wasn't until nearly six months later, when Bernadette came home for a visit, that she recognized it for what it was.

Bernadette was eight years Michael's senior but of all Annie's nine children, she was most like him. They were black-haired and round-eyed, typical shanty Irish, but beneath their fine-boned, sharp-cheeked beauty lay a shimmering brightness that went beyond straight teeth and clear skin, a shining, ethereal glow that artists ached to capture but never could. Even their photographs were different from the others'. Bernadette was the only girl, so it was natural that Annie should be partial to her unusual, slender-hipped beauty. But there was no logical explanation for the way every eye, including her own, singled out Michael in a Devlin family photo.

Clear and blue-green as the Irish Sea, his eyes, set above a prominent Roman nose and a mouth only

God could have shaped, laughed back at her. He was six feet, tall for a Devlin, and wiry thin, with straight shoulders, a deep chest and narrow hips. People were drawn to him just as they were to Bernadette. They were ambitious, these two middle children, more so than the others.

Only Michael and Bernadette had finished their schooling and gone on for university degrees, courtesy of the British Empire. Of course it was absurd for a Catholic to be ambitious in the Six Counties. Those who were, emigrated to the mainland or America. Bernadette had settled with a husband and children. Perhaps it would be better for Michael if he made his home away from Ireland. When the two were together, there had been no peace in the house, until the winter of Meghann's wedding.

At first Annie had brushed aside her misgivings, explaining away the change in Michael as maturity. He had grown up. It was past time to give up that boisterous, laughing gregariousness that lured every drunk from the pubs home to the Clonard for a wash and a fry. She had always expected more from Michael. Gifted in his field, he had produced several published volumes of poetry, two novels and multitudes of essays featured in *The Irish Press* and other periodicals, none published in the United Kingdom, of course. He was Sinn Fein, as were all the men and women of her family. No one belonging to Sinn Fein had ever been allowed a voice outside the Republic. She had reconciled herself to a lifetime of monthly visits to Long Kesh, rationalizing with her usual wry humor that as long as her children were in prison they were safe from RUC bullets. After all, beatings were better than funerals.

But when Bernadette came home and the two of them were seated together in their old place near the Aga, she realized that something was missing in Michael, something that had nothing to do with maturity. The eagerness, the laughing optimism, the magical flame that had illuminated him from birth was gone. Seeing it burn in the bright eyes and quick hands of her only daughter, its absence in Michael was all the more evident. Concentrating on exactly when the change had occurred, Annie realized that it had been missing for quite some time.

She pinpointed it to the day Michael came home with the *Times*. He rarely bought the London *Times*, preferring to read it at the library and not contribute to a British newspaper. But today he placed it on the table before her. Annie noticed that his hands shook and his face was pale even for winter. Ignoring the paper, she'd felt his forehead for fever but there was none. It wasn't until later in the evening, after the meal was cleared and the dishes put away, after Michael had gone out to one of his endless meetings, that she sat down with the paper.

It shook her, of course, but not as much as it should have. Meggie was different. She'd always been different. Causes held no allure for her. Annie had seen it from the beginning. The silent, terrified child from Cupar Street had no desire to avenge the murder of her family. All she wanted, all she had ever wanted, was a peaceful place to fit in. She'd found it in the heart of the Devlin family.

There was a time when Annie believed that Meghann and Michael would make a match of it. He was four years older, but Meghann was mature and lovely in a way that was nothing like the vivid blue-eyed Devlins. Annie never knew whether she had been mistaken in the long looks exchanged between her son and her foster daughter or whether something had happened that caused Meghann to bury herself in her books, accept the scholarship that moved her away from Clonard and the Falls to London and a world as far away in culture and temperament from the Six Counties as was humanly possible.

After she realized the true nature of her son's feelings, Annie resolved, for both their sakes, to forget she had ever known Meghann McCarthy. Until now she had kept her promise. Meghann had been widowed for a long time and Michael had never married. Annie knew the stakes were high but she had little choice. Personal feelings were of no consequence when weighed against a man's life, especially when that man was her son.

Michael had been silent for a long time. One arm was thrown over his eyes and the other ended in a clenched fist by his side. "Are y' finished with yer sulkin'?" his mother asked.

"Why would she agree t' come?"

"If y' have to ask that, then y' don't know Meghann."

His laugh was bitter, twisted. "I'll not argue that point. When did any of us know her?"

Annie looked down at her hands. Time was running short. He had to accept Meghann's help. "I had no idea y' were so angry," she said softly.

"And why not?" He pulled himself up against the pillows, grimacing against the pain. "She lived with us for years, accepting our food, our lodging, our friendship, and then she betrayed us by becoming English t' the core."

"I'm not angry, Michael," his mother reminded him. "Meghann saw her family and neighbors murdered, her home burned. I understand her choice. Perhaps she felt she had no other."

"She had another," he muttered, closing his eyes once again.

"Did she?"

"Aye."

Annie waited, but this time Michael had finished. "Well, then," she said crisply. "I'm sure y'll remind her of that when she comes. I suggest y' change yer attitude, Michael Devlin. Because this time y're in more trouble than you've ever been. This isn't ten years in the Maze, my son. This time they want you t' move in permanently. And if Meghann McCarthy was nothing more than a Catholic solicitor practicin' in Belfast, y' wouldn't have a prayer of a chance. So count yer blessings. Y've a few more days before they release you. Meggie will see y' after y've been transferred back t' the Maze."

With that, she leaned over, kissed his cheek and left the room.

Michael shifted his body so that he lay flat on the bed once again. The light from the window told him it was late afternoon. He remembered that the season was spring. It had been a late afternoon that spring when Meghann no longer smiled at him or talked to him or even acknowledged his presence. Soon after, she'd earned a scholarship to Saint Louise's Catholic Preparatory for girls. She planned it so that her visits home no longer coincided with his and after her term at Queens, she never came home again.

He knew why, of course. He had always known why. Meghann was as opposed to violence as he had been convinced of its necessity. But he never imagined that she would put him away, out of her mind and heart and memory, as surely and completely as she had the tragedy of Cupar Street when the loyalists revolted, burning and killing women and children while the police, Belfast's RUC, and British soldiers stood by and did nothing.

At first, Michael believed that he could change her mind. But she continued to elude him until one day, determined to speak to her, he waited from morning until nearly dark, his collar turned up against the rain, in front of her lodgings at the university.

She came alone, as he knew she would. He never suspected a rival or even a friend. Meghann had no time for relationships. She was driven to earn her degree and escape the curse of Northern Ireland. Wrapped in a knee-length belted raincoat, her face hidden beneath her umbrella, she didn't see him until she was almost on top of him. Without a word, he reached out and grasped the umbrella handle, transferring it from her hand to his.

"My goodness. *Dia duit*, Michael." She laughed self-consciously. "You're the last person I expected to see."

He returned her greeting in the Irish they'd learned as their first language. *"Dia is Muire Duit*. Now, why is that, Meggie, my love?"

Meghann ignored his question, fumbled for her key, unlocked the door and left it open. He followed her inside, closed the door behind him, folded the umbrella and left it in the hall.

"I'll make tea," she called back from the kitchen. "Is everything all right at home?"

"Ma's grand. The others are the same as always." He followed her through the shabby studio flat and stood in the doorway, watching as she spooned tea leaves into the pot and added hot water. "It's been a long time since anyone's heard from you."

"Not really. I met Annie for tea two weeks ago."

Michael digested that interesting bit of information. "She didn't mention it."

Meghann poured the tea, took several biscuits from a tin on the counter and set them out on a plate. Then she motioned him to the table. "What are y' really doing here, Michael?" she asked, fixing her gold-flecked eyes on his face.

He stirred milk and sugar into his cup. He'd intended to bait her, to draw her out until she lost her temper and admitted she would have nothing to do with an IRA man. The way to Meggie's soul had always been through her temper. She was slow to anger but when it hit, everything in her mind was blazingly, furiously evident. Without the rage that slow-burned within her, Michael knew he didn't have a chance at making her see there was nothing less that an Irishman could do and still call himself a man. She wouldn't want him if he were anything less. He had to make her see. But first he had to reach her. "Do y' realize this is the first time in two years that we've been alone together?"

"Surely you're mistaken."

Michael shook his head. "No. I'm not. Are y' deliberately avoiding me?"

"Of course not."

"Then why haven't y' come home?"

"I'm studying, Michael, and working." He watched her hands. Not a tremor to them. "There isn't time for everything."

"Shouldn't old friends be a priority?"

Again, her eyes met his. "I told you that I met your mother for tea, and Bernadette calls me every week. Perhaps it's you who don't go home enough."

Her words shook him. She'd kept up with his mother and sister, and neither had mentioned a word to him. He couldn't look away. Meghann McCarthy had not been what anyone would call a pretty child. Her expression was too serious, and her eyes above her short, freckled nose had taken up her entire face. But one drizzly afternoon when they had been alone together in the house, she'd read to him from her poetry text in the low, husky tones she would have when she was grown. He watched her push the heavy mass of russet hair away from her face and look up at him from beneath feathery lashes. He'd swallowed, reached out to pull her close, and like Adam to Eve's apple, bent his head to her open, willing mouth.

Nineteen was not an uncommon age for a man to marry in the Falls, but Meghann was only fifteen. There had been more than a few women in Michael's life, but never one who meant anything more than an evening of *craic* at the pub. A revelation struck him, and he realized now why that was. He had waited for Meghann to grow up, and she was very nearly there.

Two months later he'd joined the IRA and Meghann shut him out. There were no more stolen afternoons in the Falls Park or carefully planned meetings at the ice cream shop on Divas Road. No more holding her slight body close to his chest. No more listening as she read Yeats in her sultry woman's voice. No more tasting the insides of her sweet mouth. No more feeling the slide of cool hands on his neck. No more seeing her across the room or down the street or across his mother's table and knowing that the thick fall of copper-tinted hair, the leggy beauty of her maturing body, the banked heat in her whiskey-colored eyes and the promise of her wide sensitive mouth were his to touch and taste and pleasure. She behaved as if they'd never been, as if his tongue had never slid between her teeth, as if his hand had never felt the firm roundness of her breast, as if the promises they'd exchanged were never made. She did it by surrounding herself with his family and, because there were so many of them and because housing was so short for Catholics in Belfast, she was completely successful.

Michael, in love for the first time, found himself stymied at every turn. Frustrated, he decided to wait, to lull her into complacency, to force her into needing him as much as he needed her. And so he waited and watched and went about his activities for three long years until he could wait no longer. She had turned eighteen. He was nearly twenty-two. He wanted a wife. He wanted Meggie.

He reached out to touch her hair. She didn't move. "You're beautiful, Meggie."

She lifted her cup and sipped her tea.

"Do you have any idea what y're doin' to me?"

Still she said nothing.

"I want you t' marry me, Meggie."

That did it. Her eyes blazed gold with anger.

"How dare you?" she gasped. "How dare you come t' me after three years and ask such a question?"

"It isn't the first time I've asked."

"The circumstances are not the same."

"Why not?"

Pushing herself away from the table, she stood and picked up his plate. "Tea is over, Michael. You can go now."

"I'm not goin' anywhere. Why aren't circumstances the same, Meghann?"

Without answering, she stalked to the sink and began washing the dishes. Slowly he came up behind her, resting his hands on the curve of her waist. He felt her tremble and moved closer, his breath soft on the lobe of her ear.

"Why aren't circumstances the same, Meggie?" he whispered, sliding one hand up the side of her rib cage, the other to the base of her spine. "I love you. Y' know that. Y' must know that."

"I know that you believe it, Michael."

"There isn't anything I wouldn't do for you."

"Don't be ridiculous."

He found the bare flesh of her middle and she shivered. When he turned her around to meet his kiss, she came willingly, pressing against him, winding her arms around his neck and kissing him back. Meggie always had been a fool for affection.

Michael was on safe ground now. He hadn't planned this, but nothing short of an act of God would make him throw it away. He knew what to do, and words had no place in the heat-filled, dizzying pleasure of this moment. Lifting her in his arms, he carried her to the couch, unbuttoned her sweater and freed her breasts. Burying his face in the generous curves, he pulled open her wrap-around skirt, stroking her skin, fondling and murmuring encouragement until she was more than ready.

Removing his own clothes, he kissed her lips, her throat, her breasts and, when he felt her open beneath him, positioned himself between her legs and for the first time, came completely into her.

She gasped and went still. He waited until he felt her relax before resuming his slow, reassuring movements. She tightened her legs around him, heard his low groan and felt the shuddering warmth of his release.

"Y' do love me," he murmured, collapsing against her shoulder, his lips on her throat. "I wasn't sure."

She said nothing.

He lifted his head. "Say it, Meggie. I need t' hear the words."

Reaching up, she brushed away a lock of hair that had fallen across his forehead. "I do love you, Michael. I love y' so much that it frightens me."

"Why would it frighten you?"

She turned her face into his bare shoulder. "No one should love another person this much. It's too dangerous."

All at once he understood. "I'm not goin' anywhere, Meggie," he said gently. "I'll always be here for you. I promise y' that."

"No one can promise that."

"I—"

She pressed her fingers against his mouth. "Don't," she whispered. "Don't say anything. Just know that I love you. No matter what happens, remember that."

To this day, Michael still had no idea what happened. He went over it, again and again, in his mind. He would have sworn, when he left her, that their future was settled. One day he was sublimely happy, planning his life with the woman he'd practiced a lifetime of celibacy for. The next she left for England without so much as a good-bye or a forwarding address.

At first he was bewildered, then, in stages, hurt, angry and indifferent. Still he waited, hoping for a letter, a call, anything. Finally he told himself he was over her, believed it too, until five years later when he saw her wedding picture in the London *Times*.

Now she was home to defend him. Michael smiled at the irony of it. She, who had worked so diligently to eradicate her past, found herself dumped right back in the ugly center of it. His smile widened. God worked in mysterious ways.

3

Meghann leaned across the table, her eyes intent on Annie's face. "Are you sure that I should go alone? Michael and I didn't part on the best of terms."

"And why is that, Meggie?" Annie poured milk into two teacups, deliberately avoiding Meghann's penetrating gaze.

Meghann lied. "I can't remember."

"Then it can't have been very important, can it?"

Annie always ended every answer with a question. Meghann had forgotten that. She was also very elusive about her answers. But that was to be expected in a nationalist family. Self-preservation had forced her to become adept at avoiding the truth.

Meghann sighed. She wouldn't find out any more than Annie intended she should know. "What if someone recognizes me?"

Looking up, Annie perused her carefully from head to toe. She looked nothing like the girl who'd left the Falls eighteen years before. It was more than expensive clothing and her hair, more red today than when she first arrived, that separated her from the residents of Clonard. Meghann carried herself differently than she had when she lived in Belfast. She exuded the kind of confidence that came with education, money and influence, the same confidence Bernadette had after her maiden speech on the floor of Parliament. Involving Meghann had been the right thing to do. If anyone could save Michael, Meghann could.

"Y' don't look much like your pictures now that yer hair's lightened up a bit," Annie said. "Besides, no one will suspect Lady Meghann Sutton t' show up in the Maze. The lads in prison with him wouldn't betray Michael, even if they did recognize little Meggie McCarthy from Clonard."

"I wish you would go with me."

Annie filled the pot with boiling water and wiped her hands on her apron before turning back to Meghann. "I've already told y', love, they only allow one visitor a month."

"But I would visit as his lawyer. That shouldn't preempt family visits."

Annie's eyebrows drew together. "Have y' forgotten so much, Meggie? This is Ulster. Rules aren't the same here."

Anger flashed through Meghann's eyes, turning the rich whiskey color to a brilliant gold. "We'll see about that."

"I knew y' would," Annie said softly. "That's why I sent for you." She glanced guiltily at the bulky fisherman's sweater and cotton skirt Meghann wore. "How do y' like the clothes?"

Meghann lied again. "I like them." At this rate she'd be in Purgatory for the rest of her life. Wasn't there anything she could be honest about?

"They're not what y're used to, but at least they're clean."

"They're grand, Annie. Really." Meghann ran one hand up the rough wool of her sweater. Nothing was worth hurting Annie's feelings.

"They're warm and y'll need all the warmth y' can get in the cages," Annie continued. "I don't think they have any heatin' at all in that place."

Meghann shuddered. "I'm not sure that pretending to be someone else is the right way to begin."

"It's the only way. If y' tell anyone that y're representin' Michael, they won't let you in. Talk t' him first, Meghann. Find out what happened." Her lip trembled. "We don't even know why they've accused him."

Meghann had a very good idea, but she didn't voice her sentiment out loud. Hooking her purse over her shoulder, she reached for the umbrella, hugged Annie fiercely and started toward the door. "I'll be back after I've spoken with him."

Annie nodded. "Godspeed."

Meghann hadn't been on a coach since before her marriage. She stared out the window at a Belfast she didn't recognize. Tidy brick homes replaced the waterless tenements that made up Andersonstown, Little India and Shankill's Sandy Row. Grass grew in city parks on both sides of the Peace Line, a brick and wire structure that had little to do with its name, and women with baby prams thronged both Catholic and Protestant shopping areas, apparently unafraid of separatist retribution.

Fifteen years ago the octagonal guard towers were filled with British soldiers, their guns pointed at Catholic women and children as they shopped, attended Mass and played in the schoolyards. Police, afraid to leave the protection of their vehicles, patrolled in armored Land Rovers. Barbed-wire barricades kept intruders from coming into the Falls after curfew, and the stench of gasoline bombs permeated the streets.

Eighteen years ago, Clonard, with its columns of row houses—one family lined up against the next, no hot water or bathtubs, toilets in the back, fifteen streets and sixteen trees—had been home to two thousand Catholic residents. Fire trucks and police cars singsonged as they passed one another, some going to East Belfast or the Shankill on missions of mercy, others to Andersonstown or the Falls to bring English justice and retribution. The barricades were gone now, as were the row houses. The soldiers had pulled out in the wake of a peace initiative that everyone except the extremist right wing of Ian Paisley's Protestant Unionists supported.

Above it all, and yet still part of it all, on the border of Catholic Clonard and Protestant Shankill, was a dark turn-of-the-century brick monastery built by the Redemptorists, an order aptly dedicated to the service of the most abandoned souls. If it hadn't been for the courage of a Catholic priest and a fourteen-year-old boy, Meghann would not be on this coach weaving expertly through the streets of Belfast toward the Maze. She would not be anywhere at all. For that alone she would do whatever was necessary to keep Michael Devlin alive.

Meghann reached for the delicate locket she wore on a chain around her neck. The chain was new, but the thin gold oval with the Celtic markings was very old. She didn't know how old. It had been her mother's and her grandmother's and her great-grandmother's, all the way back to a time she knew nothing about. No one remembered where the locket had originally come from. It was passed down to the females in her family, mother to oldest daughter, one generation to the next, in an unbroken line of succession until the night of Cupar Street. By rights it should have gone to Kathleen, the oldest girl. But after that awful August night, Kathleen had taken one look at the haunted expression on Meghann's face and another at the white-knuckled fist clutching their mother's brooch, and told her to keep it.

There had been someone else with Meghann that

night, someone other than Father Alex and Michael, someone who continued to appear at various timely intervals throughout her life. Father said it was Saint Brigid, Meghann's own guardian angel, keeping her from harm. But the round face and sweetly pious features on the stained glass panel of the inner sanctuary of Saint Stephen's Cathedral bore no resemblance to the woman who had appeared out of the mist to save her from the carnage on Cupar Street.

That woman, dressed in the robes of a postulate, had a striking high-boned face, glittering green eyes and red braids, twisted with gold thread, as thick as a man's hand and so long they reached below her knees.

After Meghann left Ireland, she had never seen her again. With every passing year the woman's memory had dimmed until Meghann had almost completely forgotten her. Odd that she should remember, now, the youthful fancy of an introverted child's imagination. Meghann stared at the rivulets of rain running down the wet curbs into the gutters and examined the facts surrounding the Killingsworth murder.

Britain no longer wanted the expense of maintaining troops in Northern Ireland. The British government had no stake in the murder of James Killingsworth. Meghann didn't believe Sinn Fein was responsible either. While Killingsworth was not a supporter of the party, he planned to travel with them in the same direction. Moving rapidly through her list of suspects, she discounted the IRA. Although they claimed independence from Sinn Fein, they were one and the same. She had seen the coffins of men adorned with the black jackets, gloves and berets of the organization and knew them to belong to the same men whose faces appeared on political posters. That left the Unionists, the land-holding, job-holding Protestant loyalists represented by Ian Paisley. Who had better reason to assassinate James Killingsworth than those who had the most to lose?

She sat back in her seat and closed her eyes, depressed by the sight of the rain-drenched city that no longer looked familiar. Michael would know who had done it. If she could just get beyond the past, she might be able to save him.

Meghann changed coaches at the end of Ormeau Road. The only passengers left were those on their way to Long Kesh. The familiar banter on the public motor coach stopped altogether as the eight women closed into themselves, preparing for their monthly visits. Meghann pulled a tissue from her purse and surreptitiously glanced around. They were all young, in their early twenties, and not one had a decent coat or a well-heeled pair of shoes. Silently, she blessed Annie for suggesting a change of clothing. It would be difficult enough to blend in without the tailored wool slacks and cashmere jumpers she had packed in her bag.

The coach stopped outside an iron gate. Ahead, on the M1 north, travelers would pass through the post-card beauty of the Glens of Antrim. Behind the gated camp a church, pristinely whitewashed, shown purely against a field of green. Meghann drew a deep breath and forced herself to look at the rows of cages that had housed three generations of her family. Black-tarred and gray metallic roofs, tinny cold huts that broiled in summer and froze in winter, furnished with cots, meager blankets, a hot plate and one small black-and-white television.

The women hurried to a door where a guard scrutinized their papers before ushering them inside. Meghann was careful to be neither first nor last. Her hands were lumps of ice. Fifteen years in England had not cured her of her terror of Northern Ireland's yellow-vested police force. Today she wasn't Meghann McCarthy, London barrister. She was an Irish Catholic visiting a prisoner accused of killing a British politician.

Eyes lowered, heart hammering, she prayed that the guard noticed nothing more on her identification papers than her birthplace. A minute passed and still he examined the document. Perspiration gathered between her breasts. Nausea rose from the pit of her stomach.

Breathe, Meggie, she told herself. She was becoming irrational. Worst case would be that she was sent away and told to apply for visitation privileges through proper channels. There would be publicity, of course, and she wouldn't be able to see Michael unless she came out publicly as his attorney. Theodore wouldn't like it. She brushed that away. Theodore's prejudices had ceased to worry her long ago.

The real problem lay with Michael. If he had murdered James Killingsworth, no power on earth, not even Annie's pleas, could talk her into defending him. Once, Meghann had known Michael Devlin better than anyone. She was counting on that now. Only by seeing him face-to-face would she know if he was innocent.

"Move on," the guard said abruptly, motioning her through the door. Meghann was so nervous she could barely stand. Carefully, she placed one foot in front of the other until the door closed behind her. Then she leaned against the wall, drinking in deep sustaining breaths until her heart resumed its usual cadence. The communal visiting room was near the end of the hall. A guard stopped her at the entrance. "Who do you want?"

Meghann wet her lips. "Michael Devlin."

The man directed her to a door around the corner. "Political prisoners wait there."

Murmuring her thanks, Meghann walked to the closed door and pushed the button. She heard footsteps and then the sound of keys in the lock. She tensed.

Again, a guard answered and motioned her inside.

Two more armed men stood behind him. One of them stepped forward, grabbed her shoulders, turned her around and pushed her against the wall, holding her arms above her head.

Meghann was no longer a Catholic schoolgirl from Clonard. Rage and logic warred with each other in her brain. She opened her mouth to protest when a meaty hand pressed up into her armpit and down her rib cage, boldly squeezing her waist, her hips and thighs before moving to her other side.

Awareness exploded in Meghann's mind, shaking her as much as her moment of anger. The man was frisking her. A male prison guard was actually frisking a woman visitor. She filed the details in her mind and forced herself to endure the indignity of blunt fingers digging into her flesh. Finally, it was over. Another door opened and she was motioned inside. Behind her a lock clicked and the bolt slid into place.

At first she was disoriented. The room wasn't as bright as the hallway had been. She blinked and looked around. It was empty except for a small table and two chairs facing each other. Where was Michael? For the first time she felt the cold and rubbed her arms. Again the door opened and two men stepped inside, one wearing a guard's uniform, the other dressed in faded jeans and black jacket, official garb of the Irish Republican Army.

Without a word, the guard removed the handcuffs from Michael's wrists and disappeared out the door, leaving Meghann staring at the floor with burning cheeks, wondering what on earth could have possessed her to come here and face him. Fifteen years of telling herself that Michael was a man like any other, that her obsession was hero worship and nothing more, that when compared to others more sophisticated, more educated, more diplomatic, he would fall short. He couldn't possibly be as handsome as she remembered. Eyes could never be so blue nor teeth so white nor a grin so dangerously disarming. And yet here he was, in the flesh, as vital and potent and glittering as ever, as if this were some practical joke and he'd never been arrested, never been accused of a terrible crime and beaten to within an inch of his life, never lost a spleen and copious amounts of blood in the operating room at Royal Victoria Hospital.

"Dia duit, Meghann."

The lilting beauty of the ancient words blending with the richness of a voice that could never be mistaken for anyone else's washed over her. She swallowed and raised her eyes to his face, wondering if she could still form the syllables of her first language. *"Conas ta tu?"* she managed.

He shrugged. "I've seen better days."

"So I've heard. Can I help?"

Something flickered in his eyes, something deeply personal and shockingly intimate. "Do y' want to?"

She wet her lips, forcing herself to hold that mesmerizing blue stare. "Yes."

"Why?"

Meghann's throat worked and she turned away to hide the unexpected tears so appallingly close to the surface. *Breathe,* the voice of a fourteen-year-old boy from long ago Cupar Street sounded in her ear. *Breathe and the pain will stop.* She breathed. The tears receded and her voice returned, but the words she spoke were low and close to her heart, not the ones she'd intended for him to hear. "If I owe anything to anyone in this world, it is to you and to Annie. Let me pay my debt, Michael." She turned back, forcing herself to meet the remote, archangel beauty of his face. "And then you must let me go."

For an instant, before the shutters fell again, his eyes blazed like living blue flame. "You've already gone," he said softly. "Y' left your family, your religion and your heritage t' live in London and marry a bloody Brit. You've money and a title and all the respectability that beauty and brains and an Oxford education can bring. Just how much farther can a Catholic from Clonard aspire, Meghann? Are y' itching t' become prime minister?"

"I've no desire to have my body parts blown up all over Malone Street." She winced, despising the sharpness in her voice.

He grinned. "You've changed, Meggie. But I don't mind. I imagine your tongue will serve me well." The grin faded. "I didn't kill him."

Relief washed over her. She believed him. "Who did?"

Michael pulled an unfiltered cigarette from his jacket pocket, swiped a match against the concrete floor, brought the two together and inhaled deeply.

"No, thank you," Meghann said sweetly. "I don't smoke."

He blew out a blue-tinted curl. "I know. Not that I would have offered. We're rationed in here, or maybe y' didn't know that. Maybe y' think we get Guinness and lamb chops twice a day."

Meghann released her breath. "Of course, I don't think that. You haven't answered my question. Who killed James Killingsworth?"

Michael shrugged and leaned back against the wall. "Not the Brits and not the IRA. Maybe Paisley's group. I don't know."

They were getting nowhere. "Come, Michael. If you don't know, no one does."

"You're giving me more credit than I deserve."

Meghann shook her head. "I don't think so. News does reach England. I know very well what you've become."

For an instant the blue eyes flamed again and Meghann thought she saw the old Michael. But then his flash of temper disappeared, except for a slight flaring of his nostrils. When he spoke, sarcasm and the accent of West Belfast were thick in his voice. "I'm flattered that y've kept up. What do y' do with y'r spare time, Lady Sutton? Read *The Irish Times* or, better yet, the Sinn Fein home page?"

Gritting her teeth, Meghann willed herself back into the control for which she'd earned her reputation. She pulled out a chair, using it as a footrest while she sat on the table. It was an awkward postion, but Annie's shoes made her feet hurt and she wouldn't give him the satisfaction of towering over her. "Tell me why they arrested you."

"I was in the area."

"Doing what?"

"Listening to a speech."

"Whose speech?"

"Killingsworth's."

Meghann's eyes widened. "Good Lord, Michael. Don't tell me they caught you inside."

He flicked the cigarette into the far corner of the room and shoved his hands deep into his pockets. "Christ, it's cold," he complained. "Of course they caught me inside. I was on the guest list."

Pressure was building inside Meghann's head. "How could you possibly afford a five-hundred-pound-a-plate dinner?"

His mouth tightened and a muscle below his right eye twitched angrily. "None of your bloody business."

She forced herself to speak calmly. "I'm afraid it is. That's the first question the prosecution will ask."

"Let them. Their courts have no jurisdiction in Ireland."

This time her voice rose. "Do you want to go to prison for the rest of your life, Michael?"

He didn't answer, which only infuriated her more. Kicking the chair away, she slid off the table and stood before him, her head tilted to look up into his face, her shaking finger pressed against his chest. "How dare you do this to us? Your mother has aged ten years. She can't sleep at night, which might be due to worry over you or it might be because every one of your brothers is home pretending to give her emotional support while eating her out of house and home. Even Bernadette came, and you know how dangerous it is for her to be in Belfast. As for me, I've lied to my associates, my housekeeper, my clients and all of my friends, not to mention the fact that I'm here, in a prison, under false pretenses. I'm trying very hard to help you, Michael Devlin, but if you don't want my services, please let me know."

Her words echoed against the metal door, reverberating off the walls, making the silence that followed appear even deeper than it was.

Michael stared at her, noticing for the first time how her mouth quivered and how the blood leaped in the hollow of her throat. Her hair was darker than he remembered and shorter, cut into a whispy, layered style that framed her face and rested on her shoulders. Her cheeks were flushed, but beneath the scarlet her skin still had that curious golden sheen that only the darkest redheads have. Michael did not have the words to describe Meghann's eyes—Irish eyes. They were no true color, but a combination of green, gold, hazel and amber, clear brook water running over peat moss shot with silver, only brighter, clearer, changing with every mood. Just now they were black with anger and something he had seen too often to deny. Meghann was terrified. She had moved to the other side of the room, as far away from him as possible.

Hand outstretched, he moved forward, his only thought to offer comfort. He stopped in midstride, turned his head to the window and listened. Without warning his hand snaked out, grabbing Meghann by the wrist, pulling her into the nearest corner. "Pretend y' like it," he muttered, before his arms wrapped around her and his mouth came down on hers, hard.

At first Meghann was too shocked to protest. Then the door opened behind her and she understood.

Reacting instinctively, she pressed herself against Michael's chest, slid her arms under his jacket and kissed him back. His mouth gentled and moved against hers and for a moment Meghann forgot she was in prison under false pretenses, forgot that the man whose lips and hands were taking such shocking liberties was her client, forgot that eighteen years had passed since she'd kissed anyone with such wanton abandon.

"Are you all right, miss? We heard you call out." The guard's sincere voice broke through her reverie.

Michael broke the kiss, lifted his head and lashed out angrily. "Get out, y' bloody screw. Find your own girl. I'm allowed my thirty minutes."

Purple with embarrassment, Meghann hid her face against his shoulder.

The guard, no more than a schoolboy, backed out of the room, apologizing profusely. He stopped for one brief look from the outside window. Michael saw him and deliberately turned his back. Threading his fingers through Meghann's silky chestnut hair, he pulled her head back and kissed her again.

Later, after the silent bus ride through the rain-wet streets and the long walk up Divas Road to Clonard, when she was back in the safety of Annie Devlin's kitchen, Meghann wondered why it had never occurred to her to stop him.

4

"I can't do anything without a full investigation, Annie." Meghann paced back and forth in her hostess's small kitchen. "I need information, witnesses, anything. The only way to free Michael is to prove it might have been someone else. What we don't want is a Diplock Court. Without a jury, he won't have a chance."

"I'm thinkin' that he'll be made to confess."

Meghann frowned. "What do you mean?"

Annie's hand shook as she folded towels. "We still live under the Emergency Provisions Act. The limit is seventy-two hours without a lawyer. Michael can't take another seventy-two hours of torture. The last beatin' almost killed him."

"A case of this magnitude will have the eyes of the world on it. They can't touch him if they know someone other than a court-appointed attorney is watching out for his interests. It's the only way, Annie. Unless I come out in the open, my hands are tied. I can't request any files from the prosecution without legal authority."

Annie shook her head. "Y'll have no peace, Meggie.

Connor says they'll bring out the big guns if they know y'r on the defense. Wait a bit," she pleaded. "See if y' can find out more before they find out about you. Bernadette and the boys are workin' on it. They'll be here for supper. Please stay."

Meghann sighed. Had it always been this difficult to get them to move forward? She couldn't remember. Maybe it was different looking out from the inside. Thank goodness for Bernadette. As a past Member of Parliament, she would offer a perspective that none of the others could.

When the news hit and Michael's face appeared on national television, Bernadette Devlin McAliskey had left her husband and children in County Tyrone to be with her mother. For Meghann, she was a breath of life and sanity among the sober, tight-lipped Devlin males. With a sense of déjà vu, Meghann looked around the table with its cloth napkins and lace-trimmed linen. Nothing had changed in fifteen years. They were older, of course, and although Dominic and Liam had the thick, straight Devlin hair, both had gone completely gray. Connor was an older, less personable version of Michael. Sean and Niall were dead, killed in a pub bombing on Divas Street. Cormack and Davie, the merry, freckle-faced lads who had played soccer in the narrow streets of Clonard, were now hollow-cheeked, hard-eyed men who wore the traditional black jackets and blue jeans of the cause.

Meghann stared at her soup. How could Annie bear it? Nine children and all of them marked targets. Later, while walking down the lamp-lit streets of Clonard, she posed the question to Annie's only daughter.

Bernadette linked her arm through Meghann's and shrugged. "She bears it because she was born to it. Every mother in West Belfast knows that her children will struggle with the notion of joining the IRA. Some will join, others find it doesn't suit them. Think of our history, Meghann. Two hundred years ago, a woman knew that only two out of her ten children would live past their fourth birthdays. We accept what is. There is no other alternative."

"There was for me," Meghann reminded her, "and for you."

Bernadette laughed, a rich, clear sound that lifted Meghann's spirits and brought answering grins to two shaggy-haired young men sharing a smoke and a Guinness in the doorway of Feeney's pub. "We're the two, Meggie. Don't you see? We're the exceptions. You more than I. Never once were y' tempted out of your cerebral calm. 'Tis nothing short of a miracle, considering what happened t' your family."

Meghann looked straight ahead, hoping Bernadette wouldn't notice the telltale blush staining her cheeks. Was that really how she appeared to the passionate, opinionated Devlins? Were they all so filled with themselves that they hadn't seen how it was between Michael and an orphaned refugee from Cupar Street? "I was tempted," she confessed. "It just didn't work out the way I expected."

"If you're telling me that you were in love with my brother, I already know that," announced Bernadette matter-of-factly. "It was inevitable. The signs were all there for anyone with eyes t' see them. How could Michael, who read Yeats and Joyce until his eyes burned, whose mind was filled with rage and passion and romance, possibly overlook a girl like you?"

Meghann shook her head. "Michael was not a womanizer."

"Of course he wasn't. But there y' were, living in his house, all wide-eyed and autumn-colored, with gorgeous legs and budding breasts. Only an idiot wouldn't jump at the opportunity."

"The others didn't."

"Now, Meggie." Bernadette patted her hand. "I

know he loved you, too. He told me the day he was going t' ask you t' marry him. I tried t' stop him, y' know."

"Why?"

"Because I know you. Y' wanted no part of Belfast, at least y' didn't then. Michael had enormous potential t' help us. We needed him here."

Meghann no longer felt the cold on her legs. They had walked much farther than they had planned. "Why do you think I want any part of it now?"

"Because you're here." Bernadette stopped and stepped in front of Meghann, forcing her to stop, too. "I know y', Meggie McCarthy. Y' aren't here because my mother asked for you. Y're here because y've stopped running away. Y've bedded down with the enemy long enough. It's time t' reconcile Cupar Street."

Bernadette Devlin was forty-six years old, but Meghann couldn't see it. Her blue eyes flashed with the same fire they had twenty-five years before when she crossed the floor of the House of Commons to slap Reginald Maudling, the Home Secretary, after he had minimized the massacre of Irish Catholics at Free Derry Corner. She'd been twenty-one at the time, the youngest MP to be elected in over half a century.

Sixteen-year-old Michael had fairly burst with pride when he told how his sister, impervious to tear gas, had led the Bogsiders' resistance in the Rossville Street area of the main war zone. Pictures taken of her breaking bricks to throw at the police earned her a six-month jail sentence in Long Kesh.

Now those remarkable blue eyes, so like her brother's, were staring at Meghann, insisting on a commitment the younger woman was not sure she could even begin to make.

Meghann wet her lips. "I'll do everything that I can for Michael. You know I will."

Once again, Bernadette linked her arm through

Meghann's, turning them back in the direction from which they had come. "I wonder if y' have any idea how much it will cost, Meggie."

In the weeks to come, as Meghann waded through paperwork at her London office, commuted to Ireland on the weekends and endured the ghastly bus rides to the Maze and the even more ghastly interviews with an increasingly uncommunicative Michael, she was to think often of Bernadette's words and wonder where the woman had acquired her omniscience.

At the end of Michael's seventy-two-hour internment, the Crown appointed a lawyer to defend him. Miles French was a capable, soft-spoken Irish Protestant who, to his credit, believed in fair representation for Catholics. Meghann chafed at his inexperience and at the limitations the Devlins had placed upon her. But memories were long in the Six Counties, and until Michael gave the word, she would not divulge her role in his defense.

When Bernadette introduced her as a family friend, the young barrister had looked at her curiously but kept his thoughts to himself. If he wondered at her grasp of the facts or the pointed questions she asked, he never hinted that anything was other than it should be. Meghann didn't like deceiving him, but her loyalty was already determined.

She knew that, eventually, her services would be needed. Miles French was a fine lawyer, but he would never command the media attention needed to save Michael's life. Only Meghann could do that, and until she had something to go on, something other than an instinctive belief in Michael's innocence, she was like a swimmer floundering in a merciless current.

It turned out that maintaining Meghann's anonymity had been a wise decision after all. While ten-year-old Susan Killingsworth continued on life support,

London buzzed with speculation about her father's murder. Meghann had no doubt that she would have heard none of it had she come out publicly as lead counsel for Michael's defense.

Meanwhile, inside the confines of the H-Blocks, Michael refused to compromise his prisoner-of-war status, thereby losing his monthly visitation privilege. Annie was terrified, Bernadette jubilant, and Meghann, when she found out in the receiving line at the St. Johns' ball, furious.

Theodore Thorndike had just introduced her to Lillian St. John's eldest daughter when the news broke, electrifying the crowd like a lightning bolt. The hunger strike of the eighties that had immortalized Bobby Sands and increased membership in the IRA a thousandfold was resurrected as the primary topic of conversation.

Meghann excused herself, found the study and, in the middle of a dozen cigar-smoking aristocrats, listened as the anchor reported the latest news from the Maze.

"The clever bastard," she heard someone say.

"It won't help," said another. "He's a marked man. He won't be set free, even if he didn't do it."

Meghann turned, a slim regal vision in green satin. She recognized every man in the room except one. "On the contrary, gentlemen," she said coldly. "This isn't 1974. The eyes of the world are upon us. We've a great deal to answer for after the Guildford debacle. If Michael Devlin is innocent, he will go free."

"Come now, Lady Sutton," Robert Gillette protested. "He's a self-proclaimed member of the Irish Republican Army. Who else would have done such a thing?"

Just in time, Meghann realized where she was. Her eyes widened and the corners of her mouth tilted in a smile intended to charm. "Who indeed?" she asked demurely.

Collectively, the men laughed and the tension lifted.

* * *

"Bloody Prov. Have it your own way." The guard backed out of Michael's cell, leaving the chamber pot unemptied.

Michael tucked the thin blanket around his legs and lowered himself back down on the concrete floor. The cell was completely barren, stripped of furniture, books, clothing, everything except a chamber pot. The inmates had been on the blanket protest for six weeks now and the no-wash for two. Rather than wear prison issue that labeled them common criminals, they wore nothing at all except blankets. They would have washed, but the guards refused them new towels and they refused to wrap themselves in wet ones on their way back from the showers. Michael no longer smelled his own filth, but he could tell from the strained looks on the guards' faces that he stank like a pig. He grinned. It amused him to think he offended Protestant noses.

His cell wasn't as bad as some whose slop pots had overflowed. Some of the more outrageous had smeared fecal matter on the walls beside their mattresses, risking disease and body orifices filled with maggots. Cardinal Tomas O Fiaich, who on his last visit barely managed to avoid vomiting, had compared prison conditions in the Maze to those of refugees living in the sewer pipes of Calcutta.

His grin faded. It was bloody cold here on the concrete. Soon Miles French was coming to go over his defense. Swearing under his breath, he consigned the young lawyer and his endless patience to a swift and merciful end. How often did he have to tell them, he wanted no English lawyer?

Flanked by two screws, Michael made his way down the hall to the visitation room. Miles French, briefcase in hand, waited for him. He stood when Michael entered and held out his hand. Michael stared at it pointedly but did not take it. For a long moment the two men stared at each other, one nattily dressed in tweeds and smelling of cologne, the other unshaven, filthy and naked except for a gray wool blanket wrapped around his waist and another across his shoulders.

The barrister cleared his throat. "I've arranged for a court date on the seventeenth of June," he began. "You'll be asked for your plea. I don't think there is any point to pleading guilty in the hopes of commuting your sentence. The press has already crucified you. The defense is asking for the maximum. They want to make an example of you."

Michael continued to stand, saying nothing.

The lawyer balled his fists and shoved them deep into his pockets. "Does any of this matter to you, Mr. Devlin? Do you understand that unless you can come up with a reasonable suspicion of evidence that someone else was responsible for this act, your life as you know it will effectively be over?"

"I understand."

"Then why won't you cooperate?"

Michael frowned, narrowing his eyes until the brilliant color appeared as a glittering turquoise line. "How long have y' been practicing law, Mr. French?"

The barrister flushed. "Four years."

"Is this your first murder case?"

The flush deepened. "Yes."

Michael laughed, pulled out a chair and sat down, motioning for the younger man to sit opposite him. "I'd like a smoke, if y' don't mind?" he said when they were settled.

French reached into his pocket and pulled out a pack of American Camels, offering one to Michael.

After several satisfying drags, Michael blew out a ring and considered the glowing tip as he spoke. "Don't lose sleep over this one, lad," he advised. "There isn't anything anyone can do."

"What do you mean?"

"I'm done for. They have their scapegoat."

"But, if you're innocent—"

"From where do y' hail, Mr. French?"

"I was born in Belfast."

"But recently returned, if I'm not mistaken."

"How can you tell?"

"Y' know nothing about us."

The barrister sighed and sat back in his chair. "I've been practicing in Manchester for the last three years. Before that I clerked in London."

Michael's eyes narrowed. He tapped the ashes of his cigarette against the table leg. "London, y' say?"

"Yes."

"Have y' told Meggie?"

"I beg your pardon?"

Michael ground out his cigarette underneath his chair and leaned forward. "Have y' told Meghann McCarthy that y' know who she is?"

Again, the silence dragged out between them. "No," French admitted at last.

"Why not?"

Miles French frowned and shifted in his seat. "At first, I wanted to know why she was involved at all. I didn't buy her story of an old family friend."

"And now?"

French squirmed with discomfort. "I don't really know. It doesn't seem right to tell her when she obviously doesn't want me to know."

"Do y' buy her story now, Mr. French?"

The younger man looked surprised. "Of course. I've seen her with your family. They trust her. There could be no other reason for her interest."

"What would y' say if I told y' that Meghann is trying t' secure my release?"

"I'd say you were one hell of a lucky man, Mr. Devlin."

"Do y' think I'm guilty, Mr. French?"

"Of course, Mr. Devlin."

"Why haven't y' informed against Meghann?"

Beneath his wire-rimmed glasses, the lawyer's eyes

misted with excitement. "Are you insane? This is the case of the century. Meghann McCarthy is the best legal counsel in England. With her help, we can win this. And if we win, you won't be the only one to benefit, Mr. Devlin."

"Y' have everything figured out, do y', Miles?"

The young man looked very pleased with himself. "Yes. I suppose I do."

Holding the blanket like a shawl around him, Michael stood, walked to the window and pounded for the guard. Before the door opened he turned back to address the lawyer one more time. "Do y' know what they say about the best-laid plans, Miles?"

"What's that?"

"Be sure all the players learn their lines."

"I don't understand."

"I'm not guilty, Miles. But y' should ask yourself why I'm the one standing for the crime."

"He told you himself?" Meggie stood against the beautifully mounted Georgian window in her office, her charcoal gray jacket and skirt suitably framed against a backdrop of London fog.

"Yes, he did. Volunteered it, actually." To Miles French, Meghann looked to be the epitome of corporate efficiency with exactly the right amount of feminine softness. He liked the way her red hair brought out the green in her whiskey-gold eyes. How would a woman like that, the wife of an English peer, know the Irish Catholic Devlins?

"Well then, Mr. French. It appears that my time has come. The next time you visit the Maze, I'm coming with you." Meghann picked up the telephone. "Better yet, I'll go alone. There are a few things I'd like to discuss in private with Michael Devlin."

"You had better take an oxygen mask when you do that. The reek of the place will kill you."

Meghann felt no need to mention that she had been

brought up in the slums of West Belfast, where nine families shared one latrine located no more than ten feet from the back door.

When Mrs. Hartwell brought in the London *Times* with her tea the following morning, Michael's picture was featured on the front page. He had called a hunger strike. Unless the British government agreed to his demands, all of which seemed perfectly reasonable to Meghann and therefore impossible for the government, four men would refuse all food until they starved to death.

Meghann knew that hunger strikes were common in Irish history. The early Celts used self-immolation as a way of discrediting someone who had done them a disservice. An unpaid poet or tradesman would starve himself in front of the residence of an uncaring patron, the result being either death for the tradesman and a ruined reputation for the patron or payment for services received. Bobby Sands's death by starvation made world news in the eighties.

Meghann pushed aside her cooling tea. She was well aware that in order to make the front page of the *Times,* the strikers had already gone weeks without food. God alone knew what Michael's physical condition was at this moment. "Mrs. Hartwell," she called out.

The housekeeper poked her head through the kitchen door. "Yes, Lady Sutton?"

"Call my office, please. Tell them I've been called away rather suddenly. I'll be in touch within the week."

"As you say, ma'am." Not by so much as the lifting of an eyebrow did the well-trained Mrs. Hartwell suggest that Meghann's announcement, the third such in three months, was the least bit unusual.

The phone rang just as Meghann was leaving. When she learned that it was Cecil Thorndike, she debated with herself before picking up the extension in her bedroom.

"Meghann, what the devil is going on?"

"I'm in a bit of a rush, Cecil. What do you mean?"

"Why the sudden need for another week away from the office?"

Meghann's voice cooled. "I can't imagine why my travel plans should be any concern of yours."

The long silence on the other end of the line unnerved her until she reminded herself that it was Cecil on the other end and he wasn't in the least bit intimidating.

"I thought we were friends as well as associates, Meghann," he said at last.

"I'm sorry, Cecil," she said, instantly contrite. "Please forgive me, but I really don't have time to discuss this now. I'll give you a full accounting when I return."

"Are you all right, my dear?"

"Yes, quite. Thank you for asking."

"What shall I tell my father?"

Meghann bit her lip. She was going to miss the flight. "Tell him I'm taking care of a legal matter for my family."

"So that's it." Cecil sounded relieved. "Is it one of your sisters in America?"

"Cecil, I really must go. Be a love and hang up the phone."

"Very well. Call if you need anything. Where can I reach—"

"Good-bye, Cecil," she said quickly and hung up.

Meghann waited until after she'd paid for her ticket before phoning the Devlins. Briefly, she explained her plan and requested that the entire family be present when she arrived.

This time she flew into Belfast, looked for a taxi sporting a red poppy to take her to the entrance of the Falls Road and then flagged down a black taxi to take her up the road to Annie Devlin's house.

The door opened before she knocked. The entire family was assembled in the shabby living room. Annie, with her beautiful manners, had prepared a lovely tea.

Meghann dropped her bag and sank down into a chair with frayed upholstery. "How is he?" she asked.

Cormack leaned forward, blue eyes blazing, dark hair falling across his forehead. "We haven't seen him since he's been on the protest. He's not allowed visitors."

Meghann frowned. "Surely we can get someone in. What about the men who are with him? Don't they have visitors?"

"They're watched very closely, Meggie," Annie reminded her. "We can't ask anyone to take such a risk."

Meghann stirred sugar into her tea. "How long has it been?"

This time it was Liam who spoke. "Thirty-two days."

Meghann froze. She couldn't have heard correctly. "No." She managed to form the single syllable.

Bernadette nodded. For the first time in her life she was unable to speak.

"Why didn't anyone tell me?"

"What could you have done?" Annie asked reasonably.

Meghann stood and walked to the mantel where a picture of the Virgin Mary stood framed in cheap plastic. "Is he prepared to die?"

"When has Michael not been prepared to die?" replied Bernadette grimly.

Meghann turned around and faced Michael's family, seven pairs of identical blue eyes. "I mean to save him," she said quietly. "Will you help me?"

A collective sigh eased the tension in the room.

"What do you want us to do?" Davie asked.

"I'm going to bring him out." She looked straight at Connor, the brother who most resembled Michael. "You'll have to come with me. Hopefully, it will only be for a few days. But I can't promise that."

Annie gasped but Connor only nodded.

"But Meggie," Annie protested. "Connor is nearly as well-known as Michael. What do y' intend t' do?"

Meghann pushed a curl behind her ears and leaned forward. Her eyes glowed, and the soft lamplight picked up the burnished red in her hair. It seemed to Annie that all the energy in the room was concentrated in Meggie's slight person. When she spoke her voice was low, deliberate and very calm. This must be the way she was in the courtroom, assured, convincing, with an edge of repressed excitement. Annie shivered, eased down the sleeves of her pullover and forced herself to concentrate.

"Do you know anyone who can come up with identification by Wednesday?" Meghann asked. She was not surprised when every head in the room nodded. She continued. "Michael's condition will be very poor. We must make it seem dangerously poor, so that removing him to Victoria Hospital is necessary. No one will question it if Miles French insists. Organizing an escape from Victoria Hospital will be much easier than from the H-Blocks."

"What about you, Meghann?" Bernadette interrupted. "They'll be suspicious if you announce that you're Michael's lawyer and suddenly he can't be found."

Meghann laced her fingers together into a braid of white-knuckled, interlocking joints. "I have no intention of letting anyone know that I'm involved."

Liam, the eldest Devlin brother, spoke. "Will French cooperate?"

"He will know nothing about this. Fortunately, Miles is a humanitarian. The right words in his ear and he'll play into our hands."

Annie twisted the wedding band on her finger. "What if Michael refuses t' see him? It's happened twice this month already."

"We must wait until Michael can no longer make his own decisions."

Annie gasped. "Y' mean until he falls into a coma?"

The throbbing ache in Meghann's temples shifted to one side and increased in intensity. "The moment that happens, you must take him off the strike, Annie. You're the next of kin. The English don't want a martyr. They'll listen to you."

"I don't know what Michael will do when he learns we've betrayed him," said Bernadette.

"This isn't a war crime," replied Meghann, "and it isn't IRA business. This is about murder. Someone will pay for James Killingsworth's death. Do you want it to be Michael?"

The silence in the room was deafening.

One week later, despite her surface-level confidence, Meghann's nails were bitten down to the pink as she waited in a small rental car off Grosvenor Street. It was past midnight and they were already fifteen minutes late. What could have gone wrong?

Miles French had asked an enormous amount of questions which Meghann had answered, for the most part honestly. But it wasn't until she explained that this case would hold no résumé-building rewards for anyone if the defendent died, that Miles agreed to authorize Michael's transfer to Victoria Hospital. The medical staff had grown accustomed to the frequent visits of Michael's defense team. If Mr. French looked a bit more stooped than he had the day before and if Mr. Bennett, his assistant, walked a bit more slowly, these inconsistencies were explained away as natural side effects of exhaustion. The poor men really had an impossible case.

Two dark shapes rounded the corner. Meghann sat up, her hand settling on the key in the ignition. She didn't turn it until the car door opened and an emaciated Michael was thrust into the passenger seat.

"Hurry," a raspy voice insisted. "I don't know how long you have."

Meghann didn't recognize the man in the black jacket, but she knew he was IRA and her heart sank. "What happened?"

He slammed the door and thrust his face through the window. "Let's just say that everything didn't go according t' plan. A nosy nurse is trussed up in the linen room. Go along now."

Meghann was terrified. Had the entire city been alerted? Were British tanks already positioning themselves at the checkpoints? She stared at the ravaged being seated beside her. His eyes, now closed, seemed to float beneath their lids in overly large sockets. The shirt, purchased specifically for Connor's solid proportions and buttoned to the top, stood a good two inches from Michael's throat. Could this living carcass really be Michael Devlin? He was close to death. What in the name of heaven had she done? How could she possibly take care of him?

Forcing herself to behave rationally, Meghann eased out onto Grosvenor Road and looked for highway signs. She was past Donegall Square near the turnoff to the WestLink when Michael spoke for the first time.

"Where are we going?"

"To Donegal." Meghann recognized the exit to the M1 and turned the car to the right.

"The Republic or the North?"

The headlights reflecting in her rearview mirror were blinding. She turned the mirror up. "Republic," she answered shortly.

"Bad choice, Meggie. There are guards at the borders."

"Bernadette arranged it. We're staying in a cottage near the River Eske." She bit her lip. It would do no good to worry him. "I'll handle the guards."

"I'm sure y' will," he said softly, leaning back against the headrest. "Wake me when it's over."

5

Meghann never knew what made her turn north toward Tyrone instead of taking the more direct route through Armagh. It wasn't as if she had missed the signs or even made a conscious decision. She just found herself there, traveling through the beautiful sheep country of what had once been the last Catholic kingdom of Ulster. She took comfort in that and in the knowledge that anyone following Michael would assume he was headed south toward the Republic.

Cautiously, she reached out her hand to touch his forehead. His temperature felt normal and his chest moved in and out, a testimony to the strength of the life force within him. How could anyone so thin still breathe? He stirred, and she moved her hand back to the wheel. It was almost time to pull over and wait for a decent time to pass through the border checkpoint. A solitary car with a woman driver and a half-starved man attempting to cross over into the Republic at three o'clock in the morning would be like waving the tricolor in front of Ian Paisley. Michael would be back in Long Kesh and God alone knew what would happen to her.

Not for the first time, Meghann reflected on the insanity of her actions and what it would mean if she was caught. She looked at the man sleeping soundly beside her. He slept as if he were safely inside Buckingham Palace, an honored guest of the queen. She shook her head, saw the turnout, and pulled the car off the road and down an incline behind the hill. The car was completely hidden from both sides of the road. Meghann reclined the seat, pulled a blanket from the back, clutched the golden oval that had settled in the dip of her throat and slept.

A song woke her. The voice belonged to a woman, and her lyrics were pronounced in the unusual Irish spoken on the Aran Islands, thick with "h" sounds and heavily accented vowels. Meghann could make out only half of the words, but the melody was beautiful, the voice clear and high like a choirboy's at Midnight Mass. She glanced at her watch and looked around. It was six o'clock in the morning and Michael was still asleep.

Quietly, Meghann opened the door and stepped outside into the long wet grass. She breathed in lungfuls of fresh, sea-scented air. The voice was closer now. With one anxious backward glance to be sure Michael hadn't changed position, she walked toward the sound. The hill rose, dipped and rose again. Meghann walked steadily for several minutes, following the voice to another rise. There, she saw a huge, flat boulder with coppery lichen running down its northern side. Leaning against the rock was a young girl, still in her nightgown, playing what looked like a lute. Caught up in her song, the girl hadn't yet realized that she wasn't alone.

Unwilling to explain why she was walking the hills at dawn, Meghann started to back away, but her movement must have startled the girl because she looked up, her fingers motionless on the strings. Meghann relaxed. She was a child, barely into her teens, and she was very lovely. "You play beautifully," she said in her best schoolgirl Irish.

The girl straightened and tucked the instrument under one arm. "Thank you," she replied in the same tongue.

Meghann stared at her curiously. She looked familiar and yet she would never have forgotten such a face. There was something unusual about this child, something more than the absurd way she was dressed and the fact that she wore no shoes even though it was bitterly cold.

She was small and wraithlike, with a delicate gamin's face and hair so gloriously long, thick and red that it looked like a living thing. But it was her eyes that kept Meghann silent, that caught at her breath and held it when she would have spoken. Those eyes had seen things that a child should never see. Staring into that ageless green gaze was like taking the first step into a journey that, once begun, could never be abandoned.

"Who are you?" she whispered. Effortlessly, the crystalline silence carried her words across the distance that separated them.

The girl's expression changed to one of amazement. "I am Nuala O'Donnell, of course. Who are you?"

Meghann hesitated. "My name is Meggie. Can you tell me if there is another way into Donegal?"

"Aye." Nimble as a mountain goat, Nuala turned and climbed to the top of the boulder, pointing her finger to a spot somewhere to the northwest. "Follow the River Eske away from the main road toward Tirconnaill. You'll be safe enough from the English."

Somehow the child understood what Meghann had been afraid to voice. "Thank you," she said again, but Nuala had slipped behind the rock and disappeared. Disappointed that she hadn't offered a proper good-bye, Meghann walked back toward the road and Michael.

The lurching of the car over the rocky, unpaved pony path woke him. "Where the devil are we?" he asked thickly.

"We've crossed over the border into the Republic by way of Tirconnaill."

He frowned. "What did y' say?"

"We should reach the cottage shortly. Someone should be there. I'll leave immediately in order to establish my alibi, but I'll be back, and then we can really get to work—"

"That's not what I meant."

"I beg your pardon?"

"Y' said we were in the Republic by way of Tirconnaill."

"That's right."

Michael grinned, a tight terrible pulling of thin flesh over prominent bones. "Good Lord, Meggie. I hope your sense of direction is better than your geography. Tirconnaill no longer exists. The last time it appeared on Irish maps was before the Flight of the Earls in the seventeenth century."

"That's impossible."

Michael shrugged. "Check it out yourself. By now y' must be an expert at research, although I'm appalled t' find an Irish woman so woefully ignorant of her own history."

"History is not my specialty," she said stiffly.

"Neither is it mine, but I still know it," countered Michael.

"It's possible that the residents still refer to the area in the old way."

"I doubt it. Where did y' come by that interesting bit of information anyway?"

"A young woman told me. Her name is Nuala O'Donnell."

This time Michael didn't laugh. Instead, he studied her profile thoughtfully. "It's possible, of course," he said. "This is O'Donnell land and the name is not uncommon in Tyrone."

Intent on maneuvering the car back onto the main road, she barely paid any attention to him. "I did it," she said when they were on smooth ground again. "I actually got us around the checkpoints." She looked over at Michael. "I'm sorry. What were you saying?"

"You're an odd one, Meghann McCarthy," he said wearily. "Nuala O'Donnell of Tirconnaill died nearly four hundred years ago."

For a single frozen moment she allowed the words to wash over her, to carry her along and sweep her up in the chilling, eerie sensation of a circumstance too bizarre to be coincidental. And then her own sense of the absurd resurrected itself and she laughed. "Don't be ridiculous."

Michael shrugged. "I'm merely repeating historical fact." The effort of holding his head up became too great and he leaned back against the seat.

"Don't tell me you've become superstitious in the last fifteen years."

He spoke with his eyes closed. "All the Irish are superstitious, and I've become many things in the last fifteen years."

Meghann changed the subject. "Are you hungry? Your mother made soup. It's in the thermos."

"No. I haven't been hungry for a long time."

Meghann's hands tightened on the wheel. "I didn't smuggle you out to watch you die."

Michael opened his eyes and turned toward her without lifting his head. "Why *did* you smuggle me out? In the excitement of the moment I forgot t' ask."

She ignored the sarcasm in his voice. "I need time to build a case, and I can't do it by talking with you for thirty minutes once a month. We need witnesses who saw you at specific times during the day. I need authority to request copies of the files. There must be a reason why you're the only suspect. Motive is extremely important in a case of this nature. Motive must have been established. Without access to the prosecution's files, I'm in the dark."

Michael was uncharacteristically silent.

"Can you tell me anything at all?"

"No," he said shortly.

"Are you all right, Michael?"

"Tell me why you're coming out for me, Meggie."

Heat colored her cheeks. "I've already explained all that."

"It will mean professional suicide. You could drag the Thames for clients and no one would hire you. Everything you've worked for will be gone."

"Thank you for the vote of confidence. The next time I organize a prison break it will be for someone who appreciates me."

Michael swore weakly and stared out the window at the gray skies of Donegal. He hadn't meant to hurt her. Oh, Christ, maybe he had. The best he could hope for was that she would give up on him before anyone found out about her involvement. No one could win this one, not even Meggie.

He was so very tired. It didn't really matter what they did to him. All he wanted was to sleep. Lord, she was blethering on again. The woman had a mouth that wouldn't quit. Odd that he didn't remember Meggie as a talker. She had been a quiet little girl and a serious young woman. It must be the British influence. All Brits were thick as champs because they never listened. Michael believed in listening. He had never learned anything new by talking. Pity. Meggie was a taking little thing. Too thin, but still appealing. Her kissing needed improving, but that was to be expected. After all, she'd married a Brit. He wouldn't mind having a go-round with her again, but then it wouldn't bother him if it never happened. Nothing bothered him much anymore. All he wanted was sleep, sweet, uninterrupted sleep.

Meghann drove past the town center and into the castle carpark. She turned off the motor and waited. Michael was asleep again. He slept a great deal, but then it was probably good for him. If only he would eat.

The River Eske pooled into a small lough that had once served as the castle moat. The landscape was lovely in a wild, remote sort of way. The castle itself had been remodeled by an Englishman, but if Meghann remembered her history correctly, Donegal had originally been the ancestral home of Rory O'Donnell, one of the last Catholic earls of Ulster. Rather than have an Englishman inhabit his castle, he'd gutted and burned it before leaving for Italy. She had an overwhelming desire to see inside the walls.

Through the rearview mirror, she saw a young woman with black, short-cropped hair cross the street and enter the park. Her long, denim-clad legs covered the distance to the car in smooth, efficient strides. After a cursory glance at Michael, she motioned for Meghann to roll down the window. "Step outside," she ordered in a curt, authoritative voice. "Bring your bag with you."

Meghann did as she was told. The woman climbed into the car and turned the key, gunning the engine. It sputtered, hesitated and caught. "There's a blue Saab waiting for you by the monastery," she said. "Leave it in the dropoff lot at Shannon."

"How will I know where to find you?"

"That's not my problem."

"Wait." Meghann called after the moving car. "Will you be the one caring for him?"

Without answering, the woman rolled up the window and drove out of the park, leaving Meghann staring helplessly down the road after the disappearing car.

She stood there for a long time, reliving the events of the past six hours, unable to muster the energy to move. Fatigue washed over her. Her hand reached for her brooch. The smooth gold felt unusually warm. A solitary curlew circled and called overhead. The wind rose and lifted the hair from her cheeks. Just ahead loomed the castle walls. Soft insistent whispers urged her toward the portcullis gate.

Summoning the last reserves of her strength, she walked to the entrance, paid her fee and passed through the gate of Donegal Castle. The pamphlet was brief. The castle had originally belonged to the O'Donnells. After the Flight of the Earls in 1607 it had fallen into the hands of an English family, the Burkes.

The gardens were completely empty. To the right, a twisting staircase beckoned. Ducking her head, she made her way up the narrow steps to a large refurbished chamber that was once the Great Hall. A massive oak table set with trenchers and goblets dominated the room. Somehow, Meghann knew this wasn't what she had come for. Continuing up the stairs, she bypassed several smaller rooms until she came to the end of the hall. Disappointed, she turned back. There was nothing of Ireland or the O'Donnells in this refinished, glossy-coated mansion.

Absorbed in her own thoughts, she almost missed it, the sharp turn where none was before, the roughly hewn walls, the narrow, low-ceilinged hall, the glow of a hot peat fire, the leap and gutter of torches throwing light on a laden banquet table and rush-strewn floor. Meghann had the childish urge to rub her eyes. Something was wrong with her. Shadows moved along the walls and then, assuming shape and dimension, stepped away, taking their places on the low benches. Warm laughter, slurred voices and odors, pungent and human, filled her senses.

The hearth dominated an entire wall, a blazing fire throwing arcs of light across the room. Caught in a ruddy beam, silhouetted against its glow, a man dressed in period costume was fingering the same instrument that Meghann had watched Nuala O'Donnell play earlier that morning.

Her heartbeat drummed in her ears. It had to be a reenactment, and yet she was the only audience. The players, caught up in their drink-induced camaraderie, seemed unaware of her presence. Meghann found a stool in the shadows and sat down, her eyes on the musician and the small crowd that took their places around him.

His voice was rich and clear, and soon the only sounds in the chamber were his words and the lilting notes of his music. Meghann closed her eyes and listened. The man was very skilled. Her breathing quickened as he sang of a mighty castle, secret glens, silver lakes and the treasures found to the east in the O'Neill kingdom of Tyrone.

She must have dozed off because she no longer felt tired. The music had stopped and a man stood before her. Not really a man, she decided after looking more closely, but a boy, barely out of his teens, with hair so light it fell like spun silver to his shoulders and eyes as hard and blue as winter ice. He was very tall and lean, and the sun-darkened arms and chest exposed at the neck and wrists of his rough linen shirt showed the promise of powerful muscle. Fur trimmed his boots, and the leather scabbard at his waist carried the deadly, winking gleam of steel. The clothes and hair were sixteenth century, but even if she hadn't known that, she would never have believed that this incredible young man standing before her was English.

Meghann swallowed and would have spoken, but before the words could come he spoke instead, but not to her. She did not exist for him. Intrigued, she sat back and waited, her own reality suspended for one timeless, inescapable moment.

"Sing to me again of Nuala O'Neill," the boy demanded.

The bard strummed his lute and stared into the fire. "You've heard enough of the glories of Tyrone," he grumbled. "Your father will have my hide if he hears more."

"Come, Ruidarch," he coaxed him. "Father sleeps. 'Tis I you must entertain."

"Nay, Rory. 'Tis Kieran you will wed. I will sing to you of Kieran O'Neill."

Cursing, the boy spat into the rushes. "The taste of ale coats my mouth. I never chose to wed Kieran O'Neill."

"There now, Rory," the bard soothed him. "Those who are born to the nobility rarely take part in the choosing of their brides. Your troth was plighted the moment she was born, an earl's first son to marry an earl's first daughter."

"They tell me she is lovely, with a quiet beauty like the coming of a silver dawn, but even were she born with the face of legends, I would not take her. My soul burns for a lass called Nuala."

The old man nodded. "They say Nuala is most fair, beyond the fairness of mortal women," he mused. "Beggers leave the castle gates of Tyrone with bread in their bellies and coppers in their palms. But I know you better than yourself, lad. 'Tis not compassion you desire in a woman, nor is it accomplishment." He leaned forward, his instrument forgotten. "What is it that makes you seek out the O'Neill's second daughter before all others?

Rory clenched his fists. Ruidarch was all he had ever known of a mother and a better father than his own. If he could not unburden his heart to him, he could do so to no one. "She is of Brian Boru's seed," he said. "Her courage in the teeth of her father's submission to Elizabeth and her loyalty to her mother's people are the stuff of legends. Kingdoms are lost for the lack of those qualities in the bloodlines of our noble houses. I want Nuala O'Neill for the children she will give me." He stood. "I will go to Tyrone and I will bring her home as my bride or I will bring back no one."

The old man's gasp was like heady wine to the brash, unschooled heir of Tirconnaill.

Nuala O'Neill, Tyrone, 1588

My sister was sixteen summers to my fourteen, but she was still a timid fool. Watching her sob into the bed linens, I felt only contempt for her plight. "Why didn't you tell him from the beginning?" I asked. "Father is not a cruel man. He would have welcomed a daughter with a vocation."

Kieran shook her head. "I could not. He always meant me for Tirconnaill. I've known since I could understand the words."

"You might have tried," I said reasonably. "'Tis no small thing to have a daughter enter a convent."

"I am not you, Nuala," Kieran muttered. "Father does not grant my wishes."

Flipping my braid back over my shoulder, I stood and looked down at the mewling woman who called me sister. "Men do not care for tears, Kieran, and our father is every inch a man. It would serve you well to remember that."

Kieran lifted her tear-swollen face to look at me. "Do you fear anything, little sister?"

I shrugged and considered her question. In truth, there was very little in life to fear. Born of the union between the Earl of Tyrone and an Irish princess of Munster, I was allowed my lead from the time I was a wee lass. From the kitchens to the stables to the Great Hall, I listened and learned until the smallest detail of my father's castle was as commonplace to me as the tales I learned in my mother's solar. It was she, a woman of Brian Boru's line, who taught me the power of language, the art of courtly politics, the value of loyalty and the terrible, unalterable price of a woman's honor.

To uphold her honor, Kieran was forced to a troth she had no wish to keep. That same honor silenced my mother's tongue when she would have spoken on her behalf, and it was honor that sent me to the glen on that mad, diabolic flight across marshy bogs and moss-wet stones to face the man who would be my sister's husband.

Until that night of ghost-touched mist and leaves faerie-painted with moonglow and ash, I had no knowledge of Rory O'Donnell, only of the plan I would unfold before him. I remember wondering how I would know him, and then, when at last he stood before me, I feared that I might never forget him.

Honor had no place that night in the netherworld glen nor in the words that passed between us, only a wanting and a slow, sweet ache that began deep in my core, swelling and spreading until it burned with piercing clarity as if to proclaim to all of Tyrone that Kieran O'Neill would become a nun after all.

They had camped on the northern side of the glen, nearly two leagues from the castle gates, two men and Kieran's betrothed, the man they called Rory O'Donnell. I walked carefully around the horses to be sure they alerted no one to my presence and settled behind a boulder to watch as they conversed by the fire. I wanted to speak with O'Donnell alone, to sense the measure of the man he was. Finally, after an interminable time, he stood and stretched, bidding his companions good night. Again I waited while the men settled into sleep, silent lumps beneath woolen blankets on the nettle-soft ground.

Cautiously, I approached him, crawling the last few paces on my hands and knees. Then I crossed my legs beneath me and willed him to feel my gaze and wake.

The man slept soundly on his bed of nettles. Inching my toe forward, I prodded his shoulder. Still he slept like the dead. Frustrated, I grew bolder. Leaning over him, I brushed his face with the end of my braid. And then in the space of a heartbeat it happened. Hurting hands gripped my shoulders, flipped me over and threw me to the ground. When I could breathe again, my wind came in deep uneven gasps.

"What do you want?" he demanded, holding me down with a grip of steel.

The weight of his body crushed the speech from mine. I opened my mouth to tell him but the words refused to come. Somehow I managed to communicate my discomfort for he moved slightly, keeping his hands on my wrists. I breathed again and found my voice. "Why do you camp here in the glen when the castle is so near?"

" 'Tis rude to come to the O'Neill at night after the gates are closed." His hands tightened and he grinned. "If you seek to rob me, lass, I tell you now, 'tis not your sport. You are too loud."

The man was insolent. I struggled to a sitting position and he released me. "I have no need of money, sir. I am a daughter of the castle."

He frowned. "You are Red Hugh's daughter?"

"Aye."

He reached out and gripped my chin, forcing me to look at him. " 'Tis too dark," he muttered, "I cannot see your face."

His fingers on my flesh and his face so close to mine

unnerved me. "The fire is out," I whispered, wondering what it was about this man that sent the shivers down my spine.

"Aye," he whispered back, "but the sunrise will come."

Alarmed, I came to my senses. "I cannot stay the night with you. My maid will miss me. I came only to bring a message."

His hand moved across my face, a hard callused hand, testing the shape of my nose and the bones beneath my cheeks. "What message do you have for me, fair Nuala?"

"'Tis from my sister, Kieran. She has the calling and does not wish for marriage." I swallowed. What I had come to say was not as easy as I had imagined it to be. Still my mind was the same as it had been when I left the castle, and I was not one to dissemble. The worst he could say was nay. I lifted my chin bravely. "I thought, that is, I hoped you would have me instead."

I had no idea what it was that caused the laughter to rise from his chest and spill out into the night. But it did. And before I could ask what humor he found in my words, he was no longer laughing. For the first time, I learned that the lips of a man tasted like cool rain and clean wind and the promise of something warm and wild and uniquely different from anything I'd ever known.

Later, much later, when I could think again, I heard his words, unsteady and muffled against my hair. "I would be honored to take you, lass. 'Tis what I intended all along."

6

Completely oblivious to everything but her own fatigue, Meghann dropped the Saab at Shannon Airport, purchased her ticket for the brief flight home and hailed a taxi to her London town house. All she wanted was sleep. Mechanically, she greeted Mrs. Hartwell, refused her offer of tea and went straight to the bedroom, where she collapsed in the large fourposter for fourteen hours of uninterrupted sleep.

All that week she was careful to make regular appearances at the office, to inform her new associate of the details of her most pressing cases and to lunch with Cecil at least twice. It was not that difficult to hint at family difficulties, and although it was embarrassing to listen to his sincerely sympathetic condolences, she wrote them off as a necessary liability. It was not so easy to disregard the guilt that nagged at her conscience for deceiving him.

Meghann meticulously scanned the newspapers, but to her surprise no mention was made of a successful escape from the Maze. For some reason, British authorities wanted to keep this one quiet, and British Broadcasting was cooperating.

Pulling the zipper of her suitcase closed, she looked around to be sure she hadn't forgotten anything. A wave of premature homesickness swept through her. Before Michael Devlin had stepped into her life again, her days had been so wonderfully predictable. Mrs. Hartwell's tea and toast in the morning, the drive to her office in the expensive Jaguar Charles had purchased the year before his death, the whisper of soft cashmere against her skin, the chime of Waterford crystal, the bone china filling every cupboard, the gleam of fine silver, the scent of lemon polish on eighteenth-century furniture and the delicious wanton pleasure of purchasing anything she could ever want.

Not that she had, of course. An unusual phenomenon had occurred once she found herself with the means to ignore anything so ignominious as a price tag. It seemed to Meghann that the ache of desire mysteriously evaporated. Since she was inherently frugal and her career took most of her time, she considered it a blessing. Still, she would miss the convenient elegance of her home and the redoubtable Mrs. Hartwell. Meghann couldn't remember the last time she had cooked a meal or managed the laundry. With a sigh, she lifted her bag to her shoulder and walked past her Sevres china vases and Queen Anne chairs, through the tasteful living room and out the door to her waiting taxi.

Her drive to the beach cottage was not without incident. It was surprising that she found the place at all. The directions had been whispered over the phone, the voice muffled with something that made detection impossible. Not that it would have made a difference. Meghann was not a private investigator nor a police detective, and she knew no one actively involved in nationalist politics.

She almost turned down the road that would have taken her in the opposite direction toward Ballybofey and British-occupied Ulster when something stopped her, an urge, no, something stronger than that, a force, compelling her to pause, pull over and look at the map more carefully.

While she was in the convenience store asking directions, a British patrol rolled by. Meghann felt the blood leave her hands. She watched as a car bearing an Armagh license plate was commandeered to the side of the road and the driver questioned. Shivering, she busied herself by examining the store's inventory until the patrol moved on. The clerk looked at her curiously. "May I help y', lass?" he asked.

"Yes, please." Hastily grabbing two pints of Guinness, a dozen eggs, a loaf of bread and a tin of tea, Meghann carried them to the counter, paid cash and walked quickly to the car. After stowing her purchases in the backseat, she slid behind the wheel and turned the key. Her hands shook. Leaning her forehead against the steering wheel, she took several deep, sustaining breaths before pulling out onto the road. An encounter with the British army and the inevitable questions for which she had no answer was something she wasn't prepared to face.

The man's directions were flawless. Meghann drove to the back of a whitewashed cottage with a thatched roof and parked the car in a shed. Pulling the strap of her travel bag over her shoulder, she gathered the groceries and made her way across the long grass to the door. No one answered her knock.

Shifting the bag to one arm, she fumbled with the latch, lifted it and pushed the door open. The room was empty but very warm. A peat fire glowed in the hearth. She noticed the dishwasher and immediately relaxed. A more thorough inspection revealed an electric can opener, a coffeemaker, a toaster oven and a blender.

She set the groceries on the table and walked into the living room. The cottage was two-storied, with a shining wooden floor stained honey-gold. Hand-painted birds had been painstakingly stenciled around floorboards, and large, multipaned windows took full advantage of the light. The wood furniture, while not expensive, was old and sturdily built, and the sofa with its plump pillows looked comfortable. A cozy fire provided most of the warmth, but evidence of gas heat could be seen in the narrow pipes running along the ceiling. Fleece throws hung invitingly over the chairs, and scenes of fishermen hauling in their catches lined the walls.

A stairway with a substantial guardrail twisted its way to the second floor. Michael would be at the top of those stairs. Michael with his caustic conversation, his fundamental chin and that penetrating blue gaze that saw through all her layers without revealing anything at all of himself.

Meghann squared her shoulders. This time it would be different. This time she would have weeks to find the answers to this maddeningly elusive case that made no sense at all. Fifteen years ago she would have sworn that Michael Devlin was no murderer. Now, she wasn't so sure. Fifteen years in Belfast with no hope for anything better would lay their mark on a man. It was no accident that IRA men were heroes in the Falls, no accident that those who did time in Long Kesh and the Maze were welcomed back into the community, given respect, lodging, food and what living there was to give, until the next time they were arrested. Paramilitaries learned their trade behind bars, and they learned it well. The Irish Republican Army was acknowledged the most thorough, the most efficient and the most deadly guerrilla force in the entire world.

It suddenly occurred to Meghann that she should be afraid. Although the Provisional IRA did not intentionally harm civilians, especially women, she was not the average civilian. She was one of their own who had turned her coat, a traitor who left the Falls and married a British lord, one of the hated establishment who, through sheer ignorance, neglect and a touch of cruelty, had kept them in a state of feudal serfdom up to the present day.

Slowly, she climbed the stairs. The door to a modern bathroom with thick yellow towels and a fluffy rug stood open. A wide hall led to a single room with a double bed, a nineteenth century armoire, a dresser and a washbasin. Michael stood by the window staring out at the gray sea.

"Hello, Meghann," he said without turning around.

She lowered her suitcase to the floor and rubbed her shoulder. "Hello."

He turned and a shard of relief pierced her chest. He was still dreadfully thin, but he looked like the old Michael, the one she had seen the first time she visited the Maze. Faded denim jeans hung on his emaciated frame, and the rolled-up sleeves of his flannel shirt revealed bony arms with atrophied muscle and no fat at all. He stood straight and tall without support, and before they went blank the blue eyes staring into hers had, for an instant, blazed just as they had the night he'd waited in the rain in front of her lodgings, the night she'd sent him away forever.

"How are you feeling?" she asked in Irish.

He shrugged. "Well enough. And you?"

"I'm well, also." Meghann looked around. There was only one bed. "I'll put my things in the closet downstairs and fix us something to eat."

"I'd play the gentleman and offer up the room, but I spend a great deal of time sleeping and you'll be about more than I will. Don't bother about the food right away unless you're hungry." He looked pointedly at her slender figure. "It doesn't look as if y' bother with food much. You're thinner than y' were as a girl."

Meghann ignored his last comment. "Actually, I am hungry. I'll make us some tea. If there's soup and bread I'll make that too. As soon as I find out where everything is I'll call you, unless," she tilted her head and looked at him speculatively, "you want to keep me company."

He shook his head and turned back to the window.

Suddenly Meghann was stricken with doubt. What if he wouldn't talk to her? She took a step forward and stopped. Michael had been through a tremendous ordeal, and it was far from over. Perhaps he needed time. Resolving to curb her impatience, Meghann picked up her suitcase and walked back down the stairs, leaving him alone.

Tins of soup, fruit, vegetables, tea, oats, biscuits and a basket of potatoes filled the cupboards. An inspection of the refrigerator revealed a half-dozen eggs, a pint of milk, a package of butter, two packages of cheese and several pounds of beef, lamb and a pork roast. They definitely wouldn't starve.

Meghann unpacked the groceries she had purchased and opened a tin of potato soup, added grated cheese, a tin of corn and some salt. She ladled the soup into bowls, set out some sliced wheat bread and two glasses of Guinness and called to Michael to come downstairs.

Five full minutes passed before he arrived at the table. Meghann's cheeks were pink with temper. Too bad for him if it wasn't hot enough, she fumed silently. If he didn't care enough to come when she called, he could just eat it cold.

He ate sparingly, efficiently, making his way through the creamy soup and buttered bread with minimal motion. She noticed that he barely touched his ale.

"You're not drinking your Guinness. Would you like some tea?"

Michael looked up, startled, as if he'd forgotten that someone else was in the room. A minute went by, and the bewildered look on his face vanished. "Aye. I'll take a cup of tea. I'm not much for Guinness, or spirits for that matter."

"What kind of Irishman are you," she teased, busying herself with the tea, "to be refusing the drink?"

"A practical one, I hope," he retorted with a spark of the old fire. "God, Meggie, I would have thought you of all people would be encouraging temperance."

She set the teapot on the table along with two cups, spoons and saucers. "I wasn't serious, Michael. Can't you laugh anymore?"

"In case y' haven't heard, there hasn't been much t' laugh about in my life lately."

She poured milk into each cup and then added the tea, in the orderly symbiosis she'd learned at her mother's knee. Only her voice revealed her emotions. "I'm trying to help you," she said quietly.

"How magnanimous of you. I must remember that."

Meghann sat down across from him and lifted her cup with icy hands. "You don't like me much, do you?"

A shock of black hair fell across Michael's forehead. Impatiently, he tossed his head back and glared at her, naked anger in the storm-tossed turbulence of his eyes. "Should I? Y' took your education and your talent and left us. That's such a Protestant thing t' do, Meggie. There isn't one doctor or lawyer or teacher in the Shankill. They all left for better neighborhoods. That isn't what we do. We help our own. Maybe there's bad blood in you. Is that it, Meggie?" His cruel emphasis of her childhood name sickened her. "Maybe there's always been some Prod in you, more, that is, than Lord Sutton's endowed patrician di—."

"That's enough! My husband was the kindest man alive, and I won't let you insult him." She wasn't aware that she had leaped to her feet, the chair knocked over and forgotten behind her. She leaned forward, the weight of her body balanced on her curved fingers.

"Yes, I left the Falls, and there's not a moment that I regret it. I have a life, Michael, a life that's clean and purposeful, away from women who never sit because all they do is cook and clean and wash in houses that run with rain in winter and have no indoor plumbing. You remember those women, Michael, the ones who bear a new child every nine months and find jobs away from those children so they can bring in more than the thirty shillings a week their husbands bring home on the dole, if they don't stop at the pub on the way home. Have you forgotten, Michael, how your mother and mine gave up their chairs so their men could sit in the sun on fine days?"

Her lip curled contemptuously. "Have you forgotten how those poor, burdened men wore themselves out walking to the Labour Exchange to sign for their weekly dole and then wondered what to do to fill the rest of their hours, besides talking about the world's problems with other men just as worthless and just as drunk? Maybe that's what you wanted for me, Michael, a man who educates himself all day in the Linen Library instead of looking for work, because God forbid that a man on the dole appear ignorant. He needs to know all about world affairs in case Bosnia falls or the United States declares war or apartheid in South Africa begins again. It's all right that his children drink sugar water instead of milk as long as he can sit in the sun with his cigarettes and Stout and demand that his sons prepare themselves to fight for Ireland. It's all right that he gambles and drinks away his pay and that his wife will die young in a cold-water flat because every year there's a new baby, no birth control and no divorce, and because all she has to look forward to is the knowledge that someday her children will all die for Ireland."

He stared, arrested, at the rage and heartbreak in every strained tendon of Meghann's slight body. Impassioned disclosures were not typical of the Meggie he'd known. In fact, it was her detached remoteness, so different from the loud cacophony constantly permeating the Devlin household, that had attracted him in the first place. Meghann was never loud or rude or opinionated. In the entire time she had lived in his mother's house, he couldn't remember her disagreeing with anyone, a difficult feat considering that none of the Devlins ever agreed with one another.

He remembered a certain Christmas Eve Mass when he'd stared at a stained-glass window with its depiction of the Virgin Mary and Jesus. Something had flashed in his mind that he'd never thought of before. Meggie, with her halo-lit hair, her serene lovely face and her slow, secretive smile was Mary of the New Testament. Mary, the quiet, long-suffering mother of Jesus and wife to Joseph who never complained, never spoke her mind and never lost her innocence.

"That was quite a speech," he said quietly. "Too bad you've no desire for political office."

She stared at him. "When did you become such an unfeeling bastard?"

It was the day he made love to her. She'd told him that she loved him and then, without a word, packed up and moved away. But he'd swing by the neck before telling her. "Not all men are drunks, Meghann," he said instead.

"No, just Irish men."

"Come now, Meggie, you're the one who drank the Guinness."

"If that's supposed to be a stab at levity, it won't work."

"Very well then," he said. "Here's a fact for you. Poverty exists in London just as it does in the North."

"I'm not talking about poverty," she said stiffly, in control of herself once again. "I'm talking about desperation and futility."

"You're exaggerating."

She began clearing the dishes. "You forget that I speak from personal experience."

"Why did you agree to stay here with me?"

"There was no one else we could trust. Your family

would have been watched. There is no possibility of anyone connecting me with you."

"You're far more sophisticated than anyone in my family, Meghann. Did you tell them of the risk you're taking? After all, I'm a fugitive. You could lose everything you've worked for as well as go to prison."

She stared at him. Was this Michael Devlin talking? The boy who had risked his life to find her amid the death and rubble of Cupar Street? Had he any idea what his family meant to her? "That isn't likely to happen," was all she said.

He stood up. "I'm tired. Come into the sitting room and read t' me until I fall asleep."

Meghann pushed a wisp of hair off her forehead with a soapy hand. "Is something the matter with your eyes?"

"Someone forgot t' tell me I was leavin' in a hurry. I left my reading glasses in the Maze."

"I need to ask you some questions, Michael. This won't go away, and I can't stay forever."

He brushed her protests away with a lift of his hand. "Not now. I feel like a novel. There's some good literature in the bookcase. How about it, Meggie?"

She sighed and turned back to the sink. "You go ahead. I'll be there as soon as I finish the dishes."

After wiping dry the last bowl and stacking it in the cupboard, Mehgann surveyed the bookshelf in the hallway. She was drawn to a small volume entitled *The History of Ulster*. Michael's derisive taunt about her ignorance hit very close to home, although she wouldn't give him the satisfaction of telling him so. By the time she walked into the living room he was asleep. A fine sheen of perspiration covered his forehead, but when she touched his cheek it was cold. Replenishing the fire had obviously taken up whatever reserves of energy he had. She tucked a throw around him, pulled her chair closer to the fire and stared into the flames.

The light was lovely, copper-tipped and black-centered, with the lines of deep royal blue so often seen with peat fuel. It was odd, really, the way she had no desire to do anything but stare into the center of that sweetly scented fire. Normally she wasn't the kind to waste a minute, but just now it felt right to do nothing but sit without thinking, mesmerized by the play and dance of light against the darkening walls. Her eyelids felt heavy and she was finally warm. Through spidery lashes she saw the flames leap and dance inside the brick hearth, taking one shape and then another. She smiled. Involuntarily, her fingers moved to the gold circle resting at the base of her throat. Her eyes closed and her head fell back against the chair.

She heard rain slant into the chimney. The fire sizzled, its black center swirling and melding into a feminine form, the copper borders framing a woman's face like braids of flame-red hair.

She stood beside Rory O'Donnell, a child-woman with eyes as clear as glass and a delicate mobile face that with every changing nuance spoke of Ireland.

Nuala O'Donnell, Tyrone, 1588

We faced my father together. I saw Rory swallow and step forward. He reached for my hand and whispered that we would see this through together.

Hugh O'Neill was a massively built man, with hair the same shocking red as my own. His neatly trimmed beard was a shade darker, with streaks of white, and his eyes were the hard, cold gray of the North Sea beneath a cloudy sky. He would be a formidable opponent in any mood, but now more so because he stood in the throes of a raging temper. I glanced at Rory and felt a surge of pride. He was not afraid of Red Hugh O'Neill.

"You dare come to me with this outrageous proposal!" my father roared, towering over me.

Rory stepped between us, braver than he was wise,

for although the two men were the same height, the O'Neill was twice his girth.

"Who are you?" my father demanded.

"I am Rory O'Donnell of Tirconnaill, and I have come to wed your daughter."

"'Tis time you came. You are her betrothed."

From what little I knew of Rory, I had already guessed that diplomacy was not his strength. I sensed what he wished to say and with a few whispered words brought him all that he desired.

"The O'Neill is blessed in his daughters," he began, struggling at first with the words of a courtier. "Gentle Kieran will serve you well with the holy sisters. Her prayers will surely reach the ears of our Lord when we unite against the English. 'Tis Nuala I would wed. Tirconnaill needs Nuala. She will bring kingdoms to our way of thinking."

The O'Neill's bushy eyebrows drew together over his nose, and he glared at the two of us for a long time without blinking. "You have met before?" he asked suspiciously.

"Nay, my lord," I said quickly, refusing to be the first to look away.

He stroked his beard and motioned Rory to a chair beside his own. "You would wed this wild piece?" he asked, gesturing toward me.

"I would."

He stared at Rory, missing nothing. Lowering his voice, he spoke. "She is young and you are burly. Fourteen summers is too young for bearing."

Rory nodded. "Aye."

"If I agree to your troth, you will not bed her until the spring."

"Until next summer, if you wish."

Red Hugh nodded. "The English queen is my enemy. She seeks to join my lands with her own."

"Aye, mine as well."

"Swear that you'll bring the might of Tirconnaill against her if I ask it."

"I swear."

My father held out his hand and Rory grasped it. "You may have my daughter, O'Donnell," he shouted for the entire hall to hear. "The wedding will take place in a fortnight."

"My father is ill," Rory protested. "I cannot be away so long, and I had hoped to take Nuala with me when I return."

The O'Neill weighed his words for a long time. "So be it," he said at last and motioned to my mother, cool and silent, standing behind him. "What say you, Agnes? 'Tis our Nuala who will wed the O'Donnell and Kieran who will be the nun."

Her soft musical laugh charmed everyone. I saw that Rory was already bewitched by her.

"I say, 'tis better than the other way around." She kissed Rory on both cheeks. "Welcome to Tyrone, my lord."

"Nuala, wake up." Kieran's cool hands touched my face.

"What is it?" I grumbled. "Surely 'tis the middle of the night, Kieran, and no time for conversation."

"I must know. Did you do it for me? Before God, much as I wish to devote my life to Christ, I cannot allow you to make such a sacrifice. You are so young, Nuala, and so very small. The man is a giant."

I struggled into wakefulness, rubbing my eyes and pushing back my hair.

"Please tell me, little sister. Is this truly your wish?"

I stared at her, her features gaunt with worry in the dim light of the candle she carried. Was she blind that she couldn't see the manner of man she had given up? Perhaps she truly was called to God. I smiled. "I am doubly grateful for your calling, sister. Because of my nature, I shall need all of your prayers. And it is I who should thank you for Rory O'Donnell. He suits me well."

"Truly, Nuala?" Tears gathered in the corners of Kieran's dove-gray eyes.

"Truly."

Her breath came out in a small rush of air. "God be praised." She raised her eyes to my face. "The wedding is tomorrow, and tomorrow night—" She shuddered. "Aren't you afraid, Nuala?"

I thought back to the strange trembling that began in my stomach when Rory kissed me. "Nay," I said truthfully, pulling my nightshift tight against my body. "I only hope that I please him. As you say, I am small."

"But beautiful," Kieran protested fiercely. "The most beautiful lass in Tyrone."

"You are my sister, Kieran. Your sight is colored with affection."

"The bards sing of you, Nuala. You know what they say."

She spoke the truth, and I suppose it could be said that I was unusual in my appearance. Not many were blessed with white, even teeth and unmarked skin, except for the freckles on my nose and cheeks. Red hair was common in Tyrone, but more often it came wiry and coarse, twisting into tendrils even when pulled back into a tight plait. Mine was thick and straight and very fine with a dozen hues of red from darkest claret to the lightest copper. Yes, I was fortunate in my hair and in my eyes, clear and green as Irish grass. Perhaps it was enough and I would not need full breasts and rounded hips to keep Rory O'Donnell in my bed. I prayed it might be so.

I felt Kieran's soft kiss on my cheek. "Good night, my love."

"Good night, Kieran."

7

Nuala O'Donnell, Tyrone, 1588

We were wed by the parish priest. There was no time
for the cardinal to make the journey from Armagh to
Tyrone. The day was long. Wine and ale and fiery
spirits that burned a path to the belly flowed freely
within the castle walls. By night, men and women
alike lay on the rushes, stretched out among the dogs
in drunken stupors.

I had eaten and drunk very little, my concentration
centered on the man who was now my husband. He
sat by my side at the banquet table, sharing my
trencher, eating a bit more than I but drinking little. It
pleased me that he had little appetite for spirits. It was
nearly time to retire, and a strange breathlessness
knotted my stomach. Perhaps I was just the tiniest bit
afraid.

From across the room my mother signaled and left
the room. I rose and the hall resounded with ap-
plause. Rory stood and slipped his arm about my
waist. Kieran lifted my train and screamed at me to
run. Out the door I ran and down the long hallway,
followed by a dozen shouting women and half the

men in the banquet hall, up the stairs to the landing and then up again, down another hall to the room that was to be my bridal suite. My mother slammed and bolted the door behind Kieran and me. We leaned, panting, against the door.

"Make haste," my mother said, loosening the ties at my neck and lifting the wedding gown over my head. I would have lifted off the shift, but she shook her head and folded back the bedclothes to remove the warming pans. "There is no need. Wait for your husband in here."

I climbed into the high, curtain-shrouded bed and leaned back against the pillows. The sheets were warm. Candles of the finest wax flickered on small tables, and a flask of wine with two goblets waited on a chest at the foot of the bed. A fire burned cheerily in the brick hearth, and the smell of sandalwood perfumed the air. I shivered with anticipation. Tonight I would learn what it meant to be a woman.

Laughter and ribaldry sounded from the hall and someone pounded loudly at the door. With a quick kiss on both cheeks, Mother and Kieran lifted the bolt and stepped out, then my husband stepped inside. I sat up and watched as he closed the door and walked across the room to the bed.

"Hello," he said softly, touching my cheek with the back of his hand.

I could feel the tickle of fine hair that grew from his skin. "Hello," I answered.

Turning, he lifted the flask and poured two glasses of wine. Drinking his own in a single gulp, he offered the other to me. I shook my head, and he drank mine as well. First he removed his shoes and then his tunic. My throat went dry. I had never seen a naked man before, but even I knew this one was extraordinarily well formed. He blew out the candles. After a long moment I felt one side of the bed give and then I felt his body, naked as the day he was born, warm against my own. I could scarcely breathe, so great was my excitement. I wanted to touch him but did not, fearing he would think me immodest.

His lips were warm against my forehead, my cheeks, my neck and uncovered shoulders. When at last they settled on my mouth, I couldn't help the moan that came from deep inside my throat and my arms reached out to pull him closer.

I know not what I did to displease him but the instant I melted against him and my body felt as one with his, I heard his strangled cry and felt strong hands push me away from his warmth to the cold side of the bed. His breathing was rapid and shallow, as if he had run a great distance. So great was my shame that even tears eluded me. Hours later, when I was sure he slept, I closed my burning eyes until morning.

Even before I was fully conscious, I felt his eyes upon me. Somewhere in the night his body had once again moved close to mine. I could no more stop the red from staining my throat and cheeks than I could stop the sun from shining down on County Tyrone. It appeared that Kieran was wrong, and my doubts had been well founded. Red hair and green eyes did not make up for those other womanly traits I so obviously lacked.

The night had been a long one. I had never slept beside a man before and wondered if they all tossed and turned, grumbling and cursing the night through as Rory had.

Finally I managed to sleep for a few brief hours but woke again when I felt his eyes upon me. I felt the color rise in my face even before I opened my eyes. He was awake, staring at me, and I was very conscious of his body pressed against mine.

"Was your sleep pleasant?" he asked.

"It was," I lied. "And yours?"

"I slept well."

It occurred to me to ask why he lied when I

remembered that I had as well. "When do we leave for Tirconnaill?" I asked instead.

He leaned close to me and breathed deeply. "After Mass. Your hair smells like sunlight."

I pushed the red weight of it away from my face and sat up. "Tell me again of your family."

He pulled me against his chest and settled back against the pillows. "There is only my father at Dun na Ghal. His health is poor and he rarely leaves his chambers." My hand moved across his bare chest. He kissed the top of my head and then lifted my chin and kissed my mouth, pulling away quickly. "You tempt me to take more than I should, lass."

I summoned my courage and asked the question that burned in my head. "Are all wedding nights like ours?"

He reddened. "Nay."

"How are they different?"

He muttered something under his breath.

"Rory? Have you heard me?"

"By the beard of Christ! Where has your mother been? I cannot speak of such matters to a girl who is not yet a woman."

"I cannot see how what happens on our wedding night concerns my mother. You are my husband, Rory. Who better than you to tell me?"

He was silent for a long time. I could feel the demons of logic and pride warring within him. Finally he cleared his throat. "A wedding night is when a husband takes his wife's maidenhood," he said stiffly. "Their bodies become one." He shifted me in his arms to better see my face. "Do you know what I speak of, Nuala? Surely you have seen animals."

I nodded and saw that the color had faded from his cheeks.

"Words do not come easily to me," he confessed.

I sat up and looked directly at him. "Do you find me distasteful, Rory O'Donnell?"

His eyebrows flew together. "Nay, lass. Why would you ask such a question?"

"Why did you not take my maidenhood?"

There was nothing wrong with my understanding. Written in the twin flames of his eyes was regret.

Slowly, carefully, as if I were made of delicate porcelain, he reached out to trace my brows, the thin bridge of my nose, my lips and the sharp lines of my cheeks and chin.

"The Blessed Virgin herself could not have been more lovely than you are to me, Nuala," he whispered. " 'Tis not for lack of wanting that I keep myself from you."

"Then why—"

His fingers brushed across my mouth. "You are too young for bearing. Too many are wed one year and dead the next. I would have it go differently for you."

A warm glow spread through my breast. "Truly, Rory? Is that your reason?"

He laughed and pulled me close. "Truly, Nuala."

I leaned into his lips. After all, there was no harm in kissing.

Meghann woke to the tapping of a tree branch against the windowpane. She had never dreamed this way before, so clearly and in chronological segments, as if she were viewing a film. She turned toward Michael and found him staring at her. Disconcerted, she behaved as if it were perfectly natural to wake and find a man's eyes upon her. "Have you been awake long?"

"No."

"Can I get you anything?"

"No."

She set the book on the table beside her and folded her hands in her lap. "I'd like to ask you some questions, Michael."

He reached over and picked up the history book. "Were y' looking for something in particular?"

She hadn't intended to tell him. The words just popped out. "I wanted some information on Nuala O'Donnell."

He smiled and ran his thin, long-fingered hands tenderly over the book cover. "Nuala, lady of legend."

"Why do you say that?"

"Nuala O'Donnell is an Irish legend. She kept Ulster out of English hands for fourteen years, long after everyone else had surrendered t' Elizabeth Tudor."

"What happened to her?"

"After the Battle of Kinsale and the importation of Protestants into the North, she and her husband escaped t' Italy. I believe she died there."

"Did she live in Donegal?"

"Aye. She was Rory O'Donnell's countess, and he was the last Catholic earl of Tirconnaill."

"Was the marriage a happy one?"

Michael shrugged. "Most noble marriages of the time were political matches. There is no evidence t' suggest that theirs was different."

He grinned and Meghann felt the stirring deep within her. It came whenever Michael unleashed the charm that had once been her undoing.

"They had nine children," he said. "I suppose they felt some affection for each other."

Meghann was instantly suspicious. "Are you making this up?"

"Not a bit of it."

She looked skeptical. "It's strange the way you know so much about whatever it is I ask about."

He looked surprised. "I told you. I know Irish history."

"Your education was certainly better than mine," she observed thoughtfully. "We learned next to nothing about Ireland."

"I didn't learn it in school, Meggie. All Irish prisoners of war learn their history in prison. It's what we do t' pass the time. While the Brits are learning about computers or electronics, we're learning the stories of our people along with a healthy dose of political science. It's what keeps us goin'. It's why they won't let us on their networks. The BBC knows that we can debate our cause with the best English minds and win."

Meghann wrinkled her brow. "When I saw you in the Maze you were isolated. How could you possibly conduct classes?"

"Through the walls," he said deliberately. "We shout the words through the pipes and memorize them."

These men were her countrymen. Men like her father, her grandfather and her brothers. Meghann didn't know why she felt the sudden, overwhelming surge of pride flare up inside her chest or why the tears burned beneath her eyelids. She only knew she had to turn away, change the subject, leave the room, something, anything, so that he wouldn't see just how deeply his words had affected her. "Tell me about Nuala O'Donnell," she said, wiping her eyes before she turned back to face him.

Michael was a born storyteller. It was so much a part of him that Meghann wondered how she could have forgotten. The timber of his voice was wonderful, clear and beautifully pitched, and he knew just how to expand a moment. She could have listened to him forever, forgetting London, her work, her life, the reason why they were there, the two of them, in this isolated cabin on the edge of the Irish Sea with its lovely wood floors and tasteful pictures of shorelines and seabirds, of men with cable-knit sweaters and sunburned faces running with Irish rain.

He began slowly, warming to his subject just as the last rays of waning light left the darkening sky.

Firelight played on his face, highlighting the bones, shadowing the hollows beneath, picking out the length of his chiseled nose, the squared-off substantial chin, the mobile, beautifully formed mouth from which the words, always the words, intense and lyrical, rose up and poured out, sliding off his tongue as if there were a deep wellspring somewhere within him and a dam had broken.

"Legend says she was the light of Tyrone until Rory O'Donnell made her his wife and brought her home to Donegal. She kept the faith even when Niall Garv, her husband's cousin, held her captive in her own castle. She starved along with her people when the blight of sixteen hundred destroyed the potatoes. And she was the reason the English queen found no toehold in the north of Ireland."

Meghann closed her eyes and gave herself up to the magical quality of his story and the images his words evoked. She felt heat from the fire and mist on her cheeks, and behind her eyelids colors leaped and danced and settled until everything was once again completely clear.

Nuala O'Donnell, Tirconnaill, 1589

At first glimpse, Tirconnaill seemed much the same as Tyrone, wilder perhaps and a bit more primitive, but not so different that one would think longingly of home. I was not at all homesick. There was too much to do.

Dun Na Ghal Castle stood, a stark sentinel, gray and forbidding, in its place on the River Eske. Rain seeped through the mortar and collected in muddy pools beneath the rushes. Walls wept with the wet, and rats scurried in dark corners. The only warmth to be found was on the top floor, where everyone, nobles, soldiers and servants, slept on flea-ridden rushes before enormous fires. In truth it was a somber place and would take more than a cursory scrubbing. I forgot about Rory and went about the task of setting it right.

'Twas nearly a year before I could look around with pride at whitewashed walls and sweetly scented rushes covering the Great Hall floor. Finally the rooms were dry, woven tapestries kept out the drafts and jewel-bright carpets, pleasing to eyes hungry for color, warmed cold feet. Plate and silver filled the pantry, bedchambers were furnished and the larder well stocked.

When the domestic work was done, I took a moment's breath to look up from my chores and saw the frightening chain of events that had transpired in Tirconnaill, events that would set Rory and me on a journey that could end in only one way.

I was the countess of Tirconnaill, a married woman bound to Rory O'Donnell by ties that could be severed only by God. It never occurred to me that Rory would take our vows less seriously than I. He was a wonderful companion and very discreet. I had just passed my fifteenth year when I learned that marriage meant something different for him than it did for me.

When Siobhan, with her apple cheeks and full curves, brushed against my husband and offered him her lips, and when he took them as if it were the most natural thing in the world and when his hands cupped the cheeks of her voluptuous backside, I knew what it was to feel the bloodlust rise within me. My fingers itched to claw her eyes and mark her cheeks, and surely if I'd been skilled at the dirk, Rory O'Donnell would no longer be a man.

But I was my mother's daughter and did none of those things. Instead, I looked away and pretended not to see what he did with Siobhan, with Jane, with Mary and Fiona and countless others who lived under his protection and mine in that unholy castle by the River Eske. I suffered my humiliation in silence until the day a messenger came from Tyrone, bearing gifts from my mother and a note from my father.

Send your husband with your blessing, little Nuala. Ireland has need of its warriors. Pray that your womb be fertile lest Tirconnaill be left without an heir.

It was then that I realized how long Rory and I had played at this game and what I must do to end it, or the heir to Tirconnaill would be no son of mine. The gypsy woman helped me, as I had helped her when her children had no bread. She told me how to please, where to touch with lips and tongue and slow, seeking fingers. I planned it well, wine, fresh sheets, fragrant candles, perfume. I would be willing, seductive, mature, never revealing what I knew of the women who had shared my husband's bed and the ache it brought to my heart.

All would have gone as it should if Rory had come at his usual time, but he was very late. He smelled of spirits and women and the rage I'd cultivated was something he'd never seen before.

"Good night, Nuala," he said.

"Is it?" My voice sounded odd even to my own ears but such was Rory's bout with the drink that I wondered if he would notice.

"Are you well, my love?"

"Quite well."

He stepped backward and tripped over a footstool. Struggling to regain his footing, he stood and swayed on his feet. "Since you are well, I'll leave you to sleep," he said.

"Sleep?" I walked across the room and stood before him, hands on my hips. "You expect me to sleep while my husband turns from me and ruts with half my household?"

I felt very small and alone standing there in my white sleeping gown, spewing venomous accusations as if I were an angel condemning Lucifer to a fiery hell. I wondered what he would say to defend himself.

"Do you deny it?" I demanded.

His smile was tender. "Surely not half the household, Nuala."

"Do not jest, Rory. An unfaithful husband is a sin."

My cheeks were cold and I felt my lower lip tremble. I looked down at the floor. When would he see that it was more than anger that moved me? I was hurt, deeply hurt. For what had Rory made his wild impetuous ride across the moors to claim me as his bride?

I had done much for Tirconnaill in one short year. Dun Na Ghal was no longer a fortress. It was a palace fit for an earl, with candles of the finest wax, food set for a king's table, an abbey where daily mass was offered and a library where books in four languages could be read. Every peasant who worked the fields had woolen blankets and meat three times a week. I knew when a tenant needed a new roof, when to administer justice between feuding neighbors, which fields should be tilled and which should be left fallow. For the first time, disease had passed us over and no infants were buried in the castle graveyard.

The peasants called me a miracle, beloved to all in Dun Na Ghal, from the lowliest serf to Rory's father, the O'Donnell himself. They said I was goodness and beauty and wisdom and yet I was fifteen years old, a married woman and still a maiden.

He reached for my hands. "I am not your husband yet, Nuala, and therefore I have not been unfaithful."

I would have spoken, but he held his fingers against my mouth and spoke for me. "And you are not a wife."

Then I looked at him. Everything I hoped and felt I

willed him to see in my eyes. "I wish to be," I whispered. "I have waited long enough."

I had waited more than long enough, but still he did not speak. "Why did you come to Tyrone to ask for me, Rory, if it is not me you want? Kieran would have served you just as well."

"I did want you," he protested, holding my hands tightly in his. "I do want you. By God, Nuala, I want you so much my heart aches."

"Then, why—"

He groaned. And then the words came, stilted and awkward, but from his heart. "I have never known anyone like you. You have wisdom beyond your years. There is nothing I can give you. How can you want me, Nuala, a man so far beneath your touch?"

My eyes widened and for a long moment I stared, doubting my own ears. Then I smiled and stepped close to him again. The top of my head came to the middle of his chest, but I stood on my toes and pulled his head down to brush my lips against his. "You are a fool," I whispered against his mouth. "There is a great deal I know nothing about and which only you can teach me." And then I uttered the words that I had kept in my heart during that long year in Tirconnaill. "I love you, Rory O'Donnell. I love you so much that I can no longer bear it."

Somehow, I was in his arms and he was kissing me as if he had never kissed anyone before. I was small and he was not, but we fit together as if we were made for one another. When he touched my breasts, my waist, the inside of my thighs, I knew a pleasure that I had never imagined. He took me slowly, with gentle caresses and a saintly patience that seemed new to him, but then never before had Rory set out to seduce his own wife.

And when it was time, when he'd tasted every inch of my skin, when he'd whispered words of love and need against my throat, when my back arched and the heat flowed within me, when I laughed and cried and laughed again, when he was so far inside me that I saw the gates of heaven, the life force filled him and he held back no longer. I clung to him as the raging tide rocked us, moving from his body to mine and back again until we swirled in a maelstrom of color and heat and passion and, strangest of all, humility.

This was what I'd waited for, yearned for, dared my father's rage for, this union of body and spirit and mind and heart. Never again would my soul be my own.

8

Meghann lifted her head and smiled dreamily at Michael. "That was beautiful. You're a marvelous storyteller."

He waved aside her praise. "History has a way of rounding out a tale."

"History doesn't turn a phrase or color it alive the way you do. I can see Nuala and her Rory just as clearly as if they stood before us." She hesitated.

"Go on."

"It's nothing."

"You were about t' say something, Meghann. Say it."

"It's just that you're a born politician, Michael, one of the inner circle. How did you let yourself get into this mess?"

"Isn't that what I have you for, t' figure out the answer t' that question?" His voice was flippant, guarded, completely removed from his earlier eloquence.

Meghann chewed her bottom lip. "You're not disclosing enough for me to find anything. It's almost as if—" She stopped.

The silence extended beyond normal limits. "Say it, Meggie," he said impatiently. "There isn't anything y' haven't already said."

There was a great deal she hadn't said, nor would she. Meeting his gaze directly, she asked, "You do want to be cleared of this murder charge, don't you, Michael?"

"What an odd question."

"You haven't answered it."

He leaned his head back against the pillow and closed his eyes as if the entire conversation wearied him.

Meghann saw the way the skin stretched across the bones of his face, and her throat tightened. Why wouldn't he answer? "Michael?" she whispered across the space of silence that cloaked them.

"I'm awake, Meggie," he said slowly, "and I'm trying very hard t' give you the answer y' want. The truth is I just don't care. I don't seem t' care about anything anymore."

Her heart hurt. There was no other way to explain it. It was a pain as physical as if her chest had caved in and squeezed the arteries dry. Nothing that she knew of Michael's life, not his affiliation with the IRA, not his years in the Maze, not this absurd murder charge, terrified her as much as this uncharacteristic apathy that held him in its grip.

"You're still not feeling well," she said bracingly. "You'll see. When your strength comes back you'll feel differently."

"Perhaps." He didn't lift his head.

She stood. "I'll fix you something to eat. The lamb chops look wonderful and there's a microwave. I'll defrost them and we'll have a meal in no time." She paused and rested her hand on his shoulder. "Would you like a drink before dinner?"

He shook his head.

"Please, Michael." She could hear the desperation in her voice. "There are calories in alcohol."

"Let it be, Meggie. Why did y' have to come? I was fine on my own."

"You really are the most ungrateful person I've ever known," she snapped. "You couldn't manage one day by yourself. What would you eat? How would you wash clothes or shop?"

He lifted his head and stared at her. "I managed quite well before you came."

"What are you talking about?"

"Y' heard me well enough."

She must have misunderstood. "Someone was supposed to be with you."

"No one has been here except me."

She sank down on the couch beside him, allowing the full, horrific meaning of the words to sweep through her. Michael, emaciated, unable to stand upright for more than a minute. Michael, dehydrated and near death, left alone to fend for himself in a house with stairs for nearly ten days. "Something is wrong," she said out loud and turned her head to look at him.

"Y' always were a bright lass."

"Stop it." Her eyes were wide and gold in the pale oval of her face. "Stop joking. You must know what this means."

"I know what it means."

She must think. She couldn't think. Dear God, why couldn't she think? *Dear God, dear God, dear God.* The phrase repeated itself over and over in her brain. She pressed her hands, open-palmed and hard, against her mouth and rocked back and forth on the couch. The pressure brought back a measure of reality. "What are we going to do?" she asked when she could manage the words.

Again he shrugged, that fluid masculine lifting of

the shoulders that no loss of flesh or muscle could completely destroy. "There isn't anything to do."

"We've got to get away from here. It isn't safe."

"Don't panic on me, Meggie, and don't jump t' conclusions." He sounded like the old Michael, completely confident, completely in charge. "This place is as safe as any. We're in the Republic. You're an English barrister. No one would dare harm us."

"Are you insane, Michael? They killed Mountbatten and Killingsworth. For God's sake, they nearly killed Margaret Thatcher. Do you really think they care that I'm a barrister?"

"Aye," he said evenly, "I do."

"How can you possibly know that?"

The lines of his cheeks and jaw were very pronounced beneath the drawn tightness of his skin. "Don't ask a question if you can't take hearing the answer."

"I can take the answer."

He sighed and looked away. "At one time informers were a problem for us. It was decided that the fewer people who knew about a target, the more likely an operation was t' be successful. I wouldn't worry about our safety, Meggie. It's likely that the decision was made to involve no one else. There are fewer questions this way and fewer witnesses when I go to trial. It changes nothing for us."

"Of course it does." She reached out to grasp his shoulders, to shake him into reason. The shirt was soft under her hands, a contrast to the hard line of bone beneath the wool. "You never agreed to this, Michael. Tell me you didn't agree to become some sort of Irish martyr sacrificing yourself for a noble cause."

"All right, Meghann. I'll tell y' anything you want."

"But is it the truth?" She had never been so frustrated. "Please, tell me the truth. You owe me that."

He stared at her, as if understanding her fear for the first time. "I suppose I do," he said softly. Prying her hands from his shoulders, he held them between his own. "The truth is I never volunteered for this. I had no idea there was t' be an assassination attempt on James Killingsworth's life. I wasn't a part of it, and I know of no one who was. I speak from experience, Meghann. The Irish Republican Army does not set out to harm women and children. When it happens, and it does far too often because they are a civilian force and many times their war is waged against civilians, they deeply regret it. Not only because of the loss of life but because it looks very bad. The danger you feel has nothing t' do with fearing for your life. I believe y' already know that."

Perhaps he didn't understand. She moistened her lips and placed her palms against his cheeks. "They mean to kill you, Michael. Don't you understand? They want you to take responsibility for this murder. That's why there isn't anyone else here. That's why they don't care about keeping you alive."

His hands came up to cover hers. "We don't know that. Besides, everyone dies eventually, Meggie. I never expected a long life. I don't mind if it means something."

"But it won't." Tears burned beneath her eyelids, and when they streaked down her cheeks she didn't brush them away. "What good could it possibly do to have the world think you killed a man who had your party's best interests at heart? James Killingsworth was a fair man. To kill him is to set our political situation back to where it was twenty-five years ago. There won't be any sympathy for nationalists if one of their leaders is convicted of this murder."

"Careful, Meggie. Are y' with us now?"

She dropped her hands and stood, rubbing her cheeks dry. "Now you're being ridiculous. I'm going for a walk. I can't think properly when I'm around you."

He watched her grab her coat and muffler before walking out the door. "There is that, at least," he muttered under his breath before stretching his legs and closing his eyes once again.

Meghann cursed under her breath and strode head down along the hard, damp shoreline of Donegal Bay. The shadowy ruins of an ancient monastery hovered on the hillside above. It was bitterly cold. Icy winds whipped the seawater into a spray that stung her cheeks and left the taste of salt on her lips. Caught up in her own private battle, competing against the roar of the waves, she railed against the randomness of fate and her own desperate fear. She argued with herself, hammering and shaping her logic as if she were in the privacy of her London office.

"The Crown needs a scapegoat for Killingsworth's murder, and the sooner the better," she muttered, her words drowned by the keening of the wind. "Negotiations with Northern Ireland have come to a standstill. What better way to terrify everyone into returning to the bargaining table than to assassinate a powerful political figure? But why Killingsworth? He was the only legitimate politician willing to deal with Sinn Fein."

She considered Ian Paisley's group but couldn't formulate a serious argument. It was too obvious. This time County Antrim's loyalists seemed to be in the clear. A thought, still hazy and half-formed, took shape in her mind, a thought so terrifying, so incredible that it had no place in the forefront of her brain, where rational ideas evolved. She pushed it away and started over. "There are plenty of conservative MP's in Ireland," she said out loud. "Why haven't the Provisionals gone after one of them? Why would—"

She stumbled and bumped against something hard. "I'm terribly sorry," she began, reaching out to steady what was most definitely a human form.

Before she could touch her, the woman stepped

back. "My fault," she apologized, "I wasn't watching where I was going."

Meghann stared. She had seen that face before, green eyes and pixie features framed by striking red hair. The woman smiled, and a vague image clicked in her memory. It was the girl who had showed her the back roads into the Republic, away from British patrols. Meghann frowned. But it couldn't be. This woman was older by twenty years, possibly more. Perhaps she was a relative. "Do you live around here?" she asked casually.

"Not anymore," the woman replied. "I'm just visiting, and you?"

Meghann improvised. "My husband and I are renting a cottage on the edge of the bay. He's recovering from an illness."

The woman nodded and turned to face the sea. Meghann noted her long wool skirt and the old-fashioned shawl wrapped around her body. The silence lengthened, but Meghann felt no awkwardness. There was something oddly comforting about someone who had the ability to stand so utterly still without speaking. "Who are you?" she asked at last. It was a question she wouldn't ordinarily ask under the circumstances, but somehow she knew her curiosity wouldn't be held against her.

The woman turned, fixing her green gaze on Meghann's face. "My name is Nuala," she said simply.

Meghann's throat went dry. Michael's words, filed away in the recesses of her brain, floated to the forefront. *Nuala O'Donnell of Tirconnaill has been dead for nearly four hundred years.* Sanity returned. She swallowed several times before speaking. "I suppose Nuala is a common name in these parts."

The woman nodded. " 'Tis so."

There it was again, that old-fashioned speech pattern no longer used outside the western isles. But she claimed to be from Donegal. Meghann couldn't stop herself. She had to know. "Two weeks ago I met a girl who looked very much like you. Her name was Nuala O'Donnell."

Nuala smiled. "That is hardly unusual. There have been O'Donnells in Donegal since the days of Brian Boru."

"But, Nuala O'Donnell?"

"As you said, Nuala is a common name." She tilted her head. "Is something troubling you, Meghann?"

Meghann couldn't begin to explain why she couldn't stop the words pouring out of her, dangerous words, revealing words of Michael's identity and her role in his escape, words she would never have considered sharing with anyone outside the confessional, and since she hadn't stepped inside a Catholic church since leaving Belfast fifteen years before, that event wasn't likely.

When she finished speaking, she sank to the sand and stared out at the bay, aghast at her shocking disclosures. What had come over her? She was a barrister, for heaven's sake, professionally trained to keep her mouth shut, her ears open and her face expressionless. What must this woman think of her? More importantly, how could she have risked Michael's life so carelessly? Squeezing her eyes shut, she wrapped her arms around her knees, hid her burning face and prayed for Nuala O'Donnell to disappear into the mist.

Gentle fingers sifted through her hair and a voice, low and comforting, reached her ears. "Poor lass. Nothing is ever as dark as it seems. Take your time and everything will come about. There is no need for haste."

"I don't know what came over me," Meghann mumbled. "I didn't mean to burden you. Please, don't concern yourself about any of it."

The voice was more definite now. "I shall help you." She sat down in the sand beside Meghann. "It was my intention all along, but I had a different course in mind. For now, I believe you should concentrate on healing your young man, his body and his spirit. Later, we shall work on your problem with, what did you say it was called, Sinn Fein? *We Ourselves* I believe it means in English. What an odd name for a revolutionary society."

Meghann lifted her head in astonishment and stared at Nuala. How could anyone live in such isolation that she had never heard of the nationalist party? "Why don't you know about Sinn Fein, and why am I telling you everything I know?"

The woman's eyes widened, filling her small face. "I already told you. I am Nuala O'Donnell of Tirconnaill."

"There hasn't been a Tirconnaill since the seventeenth century," Meghann said flatly.

Nuala laughed, stood and brushed the sand from her skirt. "Don't be absurd," she said and began walking down the beach. "There will always be a Tirconnaill."

"Wait." Battling the wind that didn't seem to affect Nuala at all, Meghann struggled to her feet. "I don't know where you're staying," she shouted. "How can I reach you?"

"No need to worry, Meghann," Nuala called over her shoulder. "I'll be the one reaching you."

Something didn't make sense. Nuala was definitely odd, but people inhabiting the more primitive parts of Ireland had never really caught up to the rest of the world. Imagine knowing nothing about Sinn Fein. Perhaps Nuala couldn't read. Illiteracy was not uncommon among the older generation. But Nuala wasn't old. Maybe it was something else. Maybe the woman was simpleminded or mentally handicapped. Still, she had seemed lucid enough.

Meghann's logical mind discarded solutions as

quickly as she thought of them. Eventually she put the entire matter aside. There could be no satisfying answer to explain Nuala's shocking political ignorance or her own released inhibition.

It wasn't until much later, after Meghann turned down the heat from under the lamb chops and served them up on plates, that she realized what it was that could not be explained away to oddness, coincidence or compassion. Not once, in their entire conversation, could she remember introducing herself, and yet Nuala had used her name more than once. She shook off her doubts. They were sheer nonsense. She must have told the woman her name.

Michael was subdued when she called him into the kitchen for dinner. He commented politely on the lamb and potatoes, liberally buttered his bread, ate two bites, excused himself and went upstairs to bed. He climbed laboriously, hanging heavily on the bannister, taking an inordinately long time on the stairs. Meghann listened to his dragging step, bit her lip, folded her arms tightly against her chest and forced herself to remain in the kitchen. Something told her he wouldn't appreciate her help.

Hours later she finished the last of her notes, closed her book and slipped the pen back into its leather pocket holder. The words she'd written were without substance, giving her no satisfaction. There had to be someone out there who knew something, someone who couldn't stand by and allow an innocent man to be imprisoned for a crime he didn't commit. She slipped off her shoes, pulled the ottoman under her legs and wiggled her toes.

In the fireplace, flames sizzled and licked at the peat, warming her feet through the thick wool of her socks. Rain slanted against the seaward side of the cottage and lashed against the windows, rattling the diamond panes. Already the combination of heat and moisture had fogged the glass, cocooning her in a private world of orange flame and yellow light and the clean, earth-turned smell of peat fuel.

What had Nuala meant when she said they would work on her problem with Sinn Fein? How absurd to think a small, oddly dressed woman with an archaic speech pattern actually believed she could help. She'd said it with complete confidence, as if all she had to do was decide and whatever she wanted was accomplished. Wouldn't it be wonderful to live with that kind of certainty, to believe that wanting was the same as having?

It seemed to Meghann that she never had that confidence, that she was born old, that laughter and the easy, carefree, exhilarating trappings of childhood had always eluded her. Annie lived in the present, as did all the Devlins. Meghann remembered what it was like to be drawn into the warmth of their vital sense of awareness, tasting sweet on the tongue, feeling cold on the skin, hearing music in the soul and knowing that the slow, delicious bubble of humor would rise within and spill out into the air with the clear magical clarity of a choirboy's hymn. Even in times of desperation, the barricade of the Lower Falls in West Belfast, the riots in Andersonstown, Bernadette's time in prison, the funerals of Annie's two sons, Michael's arrest, the dreadful hopeless poverty of living as a Catholic in Belfast, the Devlin family was alive in ways that she had never been.

In all her years in Annie's house, living in the midst of the raw purity of Devlin emotions, Meghann could count the moments when she had allowed herself to feel even a small measure of what Michael Devlin felt every moment of every day. Even before the events of Cupar Street had wiped out her world as she knew it and irrevocably changed her life, Meghann wondered if she'd ever known that kind of awareness. She wondered if she ever would. Perhaps if she knew what it was they felt, if she could experience a small portion of it, if she could understand why people as brilliant and talented and devoted as the Devlin offspring would offer up their lives on the altar of Irish patriotism instead of leaving for London, America or Australia, she might just be able to help Michael through this mockery of a murder trial.

9

Nuala, Tirconnaill, 1590

It was nine months to the day after we bedded that our son was born, a healthy lad made in the image of Rory, with a head of silver-gilt hair and eyes the blue of the Irish Sea. We named him Patrick. I, who had worried that my temperament was not suited to motherhood, understood for the first time what it meant to love a child.

Rory was more than pleased. It was as though no one had ever before sired a son. I'll warrant the matter of an heir was of some importance. Rory's father had succumbed to the fever, and there was the earldom to consider. Still, Patrick was just a wee babe, and when I think of the months that followed, Rory should have taken more care and I should have weaned my babe from the breast and insisted that he stay behind where it was warm and safe.

Ireland's troubles began long before I was born. Elizabeth Tudor was always one to meddle, even when her gain was less than a morsel of the vast holdings that were already hers.

To be fair, everything my father had, even his life,

he owed to her. He grew up at Whitehall under the queen's guardianship after Shane O'Neill, his uncle, would have slain him as he did my grandfather. It was at the English court that my father learned the manners of a gentleman, kept his holdings and came back to Ireland with his title and lands intact. But that was a long time and many promises ago. Elizabeth became greedy, and in her place she sent her man Sir Philip Sidney, who tried to push the Irish west of the River Bann and settle Englishmen on the coastlands of Antrim and Down.

But the Irish are fierce fighters and not so easily subdued. Sir Philip went home in disgrace, and Sir Thomas Smith was sent in his stead. Again, 'tis hearsay I repeat for I was not yet born, but the bards are skilled and the tales they tell no one can dispute. Sir Thomas wished to sweep away all the native Irish except for peasants to till the fields. Every Irishman born in Ireland or of Irish descent was prevented from purchasing land, holding office or bearing arms upon pain of death. Sir Thomas did not live long in Ireland. My father killed him in the year fifteen hundred and seventy-two, shortly after my sister Kieran was born.

After Smith's death the queen gave Walter Devereux, Earl of Essex, all of Antrim to pursue Smith's evil policy. Essex made the most dreadful of mistakes and in so doing forever alienated my father and the O'Neills from the English crown.

It happened the night I came into the world. My father would have gone to Belfast Castle to sup with his cousin, Brian O'Neill, who had offered the hand of friendship to Essex. But out of consideration for my mother's difficult birthing he stayed behind. The morning after, a bloodstained herald rode across the drawbridge and told of betrayal and murder, of Brian beheaded and Maired, his wife, beautiful, laughing Maired, raped until her screams sent the pigeons from the rafters. When her captors would hear no more they cut out her tongue and left her bleeding to death on the Great Hall floor while they burned the castle around her.

In a fury as white-hot as the flames that destroyed his clansmen, my father rode to London with his witness and shamed Elizabeth before her entire court. She withdrew her support from Essex, but she never forgave my father. From then on they were enemies, and the bitterness of their feud lasted for the next sixteen years until it swept throughout Ireland like a mighty wave, destroying everyone in its path without regard for rank or station. All of us fell in, in one way or another, without protest, even I. For I was born in the midst of my father's enmity for Elizabeth and knew no other way. It wasn't until her icy fingers closed over Rory and my innocent baby son that the rage grew within me, and all of Ireland learned why the bards called me my father's daughter.

Motherhood changes a woman. From the moment Patrick was born I could feel the difference in me. It was not that I loved the babe more than Rory, it was just that he needed me so much more than I had ever been needed before. It was frightening, the enormity of his need. The newness of him and the dreadful possibility that his fragile life could be immediately snuffed out consumed me until I was either with him every waking moment or counting the time until I could be.

Not that Rory complained, of course. He knew that it was a woman's way to care for her child until it grew out of infancy. Too many died in their first winter after they were taken off the breast. He would not have it so with his son. But he did think that my refusal to dine with Sir John Perrot on his Spanish galleon was exercising caution to the extreme.

He followed me into our bedchamber and there he tried to reason with me. "'Tis only for one night, Nuala. The boy has his nurse. He won't miss you."

"There is more to this than leaving the bairn." My

words were deliberate, as if I were explaining my thoughts to someone slow to understand. "Perrot has been seen with Captain Willis, the same Captain Willis who sent his men to raid and debauch on our land. I trust him not, Rory, and you are more the fool if you do. Besides, Niall Garv will be there, and he has not forgiven my father for allowing me to marry you."

"Niall is my own cousin. You have nothing to fear from him," he said stiffly. "I love you dearly, Nuala, but you are a woman and I will stand no woman on earth to call me fool." He pulled a fresh tunic over his head. "Stay here if you must. I go to sample the sack without you. 'Tis said to be fine wine. Perhaps I shall bring some back to the cellars."

"Rory." There was desperation in my voice but he heeded me not. "Please don't do this. Patrick is too young. I cannot hold Tirconnaill for him if you are taken."

"Nuala, Nuala." He sat down beside me on the bed and drew me into his arms. "You make too much of this. I will return before midnight."

I lifted my face for his kiss and heard his breath shorten. "By God, Nuala, what have you done to me?" he muttered. "I have no desire for Perrot's wine. I want only you."

My mouth opened under his. "Stay with me," I whispered against his lips.

Reluctantly he pulled away. "I cannot. Wait for me." I hesitated and then nodded. "I shall wait, Rory, and I'll not rest until I have you safe at home again."

It was two years before I saw him again. Two years during which he endured filth and darkness, freezing rain and biting wind and ragged clothing. Two years of lice and mealworms in his bread, of seeping wounds and iron shackles and wet stone floors. Two years of starvation, of begging for alms. Two years of wondering whether he'd been left for dead and whether the bairn who had just begun to smile would ever know his father.

The treachery began with a meal and a greeting and a goblet of the finest sack ever to find its way to Donegal harbor. The McSweeneys had also been invited, and together the men raised their goblets many times until they forgot the number. It was late when Rory first knew that something was wrong. He told me of how the deck rolled beneath his feet and how he felt the wash of a wave against the hull. His feet were too heavy to lift, and as he sat there pondering the reasons for the strange noises he heard, their hosts left them. The door to the cabin was locked, and they were alone for days until they sailed into Dublin harbor.

There, they were shackled with irons, marched to the prison surrounded by water and left to starve with the thirty or so pathetic souls who had been pledged to the Crown as hostages. Among them were Art and Henry O'Neill, my brothers. There was no hope of escape, no contact with the outside world. Every twenty-four hours a guard examined their irons to be sure they were intact. Time passed, month after month, season after season, until I despaired of seeing Rory again.

Tyrone, 1590

I faced my father bravely, for I had little to lose. "He is my husband, your ally. Will you leave him to die?"

His wide forehead was furrowed and grave. "I have done all that I can. Two thousand pounds bounty is no small sum. Elizabeth refuses us. She was always obstinate."

My foot itched and I longed to stamp it, to throw myself upon the floor to kick and scream, much as I had as a child. But I was twice a mother, or nearly so, and my screaming days were over. "Why will she not take the money?" I asked quietly.

My father shrugged, and for the first time I saw his age. "She will not listen to me. 'Tis your mother's MacDonnell blood she despises. The massacre at Rathin is still fresh."

"The MacDonnells were killed, not the English."

Red Hugh shrugged. "She holds it against us."

Helplessness washed over me. "What can we do?" I asked.

"Wait and pray."

The temper rose within me. "God is not so poor-spirited, Father. I'll not sit and wait until my husband's soul has left his body."

"What will you do, Nuala?"

If he would not help, I would not answer. My plan was simple, but first the child would be born. I returned to Tirconnaill and she came within the week, on a day so cold the trees snapped as ice swelled within their trunks, a small red-haired girl, blue and weak from seeking the mortal world too soon. She took a breath, opened her eyes and saw that this place outside the womb was neither warm nor kind and quietly slipped away. I named her Joan and buried her in the monastery crypt.

My heart was sore, but my breasts were full and Patrick had been weaned too soon. He thrived on the milk that belonged to my small dead daughter, and I could not be sorry that he looked so well. God willing, there would be more children. For now, Elizabeth waited in London, and if she refused me, there was always the hope that with luck and a strong rope smuggled in at just the right time, Rory would escape.

London, 1591

Elizabeth was nothing like I imagined. She had little beauty, and with her shaved skull and the stiff ruff that forced her chin up into an unnatural angle, she looked particularly odd. So this was the virgin queen who would take no man to her bed. More likely it was the other way around. I sensed that she knew my thoughts, for her lips tightened and her eyes narrowed into tiny slits. Much later I learned that it was not the workings of my mind that bothered her. It was my youth, my red hair so different from her own and the rather startling effect my appearance had on the men at court.

I had never known men like these before. Growing up in Tyrone, I was protected by my father's rank. As Rory's wife, no one in Tirconnaill would dare shame me with their suggestive looks, their ribald whispers and their wandering hands. The queen could not know that I preferred the company of my husband and therefore looked at me, her supposed rival, with dagger eyes.

My audience with her came sooner than expected, most likely because she hoped to send me home as quickly as possible, a hope I heartily shared. Patrick did not thrive in the dirt of London, and there were more hacking coughs at Elizabeth's court than in the entire county of Tirconnaill.

I wore my finest gown, an absurd act of vanity. Elizabeth did not care if I dressed in rags. I knelt at her feet and waited for several minutes before she spoke.

"Rise, child," she said in her dry, cracked voice. "What is the reason you have sought audience with the Crown?"

I kept my eyes on the floor. Elizabeth approved of humility. "My husband, the earl of Tirconnaill, has spent the better part of two years imprisoned in Dublin Castle. He has done nothing to warrant this outrage, Your Majesty. He is a loyal subject of the queen. Never once has he taken up arms against your Royal Highness. I beg you to release him."

Not by the blink of an eyelash did her thoughts reveal themselves. The tapping of her fingernail against the carved oak of her throne was the only sound in the hushed room. I thought it odd that she should meet with me alone, without the lord chamberlain at her side to advise her.

After a long time she spoke. "Your are Red Hugh's daughter, are you not?"

"Yes, Your Majesty."

"Your mother is the Lady Agnes MacDonnell, kin to the MacDonnells of the Isles."

"Yes, Your Majesty."

"Your father has written me many times hoping to secure your husband's release. Why should I do this for you if not for him?"

I lifted startled eyes to her face. "Rather should you ask why you haven't done it already, Your Majesty."

Her scarlet-tinted mouth tightened. "Insolent one. Do you hope to release your husband by insulting me?"

"Never, Your Majesty. It is said that you are England's wisest monarch. I had hoped to prevail upon your sense of justice. My husband has done nothing more than marry my father's daughter. Why would you imprison a man for that?"

"Your father can no longer be trusted. He will not put aside his MacDonnell wife."

"We are Catholic, Your Grace. It is not possible to dissolve the bonds of marriage when a man and woman have been wed for five and twenty years."

Again Elizabeth tapped the armrest of her throne. I waited in suspense for her reply. Finally she spoke. "What manner of man is your husband?"

This time I was caught. I had not expected such a question. "Why, he is a good man, Your Grace," I stammered, "although nothing like my father. He is a warrior and his loyalties run deep." I gained confidence as I thought of what Rory meant to the people of Tirconnaill. I could not tell her that my husband, as hotheaded and passionate as my father was cool and cynical, was fast becoming a legend in Ireland, the image of a warrior clansman who could stir the common folk into a patriotic fever not seen since the days of Brian Boru.

"He is content to stay in Tirconnaill and administer to his lands and his family," I said instead. "We are wed but four years, Your Grace. I know little of running an earldom." I sensed that these words alone would not free my husband. "Rory is a popular lord," I continued. "He rallies men to his way of thinking. Ireland is many leagues from London. It would be a foolish ruler who makes an enemy of Rory O'Donnell."

She took less than a minute to decide, and when she did I wasn't sure that I had done the right thing. But it was too late to take back my words, and if it brought Rory closer to freedom, I could not be sorry.

"I would meet this husband of yours," she said. "I shall send the missive today. You may stay at court as my guest until he arrives. Then I shall make my decision."

I bowed my head. "You are too kind, Your Grace. I thank you from the bottom of my heart."

She nodded and waved her hand in what I took to be a gesture of dismissal. Back in my apartments at Whitehall, I could barely contain my glee. Rory was coming to England. For the first time in two years I would see his beloved face.

The royal edict came in February. Elizabeth Tudor requested Rory's presence in London. His clothing was in tatters, and the winds from the North were icy. A guard took pity on him and found a spare blanket and boots that were too small but offered some protection against the bruising snow. By the time he reached London he had become accustomed to a horse beneath him again. His muscles had hardened, and although there was not an ounce of spare flesh on his body, he no longer looked like the skeleton my father saw when he traveled to Dublin in hope of securing his release.

Rory was taken directly to the palace where, for the first time in two years, he bathed. A velvet doublet, matching hose and a stiff pleated collar called a ruff were laid out for him. He shocked the servant sent to help him dress, and the barber even more, by refusing to clip his hair above his shoulders. Rory would always be an Irish chieftain.

After dismissing the servants, he lay down on the bed to wait. It was then that I learned of his arrival. Flinging open his door, I threw myself upon him. He bent his head to my hair and breathed in.

"Nuala," he whispered in wonder.

My head moved against his shoulder.

"Nuala, my love, is it you? What are you doing here?"

I looked up, my face wet with tears. "I came to ask Elizabeth to release you. She would not unless she saw you first. Oh, Rory." My arms tightened around my waist. "I've missed you so."

"I, too." His voice choked with emotion, and as he lifted my face to his lips, I felt the familiar stirrings of desire that had lain dormant for such an endless length of nights and days. This was Rory, my husband, and I hadn't touched him in two years.

The fire was low and the temperature of the room dropped, but neither Rory nor I felt it. The clothes I had donned with such care lay in a crumpled heap on the floor. I cared nothing for that. Instead I touched every beautiful inch of my husband's body with the reverence of a sinner who has found salvation at last. I could have stayed there forever, worshiping him with my eyes and mouth, but he wanted more and showed me with skilled hands and seeking lips. He raised in me a flame that could be quenched in only one way. We came together in that small elegant room at

Whitehall, forgetting all that had passed between us except the heat of our embrace, the piercing sweetness of our mating and the final explosion that rocked us in its grip until we slid back to reality once again.

"How long have you been here?" he asked when he could manage his voice once again.

"A bit over three months."

He lifted my head. "Three months. Christ, Nuala, what of Tirconnaill?"

"The steward will manage until we return."

He rested on my elbow and looked down at my face. "What if I do not return?"

I clutched him fiercely, and the color came and went beneath my skin. "You must return. Elizabeth is a woman, Rory. You must please her, pretend loyalty if you must, but please her. Do whatever it takes. I cannot bear life without you."

He held me close and whispered against my hair. "I will try, Nuala. I will try. Will you bring Patrick to me?"

I hung my head and a tear slid down my cheek. "Patrick is dead, Rory. He caught the fever less than a month ago. I could not save him." My throat worked and all the words I would have said stayed inside my heart.

"There is more," I said, my voice muffled against his chest. "There was another bairn, born after you were taken. She didn't last the night."

He pressed my head against his shoulder as much for his own sake as to comfort me. "I'm sorry, lass," he said brokenly. "I'm so very sorry I wasn't there for you, but there will be more children. I swear it. Perhaps even now my seed has taken root in your belly."

I smiled, kissed him on the mouth and reached for my clothes. "It grows late, and Elizabeth will not be kept waiting. I shall come to you tonight and never again will they part us."

From the bed, he watched as I dressed and I could tell from his eyes that he wished for more time. But it was not to be. He pulled on his garters and hose and stepped into the velvet doublet. I would have helped him with the ruff, but he refused to wear it. Without speaking, we held each other close until a heavy fist pounded on the door.

"Speak wisely, my love," I whispered as the guards took him away.

His escort, complete with helmets and spears, closed around him and together they marched to Elizabeth's private chambers. I did not learn what happened in that room until nearly a year later.

Elizabeth reclined on a long chair and she was alone. He lowered one knee to the floor, but she motioned him to her side and held out her hand. He lifted it to his lips. She patted the space beside her.

"Sit down beside me, Rory O'Donnell," she said in a low, husky voice. "You certainly are handsome. Nuala didn't do you justice. Are you as loyal as your wife claims?"

He sat in the spot she indicated, a mere inch from the exposed skin of her breasts. "I am extremely loyal, Your Grace." Fortunately for him, she did not ask to whom.

Her hand found the column of his throat and her fingers caressed him. He moved back slightly. She frowned and lowered her hand.

"Such a handsome boy and such an unfortunate set of circumstances," she purred, looking up through her sparse eyelashes. "Do you find me attractive, my lord?"

He stared down at her, hoping his revulsion didn't show in his carefully arranged features. She was old, old enough to be Rory's mother's mother, and the heavy paint she wore emphasized every line. What hair she had was dyed a most unnatural red, and the veins under her bald skull pulsed beneath her pale skin. She was hideous and even though the promise of freedom faded like an impossible dream, he could not bring myself to do what I asked. Rory was a warrior, not a diplomat. He told me how the heat rose in his cheeks and how difficult it was to speak. "Surely a woman who has ruled for decades has more need of wisdom than of beauty."

"No woman is ever too old to be told that beauty still lingers. Come, my lord. Do I find favor in your eyes or do you only find children, like your Nuala, attractive?"

I was not a vain woman, but no man alive would prefer a woman Elizabeth's age over me. This woman, this queen, with her twisted lips and feral predator's gaze profaned our love. Still, he could not spurn her completely. "For a woman of your years, you are most attractive, Your Grace."

She rested her hand on his knee, squeezing lightly. "I thought Irish chieftains were virile, primitive men. Are you such an innocent that you know nothing of what I want, Rory O'Donnell?"

"We cannot all have what we want, Your Grace."

She flushed angrily. "I am Queen of England. Nothing is beyond me. I want you to pleasure me, O'Donnell. When the season is out, I shall tire of you. If you have serviced me well, you shall return to Tirconnaill. If you refuse, you shall go back to Dublin and serve your sentence."

He stood and bowed low before her. "I thank you for the clothes and for the bath, Your Grace, but I must decline your offer. I am a married man and loyal to the Church of Rome. In Ireland we take our vows seriously. I cannot help you."

Her mouth opened and she rose from her chair. A shriek more animal than human came from her mouth. "Guards. Guards. Take him. Take him and return him to Dublin."

10

〰〰〰

Meghann was becoming obsessed with Rory and Nuala O'Donnell. She didn't intentionally think about them, but somehow they managed to drift into her consciousness just before she fell asleep. From there her imagination took over, playing out a story that was vivid enough to belong on a movie screen. At first the images were intriguing. She'd even begun to write them down as she saw them. But the last two nights were different. The essence of what she saw had changed, becoming stronger, clearer, more visually graphic. She could no longer control what she saw and it frightened her.

There was something else, too. History had never been Meghann's strongest subject. She knew the highlights of the expulsion of the Catholic earls of Ulster from Ireland. What schoolchild didn't? But she was positive the nuns at St. Mary's Hall had never discussed the rape of Maired O'Brien nor Queen Elizabeth's attempted seduction of Rory O'Donnell while his wife was in the castle. Were those events a product of her imagination, or had they really occurred? And if they had, where had she heard them before? Her first spare moment in London she would visit the library.

Other than a nagging worry about her sanity, Meghann was happy, not contented or satisfied, not ecstatic or delirious, just happy, with a warm glow that began when she woke each morning, set Michael's eggs, ham and porridge before him, toasted half a loaf of bread and spread it liberally with lemon curd and watched him clean his plate.

He was healing. His chest had filled out, and the muscles along his arms and thighs were clearly defined again. The sunken hollows beneath his eyes had disappeared, and his skin was tanned from the long daily walks she insisted they take on the beach. He had even hiked into town with her to carry groceries back. She had worried that someone would recognize him, but it was just as he had explained it. The residents of a small town in the Irish Republic knew nothing of Michael Devlin, and even if they did, they did not recognize him in this lean, black-haired stranger with the healthy tan and brilliant blue eyes.

Meghann's life in London seemed very far away, and occasionally, when she allowed her brain to relax, visions of what might have been if Michael had never joined the IRA came to mind. She pushed them away quickly, of course, but she was never able to make them disappear completely.

Other than Michael's actions the day James Killingsworth was murdered, she hadn't been able to gather anything substantial. There were witnesses, but until she interviewed them it would be impossible to tell whether or not they knew of Michael's whereabouts at the exact time of the murder. It was quickly becoming apparent that the prosecution's files were vital to building her argument.

Still, it was pleasant to do nothing but read and walk, cook simple meals in this lovely kitchen and share dialogue with Michael. For the most part his defenses had come down and he was the old Michael, the boy she'd grown up and fallen in love with, a bright witty conversationalist whose sense of humor eased their political differences and whose quick understanding often finished sentences for her. Occasionally, she would look at him and there would be something in his eyes, a guarded expression, a hint of suspicion that she couldn't penetrate. Not that she tried very hard. Meghann had no desire to rehash those confusing years before she left Belfast when she wasn't sure of anything, including her own emotions.

She stacked the rinsed plates and reached for a towel, mechanically wiping them dry. He was probably reading at this very moment. He read constantly, more than anyone she'd ever known, and Irish men were known for their reading. The reading rooms in the Linen Hall Library were filled to capacity with men from the Falls perusing newspapers, novels, periodicals and essays written by the finest minds in the British Isles. Often they read the day away, drinking copious amounts of sustaining tea, with an occasional step outside for a smoke, a Guinness and a bit of conversation. Few were employed, and none would think of caring for their brood of children while their wives worked. For some reason, women from the Falls rarely had trouble finding work.

Meghann wiped down the counter, folded the towel into a precise square, hung it on the rack and walked into the cozy living room. Sure enough, Michael was reading. On her last trip into town she'd purchased a pair of reading glasses for him. They weren't prescription, of course, but they seemed to do the trick. He wore them constantly and never complained.

Unobserved, she watched him. His hair had fallen over his forehead, and his brow was creased in the frown he wore when concentrating. He needed a haircut. Perhaps she should offer to give him one. She hesitated. He looked so peaceful sitting there by the fire, his feet on the low table, a pot of tea by his side. How long had it been since he was able to relax, with nothing to do but read and sleep and walk and decide what kind of sandwiches to eat with his soup?

"How about a walk?" she said, breaking the silence.

Michael lifted his head, removed his glasses and smiled. "All right."

Meghann's heart swelled, and warning bells sounded in her brain. Slowly, slowly, she reminded herself. After all the heartache and all the years that came after, she refused to fall apart over a smile.

"I'll get our coats," she stammered and hurried up the stairs.

Michael watched her retreating figure curiously. Meghann wasn't usually tongue-tied. He stared for a minute at the page he'd been reading, but the words made no sense to him. He was thinking of Meghann and how she'd cared for him, persuading him to eat her food, cooking delicacies to coax his appetite, buying glasses so he could read comfortably. She was as good at what she did for a living as she was at domestic chores. For reasons he couldn't explain, he didn't mind answering her questions. She was a good listener. Whether or not she was truly interested, she listened to his stories with the same flattering intensity as she did his answers to her questions. It was comfortable living with her, even natural, eating, sharing conversation, walking on the beach.

Not everything was perfect. For a long time he hadn't been able to put his finger on it, but today, for the first time since he'd gone on the hunger strike, he recognized what it was, the edge that wouldn't allow him to relax completely.

When Meghann stood in the doorway in her faded denims and fisherman's sweater, her hair loose and glowing with the russet tones he remembered from childhood, desire, repressed and long dormant, rose within him. He wanted her, just as he always had, and it was still impossible, just as it always was. She'd left him before just when he'd felt secure about her feelings for him. There wasn't a prayer of a chance that she'd want him now, with Killingsworth's murder over his head. There was no life for him outside the Six Counties. There was probably no life for him anywhere at all.

She came down the stairs wearing her parka, carrying his. Without speaking, he stood and allowed her to slide it up his arms and over his shoulders. Leaving it unzipped, he walked to the door and held it open for her. They walked side by side without touching until a gust of icy wind blew with such force that Meghann was propelled backward.

Michael reached for her hand, laced her fingers with his and drew both hands deep into his down-lined pocket. Meghann's cheeks were pink from the wind or embarrassment, he couldn't tell which, but she didn't pull her hand away. It felt good to have her lean on him, good to have enough strength to support her. He knew that she would leave as soon as he could manage on his own. But he intended to postpone that day for as long as possible.

Meghann broke the silence. "It's cold for this time of year."

He nodded in agreement. "Aye. Shall we go back?"

She laughed. "No. Walking on sand is good for you. It will bring the rest of your strength back. We'll be warm if we move a bit faster."

"Y' don't want me t' have a relapse, do you?"

Burrowing her right hand deeper into his pocket, she reached over and slipped her left hand through the crook of his arm. "There's no danger of that. You're completely recovered, Michael. I've never seen you look better."

"Then why are you staying?"

For a moment she looked confused. "I hadn't thought of leaving," she began, "but I suppose—"

"What?"

"I'm comfortable here. It feels like I'm on holiday."

"How long until I go t' trial?"

"Three more months."

"Will there be a trial if I don't return?"

Meghann nodded. "Yes. But it won't look good if you don't."

"What shall I do, Meghann?"

She thought a minute as if none of this had occurred to her. When she answered he knew that it had and that she had spent considerable time thinking about it.

"You'll have to return to the Maze. You were in no condition to leave the hospital on your own. There can be no doubt that you were kidnapped. If you give yourself up it will go easier for you."

"When do y' suggest I do this?"

"Not for a while. Stay here for another month at least, maybe two. That will give me a month to interview witnesses and look over the prosecution's files and another month to come up with a strategy for your defense."

"You'll be watched."

"Yes." She didn't voice what they both knew, that she wouldn't be able to return to Donegal.

"So you're leaving." His eyes were narrowed against the wind and he looked straight ahead.

"Not just yet."

The moment her words registered, the tension left his body. She wasn't leaving, at least not now. He could relax. This time he would have time to prepare for the moment when she walked out of his life and resumed the one she preferred.

Michael felt her hand tighten on his arm. He stopped and looked down at her wind-tossed head.

She leaned against his arm. Carefully, so there would be no misunderstanding his intentions, he drew her into the circle of his arms. She came willingly and pressed her face against his chest. He bent his head to catch her muffled words.

"I don't want to leave," she confessed. "I wish this would all go away and we could stay here forever, just the two of us."

He couldn't believe his ears. "Do y' mean it, Meggie?"

Her head moved up and down against his chest.

"What about your practice, your friends, the life y' have in England?"

She shrugged her shoulders, and a helpless, unintelligible sound came from deep within her throat.

Michael wrapped his coat around her and zipped it so that she was pressed tightly against the wall of his chest, absorbing his warmth. His chin rested easily on her head. Her body against his was a bit of heaven that he never thought to feel again. Every inch of him ached for what might have been. He wanted desperately to kiss her but refused to risk losing what they had slowly, painfully, fought their way back toward. He needed her presence more than he needed sex. When the time came for her to leave, perhaps he would rethink his position.

Meghann inhaled the clean scent of soap on Michael's skin. The wool of his shirt scratched her cheek. She burrowed closer, ignoring the retreat messages sounding in her brain. She refused to think about phrases like *compromising her professionalism* or *personal involvement with a client*. The assault on her senses was too much to resist. This was Michael, and it had been so very long since she had thrown caution away and taken what she wanted. When or if it would happen again was something she couldn't think about. Turning her face into his shirt, she found an open space between two buttons and opened her lips against his skin. She felt his shudder and the surging heat against the nerve endings of her mouth and knew that he wanted what she did.

"Meggie," he rasped, barely clearing the words from his throat. "Don't do this unless y' mean it."

She moaned a low protest as he put her away from him, breaking the contact of her lips against his skin. "We've somethin' to clear up between us before this goes any further," he said firmly.

Meghann put out her hand to stop him. "Don't ruin it," she began.

His arms tightened. "You left me without a word. How could y' do that, Meggie?"

She shook her head. "I don't know."

"That isn't good enough."

"It has to be. That's all there is."

He shook his head. "I asked you t' marry me, Meggie. I waited for you t' call. For years I waited, goin' over that day again and again in my mind. Did I say somethin'? Did I scare you? It was your first time. I know it was. How could y' leave after we'd been together like that?"

She wanted to explain. He deserved an explanation. But there wasn't one, at least not a good one, not one that would make him nod his head and say, "Oh, yes, now I understand." Wetting her lips, she tried to tell him what was in her heart. "I hated Belfast, Michael. Can you imagine hating the only place that's ever been home?" She shook her head. "I just never fit in. After I left your family, I had no one. People were either part of 'The Troubles' or they ignored it. Everyone expected me to be militant because of what happened to my parents and my brothers. But I didn't feel militant. All I wanted was to be away from a place where people judged you by your last name and what school you attended. I loved you, Michael, but I hated your politics. You expected me to accept them and I couldn't. I knew that if I said good-bye, or told you where I was, you would come after me. I wanted you so much that I was afraid you would convince me, and then I'd never be out of it and we'd both be miserable. I didn't love David Sutton the way I loved you, but I knew that if I married him, I could never go back to you. I know it wasn't admirable or brave, but I wasn't either of those things. I'm not now."

She rested her forehead against his chest, taking comfort in his hand stroking the nape of her neck. "I have no excuse for the way I behaved. I'm terribly ashamed and very sorry that I hurt you. You didn't deserve it. But if it's any consolation, I suffered too. The guilt never left me. You never left me. I'm trying to make amends, but I'm not surprised that you don't trust me."

"Are y' comin' back with me now, Meggie?"

She looked at him, at his too-long hair and the impossible blue of his eyes and drew a deep breath. "I've come back *to* you, Michael, not *with* you. There's a difference."

"I don't see it."

"When this is over, if everything turns out all right, I'll explain it." She lifted a shaking hand to brush away the hair falling across his forehead. "You need a haircut. Shall I give you one?"

He nodded. A haircut would occupy his mind, take away the ideas he had no business having. Absorbed in their own thoughts, they walked hand in hand back to the cottage.

Michael rested on the couch while Meghann assembled what she needed. Motioning him to the sink, she had him sit on a chair near the basin. She lifted several layers of hair, allowing the coarse, straight strands to sift through her fingers. She could see clear to his scalp. His hair was scrupulously clean. Wrapping a towel around his shoulders, she reached for the water bottle, lifting and spraying until his entire head was damp. She combed his hair forward, divided it into sections and picked up the scissors.

His arm snaked out, grabbing her wrist. "Y' do know what you're doing, don't you?"

Meghann's eyes widened innocently. "Does it matter? No one's going to see you."

"Just how many haircuts have y' given?"

She pretended to think. "You're my very first."

He started to rise, but Meghann pushed him back down into the chair. "Don't be ridiculous, Michael. How hard can it be? I won't take off too much. If it looks right and you agree, I'll continue."

"All right," he grumbled. "Don't get carried away."

Meghann handed him a small mirror and caught her bottom lip between her teeth to keep from laughing. Michael was as vain as a teenager.

Carefully, she measured off a section of hair on the side of his head, held her scissors against it and snipped. Wisps of black fell on the towel. Then she moved to the other side and did the same.

Michael held up the hand mirror, checked both sides, set it down and nodded for her to continue. Lifting, measuring and cutting, she worked her way up the sides, across the top and down the back of his head.

He relaxed. The play of her fingers moving gently across his scalp was unnervingly sensual. He closed his eyes adjusting his head to accommodate the slight pressure of her hands. The pads of her fingers, cool and deeply personal, moved against him as she lifted pieces of hair and patted them into place after she'd made the cut. It was a dance, the light, deliberate, back-and-forth motion, the stretching of damp hair, the scissor blades closing around a strand, the sharp anticipation, the brief sound of fine-grained sandpaper as his hair separated from the shaft, and the exquisite pleasure of Meghann's fingers, light and sure against his head. He found himself leaning into her, wishing she would go on forever, wishing she would knead his shoulders, rub his back, press her lips against his chest as she had done on the beach.

"I'm through," she said gently, rubbing her palms against his stubbled cheeks. "Would you like me to shave you? I don't mind, and you need it."

Dear God, could he live through it? His body was tight as a drum. Not trusting himself to speak, he nodded his head.

She was gone for less than a minute. When she returned he saw his razor and a can of shaving cream he'd never seen before.

"Where did that come from?"

Meghann shook the can and sprayed a generous amount into her palm. "It's mine. I use it for my legs."

A vision of white foam slathered over a shapely leg, one sweep revealed at a time by the swath of a razor, danced along the edges of his imagination. He swallowed, and with the discipline learned in the H-Blocks closed his mind against the image.

The foam was warm against his cheeks and throat. Slowly, carefully, Meghann moved the blade over his throat, up the line of his jaw and across the plane of his cheek. His bare flesh felt cool without its blanket of foam. He opened his eyes to see her dip the blade in water and return to a foamy spot on his neck. Another smooth, careful stroke, more tensing of his muscles, the sensation of cool against his skin before the cleansing dip into warm water. Over and over she applied the razor, focusing on the correct angle like an artisan crafting a priceless sculpture.

Michael couldn't keep his eyes from her face, the ivory skin, the wide golden eyes, the cinnamon-dark hair falling against high-boned cheeks and her small squared-off chin. Not once did she allow herself to look at him, but he knew that she was aware of his gaze. Otherwise the pink glow would have long faded from her cheeks.

When he thought he couldn't stand the nearness of her for another minute, she stepped back to survey her handiwork. With a satisfied smile she soaked a kitchen towel in hot water, wrung it out and pressed it against his face. The heat of the towel, the smell of floral perfume, the knowledge that he was close enough to bury his face against her throat nearly undid him.

He reached for her, found empty space and realized she'd stepped behind him to remove the towel, replacing it with a dry one. Michael dried his face, lifted the hand mirror and smiled. "You've made me presentable again."

Her laugh was air-filled and shaky. "You were always that."

Their eyes, whiskey-gold and blue, met in the mirror and locked. For a long moment they stared, emotions veiled from one another. Finally Michael spoke. "The paper says there's a *cruinniu* in the village tonight. Will y' come with me?"

"Aren't you worried that someone will recognize you?"

"No."

Meghann quelled her anxiety and thought of the pure pleasure of dancing with Michael. "Yes. I'll come with you."

Meghann felt comfortable in Donegal. It was a town typical of the Republic. Small houses with whitewashed walls, dark wooden doors and thatched roofs came right up to the single main street. Dwellings were attached to small businesses. Mothers attended to their children while taking cash and helping customers. There were few visitors in the northwest corner of Ireland, and most were happy to see anyone come in even if it was only to chat. Not until summer tempered the weather to a reasonable sixty degrees would the tourists come to see the castle on the banks of the mossy, tranquil River Eske.

Michael dressed for the occasion in navy denims, which nearly fit, a V-necked burgundy sweater with a white shirt open at the collar. Meghann was grateful that she'd packed a skirt. It was a calf-length wrap-around made up in a practical heather tweed, nothing fancy, but it was a skirt all the same and her sweater matched it perfectly. She'd chosen boots and her parka for the long walk into town. Nights were cold, even if it was nearly summer, and it would be late by the time they returned.

They walked companionably, Michael shortening his stride to accommodate Meghann. Her hand was tucked inside his as naturally as if they'd been together for years. When they reached the village he was sorry the distance wasn't greater.

"I haven't been to one of these since the recreation club on Divas Street," she confessed, preceding him into the church hall ablaze with light.

"Neither have I."

Meghann looked at him, startled. "Why not?"

He shrugged. "I'm not much for dancing."

"Of course you are. You were a wonderful dancer."

"Y' can't possibly remember that."

Meghann's cheeks flamed. "I remember everything about you."

"Then y' must know that the only girl I ever danced with was you."

"Why is that?"

They had moved into the coatroom. He helped her remove her coat and hang it up. They were alone for a few precious moments. Michael looked down at Meghann, and the heat in his gaze was like the lethal pull of headlights holding their victim immobile until escape was no longer an option. He leaned closer, and closer still, until she closed her eyes against the drowning blueness and felt his lips close over hers.

When he lifted his head, his voice was rough and gravelly against her ear. "I never wanted anyone but you."

The kiss had been heady, drugging, tremendously flattering, but it was his words that left her breathless, shaking and confused. Why would he say such a thing now? Had he heard what she told him on the beach? Did it mean that he would consider a different way of life, away from the North and "The Troubles"?

Still wondering, she followed him into the well-lit hall. The chairs were arranged in a large circle. First, those who wanted to perform would entertain their guests with songs, and stories. Then the chairs would be removed and the dancing would begin.

Michael found two seats in the shadows, leaving Meghann to hold the chairs while he brought back two glasses of Guinness, a pint for him, half for her. She accepted the creamy-headed dark brew with a shy smile and turned expectantly toward the impromptu stage. Two musicians, one with a guitar, the other holding a violin, pulled chairs into the center of the circle and sat down. Without sheet music, they began to play from memory. The audience listened, spellbound, as the eerie, wailing melody lifted and soared until it seemed as if the clear, piercing notes could not be held inside the four walls.

Meghann loved music. Before the horror of Cupar Street, her mother had taught her to play the piano. The Devlins didn't own a piano, and Meghann, remembering her mother's long fingers against the ivory keys, never touched one again.

The musicians were followed by three talented singers, a storyteller, another musician playing the lyre, a piper and a comedian. The residents of Donegal were an appreciative audience, and with each round of Guinness, the leg-slapping and cheers grew louder. Michael was enjoying himself. The room was warm, the mood social, the drams potent, and soon the lights would be dimmed and Meghann would be in his arms.

For a few brief hours he could forget the dark cloud that loomed over him and the knowledge that too soon it would be over and he would never feel again what he felt tonight. Michael felt the pull of his own mortality. When Meghann left for Belfast he had no intention of waiting for the axe to fall. He would find out the truth, no matter what the cost. But that was the future. Now, he wanted to forget everything but the warm camaraderie of the Irish working class, the class into which he was born.

When the entertainers finished, Meghann helped to fold chairs and Michael joined the group of men who stacked them against the wall, good-naturedly joking and ribbing each other as they worked. They were interested in visitors, and Michael, sensing they would be easier with it, reverted to the brogue of West Belfast, accentuating his *h*'s at the beginning of words and dropping the *g*'s at the end.

"On holiday, are ye?" a bearded, broad-shouldered giant with a thick head of brown curls spoke up.

"Aye." Michael couldn't be sure, but he thought he recognized IRA. Grinning engagingly, he held out his hand, offering a false name. "I'm Feeney. Thomas Feeney. We've rented a place a short walk from the village."

The man nodded and extended his hand. "Patrick O'Shea." He nodded toward the group of women stacking chairs. "Is that yer missus?"

Michael saw where his gaze pointed and followed it to where Meghann stood folding the last two chairs. He came up with an elaborate lie that felt right. "We're just married."

O'Shea chuckled knowingly. "We thought so, or we

would have been more neighborly." He offered his hand again. "Good luck t' ye and t' the pretty colleen. Don't let any of the local blokes cut in."

Michael laughed, dropped his arm to his side, and made his way through the assembling couples to where Meghann waited. She looked up expectantly.

"Will you dance with me, Mrs. Feeney?" he asked.

She picked up the cue immediately and her eyes sparkled. "I would be delighted, Mr. Feeney."

Michael led her to the floor, took her hand, slipped his arm around her waist and drew her close. The top of her head reached his chin. He lowered his cheek so that it rested against hers and silently blessed the villages of rural Ireland for not allowing popular music to destroy the closeness that a man and woman could find in each other's arms on a dance floor.

Slowly his feet moved to the music. Meghann moved with him, following his lead, her weight warm and boneless, as if she were attached to his chest. No one in the room watching the couple, so oblivious to everyone but themselves, doubted their story of a recent wedding. They were obviously in love.

Meghann's emotions were raw. Even the Guinness couldn't dull their edges. Michael's hand on her back, his lean, hard jaw pressed against her cheek and the unnerving heat and closeness of his arms and legs evident through the wool of her clothing, unleashed years of repressed longing.

Michael inhaled the scent of her skin. Her mouth was very close. If he moved his cheek just so, their lips would meet. She couldn't run away or make a scene, not after the story they'd come up with. Still, it was a risk, a risk he was very willing to chance if only he could taste her, feel the softness of her lips, take her tongue inside his mouth.

She settled against him, and the new intimacy shook him. Burying his face against her throat, he pressed her into the saddle of his hips, willing her to know what he wanted, to understand what she did to him, what they might never share again. He needed her desperately, and he no longer cared whether or not she needed him. Tonight was his. Opening his mouth against her throat, he tasted salt and moisture and the sweet, floral scent of her perfume. "Meggie," he muttered hoarsely. "I want you. I've never wanted anything more in my life. Can y' do it, my darling? Do y' understand what it is I'm asking?"

She moved so that they shared the same breath. "Aye," she whispered. "I can do it. I want to do it." Closing the space between their lips, she opened her mouth and kissed him, drawing him in, holding him inside until the room dipped and swirled and he wondered where he would find the strength to walk back to the cottage.

11

Meghann barely felt the cold. Michael's arm was tight about her shoulders while hers was under his parka, wrapped around his waist. Their strides matched easily, comfortably, as if they had walked arm in arm together for a lifetime, stopping occasionally to touch and kiss and reassure themselves that they were still of the same mind.

Clouds hid the moon, and the house was completely dark when they arrived. Michael cursed under his breath as he fumbled with the lock. Finally the key turned. He stepped inside, drawing Meghann with him, and closed the door. He heard the pounding of her heart, labored and shallow, as if she'd run a great distance, or perhaps it was his own that he heard. He couldn't be sure. Pulling her into his arms, he kissed her cheeks, her chin, her throat and finally her mouth. He lifted his head and looked down at her face, shadowy and pale in the darkness. "You're not much t' carry," he said softly, "but I don't think I can manage the stairs."

She pressed her fingers against his mouth. "I'll walk."

Michael took her hand and led her up the stairs into the room that had been his own for too long.

Meghann trembled, crossed her arms against her chest and watched him light the small gasoline lamp on the dresser. He removed his sweater and shirt and then turned to her. Wordlessly, she allowed him to gather her into his arms, to frame her face, to rain kisses across her mouth, her throat. And when she was no longer cold, she felt his hands slide beneath her sweater, rubbing her back, gliding over her stomach and tracing the swells of her breasts.

"God, Meggie," he murmured, "I want you so. Tell me that you want me."

She tried to speak and found that her voice had an airy, breathless quality, so that it came out in the barest whisper. "I want you so much that my legs won't work. It seems I've waited a lifetime to have you hold me again."

More than satisfied with her answer, he lifted the sweater over her head, unclasped her bra and buried his face in the soft valley of her breasts. Within moments the rest of their clothing was discarded and they were in the large bed, the covers around them, their seeking mouths and fingers finding the pleasure spots that fifteen years and separate lives could not erase.

Meghann was on fire. The feel of his tight, hair-roughened body against hers left her trembling with a need she couldn't control. Instinctively, she brushed aside the orderly, cautious role she'd cast for herself and moved and spoke and responded as if she'd been handed a whole new identity. For the first time she understood the enormity of what she'd given up and the sweet, stabbing pain of it filled her. Her only relief was to press closer, burying herself in the heat of his skin, his smell, the urgency of his hands caressing her body.

The clouds disappeared and moonlight streamed through the window, illuminating Michael's face and chest as he moved over her, stroking and kissing, murmuring words she never thought to hear from him again. Meghann reached up to run her fingers across his broad shoulders and chest, the column of his throat, the square Irish chin and the sharp bones of his cheeks. His eyes, clear and colorless in the moonlight, framed by the sooty lashes she had envied as a girl, were filled with a need that left her trembling. Despite the pains she had taken on his haircut, the same unruly shock that would never be tamed fell across his forehead. She brushed it back. It fell again. Weaving her fingers through the thick straightness, she pulled his head to her breast. When he slid his tongue down the generous slope, Meghann closed her eyes, giving herself up to wave after wave of undiluted sensation.

Surely it had never been like this, the searing heat, the curious throbbing, the delicious, building tension, a hard mouth gone soft with tenderness and lean callused hands reverently caressing her body as if it were delicate crystal. How could she possibly have given up this priceless pleasure for something so insignificant as peace and sanity? Meghann knew as surely as she drew breath that after tonight there would be no peace for her in all the world.

Michael was hard and hurting with the strength of his desire. He'd meant to hold out and prolong the end of their lovemaking for as long as possible. Something told him that after tonight she would leave, as much because of what was happening between them as her need to get on with his defense. If this was their last night, he wanted her to remember it.

But the wait had already been too long. He had

always been too immersed in his work to become seriously involved with a woman. The immorality of beginning a relationship he had no intention of culminating with a marriage proposal stopped him every time. Meghann was his first and last love, his only love. He wanted her, only her.

The flame inside him heightened. Her legs parted and he slid into her. It was impossible to wait any longer. The moment she arched beneath him he was lost, swept away in the undertow of his own raging current. Moving with its flow, he reached for breath, straining to imprint the rush on his brain, to store, bring out and savor when the nights were long again, this exquisite, mind-absorbing sensation. Time swelled, extending the peak, encapsuling the weightless floating descent until the last surge had settled into a relaxation so absorbing it bordered on unconsciousness. Too exhausted for speech, Michael folded her into his arms, pressed her face into his shoulder and slept.

Meghann stared at the ceiling, wide awake and terrified of losing the power of what they had shared. What if she couldn't save him? What if information was kept hidden in files to which she had no access, as in the Guildford case? How could she go on living if her defense wasn't successful and Michael was sentenced to life without parole?

In a blinding flash of clarity, she realized what had lain dormant within her for nearly a lifetime. She still loved Michael Devlin. She had always loved him, ever since that dreadful night on Cupar Street when her family was killed by British tanks and plastic bullets, the night Michael had reached out into the night and pulled her to safety.

For years she had waited for him to notice that she was more than a child, and when he did, she was ready. Even at fifteen she had known how to widen her eyes, to lower her voice, to swing her hair across her shoulders, to lean against him as if she had no idea how the feel of her skin, the scent of her soap and the curve of her virginal breast pressing against his shoulder affected him. When his voice hoarsened and the blue of his eyes became too intense for her to meet his gaze, when his conversation stopped abruptly and a dark flush rose in his cheeks, Meghann closed her eyes and leaned toward him.

Finally, after what had seemed an interminable wait, she had known what it was to feel his mouth on hers, to feel his arms close around her and to open to the gentle demand of his tongue. Her time had come. Michael Devlin wasn't a womanizer. When he claimed her, he had intended it to be forever. What she hadn't known was how long forever could be.

Dawn in Donegal was as close to heaven as anything worldly could possibly be. Varying hues of violet, peach, silver and pink steadily encroached across the indigo sky. Clouds, wispy and veiled as Irish lace, muted the onslaught of a still wintry sun, and gulls circled above, dark against the morning light. The tide was low, and thousands of scurrying water creatures scrambled for survival in the sucking, sun-stained sand. No wonder stories of leprechauns flourished in western Ireland. It seemed to Meghann, as she stood staring out the kitchen window, that the entire coastline was caught in the rays of a rising sun.

She had slept little, and when it was obvious she would sleep no more that night, she had pulled on jeans and a long sweater, slipped on wool socks and walked down to the kitchen to put on the teakettle. It was time to leave Donegal. If she waited any longer she would be unable to work on Michael's defense. She was already far more emotionally involved with her client than an attorney should ever be. If she stayed even another day there was the possibility that her bias would cause her to miss important clues, to place emphasis on details that had little value when placed before a jury. Clear, cold purpose with the right measure of professional courtesy impressed juries, not emotional rhetoric.

Meghann did not think it was possible to sit in a courtroom and listen to the Crown accuse Michael of unspeakable acts without a certain level of emotionalism. She only hoped it wouldn't jeopardize his defense. It would be much better to leave now, when she could still think rationally, when time had dulled the edges of what they had found in Donegal. She would tell him today, after breakfast.

Somehow he knew without speaking. He came down the stairs, blue-jeaned and bare-chested, with his hair falling over his forehead. His eyes, disturbingly blue, pierced through her defenses, and she couldn't wait for breakfast. She told him immediately, truthfully, without further pretense. "I'm leaving, Michael. If I stay any longer I won't be of any help to you."

He pinned her to the sink by placing both arms on either side of her. "All right, Meggie. But I want you t' know this. If things work out for me, I'll be in your debt for the rest of my life. Don't forget that. Ask for anything and I'll do it." His face was very near, his eyes intent and serious. "I want you back in Belfast. Maybe when you realize what defending me really means, what you'll face when it's over, you'll reconsider. If I'm found guilty, understand that I won't hold you responsible. I never wanted you involved in the first place."

Not one word of love or even of wanting. Nothing personal. It was over, their stolen moments together. What had he said that smoke-filled, gasoline-fumed night on Cupar Street? *Breathe.* She breathed and her heart slowed. "I couldn't have watched it from the sidelines," she said. "This way I know that if it doesn't work out, it won't be for lack of trying."

His hands moved up and down her shoulders. Something was bothering him. She waited, completely still under his touch. Finally he spoke. "Do y' still love me, Meggie?"

Again Meghann held her breath. A lie or the truth. The lie would save her pride. The truth would cleanse her soul. This might be the last time she ever saw him alone. "I'm surprised you had to ask," she said softly. "Yes, Michael, I still love you. I love you so much that I want a part of you to take away, something of you that I can mold and fit into my life."

His hands tightened on her shoulders. His smile made her chest ache.

"There was a time when I offered y' much more than a part of me," he said softly. "Why now and not then?"

"I don't know." She knew he would deliberately ignore her message, just as she knew that she would insist he face it. "The point is, I don't care." She held his gaze, forcing him to understand her meaning.

"What are you saying?"

"I'm thirty-five years old. In all that time I've never done anything so foolish as to make love without protection, except for the times I've been with you. What I'm saying should be obvious. I love you. I'll love you forever. I want to have children with you. I never stopped loving you."

He didn't want to ask, nor did he care to hear her answer, but something inside him wouldn't let her leave without his knowing. "You were married for five years."

"Yes."

"Did you love him?"

Her eyes ached in their sockets. She desperately needed to blink. "Not at first. But I learned to. He was a dear man."

His mouth thinned. "Why did y' do it? Was it the money?"

Meghann shook her head. "I needed his love and his power."

"I don't believe that for a minute. You're hardly the type who thrives on controlling others."

"You're wrong. All my life I've felt powerless. First there was Cupar Street and I was alone. Then you joined the IRA and again I was alone. At university it was assumed that I wouldn't do well because I was Irish, a woman, and alone. David offered me a job that would lead to a powerful position. Then he offered me his name, something no one could ever take away. His name gave me power. He promised to care for me, and I grew to care for him. Because he was older, I knew I would be alone again, but it wouldn't be the same this time." Her hands were trembling. "Money and position bring such power, Michael. You can't imagine the difference between having and not having until you experience both. It's like nothing I've ever known. I'm never afraid because I'm safe. Can you imagine being Catholic from the Falls, and never being afraid again?"

His face was grim, his eyes cold. "No, I can't. Children born in the Six Counties are delivered head first into fear. Some grow up and leave. Some can't escape. The pain of leaving is worse than the price of staying. How can y' do it, Meggie? How can y' leave your country without looking back? Your education and talent could help us."

"Like Peter Finucane, the lawyer with brothers in the IRA? They murdered him in front of his wife and children on Malone Street."

"Peter was a friend of mine. His wife doesn't blame us."

Meghann shook her head. "You don't understand anything about me. Countries aren't boundaries. Countries are people, Michael. Men, women and children who work and eat and sleep, people who live out the fabric of their lives just trying to survive.

Boundaries mean nothing. We can go anywhere. Everyone will be the same."

"If you believe that, how can you love me?"

He was so very dear, and his eyes were no longer cold. "How can I help it?" she whispered. "If ever I've felt passion and heartbreak and longing, it's been with you." She pressed her palm against her chest. "You will always hold a piece of my heart, Michael Devlin. It will go to the grave with you."

His thumb was on her chin, angling slowly, deliberately up her jawline and across her cheek until it touched the corner of her mouth. Meghann waited, life signs suspended, anticipating his next move. He lowered his head, and she felt the briefest touch of his lips on her throat, traveling a path marked by his fingers, down and across the shadowed hollow to the base of her throat. There he stopped, and she was aware of breathing, his or hers she couldn't tell, and a warm hand under her sweater, unsnapping her jeans, circling the spot below her navel that weakened her knees. Tangling his other hand in her hair, he pulled gently, turning her face up to the light. Bending his head to her mouth, he kissed her, claiming her with his lips and tongue and teeth, until she pulled away, desperate for air that wasn't his, air that would make her a separate person again.

"Give it to me, Meggie," he murmured hoarsely, his mouth still connected to hers. "Give me that piece of your heart to take with me."

At the sound of his voice, the last remnants of Meghann's self-control melted away. The boneless feeling was with her again. She had no weight, no matter, that was not his. Molding herself against him, she shaped herself to fill his hollows, allowed his hands to move beneath her sweater and roam across her hips. She heard the whisper of zippers, felt him lift her into the saddle of his hips and when he filled her with a single swollen thrust, she wrapped her legs around him, matching his rhythm until the laughter bubbled and the tears flowed and all that would be lost came together in a vortex of heat and tension, exploding light and physical release.

Two days later Meghann left Donegal and two days after that Michael boarded a bus to Sinn Fein headquarters in Belfast. He took nothing with him except for the clothing he wore and fifty pounds in his pocket. Meghann wasn't the only one with questions. Someone had set him up and although he had a fairly good idea why, he wanted to know whose idea it was and why he was suddenly considered expendable.

"You're what?" Cecil Thorndike's homely face twisted into a shocking grimace and his voice shook. "Have you gone mad, Meghann? This is outrageous. Our firm cannot possibly accept such a client. Father won't allow it."

"What you are not remembering, Cecil, and what Theodore will, of course, is that I own half of this firm. I choose whom I represent without any interference from anyone, not even your father."

Cecil's eyes bulged, and the pink cheeks that took ten years from his age were a startling purple. The woman before him looked the same, in her forest green suit with gold jewelry in her ears and an unusual pin of twisted gold attached to her lapel, all of which bespoke wealth, elegance and superior taste. There was something different about her hair, something not terribly obvious even though he'd noticed right away. The style was the same loose twist caught up at the back of her head, but for some reason it lit up her face in a most unusual way.

"What's come over you, Meghann? In our entire acquaintance you've never spoken to me in such a manner. I can scarcely believe it's you."

Deliberately she sat down and leaned her elbows on her desk. The tips of her fingers met to form a pyramid, and her eyes were fixed on Cecil's face. "You really don't know very much about me."

"Why, I'm sure I know everything I need to know," he sputtered. "Really, Meghann, this is most unlike you. Why should I know anything of your personal history? I'm sure you wouldn't want me prying into your affairs."

So like the British, Meghann fumed silently. How had such a conservative, retentive race managed to procreate? "Come, Cecil. Don't be shy. Tell me what you know." Meghann had never seen a man's face color such a shocking red. For a brief moment she feared for his health and considered recanting the entire conversation. Except that it was too important.

Cecil walked over to the mahogany cabinet, opened it and reached for the bottle of port. His hands shook as he poured a glass and downed it quickly. He turned back to Meghann. "I know that you were educated at Queen's University and then at Oxford. You were on scholarship and proved to be an exceptional law student. Upon interviewing you, David Sutton was utterly charmed and married you shortly after you were hired."

"Do you know that I'm Irish?"

Cecil looked confused. "I imagine so. I've never really thought about it."

"Do you know that I'm Catholic?"

"Good lord, Meghann. Your religion has nothing to do with anything, although come to think of it, you and David weren't married in a Catholic church. I thought that was a rule or something."

Meghann tapped her two middle fingers together. "It is, Cecil. It most definitely is."

He wiped his brow with his handkerchief. "Where is all this leading? I don't understand your point."

"You will, Cecil." Her eyes were narrowed and very gold in the dim afternoon light. "I grew up in the slums of West Belfast. My grandfather was James

Connelly, one of the first martyrs of the revolution, executed for proclaiming Ireland a republic. Most of the time my father, Paddy McCarthy, was unemployed, and when he wasn't he was in Long Kesh prison camp, the charge, insurrection against the Crown. My mother took in washing, that is, until British troops broke through the barrier we resurrected against the rioting Protestants and shot at every man, woman and child on the street with their plastics bullets, projectiles that can split a man's head open upon impact. Three of my brothers and both of my parents were killed that day. I would have been another victim, but a boy saved me, kept me in the shadows, his hand over my mouth, whispering over and over, 'Don't let the bloody bastards kill you, too.' His mother took me in and I lived there for years, like one of her own, until I went away to school. Would you like to know the boy's name, Cecil?"

Somewhere outside of the room a soft rain fell. Cecil's private club would be filling with men dressed in tweed and dark gray, men who walked on plush carpets, looked out windows molded with dark wood and sank into chairs conversationally arranged around comfortable fires, men who understood that the rules of etiquette included never embarking upon embarrassing topics, never involving themselves in objectionable situations and never, ever discussing religion, the state of one's finances or politics unless one was very sure one's companions were of a similar state of mind.

Within ten minutes Cecil had broken every one of those rules. His collar felt very tight and he had the dreadful feeling that after today his relationship with Meghann would never be the same again. Slowly, he nodded. He could barely manage the words. "I imagine that the boy's name was Michael Devlin," he rasped.

Meghann's eyes widened. She looked quite pleased.

"Why, Cecil, that is very, very good, and I mean it sincerely. You are surprisingly astute."

Cecil loosened his tie. It felt much better. Perhaps he wouldn't go to his club today. Yes, that was it. He felt a bit of a headache coming on. Better to go straight home and insist that he not be disturbed. "I'll be leaving now, Meghann. I'm sure you'll want to tell Father on your own."

Meghann smiled. "Nonsense." She reached for the phone. "You are a part of this firm and my very dear friend. We shall tell him together."

12

Theodore Thorndike would be a formidable opponent. Meghann knew his position in the world of business and politics had been achieved through sheer talent. He was brilliant, calculating and deceptively charming, with the manners of an ambassador and the killer instincts of a barracuda. Unlike Meghann, he rarely defended anyone he wasn't sure of clearing completely, resulting in an unimpeachable reputation. Four years ago he was elected to the Commons, and most of his legal work had fallen to Meghann, Cecil and a slew of associates at various levels of their professions. Thorndike and Sutton was an old and prestigious firm, the clients conservative and wealthy.

From the very beginning, when she was a law clerk in the office, Meghann felt uncomfortable about limiting her services to those with exorbitant bank accounts. The law was sacred and should be upheld equally for everyone. She came from a country where it was applied randomly, benefiting some and ignoring others. When she took over David's half of the firm, she decided to offer her services to certain charity clients. It was her way of atoning for the accident of birth that had given her more than enough talent and brains to rise above the circumstances of her past.

When she married David she believed that Ireland and its ghosts were behind her. But she found that a lifetime of memories was not so easily eradicated. Every round-faced woman with lined hands reminded her of Annie and deserved a bit of a rest and a cozy tea. She carried biscuits in her purse for the cleaning woman's freckle-faced children who waited patiently on the stoop for their mother to finish and because every lad in a stocking cap hawking *The Big Issue* in Picadilly could have been Michael or Connor or Dominic or Liam, she bought the entire stack of magazines and sent him home with a five-pound tip.

There was more, of course. The guiltier the conscience, the greater the contributions, and Meghann's conscience was very guilty. So every Christmas she sent a generous check, anonymously, to the Redemptorist Monastery in West Belfast, and every fall, all children with the potential to pass the rigorous course work at Saint Louise's Preparatory School were able to attend, thanks to the David Sutton scholarship fund and Meghann's staggering salary.

At first Theodore had offered an amused, raised-eyebrow objection to Meghann's philanthropic tendencies, but when he realized how inflexible she was on the subject, he withdrew his reservations and never mentioned them. He would just have to do so again, Meghann decided firmly. Michael would be her charity client.

A certain core honesty rose up within her and demanded she acknowledge the difference between Michael Devlin and the others she had defended. Michael was a well-known political figure, a member of the Sinn Fein elite. Although he had never been convicted of a crime, his voice was banned on national television and his passport had been revoked. Defending him would raise questions about her background, her sympathies, her loyalty and her religion. Once the public learned that Meghann was defending a man known for his affiliation with the IRA, a man accused of killing a popular political hero and injuring his small daughter, her clients would leave in droves. Theodore would not be pleased.

She recognized his soft knock. Cecil groaned and sank into a leather chair. Meghann lifted her chin, walked deliberately to the door and opened it.

Immediately she took the offensive. "Good afternoon, Theodore, and please come in. I have some news that I'm afraid you'll find rather shocking."

"Really?" His dry, controlled voice carried a trace of amusement as he stepped into the room and walked to the liquor cabinet. He neither spoke nor turned until he'd filled a tumbler with whiskey, straight up, and swallowed a healthy measure.

Meghann, watching the loose flesh of his throat jump, remembered Michael, his head thrown back to swallow a pint of Guinness, and marveled at how the same action in two different men could bring out such opposing emotions.

"What have you done, my dear?" he asked.

She looked directly at him. "I'm going to defend Michael Devlin."

Not by the flicker of a muscle did his expression change. He leaned against the cabinet, comfortably slouched as if she'd told him the hallway needed refurbishing. Meghann knew exactly what he was doing. It was what she would do, process the information and look at all possible ramifications before answering. Finally he spoke and his words, although she had expected them, shocked her.

"I'm afraid that's impossible."

She cleared her throat. "You misunderstand, Theodore. I've already accepted Michael Devlin as my client. I've been working on his case for several weeks now. It is impossible to back out even if I wished to."

He brushed her response aside. "Rubbish. Leave it to me. I'll secure a competent attorney for Mr. Devlin, although I doubt it will make a difference. The man's guilty. No jury in England will acquit him."

Meghann walked behind her desk and sat down in her chair. "He already has a competent attorney," she said quietly.

Theodore looked at his son, slumped and silent against the rich maroon leather of the chair. "Cecil, please leave us. I wish to speak with Meghann alone."

Meghann's voice stopped him. "I wish Cecil to stay. He has some interest in the way this conversation resolves itself. Nothing you say should be held back from him."

Theodore's gray eyebrows rose for an instant, and then his face relaxed into an expressionless mask again. "Very well, Meghann. This insanity will hurt the firm. Clients will leave us and your reputation will be destroyed, all for a man who hasn't a hope of being acquitted. You aren't a nameless nonentity any longer, Meghann. Your past is exactly where it should be, in the past. There is no atonement for leaving Belfast and making a better life for yourself. Stop punishing yourself for succeeding."

Her expression became more and more mutinous as he continued. "For God's sake, support the Irish if you must. Send donations, write letters, do whatever you wish, but do not destroy what you've accomplished for someone as worthless as a cold-blooded murderer of women and children."

"Michael is not a murderer."

Theodore's eyes lit with suspicion. "So," he said softly, "it's Michael, is it?"

Two spots of color stained Meghann's cheeks. "I

knew Michael Devlin when I was a child. We grew up together."

"I see." Theodore lowered himself into a chair across from his son. "You plan to defend a client on a murder charge with whom you have a personal relationship?"

"I haven't seen Michael Devlin in fifteen years."

"Then why the profound interest?"

Meghann saw no reason for fabrication. "His mother raised me after my parents were killed. I owe her a great deal."

He was quiet for a long time, and although his eyes were fixed on her face, Meghann knew he didn't see her.

"I'm very sorry to say this, Meghann, but I cannot allow it," he said at last. "You will not drag the firm that David and I worked to establish down into the mud."

"You forget that I have as much to say about the direction of this firm as you do."

Theodore shrugged. "Perhaps. However, I offer you an alternative. Before your client list is worthless, I propose offering you a fair price for your shares."

Cecil gasped, but his father ignored him.

"Since you are particularly astute in business matters," Theodore continued, "I needn't point out that once your name is linked with Devlin's, you will no longer be in a position to bargain. I won't throw my money into a poor investment."

Meghann's chin tightened stubbornly. "I've called a press conference for tomorrow."

Theodore rose, walked to the door and opened it. "I shall expect an answer before then. Good night, Meghann." He looked expectantly at his son. "Are you coming, Cecil?"

With a strangled mumble, Cecil stood, threw Meghann a beseeching glance, and preceded his father out the door.

Meghann's hands shook. Carefully placing one high-heeled foot in front of the other, she made her way to the liquor cabinet, poured herself a liberal glass of whiskey, added water and sank down into the chair still warm from Cecil's body heat.

An apple log fire burned in the fireplace. She loved a comfortable fire. There was something sensual about the leaping light, the crackling wood, the delicious, tension-draining warmth. She thought more clearly when she stared into a fire.

Meghann slipped off her shoes, curled her legs beneath her and sipped the amber liquid until she felt the slow, steady heat burn its path down her throat and into her stomach. She was more than tired. The emotional strain of her weeks in Donegal, the depth of her feelings for Michael and the loss of her job had taken its toll.

Her hand reached for her mother's brooch. It was unusually warm. Her head fell back against the chair, her eyelids, heavy from fatigue and alcohol, fluttered and then fell. Centuries flew past, back, back, and still farther back to when the bards sang of a lass from Tirconnaill, a lass named Nuala O'Donnell and the boy whose heart was hers.

Dublin Castle, 1591

It was Christmas, and Rory was determined to escape. The walls ran with wet, and rats scurried beneath the fetid straw upon which he slept. The rage he'd felt when he was chained and brought back to prison without seeing me had deepened into a festering bitterness that only vengeance would soften. He paced the stone floor like a rabid dog, wondering what had become of his wife and his land.

Tomorrow priests would come to say Christmas Mass. He swore, though he burned in hell for all eternity, there would be one clergyman leaving who had not come and one staying behind who did not belong. He would find a way through the sewers and return for Henry and Art, although Art would never last the journey. He coughed endlessly and the shakes were full upon him, but Rory would sooner cut out his heart than leave him to die in Dublin Prison.

Luck was with him, for of the three men dressed in the robes of Rome, one was from Tirconnaill and it wasn't necessary, after all, to do the man harm. I had sent him for the very purpose of aiding an escape. Somehow the priest had obtained a map of the prison. The sewer grates were easily removed, and the three were out of their cells and away from Dublin as easily as mice from sprung traps.

They headed south toward the O'Byrne stronghold, and snow, such as they had never seen in Ireland, fell upon them. Their feet were bare, their clothing in tatters. The air grew even colder as the snow changed to sleet and like sharpened swords fell upon them from the sky. Rory could no longer feel his toes. Art dropped, exhausted, after the first twenty leagues, and Henry and Rory dragged him between them, their footprints staining the snow with blood. When Art fell unconscious, Rory knew that they could continue no longer. The condition of his feet was grave. It was decided that Henry should go on to the O'Byrne castle while Rory stayed behind with my dying brother.

How long is a day and a night and another day in the darkness of endless sleet? Forever, it must have seemed to my brother and Rory. Time after time, in the two days before O'Byrne found them, Rory held his hand over Art's lips to be sure he still lived. His breath was faint but still warm.

After two days O'Byrne and his men found them. Their limbs were stiff and frozen, their clothing one with their bodies like another layer of flesh. Art did not live to see O'Byrne's stronghold, and Henry's grief was terrible to behold. He swore to fight the English until his dying day.

Three toes on Rory's left foot and two on his right were black and bloodless. A surgeon was summoned to cut them off. He felt no pain, but it took time to walk properly again, and the rage in his heart would not be put aside.

He stopped to see Red Hugh O'Neill before moving on to Tirconnaill. The O'Neill welcomed him like a son, thanking him profusely for rescuing Henry and weeping when he learned the details of Art's death.

"'Tis a sad day for an earldom when a son dies," he mused. "Art was ever a robust lad. Damn Elizabeth's soul for destroying my boy. I rue the day she turned against me."

"I do not." Rory spoke softly, but the rage within him would not be quieted. He too had lost a son and a daughter, and his wife was left to mourn alone. "Because of the English queen I've had no word of my wife in a year. I pledged on my honor that I would join with you against Elizabeth, and I shall. We shall make Catholic Ireland her enemy, as Philip of Spain and Mary of Scotland are her enemies."

Hugh stared at my husband from beneath bushy, gray-flecked eyebrows. "Well spoken, my friend. How many men will you raise from Tirconnaill?"

"'Tis two years since I've stepped on the shores of River Eske. I'll have an accounting by the end of the month."

He clapped large hands upon Rory's shoulders. "Godspeed, Rory O'Donnell. 'Tis good to have you home. Perhaps my daughter will learn to smile again."

My mother, the Lady Agnes, waited at the portcullis gate. Rory reined in his horse to hear her.

"Nuala spends much of her time tending the monastery gardens," she said. "Stop there first. There is more that you should see."

Rory told me later that her gray eyes were clear as glass and the sympathy in them was nearly too much to bear. "You speak in riddles, my lady. Is there something I should know that I do not?"

"Nuala has buried three sons and a daughter, my lord. She is not the same woman you once knew."

Rory must have wondered if she'd lost her mind. "We have been apart only two years," he told her. "I learned of Patrick's death and my daughter's. How is it possible that Nuala has buried two more of our children?"

"She was delivered of twin sons three months ago. They did not last the night. It was very cold and they were too young to live outside the womb." Resting her hand on his knee, she spoke clearly, deliberately. "Nuala is in great pain, Rory. I fear for her. Treat her kindly and do not leave her alone again soon."

He nodded and turned his horse east, greatly troubled by Agnes's words. The monastery grounds were desolate. Hobbling the horse, he limped through the doors into the sanctuary. There, entombed in the walls with their names engraved on plaques, was proof that he had sired four children. With trembling fingers he traced the outlines of delicate script, Patrick, Joan, Cormack and Hugh, his children, three he had never seen nor held nor buried.

I felt his presence long before I saw him, and my heart lifted. Rory was home, or nearly so, and my days of darkness were over. He would be pleased to see that Tirconnaill had been well maintained in his absence. The fall harvest was strong and profits larger than ever before. Complaints from the tenants were few. The castle had been resealed, the rushes changed and carpets beaten before the worst of the cold settled in. For the sake of economy, oil-soaked rushes lit the servant's quarters, but in the finer parts of the castle, candles of finest wax stood tapered and slim, filling wall sconces and chandeliers. My only fault was that of all the children I had borne, there was still no heir for Tirconnaill.

Darkness had claimed the land for many hours before I heard the portcullis gate creak upon its hinges. There was a shout and then a most unnatural silence. My nerves were stretched as they had never been, and I waited no longer. Pulling my fur-lined cloak about my shoulders, I ran through the long hall, down two levels of stairs, through the banquet room and out the huge oak doors into the courtyard, where I stopped abruptly.

He was alone on his knees, both hands gripping the hard-packed winter soil, his lips pressed to the ground. His horse waited patiently, in full saddle, reins dragging behind him.

I watched my husband tremble and his body shake with full rocking tremors. I heard the guttural sobs wrenched from that dark place within his heart that no mortal outside of himself could heal. Pressing my fist against my mouth, I knew not whether to announce my presence or turn away and wait until Rory had made his peace with Tirconnaill.

We were wed only four years, but we had come a long way together, Rory and I. I was Nuala O'Donnell and my husband was the earl of Tirconnaill. Still, he was only a man, a man who blamed himself for the troubles that had settled upon his people. If ever Rory and I were to reclaim what once was ours, it would start now in Dun Na Ghal's courtyard of ancient memories, haunted by generations of ghostly O'Donnell ancestors.

Silently I walked to where he lay and knelt beside him. The huge winter moon picked out the silver glints in his hair. Rory had the most beautiful hair. My hand reached out, drawn to the lovely glittering gilt color, but before I could touch it, my wrist was wrenched and I ended up flat on my back on the ice-hard ground, just as I had been the first time Rory had ever looked upon my face.

I could see his expression change from dangerous determination to dawning wonder. "Nuala," he breathed. "My God, Nuala. Tell me this isn't a vision. Tell me 'tis really you."

I laughed, and the frozen stone that was my heart began to thaw. I raised my hand to stroke his cheek. "I'm here, my love. 'Tis Nuala. I've waited so long to have you home again."

With that he stood, lifting me against his chest, and carried me through the open doors, up the stairs and into the bedchamber where I had spent so many nights alone.

His body was thinner than before, and the scars marking his skin were new. I clung to his animal-sleek leanness, my fingers circling and probing, acquainting myself all over again with the corded muscles of his back, the strength of his arms, the width of his shoulders, the taste of his skin.

His lips feathered across my forehead and down my cheeks to my mouth. I opened for him and he kissed me as if we were new lovers again, his hands exploring what his lips had already tasted.

Without speaking, Rory knelt over me, his eyes moving across my breasts, my hips, my stomach and then to the secret place below where the lives of our children had started. I saw the blood leap in his throat, the cords of his neck tighten and felt the hard length of him against my thigh. I burned to take him inside me, and when he finally did, his entry was slow, delicious torment. Too soon, I felt the pulsing of my own heat and the greater one of his seed flooding the emptiness of my womb.

I can no longer remember the words we shared during that first of many long nights of coupling, but I know that we were spent with lovemaking. It was near dawn, the firelight etching our bodies, separating them from the darkness, when I first noticed his feet. Rory slept like a dead man. I slipped out from under the bedclothes and lit a candle from the grate. Holding it close to his feet, I examined them carefully.

Only the big toe on each foot prevented them from looking like stumps. Three toes were missing on his left side and two more on the right. Mutilated skin had grown over the wounds, and I wondered how he could walk with such a deformity.

His voice came out of the darkness. "Do you find them repulsive, Nuala?"

My voice would not come. No matter. Words would not comfort Rory and make him understand what I felt. Instead I balanced the candle against the bed, circled his ankles with my hands and lowered my lips to the holes that once were toes. One by one I kissed them.

I heard the harsh intake of his breath, felt the slight jerk as he tried to pull away, but I refused to release him until I had paid tribute to every missing toe. When I raised my head, I lifted the candle and met his unblinking gaze. "Listen to me, Rory O'Donnell, and listen well," I said fiercely. "I have never loved you more, nor thought you more a man than I do now when I see what you have endured to come home to me."

His smile was very gentle when he pulled me close and wrapped the bedding around us so that we lay swaddled in the warmth of wool and bare flesh. "We shall deal with this together, my love," he whispered through my hair, "and, as God is my witness, I shall never leave your side again."

It was a promise he would break many times over. But I knew it was the nature of men to raise their weapons against an enemy. Elizabeth was evil, and she intended to strip every Irish family of its estates. The time would eventually come. Everyone saw it, I sooner than most. But first English blood would spill, generations of English blood, until our country stood alone, no longer subject to an English parliament and an English monarch.

Meghann still had library privileges at Oxford, and its humanities library was the most complete in all of Europe. With shaking hands, she clicked the computer mouse on the subject title *Hawke of Eske* and waited. Seconds later, pages scrolled across the screen. She read quickly, discarding one page, printing the next. Sixty pages of the entry *The Life of Rory O'Donnell* and twenty of *The Treasure of Tyrone* were already stuffed inside her briefcase.

Two hours later she stood before the reference librarian's desk. "Are you sure there isn't more?" Meghann asked. "Could there be a cross-reference I've missed?"

The librarian shook her head. "I'm afraid not. This is it, even the translations. There's fiction, of course, but these are the facts, history as we know it."

Meghann nodded and turned away. The small tearoom across from the park was still serving food, and most of the summer crowds were in the souvenir shops. She made her way to a table in the corner and ordered a pot of tea, a cucumber sandwich and chips. Milk-colored sunlight filtered through the window, illuminating the pages she'd pulled from her briefcase and set on the table. She ate her sandwich first, decided against the chips, sugared her tea and picked up the first page of *The Life of Rory O'Donnell*.

Her tea was cold by the time she finished. She looked at her watch and her eyes widened. Leaving a generous tip along with the amount of the bill, she hurried to her car and drove around the one-way city center to the motorway exit. English motorways were not like Irish roads. Speed limits were not observed. Unless one drove in the slow left lane, great concentration and steady nerves were required to overtake other automobiles. Meghann needed to unscramble what she'd read today. She decided to stay in the slow lane.

O'Clery's *Life of Rory O'Donnell* was a dry, uninspiring view of sixteenth-century Ireland. Battles, intrigues, betrayals, motivations, even peculiarities of dress and manner had all been meticulously documented, but that was all. There was none of the color and vibrancy, the rich pageantry, the sounds, the music, the smells, the pride and anguish of the world that came to Meghann as she slept.

What she couldn't explain away and what she had previously refused to face squarely was something that had no place in logic or scientific phenomena. She knew details, colors, odors, fragments of conversation. She had seen rain dripping on the stone stairways, smelled herbs scattered on a sickroom floor, heard words twisted in accents that had never been encountered in the twentieth century. She had seen moonlight color a boy's hair to liquid silver, watched the reverence in his eyes as he held his newborn son. She had felt his bitterness as the blade sliced through his flesh and watched the pain in his eyes as, one by one, his blackened, bloodless toes fell to the stone floor.

Where was the historian who had recorded such scenes? And if there was none, why had she seen them so clearly?

13

Nuala, Tirconnaill, 1595

My prayers were answered, and the children born to Rory and me came in rapid succession, first Brian, then Sean and the joy of my heart, tiny, golden-haired Kathleen. The boys were redheads with tempers to match and as similar in feature and character as twins though they were a year apart. They fell into constant mischief, but Rory could no more bring himself to punish them than I could. I feared they would be terribly willful. Looking back on those perfect, golden-lined days I cannot be sorry for the decisions we made regarding the small beings created in images of ourselves.

Tirconnaill was a tiny sanctuary far away from the whispered horrors of those around us. The Irish were suffering terrible persecution throughout the country but at Dun Na Ghal Castle, life was the same as it had always been. In Tirconnaill there were no evictions and no man, woman or child went hungry. We simply ignored Elizabeth's Irish Policy, and since we were far to the north, there was no one to enforce it.

Still, the stories filtered to our gates, and they were

as unbelievable as they were outrageous. Mass was forbidden lest one be stripped of his belongings. Tithing to the English church was required. Catholics were taxed and rents raised if tenants improved a landlord's property. Prisons and prison ships were filled with men and women destined for the penal colonies of the New World, charged with nothing more heinous than feeding their children rather than paying taxes.

In those first months after Rory's return I feared that Elizabeth's troops would come to take him back. But they did not, and after a year had passed, I stopped waking in the night. The English queen had more on her mind than the escape of a single Irish prisoner. She worried over Catholic Mary Stuart of Scotland, Catholic Philip of Spain and, to a small degree, the Catholic earls of Northern Ireland.

She was right to worry. While she fretted over Spain and Scotland, Rory broke with tradition and armed his peasants, training them to fight. They were known as the *buannada*. In three years he had fifteen hundred horsemen, one thousand pikemen and four thousand foot soldiers carrying arms, rolling cannons and leading packhorses. Almost every Irish family was angry over the Ulster Policy and joined Rory and my father in their fight.

In 1595, Sir William Russell proclaimed my husband a traitor and in 1596, Rory appealed to His Most Catholic Majesty, Philip of Spain.

Only because I loved Rory O'Donnell could I understand what moved him to the lunacy of following his instincts rather than his intellect. Rory was a true Irish chieftain, his reputation embellished by ancient prophecy: *When two O'Donnell earls, father and son, lawfully and linearly succeed each other, the last Rory shall be a monarch of Ireland and banish hence all foreign nations and conquerors.*

He was a man who fired the imagination of our clansmen, now turned soldiers. He gave the Irish what no English earl ever could, the figure of a popular folk hero, rooted in prophecy, born to lead them against the enemy.

The common folk turned to him with delight. They lifted him to their shoulders. They wove him into legend, reminding themselves of his destiny over and over. By ancient law and his own worthy muscle, he brought back the magic of the raider-made-king. He gave our people hope of an Irish world as familiar and warm as the glow of Irish whiskey. He was impulse and instinct, brilliance and bravery. Like a twist of lightning, Rory danced among the downtrodden, whipping them into a frenzy not seen since the days of Brian Boru.

And so, slowly, he destroyed what I had worked so hard to achieve, a detached and unemotional but intrinsically loyal facade to fool the queen. I walked the floor night after night, bargaining all that was mine, fine words, blazing temper, threats, and even my body, until finally Rory agreed to swear his loyalty to Elizabeth at Dundalk.

It was a farce, of course. Rory meant none of it. Thankfully, Elizabeth refused to give up the sophistication of London for Ireland and sent a representative in her place. Crafty with age and experience, she would have immediately seen what was in Rory's heart and in the hearts of all the Irish chieftains who swore their allegiance to her that day.

After Dundalk, there was a period of calm. Once again my belly swelled with the child I carried and my mind, usually so clear and focused on its purpose, could fix on nothing more than the babe that would come and the children I had.

I wanted a girl. Sons clung to their mothers for only a short time. Sons were born to the sword. Sons were fostered out and fell in battle. Sons cut their teeth on the hearts of their loved ones. Not so daughters. Daughters grew to womanhood beside the women who bore them. Daughters brought home their babes to be comforted in arms too long without the feel of a downy-haired infant. Daughters were safe. Deirdre I would name her, after the first of Brian Boru's wives.

Rory met more often now with my father and all the O'Neills, with John O'Dogherty, Ever MacMahon and others I knew nothing about. It was during one of his absences that Niall Garv, Rory's cousin, came once again to Dun Na Ghal.

I did not care for Niall. Perhaps it was my own conscience that troubled me. When we were young we had promised to wed, a children's promise made when both of us were innocent of the power of desire and the price of love.

The children and I were outside the castle gates near the copse of trees leading to the river when he found us. The clouds, a mixture of white and dark, boiled above the turrets, but the sky was blue and clear of rain. My boys played by the water while I rested on a blanket nearby, holding a sleeping Kathleen in the curl of my arm. I was only one season gone with child, but already my pregnancy was very evident.

"Da duit, Nuala." Graceful as a cat, Niall leaped from the back of his stallion, tethered him to the ground and walked to the blanket where my daughter and I rested. His eyes, dark and piercing as shards of obsidian, missed nothing.

I was unable to remedy my vulnerable position without disturbing Kathleen. Because I felt awkward, my cheeks burned and my voice was sharper than usual. "You are welcome here, Niall, but I fear your journey is without cause. Rory is away."

He stretched out beside me, locking his arms behind his head, his eyes closed against the sun. "You underrate yourself, Cousin. 'Tis you I came to see."

There was movement beneath his eyelids. I dared not show my discomfort. "My husband will know how solicitous you are. I speak for him and thank you."

Niall's mouth twisted bitterly. "Were he to know my thoughts, I doubt he would speak so. Keep his thanks to yourself, Nuala."

There could be no answer to such a statement, and I remained silent.

"Tirconnaill looks well," he remarked, "no thanks to Rory."

I pitched my voice low so as not to wake the child, but Niall could not mistake its ferocity. "I'll not have you insult my husband in my presence."

He swore and flung back his hair impatiently. Fascinated, I watched it fall to his shoulders, shiny-straight, black and alive as a crow's wing. If he had been anyone other than Niall, I would have reached out to touch it.

"Holy God, Nuala." His bitterness had grown worse with every passing year. "'Tis you who care for Tirconnaill. He comes home to rut and spill his seed, getting you with another child to bear alone, and then he leaves again. How can you do it year after year?"

"What choice do I have?" The words came out before I could stop them. I knew immediately that he would not hear what I had intended.

He sat up, resting easily on his haunches, and placed two fingers under my chin, forcing me to look at him. "You had a choice. I offered you all that was mine."

Only a woman devoid of all compassion could ignore the pain in his eyes. He was handsome enough, with the sharp, cold features common to those descended from centuries of Celtic inbreeding. Not so tall as Rory, his lean, broad-shouldered frame would catch the eye of many a young woman in search of a husband. Were it not for Rory, I would have looked with favor upon his suit.

"You do me great honor, my friend," I said gently, "but the time has come for you to put these feelings aside. My choice was Rory from the moment I first set eyes upon him. It was the same for him." I pulled his hand from my chin and held it in mine for a brief moment. "Take yourself a wife, Niall, and get your heirs upon her. I promise you that happiness will come."

He shook off my hand and stood. Staring across the river, he watched my fiery-haired sons skimming stones across the current.

"They should have been mine," he muttered and strode to where his horse grazed. Unaided, he leaped to his back and pulled up the reins. "There is no one for me but you, Nuala," he called out. "Someday soon I shall claim you whether or not you are widowed."

His threat, clear and loud, rang through the afternoon air and ruined the sweetness of my outing with the children. I waited for Niall and his horse to disappear over the rise before lifting Kathleen into my arms and calling the boys home.

Despite my brave front, I could not forget the look of purpose in Niall's eyes. Neither could I ignore what he had said about my husband's frequent absences. Where *was* Rory when I needed him?

When he did come home he brought unwelcome news.

"By the fires of hell, Nuala. What ails you? It is customary for a noble to foster out his sons. Sean is too young, of course, but Brian is nearly of an age to consider it. Fostering strengthens the bonds of friendship and loyalty. Brian will be chieftain of Tirconnaill. This coddling will not help him. Why must you be so stubborn?"

The thought of losing my child so early was like a knife blade in my chest. I refused to look at Rory as I reasoned with him. "I have no objection to fostering as long as the family and the time are right."

"Niall Garv is an O'Donnell, my cousin and a fierce warrior. His half-brothers are close in age to Brian. What possible objection can you have to his family?"

"There is no woman in the household."

"There are a hundred women."

I shook my head. "Only servants and children. There is no lady to oversee the castle. 'Tis a filthy hold. Many die during the fever season. I do not wish my son to be sent to such a place."

I still wouldn't look at him. He moved to my side and lifted my chin. Rory knew me as well as I knew myself. Would he see that I hid the truth? I shook off his hand. "I am the countess of Tirconnaill. Until they are grown, all matters dealing with the children will be ruled by me. 'Tis the law and, willing or not, you must abide by it."

With a curse, he left the room. It was unlike Rory to make such a demand. I wondered if he was not hiding something as well.

He found me in the kitchens instructing the maids in the making of perfume. The smell of roses wafted through the air. By the look on his face I saw that he had not given up his notion. Leaning against the door frame, he waited until I finished.

"Is there something you wanted, my lord?" My words were conciliatory, but my mind was not. As much as I wished to avoid arguing, I knew this conversation could not be postponed.

He cleared his throat nervously. "I would speak with you on a matter of some importance."

My eyes met his from across the room. "Can it wait until evening?"

"Not this time."

I wiped my hands on a towel and followed him

from the kitchen. He waited for me at the castle gates. There, he linked his arm through mine and led me down the path by the river. "It seems I am at an impasse, Nuala," he said. "I need your help."

My curiosity was piqued. "What is it?"

"Brian is young for fostering, but we may have little choice."

"How so?"

"Elizabeth demands a hostage. She insists on the heir of Tirconnaill. Only if Brian is promised elsewhere can I refuse her."

The bile rose in my throat at the thought of Brian forced to humiliation at the English court. Would she take her revenge because Rory had refused to warm her bed? I would die before sending my son into England.

Deep in thought, I walked by Rory's side, instinctively avoiding the stones in my path. I had never told Rory about Niall Garv's visit. My husband's temper was legendary, and I wanted no scandal and no killing. Niall hoped for Rory's death, nay, he more than hoped, he planned for it. I could not send Brian to the household of his father's enemy. But neither could I send him to Elizabeth. I knew the manner of woman she was and what she had asked of Rory at the price of his freedom. Although I prayed that he would consider it, secretly I was relieved that he had spurned her. Rory O'Donnell was mine, bound by more than vows of Holy Church. We had pledged our souls, and since the first night Rory came to my bed, I believed he remained faithful to me.

All these thoughts came and went as I walked beside our river, stained a brilliant bronze from the rays of a dying sun. Suddenly an idea came to me, perfect in its simplicity.

"Tell her she may have him as soon as the weakness leaves his chest. Tell her his spots come and go and we are hopeful for his survival. Tell her that only half of the maids who attend him fall down with the fever. Tell her we will pray that our son recovers his strength in order to serve her."

I raised my eyes to Rory's face and found his eyes wide with shock and something else I'd not seen in a very long time, approval.

"By God, Nuala, you are clever. If there is anything Elizabeth fears it is illness." He frowned. "But why not just tell her he is pledged to Niall?"

"Brian is no more than a bairn. 'Tis best to keep his future open. Besides, I've heard rumor that Niall has fallen in with the queen."

Rory shook his head emphatically. "Impossible. Niall is an O'Donnell."

"Rumor is never completely wrong, Rory. Watch Niall carefully and never show him your back."

Belfast, 1995

Michael Devlin waited out the afternoon in a pub on the Ormeau Road near the Lower Falls. When the indigo blue of late dusk had turned to darkness, he made his way into Catholic Belfast and walked down Divas Street, past the Peace Line and the Conway Mill, past the mural of the Madonna and Child adorning the Brickfield's Barracks, past Dunville Park, past the spires of Saint Peter's Cathedral, past the tower and its republican slogans strung along the balconies, into the headquarters of Sinn Fein. He didn't bother disguising himself or treading lightly. They had known where he was since before he left the Maze. If they had wanted him dead he would have been.

The hallway was dark, but one room would be lit. It always was. Lighting a cigarette, Michael drew in the smoke, held it in his lungs and exhaled. The rush hit him immediately. He stepped around the corner and leaned against the open door frame watching a lean curly-haired man intent on a computer screen. "Hello, Liam," he said quietly.

Liam McKintyre froze. He didn't have to turn around to place the clear, hard voice of the man who had been his idol for nearly ten years. Arranging his features in what he hoped was a welcoming expression, he stood and held out his hand. "How are y', Michael?" he asked as if they had seen each other yesterday. His smile faded as Michael's narrowed gaze moved over him. Shifting nervously on his feet, he lowered his hand and sat down again.

Michael straightened and closed the door behind him before pulling up a chair and straddling the seat. "I could be better if I knew what the hell is going on around here."

Liam wet his lips. He was very pale. "I don't understand."

"I think y' do."

Nervously, Liam reached for the cup of cold tea on his desk. "What do y' want t' know?"

"Who killed James Killingsworth?"

"I don't know, Michael. I honestly don't know."

"Do y' expect me t' believe that something that big is ordered without your knowledge?"

Liam lit a cigarette and leaned back in his chair. "It wasn't us."

Michael did not miss Liam's shaking hands and perspiring brow. "We've been friends a long time, Liam. Y've shared a fry at my home every New Year's Day since we were boys. I should know why I'm taking the hit for this one."

Liam shook his head and managed a shaky smile. "I'm not in on this one, Mick. I swear it. I don't know any more than you do. I don't believe y' did it, never did, not for a minute. I told them I knew youse, that y' couldn't have done it. What it comes down to is that y've got enemies. Lately, y've taken us down a path that many aren't satisfied with. Decommissionin' isn't the answer, not until we've got some concessions from the unionists. Maybe this is some kind of ruse t' give us leverage in the peace talks."

Michael's eyebrows lifted. "By killing the one Brit who was on our side? I don't think so."

Leaning forward, Liam gestured with the hand holding his cigarette. Smoke swirled in the air above his head. "Think of this. The election is comin' up. If the ceasefire is no longer in place, the government will be forced t' allow us int' the talks. As it is, we're at a stalemate."

"If the government moves quickly enough and the murderer is caught and sentenced, the public will be happy enough. Sinn Fein could lose a healthy dose of support."

"Not if y' acted on y'r own."

Michael's jaw tightened. "Everyone knows me, Liam. I've opposed all but defensive actions. We've had twenty-six deaths in the last five years compared to hundreds in the previous five. I've always condemned the slaughter of innocent bystanders and I'll continue t' do so, even if it means the IRA gives up its weapons first. We've gained support in every civilized country in the world, particularly the United States. Gerry Adams has been welcomed by Clinton, for Christ sake. Do y' think any of it would have come about if the same violent, indiscriminate killing had continued? Our men and women are educatin' themselves and taking that education back to the Falls. A united Ireland must include the Protestant population as well as the Catholics, with civil rights for everyone. Do y' think such a goal is even a possibility if the world continues t' think of us as cold-blooded killers? Jesus, Liam, how can y' sleep at night knowing innocent people have died on their way t' the market for a tin of biscuits?"

"They're not the only ones who've died."

"The Prods have kept their end of the bargain," Michael reminded him. "Until recently, there was no retaliation for IRA bombings. I'd say they've been remarkably patient, and I'll wager most Americans would as well."

Liam ground out his cigarette in the already over-flowing ashtray. "It's not me y' have to convince, Mick. I've always been with you, which is why I can't help y' now. They know where y've been. They'll know y've been here and it won't be me telling them."

Michael's eyes were thin, dangerous slits of blue. Liam swallowed. The rest must be said, but he'd rather not be the one saying it. He tried stalling. "Would y' care for a cup of tea, Mick?"

"Aye, I would."

Liam started to rise when Michael's hand clamped down over his wrist.

"First, tell me the rest of it."

Liam was wise enough to know that denial would avail him nothing, not even time. His throat was very dry. "They know who y've been with."

"And who might that be?" Michael's voice was cold, flat, completely without expression.

"The barrister, Lady Meghann Sutton."

"Is there something y're leaving out, Liam?" The words were deceptively soft.

"Only that we know she's Meggie McCarthy, y'r mother's goddaughter raised in y'r home."

Michael released Liam's wrist and rose. "I don't think I'll be needin' the tea after all, my friend."

"Where will y' go?"

Without answering, Michael walked out the door and down the long hall. He had no intention of divulging his whereabouts. Liam's story had been convincing. He'd nearly believed it, until his tell-tale *we*.

14

The brash young reporter wearing a badge with the London *Times* logo called out from the back of the room. "Is it Lady Sutton or Miss McCarthy?"

Meghann waited until the silence was complete before answering, a strategy she had perfected early in her career, its purpose to establish a dignified tone that few dared to cross. "Professionally, I prefer to use my maiden name," she said quietly.

Cameras flashed, momentarily blinding her. The smell of wet wool and male bodies too long without antiperspirant wafted through her spacious office. She wrinkled her nose.

Another voice spoke up. "Is it true that you are representing the IRA activist Michael Devlin?"

"Yes."

"Do you believe that Mr. Devlin is innocent?"

"I do."

"Will Cecil Thorndike be assisting?"

"No."

"Is it true that you've resigned from Thorndike and

181

Sutton and that your shares in the company have been purchased by Mr. Thorndike?"

"I have decided to resign my position from Thorndike and Sutton, but I have not sold my shares to Mr. Thorndike."

The first abrasive voice spoke again. "Were you sacked, Miss McCarthy?"

Meghann laughed, a rich genuine sound that lit her face and brought a delicate flush to her cheeks. The effect was astonishing. A collective sigh escaped from the lips of the London reporters, and the antagonism pervasive to all legal interviews miraculously lifted.

"No, Mr. Jenson." The humor was evident in her voice. "I was not sacked. As many of you know, I am accustomed to accepting certain clients without gratuity. Mr. Devlin is one of them. Because of the magnitude of his defense and the time constraints involved I will be unable to attend to my other clients. Therefore, in all fairness to them and to the firm, I have resigned."

The next question, from a man she'd never seen before, was couched in conciliatory language. "Many of us would be very interested in your relationship with Mr. Devlin and how you became interested in his defense. That is, if you don't mind, Miss McCarthy."

"Not at all." Meghann leaned against her desk, folded her hands in her lap and casually crossed one leg over the other, a deceptively innocent pose that bought her extra time and chased every thought except one from the minds of her audience—just how long *were* Meghann McCarthy's legs under her slim, form-fitting skirt?

She spoke slowly, clearly, warming to her subject as she continued. "The murder of James Killingsworth was a terrible tragedy, not only for his family and for England, but for those who believed he was the answer to the troubles in Northern Ireland. The Peace

Initiative, entered into with such hope, has foundered, leaving everyone disappointed and frustrated, none more than Sinn Fein, the political party supported by ten percent of Ulster's population. Everyone familiar with Mr. Killingsworth's policies is aware of his stand on the Six Counties of Northern Ireland. He believed in the self-determination of a secular free state, the same stand that Sinn Fein supports. As you know, representatives of Sinn Fein are currently banned from the peace talks, primarily because of the roadblocks placed in their path by Ian Paisley and the Democratic Unionist Party. Without Mr. Killingsworth's support, Sinn Fein has little hope of participating in the negotiations. To accuse Michael Devlin of murdering James Killingsworth is to ignore the last five years of Ulster's history."

Charles Denning of the *Daily Telegraph* pulled himself out of his absorption. "Why the last five years?"

Meghann ticked the facts off on her fingers. "In 1972 seventy IRA men were killed. In 1980, intelligence reports show the number of active IRA soldiers to be five hundred. By 1987, two years after Michael Devlin assumed his current position among the council members of Sinn Fein, only four killings were reported. Before 1985, IRA killings were indiscriminate. Car bombs were left in heavily populated public areas. Since then, except for admitted mistakes, targets have been limited to soldiers, paramilitaries and police. Families are left alone."

She reached behind her and held up a slim paperback. "I do not imply for a single moment that the IRA or Sinn Fein, its political arm, is blameless. What I suggest is that the mentality of indiscriminate murder has undergone a radical change for the better because of Mr. Devlin. Gentlemen, Michael Devlin's words are not the words of a murderer. I urge you to read his book."

Once again the young reporter spoke from the back of the room. "Your name is Irish, is it not, Miss McCarthy?"

Meghann's throat closed. She had expected it, even prepared for it, but to hear the actual words was disorienting. Minutes ticked by. There was no way around it. Her credibility was at stake. Better to offer her version of the truth than to have it dragged from her.

She straightened and dropped her arms to her sides. Her voice rang out clear and cold, a tribute to her years in the courtroom. "Yes, Mr. Smythe. It is an Irish Catholic name. I was born in Belfast. My family was killed on August 15, 1969, when Protestant paramilitaries rioted and broke through the protective barriers erected by Catholics in West Belfast. The incident and the events that followed are better known as Bloody Sunday. Michael Devlin's mother raised me with her own children."

The room was completely silent as if even the act of breathing had been suspended. Meghann waited until the drama of her announcement had settled before concluding the interview. "I am a barrister, and I have seen an inordinate amount of murderers in my practice. This time the wrong man has been accused." She smiled graciously. "Good day, gentlemen. Thank you for coming."

"If you please, Miss McCarthy." A red-faced reporter with a perspiring bald head blushed furiously. "Will you describe your version of the riots as you remember them?"

Meghann shook her head and lied. "I'm sorry. It was a long time ago and I can't remember the details. If you'll excuse me, I'm already late for my conference call."

Disappointed, the man nodded and followed the others out the door. Meghann waited until the sound of footsteps faded away before crossing the room to lock the door. Slipping out of her pumps, she plugged in the kettle and curled up on the window seat.

For twenty-five years she'd avoided dredging up memories of the Cupar Street riots, hoping to erase the worst of her terror. For those first few years in the Devlin household, her mind had cooperated. It wasn't until she'd lived on her own, on the outskirts of Queen's University, that her nightmares began. She would wake breathing smoke, tasting ashes on her tongue, her heart hammering, her breathing shallow and desperate, her nightgown drenched, her body drawn tight as a drum against the images that were even more colorful, more horrifying and more real than the night had actually been.

A grown woman's mind was more graphically disposed than the mind of a ten-year-old child, she rationalized. The never-ending struggle of life on the streets of Belfast and the newspapers carrying pictures of bombings and death were a constant reminder of what she'd endured. Surely, when she moved to the safety of London, where sectarian strife was nonexistent, the recurring dreams would end. And they had, until recently, after her return from Donegal.

Intuitively, Meghann knew that Michael's defense would bring back her past, and with its return her unresolved questions, her fears and long-repressed emotions would return as well.

The teakettle whistled, but she ignored it. Pressing her hot forehead against the cool windowpane, she closed her eyes and willed the memories of that warm August night to surround her.

It had begun two days earlier, on August thirteenth, the same day Free Derry was proclaimed. There had been riots in Belfast but no casualties. The following day, Thursday, the B-Specials, a Protestant auxiliary police force armed with Browning machine guns, rolled down Divas Road in armored tanks and opened up on Divas Flats, a high-rise tenement that housed only Catholic families. A nine-year-old boy asleep in his bed and a British officer home on leave were killed.

The news spread and by Friday afternoon, August fifteenth, residents of the Falls panicked. It began on Cupar Street, the border between Catholic Clonard and the Protestant Shankill. Boards were hammered over windows, furniture loaded into vans. Trucks, bakery vans and cars were hijacked, first to carry people and valuables out of the neighborhood and later to act as a barricade against loyalist marauders.

Meghann was returning home from a two-day musical competition in the city center. The day before, she'd been warned by Sister Mary Bernard that there was trouble in the Clonard and she should go straight home, but there was always trouble in West Belfast and her audition wasn't until the following morning. Still, that afternoon, she'd been persuaded to leave and walked to the bus stop only to find there were no buses running. There were no buses at the Falls Road bus stop either. Undaunted, she continued up the road at her usual pace until she heard shooting. Mill workers from Mackies were firing into the neighborhood and there was pandemonium on the street.

Meghann dropped her music and ran toward Cupar Street. There she stopped, frozen in horror. Barricades had been erected on both sides of the road, and the charred remains of Finnegan's pub were being picked over by Protestants from the Shankill. Men from Mackie's foundry, all Protestant, carried iron bars and makeshift weapons as they made their way cautiously down Cupar to the Shankill, bludgeoning anyone who crossed their paths. Flames and the stench of petrol were everywhere. Catholic homes, one after the other, caught fire, and fifteen-year-old Gerry McCauley lay on the ground in a pool of blood.

Meghann's path was blocked by flames and boys throwing stones and armed Protestants bearing down upon her. She turned and ran back toward the Falls Road to the only safety she knew, the Redemptorist Monastery. Kneeling in the shadowy pews of the church, she prayed for an end to the chaos. Time passed. Outside, an eerie silence replaced the shouting. Cautiously, Meghann walked to the door and looked out. The street was deserted. Flames lit the darkening sky. It seemed to Meghann that the entire world was on fire. Where were the fire trucks?

Rubbing her smudged cheeks, she made her way back down Cupar Street to the remains of her home. Choking back sobs, she peered into the smoking rubble, waiting for her eyes to adjust. Where was Mam and Da and the others? Two black lumps lay in the center of the floor, one on top of the other. Meghann ventured further into the room and bent down to study the curiosities more carefully. She was ten years old and had never seen a dead body. She recognized her father's jacket and trousers, but where his head should have been was a mangled pulp of mess and blood.

"Da?" she whispered, holding out her hand, afraid to touch. Beneath him lay her mother, flat on her back. Her dark hair, normally so smooth and tidy, was caked with dirt, her face gray with ashes but still reassuringly familiar.

Meghann's voice quavered. "Mam, it's Meggie. Wake up. Please, wake up." She was crying in earnest now, silver tracks running through the dirt of her face, her breath coming in great hiccuping gasps.

Through the darkness, a voice spoke and a gentle hand sifted through her hair. "There, there, child. It will all come about. You'll see."

Meghann lifted her head and stared. Where moments before there had been only darkness and silence, now stood a striking woman with long red hair and green eyes dressed in the robes of a postulate. Outlining her figure was an odd pale light, or perhaps it was only the whiteness of her clothing that gave her that netherworld aura. "My mam won't wake up," Meggie whimpered.

Her eyes warm with sympathy, the woman beckoned Meghann to her. "Poor darling. Come, sit beside me."

Meghann felt no fear. Sighing, she sat down in the circle of the stranger's welcoming warmth and leaned against her. Within seconds she was asleep. Two hours later Michael Devlin found her alone in a corner, still unconscious, her face streaked with tears, her hand clutching her mother's brooch.

In the worst of the chaos, Annie had remembered her godchild and insisted on learning the fate of her neighbors on Cupar Street. Michael volunteered to find out and when the worst of the night had passed, he slipped through the entries and the empty, burned-out homes to the waste that only yesterday had been a neighborhood of families, grocery stores, taverns and shops.

He took one look at the mutilated bodies of Meghann's parents and, for the first time in his life, cursed like a man.

Meghann woke and looked up, her eyes very bright against the black grime covering her face. At first she didn't recognize the thin, black-haired boy with fury spewing from his lips. But when his face gentled and she saw the blueness of his eyes, she knew him. She stood and ran straight into his arms.

Instinctively Michael closed them around her, holding her against his chest, feeling her tears soak his shirt. "Hush, love," he murmured against her hair. "It's all right now. I'm here t' take you home with me."

Her words were muffled against his chest. "Are they dead?"

Michael closed his eyes. Never before had such a

responsibility been his. "Aye, Meggie. But you'll see them again in heaven."

This Meghann could understand. Meghann knew all about heaven and that other place she wasn't allowed to mention.

Michael set her away from him and searched her face. "Will y' come with me now?" he asked gently.

Nodding, she tucked her hand in his and walked with him down the middle of Cupar Street, keeping well away from the dark, smoking buildings.

They were a stone's throw from the monastery when shots rang out between the men positioned at the Springfield Road barricade and the torches from the Shankill. Frozen with shock, the children watched as row upon row of homes went up in a display of fiery explosions.

Michael dragged Meghann into the church, pushed her to the floor and covered her body with his. Minutes passed, or maybe it was hours. He couldn't tell. Meggie was warm beneath him but she hadn't moved in a long time. "Meggie?" he whispered into her ear. "Are you alive?"

Her head moved up and down. He breathed a sigh of relief and reached down to help her up when he heard pounding and angry voices at the door. "Bombay Street is burning, Father," a man shouted. "Ring the bell. We need more help. Ring the bell."

The cry was taken up by a dozen more voices. "Ring the bell. Help us, Father. Ring the bell."

Father McLaughlin's resonant voice silenced them. "I've called the barracks. The army is already on its way. We can't risk the bell. They'll hear it in the Shankill and come for us."

Michael had seen British troops assemble on the Falls Road, separating the Catholics of Clonard from the Catholics of Springfield, sandwiching the Protestants in between. He shook his head at the foolishness of a British captain who couldn't read a map. There was only one solution.

"Stay here, Meggie," he whispered urgently. "I'm going t' ring the church bell. Don't move until I come back."

Again the brief nod. She was conscious. Hopefully she understood.

The door near the altar led to the belfry. Michael climbed the stairs two at a time until he reached the bell. Grasping the rope, he pulled with all his strength. The clear, piercing chimes peeled through the smoke-filled air of the Falls, across the Springfield Road barricade and the silent streets of the Shankill until even the meager showing of tourists, safe in their lodgings on Malone Road, stopped their conversations and listened.

"Mother of God. We're in for it now." Father McLaughlin crossed himself and ran to the belfry door.

As it turned out, nothing on that unholy night had been as effective. For the first time since the riots began the British Army marched toward the sound of the bell and came upon Cupar Street, heart of the war zone. Hardened men raised on stories of Irish terrorism took one horrified look at the devastation, dropped their weapons and stepped forward to wield fire hoses, lift the injured to stretchers, bandage wounds and flag down automobiles to evacuate the homeless.

The rope tore through the skin on Michael's hands. Blood ran up his arm and into his shirtsleeves before he dropped the rope and fell back against the narrow wall. His slight body shook with pain and rage and something new, something that Catholics from the Falls rarely experienced.

Father McLaughlin, his round head and frayed Roman collar appearing above the trap, recognized it immediately. Michael Devlin, fists clenched in the fighting stance that all lads in the slums learned soon after taking their first steps, appeared lit from inside with pride.

The priest climbed into the belfry, pulled out his handkerchief and mopped his brow. "As I live and breathe, it's Mick Devlin. What in the name of heaven are you doing, lad? Was it you who pulled the bell?"

"Aye, Father, I did."

"You're a brave lad, but I fear they'll be down upon us in no time."

"There's nothing worse can be done, Father. They've burned out Bombay and Cupar Streets. Half of Kashmir is gone, and most of the houses on the Springfield Road." His eyes burned. "Meggie's family—" he stopped unable to continue.

"Dead?"

Michael nodded.

"What of the little girl?"

"Downstairs on the floor."

"We'd better see to her." The priest clasped Michael's shoulder affectionately. "Come along now, lad."

Meghann was exactly as Michael had left her, with her face pressed into the crook of her elbow. Her pallor and the stillness of her body worried the priest. It wasn't until he lifted her into his arms that she moaned and buried her face in the folds of his neck. He offered up a prayer, thanking God that she was unharmed except for the hidden wounds afflicting her heart. Father McLaughlin had spent enough time in the confessional to know that she would heal, except for the scars that would mark her forever.

They passed only one patrol on the silent, burned-out streets and were allowed to pass without questioning. Perhaps the sight of a schoolgirl in a plaid jumper with flame-lit coppery hair, a sharp-cheeked boy, his mouth tight with pain, and a Catholic priest whose level gray eyes brooked no interference, shamed them. Or perhaps it was simpler than that. Perhaps they'd waged enough of King William's war that day, wanting nothing more than a dram of whiskey, a bowl of hearty stew and the comfort of a strong pot of tea.

Annie Devlin took one look at her son's face and another at Meghann's and reached out to pull them all, girl, boy and priest, inside the well-lit room. Clucking under her breath, she bustled about lighting the stove, filling the bath and pulling out clean sheets and a quilt to make up Bernadette's old room.

Not until Father McLaughlin, restored by a sweet bun and a pot of tea, left for the monastery and Meghann was washed and sent to bed did Annie sit down beside Michael and demand to know what happened.

Stone-faced, Michael spared her nothing. Words describing the horror of the night that would make television screens the world over, with the exception of those in British living rooms, tumbled from his lips.

Two of Meghann's sisters working in hotels outside of Belfast had escaped their parents' fate. But the boys were dead, two gone up in flames trying to run the barricade into the Falls and another blown up by his own petrol bomb as he lobbed it over the Peace Wall.

It was never really decided that Meghann should stay with the Devlins. She simply settled in, and by her eleventh birthday it seemed as if she had always been there. The boisterous Devlin boys minded their manners with Meghann as they never had with their older sister and some of Meggie's serious dignity wore off with the constant barrage of teasing and practical jokes administered by Michael and his brothers. Sometimes Annie would see an expression flit across Meghann's heartbreakingly expressive face that would make her bite her lip and blink quickly. But it never lasted for long. No one born in the Falls grew to adulthood without experiencing a good deal of personal tragedy. Still there was a serene, otherworld quality about the little girl that made Annie feel protective, more than with her own children.

As Meghann grew, so did her love for learning. It was quite clear that she would go on to university and, as Michael was already there, the two spent a great deal of time poring over the books. Annie smiled fondly at the two of them, their heads together, Meghann questioning, Michael pondering before answering her. It was good to see children enjoying their schooling. She had given up hope of any more of her children learning anything but the basics. With the exception of Bernadette and Michael, none of them had shown any interest in books. Not that there was any point in a Catholic educating himself in Northern Ireland. Learned or not, there were too many Protestants anxious to fill the best jobs. If Annie had looked beyond the pleasant sight of her son and goddaughter attempting to better themselves, she would have seen what was still an unformed notion in the girl's mind.

Meghann was fourteen years old to Michael's eighteen, but already she felt the tension between them and knew, long before he did, that it was only a matter of time before he noticed it too.

While Meghann was gentle, unobtrusive and enviably serene, she was also intelligent and singularly focused on whatever goal she set for herself. She wanted Michael to notice her, and she knew him well enough to understand that he wouldn't be pushed. The realization that little Meggie McCarthy was growing up must come from him. He was his own man and would not appreciate an adolescent girl setting his pace for him. Meghann didn't mind waiting. After all, she was quite young and would most likely improve as she grew older.

But Michael posed another problem. He was tall and lean as a deer rifle, and his sharp-cheeked, square-chinned features set beneath startling blue eyes were attracting a great deal of attention among girls his own age. It would not do to have him become attached to someone else before she had time to grow up. It was time to act, even if nothing could come of it until later.

And so it was that Michael, on his way home through the entry from Blaehstaff's pub, came upon Malachy Conlin kissing Meghann McCarthy as if he had been doing it for a very long time. Rage swept the shock from Michael's brain and within seconds a very bruised Malachy, blubbering that he would never do it again, ran home holding his nose.

Breathing as if he'd run a great distance and not all from trouncing Malachy, Michael turned on Meghann. "What in bloody hell were y' doing?"

Keeping her eyes on his face, she shrugged. "No one has ever kissed me before. I wanted to know what it was like."

"We kiss y' all the time."

She looked at him disdainfully. "I wanted t' know what it's like when a man kisses a woman."

Under his breath he muttered a word that Meghann had never heard. "Malachy Conlin isn't a man."

"No." Meghann rubbed the toe of her shoe in the loose dirt. Pink-cheeked at her own daring, she looked up at him through her lashes. "But you are."

He stiffened warily. "What does that mean?"

She spilled it out in a tumble of words. "If y' don't want me kissing Malachy, why don't you kiss me instead?"

He stared at her as if he couldn't believe his ears. "You're a child," he managed. "It wouldn't be right."

"I suppose not." Meghann picked up her books, dusted them off and started to walk away. "I'll ask someone else."

"Meggie, wait." Michael's hand was on her arm. "If y' really must have it, I'll be the one."

Delighted that his capitulation had come so quickly, Meghann repressed a smile, lifted her lips and waited.

Strong hands gripped her upper arms and Michael lowered his head. "Close your eyes," he said hoarsely.

She closed them and his lips touched hers in a chaste salute. The firm pressure unnerved her and after a moment she stepped back, blushing furiously.

"Well?" he demanded.

"Is that always the way it is?" she asked curiously. "Why?"

"Malachy's kiss was different. His mouth was open and he—"

Michael groaned. "Meggie. Have y' no shame?"

"Is kissing shameful?"

"No," he said, furious at his own inconsistency.

"Then why should I be ashamed?"

Michael was baffled. He'd completely lost control of their conversation and worse, he couldn't think of a single reason to dissuade her from what she was determined to have from him. He only hoped no one saw them together. His mother would kill him and there would be no end to his brothers' teasing. "All right, Meggie," he said at last. "I'll show y' the proper way of it."

Dutifully she lifted her lips again and closed her eyes.

He took the books from her arms and dropped them beside her. She waited for the grip of his hands on her shoulders but it never came. This time one arm circled her waist to pull her close and the other reached behind her to cradle the back of her head. She felt the beat of his heart against her chest. His sure fingers sifted through her hair as if he'd explored the way many times before.

This time the kiss was neither chaste nor sweet nor warm. It was electrifying and insistent, his lips moving against hers, his tongue sweeping through her

JEANETTE BAKER

mouth, tasting, filling, pleasuring, seducing until she
forgot everything, even the need to draw breath.

When Michael lifted his head and saw her swollen
mouth and dilated pupils, he realized what he'd done.
Every schoolgirl between ten and marriage believed
that tongue-kissing was a mortal sin. Meggie probably
thought she was going to hell. "My God, Meggie," he
breathed. "I'm sorry. I never meant—"

She shook her head and pulled away, hoping he
couldn't see what he'd done to her. "Don't." She
sounded nothing like herself. "It's all right. I asked
you. I didn't know—"

Michael waited for her to finish, but she never did.
Turning, she ran through the entry and into the street
without a backward glance. He picked up her books
with shaking hands and slowly followed her home.

15

Meghann remembered other riots in the Falls, the later ones much worse than the bombing of Cupar Street. But none affected her as much as the one that had left her orphaned. In 1972 the loyalists had gone on a rampage, evicting Catholic families, burning schools and bombing churches while the British Army watched from the sidelines. This Rape of the Falls, as it came to be known, caused such devastation that entire streets were leveled to the ground. The Housing Authority erected high-rises that forever changed the flavor of the community and became slums far worse than the tenements and row houses had ever been.

Cupar Street was never again inhabited by Catholics or Protestants, and eventually the row houses were torn down and a twenty-foot brick wall known as the Peace Line was erected. There was no more shopping in the Shankill for Catholic mothers, and never again did Protestants and Catholics socialize outside their own neighborhoods. Wrapped in the secure cocoon of the Devlin family and later in the haze of her feelings for Michael, Meghann healed, or so she thought. Bernadette Devlin had brought out the truth on their last walk through the Falls. Meghann had never reconciled Cupar Street. Perhaps it was time.

She unplugged the kettle and slipped on her shoes. There were very few personal belongings in her office. Except for her books, which she would have packed and delivered later, one trip to the car would do it. Tucking Michael's files into her briefcase, she walked out of the office, through the beautiful mahogany doors and down the steps to the carpark without encountering anyone.

Placing her things in the back, she slid into the driver's seat and turned the key. The engine turned over. Maneuvering the car down the exit ramp, she stopped at the guard tower and waited until the gate opened. A crowd carrying banners had gathered outside the building.

Perplexed, Meghann inched the car forward and tapped her horn, hoping the people would disperse. Instead they surrounded the car, shouting, pressing banners painted with horrid slogans against the windows and pounding on the bonnet.

Two guards rushed out from behind the gate, brandishing billy clubs at the crowd. In seconds they cleared the driveway and Meghann quickly drove through the angry demonstrators. She turned back briefly and stared at the white banner draped below the impressive logo advertising the offices of Thorndike and Sutton. In gaudy red letters three feet high, the words *IRA Murderer* leaped out at her through the rain.

Grimly she concentrated on her driving and moved ahead with the traffic. Her press conference had ended little more than an hour ago. The British Broadcasting Networks hadn't wasted any time. She wondered if Michael would see it or if this, too, would be banned in Northern Ireland.

Turning down the elegant streets of the Mayfair district where she kept her flat, Meghann drove into her garage, gathered her belongings and walked through her back door to find Mrs. Hartwell in a state of distress. Although she knew perfectly well why the woman was sitting uncharacteristically idle at the kitchen table with a handkerchief pressed to her nose, the housekeeper's sense of dignity would be offended if formality was not observed.

Meghann sighed and set her belongings on the table. "What is troubling you, Mrs. Hartwell?"

The woman could barely form the words. "Mrs. Fields from upstairs told me but I wouldn't believe it, not until I saw it all over the telly."

"I assume you're referring to the Michael Devlin defense."

She nodded.

Meghann sat down beside her. "I am a barrister, Mrs. Hartwell. Someone has to defend him."

The older woman shuddered and for the first time forgot that Meghann was her employer and the widow of a peer. "But why you? This can't be good for your reputation or your career."

Meghann was very near the edge of her control. She had expected criticism from her associates and the press. The angry mob at the office disturbed her more than she cared to admit, and now her own housekeeper was aligned against her.

A real tear trickled down Mrs. Hartwell's cheek. Meghann softened and reached out to cover the woman's hand with her own. "We've been together a long time, Mrs. Hartwell. Surely you know that I never do anything without giving it a great deal of thought."

"I cannot bear this, Lady Sutton," she sobbed into her handkerchief. "I truly cannot."

"Perhaps this is a good time for a holiday," Meghann suggested. "Your sister is in Devonshire. Why not ring her up and tell her you're coming for a visit?"

Mrs. Hartwell brightened. "Yes. That's a marvelous idea. The very thing. And when I return this will all be over."

Meghann nodded. "I hope so. In any case, I'll keep you informed. Take the rest of the day, Mrs. Hartwell. I'm sure this has been a difficult time for you."

"Why, that's very good of you, Lady Sutton. It has been a rather unusual day." She hesitated. "If you're sure. What will you have for dinner?"

"I'm dining out," Meghann lied and stood up, reaching for her briefcase. "Lock the door and ring me when you reach Devonshire."

"Of course I will." She nodded emphatically. "I wouldn't want you to worry with everything else on your mind."

Twenty minutes later Meghann was relieved to hear the front bolt snap into place. Mrs. Hartwell was gone. She had been David's choice and, out of respect for his memory and because she knew the woman would have difficulty finding another position at her age, Meghann had kept her on. What she should have done was pension her off long ago. It was a strain living with a person who wasn't a family member. She'd always been an introvert, a loner Michael had called her, happier with her own company than with anyone else.

Perhaps it was because she was Irish. The British were accustomed to servants. They thought nothing of discussing the most personal details of their lives in front of domestics as if the men and women who served them had neither eyes nor ears nor feelings. Meghann wasn't comfortable being waited on by hired help. With their lined faces and rough hands, most of the women reminded her of her mother. She wanted to close the distance between them, sit down at the table and chat over a cup of tea. That was out of the question, of course. Class differences were observed in England. Perhaps she wouldn't hire anyone at all. Her mother had cared for a family of nine. She'd managed by herself before. Surely she could do it again. In fact she welcomed it.

With new resolve, Meghann tightened the sash of her robe and marched into the kitchen to open a tin of soup. The tray she carried into the living room looked particularly appetizing. Curling up in a chair near the fire, she sipped her wine and remembered her last day with Michael. Soon, very soon, she would see him again. The thought sustained her. Nothing else really mattered. Once it had all been important, her career, the money, the clothes, the luxuries she'd always dreamed about. But that was before Donegal. Now, she'd give it all up to spend the rest of her life in a cottage by the ocean and listen to Michael Devlin read poetry.

The warmth, the strain of the day and the alcohol took their toll. Unconsciously she rubbed her mother's brooch. Dizziness swept over her, probably the effect of a glass of wine with too little food. She leaned her head back against the chair and closed her eyes.

Nuala, Tirconnaill, 1596

Once again Rory and I were blessed with twins, girls this time, healthy and more alike than any I had seen before. Tiny rosebud mouths closed around my breasts, sucking greedily until at three months, when I was exhausted and they were round and plump as Christmas partridges, I brought in a wet nurse and returned to my duties as chatelaine of Dun Na Ghal Castle and countess of Tirconnaill.

For the first time, Rory was home for my confinement. His look of wonder at the tiny bairns no bigger than the palm of his hand was worth a kingdom to me. Apparently the birth of his daughters had a sobering effect on him. For the length of the season he rested easily at home and he was not so consumed with thoughts of revenge against Elizabeth. When he left Dun Na Ghal to take up arms against the English, it was with great reluctance. Perhaps he had grown soft with the comforts of his home, or perhaps he had a premonition of what was to come. Whatever the reason, he parted tenderly from the children and from me. A fortnight passed before I received his missive telling me he would be delayed a bit longer. My father had insisted on raiding the English-occupied castle at Lorne, and Rory's men were the best warriors ever to be seen in Ireland.

I held Brian in my arms on the battlements, marveling at how heavy he was and how much he had grown in the past year. He wanted to see all of Tirconnaill, and I could think of no better place to show him than here at the castle's highest point, cold and dangerously windy though it was. I pointed west toward the sea, directing my son's gaze toward the turquoise water under a summer sun, and then north to the wild beauty of grass-covered marshland alive with fowl. To the south was Galway and the Aran Islands where Liam Flaherty ruled like the kings who were his forefathers. To the east as far as the eye could see was farmland colored in shades of palest gold to deepest green.

My eyes stung with senseless tears. Brian would never rule this land of his ancestors. Rory and I would be fortunate to live out our lives here. Even now the English noose was tightening and time ran short. More and more Irish chieftains were expatriated, their lands forfeit to the surging Protestant tide sweeping across our homeland. We were more fortunate than most. We would survive. I made sure of it. Every harvest season secret deposits of gold were sent to Rome in preparation for our exile. No one knew of my deception, not even Rory, and were the tables to turn in our favor I would gladly donate every crown to Holy Mother Church.

Brian's expression was grave for one so young. His eyes, the same brilliant blue as Rory's, were narrowed and intense. "Does all of this belong to us?" he asked solemnly.

I hesitated, searching for an answer that was true and yet not raise impossible hope. "Aye, for now," I managed.

Young as he was, Brian knew me well. "When will it not be ours?"

Pressing my cheek against his round one, I spoke gently. "Everything changes, my love. Perhaps your destiny lies elsewhere. Would that be so very bad?"

He looked up at me with his father's expression and my heart sank. "This is O'Donnell land," he said firmly. "One day it will be mine."

"What of Sean and the girls? Where would you have them go?" Brian puffed out his rounded cheeks importantly. "Sean may stay here or go to Ballymurphy. The girls will marry."

"How do you know all this?" I asked, astonished. Surely such thoughts were beyond the understanding of a small boy.

"Da said it. He made me tell him, over and over again, how it would be."

I was conscious of a flash of anger so intense that it shook me. Rory should know better than to put such ideas in the mind of a child. It was the strength of my rage that led me to turn my back on the portcullis gate, to carry my child inside, out of the light and down the stairs to the nursery where his maid dozed by a weak fire.

If I had waited but another moment, I would have seen Niall Garv's men creep silently over the hills like a scourge of the blight. Without warning they filed through the open gates into the courtyard and surrounded the castle, sealing off all escape routes.

He found me in my sitting room, wrapped in wool against the chill. I stared into the flames, so deep in thought that I heard nothing of the commotion in my courtyard. Not even the sudden draft stirred me. Not until he walked to the hearth and stood before me, fully within my line of vision, did I realize he was there.

"You're too late, Cousin," I said wearily. "Rory has already gone."

The corner of his mouth turned up in a smile. "Again you misjudge me, Nuala. I come to bear you company while your husband is away."

His eyes glittered like obsidian in his darkly tanned face, and I was afraid. Still I brazened it out. "Your errand is wasted. I need no company. Rory needs you more than I."

"Rory and I no longer fight on the same side."

I stood and faced him, pulling the shawl tightly about me. "Surely I misunderstand you," I said icily.

He shook his head, his eyes never leaving my face. "I pledged my allegiance to the queen at Falkirk."

"Rory will kill you," I whispered, "and if he does not, my father will."

Niall laughed and tossed his bonnet onto a low table. "I think not. I hold his wife and children hostage. Rory is not a fool. He knows that I would not harm you, but I have no such scruples regarding your children. He will not attempt an attack."

"You don't know Rory."

He grinned and she wondered, not for the first time, why a man as handsome as Niall Garv O'Donnell would want another man's wife when any maid in Ireland would be willing to share his bed.

"I know Rory well enough," he said. " 'Tis you I would know better."

204

"You are a traitor." I tried to walk past him, but his hand snaked out and grabbed my wrist.

He spoke through gritted teeth. "I do not give you leave to retire, my lady."

"'Tis my house. I leave when I wish."

He drew me toward him, circling my waist with his free arm, pulling me against him.

I refused to show my fear. "Please, don't, Niall," I said in a low firm voice.

"Don't what?" He pulled me closer until I felt the length of his body through my gown. Bending his head, he brushed my lips. "What is it, Nuala? Shall I not kiss you?" His mouth hovered no more than an inch from mine. "Holy God, you are beautiful," he muttered, before closing the distance between us.

I turned my head and felt his lips against my cheek. "Please," I begged. "'Tis past time to see to the children."

He released me so quickly that I stumbled against him. "Go to Rory's brats, Nuala, but prepare yourself. I will come to you whether or not you are willing."

And so began our game, the dance of two strong wills pitted against one another. Niall Garv was a master swordsman. He knew when to feint and pull back, when to parry, strike and drive straight to the heart. Everything he knew of women he applied to my seduction.

In those first weeks after his arrival I wondered why he waited so long to finish it. A man with a thousand foot soldiers at his command had no need for a woman's approval. Later, when I had no resistance left, after I'd bartered my body for the lives of my children, I realized what it was that held him back. His tremendous pride wanted me to want him as I did Rory. The moment he realized it would never be, he ended the game.

At first he was not so difficult a companion, so

solicitous of my health, so patient with my children. If I had come upon him without first knowing the set of his mind, I would have trusted him completely. But I did know him. Even so, I could not help being flattered that it was me he wanted, a woman past the first blush of youth, a woman of twenty-four years who had borne nine children to another man.

I was ripe for seduction. When a man leaves his wife as often and as long as Rory left me, he runs the risk of losing her affection to another who is more attentive. I refused to dwell on it, but occasionally a dark thought crept into my mind. Was Rory as lonely as I? Did he fight the wanting that months without release inevitably brought? Or did he seek his pleasure elsewhere, justifying his sins by confessing to his priest that he was only a man and his wife was far away? I never asked him such a question for fear of hearing the truth. It was enough that here at Dun Na Ghal he was faithful to me. Perhaps that was all a man could be.

Day after day Niall kept at his subtle flirtation. I began to listen for the sound of his footsteps in the hall. His frequent shouts of laughter were not at all unpleasant to my ears and the look in his night-dark eyes as he watched me go about my daily business left me breathless. I was constantly wary, every nerve on edge. All through the long spring nights Niall courted me, playing the gentleman, never once pressing his advantage. If I missed Rory and wondered why he did not come to rescue his wife and children from the clutches of his enemy, no word of it passed my lips.

It was midsummer when the message came. After looking in on the children I retired to my chambers for the night. Earlier, Niall and I had dined alone and I knew by the look in his eyes and the way he pressed his lips into the palm of my hand that he would wait no longer. To my shame, a part of me hoped that he would not. But another part, the woman who was

Agnes MacDonnell's daughter, the woman who had single-handedly ruled Dun Na Ghal for years, the woman who was mother to five of Rory O'Donnell's children knew better. The risks of adultery were many and the results devastating. The wisest course of action would be to stay as far away from my charming cousin as the walls of Dun Na Ghal Castle would allow. This I intended to do.

I sat down on a low stool and motioned for my maid to loosen my braids. The sensual pull of the brush through my hair relaxed me and assuaged the ache in my temples.

A knock at the door startled me. I tensed, believing it was Niall. But when it sounded again, I knew better. Niall would knock boldly if he knocked at all. More likely he would walk in without warning and arrogantly dismiss my attendant.

She opened the door, and a man with the swarthy coloring of a Romany traveler stepped inside my chamber. Holding his finger against his lips, he handed me a small piece of paper. Rory's bold script was unmistakable. My heart pounded as I held it under the light to better see the words. I read quickly, and the blood left my head. Gripping the bedpost, I swayed and would have fallen had the stranger not reached out to bolster me with an arm strong as an oak.

"Are you ill, m'lady?" the serving woman asked timidly.

I shook my head. "No, Fiona, just tired. Please leave us."

Without a word she left the room. I stared once again at Rory's words and wet my lips. "How can I possibly manage such a deception?" I asked my husband's messenger. "We are watched every moment."

"Even Niall Garv must sleep," he replied. "The O'Donnell waits with five thousand men at the mouth of the river. Tomorrow, before first light, you must bring the lads to the south entrance."

"What of my daughters and me?"

"Be ready. Your husband will take the castle in less than a fortnight. Wait for his message, then go to the children and stay with them. Fear not. 'Tis the heir to Tirconnaill that Niall Garv would hold hostage. He'll not harm you or the lassies."

I thought of the cold sculpted beauty of Niall's mouth and wondered if Rory knew him at all. There was only one way to soften the edges of Niall's finely honed sense of danger, and it came with a terrible price. Did Rory have any idea what he asked of me? And if he did, would he allow me to finish it?

That night I slept little, wondering whom I could trust to lead my sons out of the silent castle to the south entrance. I would have taken them myself but I would be otherwise occupied.

My worry turned out to be groundless. The next morning the O'Neill standard appeared at the gates and my mother was allowed inside. We clung together, Mother and I, and she whispered words of comfort into my ear. After greeting Niall Garv, she thanked him for the care he had taken of her grandchildren. He smiled pleasantly and left us alone for the rest of the day. We played gently with the children, and I told her of Rory's plan.

Agnes MacDonnell was no fool. She frowned and asked the question I feared most. "I shall be glad to help you, Nuala, but why not take the children yourself?"

My cheeks burned. Unable to meet her clear-eyed gaze, I turned away. "Niall must be kept indisposed until after the attack."

"How?"

I stared straight ahead and did not answer. She sighed and took my hand in hers. "Nuala, my love.

Women have their own weapons. There is no shame in saving your children."

"Rory will never forgive me," I said bitterly.

"Don't tell him."

The simplicity of her logic shocked me. But the more I thought, the more I saw the wisdom in her words.

We stayed with the children until they were weary of sun and play. I kissed Brian and Sean tenderly before I sent them to the nursery for food and rest.

Dinner was late, and I took more time than usual with my appearance. My gown was the green of emeralds and cut daringly low so that my breasts, full now after nursing the children, nearly spilled from my bodice. My maid darkened my eyebrows and lips and brushed rice powder across my face, throat and bosom. My eyes glittered, and in the glass I could see that my skin was very white against the green satin material. I wore no cap, and my hair hung unbound like a curtain of fire, straight and fine, past my knees. Turning away from the glass, I walked down the stairs to the small banquet hall where Niall waited with my mother.

After one shocked look at my exposed breasts, Mother pretended that all was as usual and greeted Niall with the well-bred dignity she showed to all who graced her table. If circumstances had been different I would have been amused at Niall's reaction to my transformation.

Formality dictated that he reply to my mother's greeting, but after a single startled glance in my direction, his eyes glazed over and for the remainder of the meal he was barely coherent. He ate too little and drank too much, responding to our questions with brief, clipped answers.

I also drank more than usual. Thoughts of the night to come, the fantasies of a lonely woman too long away from her husband, had once sent my blood racing. Now, in the cold realm of reality, they made me ill. I felt cold and dull, as if I stood outside my body and viewed the scene with the detachment of a spectator. I didn't notice when my mother left. Niall and I sat across from one another, our hands curled tightly around the stems of our crystal goblets.

I still remember the way his eyes glittered as they rested on my exposed flesh and the way the tiny hairs grew on the back of his lean brown hands. His black hair shone like the gleam of a bird's wing under the candlelight, and his bones were set and very pronounced as he stared at me from across the table. I watched his throat move as he gulped the last of his wine and imagined his tongue against my skin.

I had been a child when I gave myself to Rory, and our love was desperate and all-consuming. There was no love whatsoever in my feelings for Niall Garv O'Donnell. No matter that my excuse for adultery was a worthy one. What we were about to do was a terrible sin. Knowing that did not dissuade me. I could no more have changed the course of that night than I could have stopped the flow of invaders into Ireland. I would pay for my deed for the rest of my life, but tonight my body would belong to a man who was not my husband.

Without a word, Niall pushed himself away from the table and advanced upon me. He held out his hand and I gave him mine. Slowly, inexorably, he pulled me into his arms and took my mouth in a fierce kiss. I clung to his shoulders and allowed him to mark my lips, my throat and my breasts with the heat of his tongue.

I have no memory of how we ended up in my chamber, but somewhere on the stairs I felt his hands on my breasts and by the time we reached my bed he'd coaxed my traitorous body into an unwilling response. It had been too long since I'd felt my husband's arms around me. I closed my eyes and thought of Rory. It was Rory whose lips touched mine, Rory whose hands evoked such pleasure, Rory who moved over me at just the right time and spoke the fevered whispers against my throat.

Niall claimed me after his searching tongue was familiar with every inch of my flesh. Finally, when I was too exhausted to speak, he slept briefly, my body joined with his. Sleep eluded me completely and it seemed like only moments before he woke, ready for me again.

It was past dawn when the door burst open. Guards filled the room, telling of invaders in the night and soldiers at the gates. Rory's army had attacked. I hid my face in the sheets while Niall threw on his clothes and ran outside to the battlements.

I pulled a gown over my head and rushed to the nursery, praying that all had gone according to plan. The wet nurse sat wide-eyed in a chair feeding the twins.

"The boys?" I asked through swollen lips.

"The Lady Agnes took them hours ago, before first light. They haven't returned."

Sighing with relief, I returned to my bedchamber, stripped off my gown and fell into bed, praying for the sleep that had eluded me all night.

I woke to silence and absolute darkness. Fearing the worst, I reached for the candle, but a firm hand closed over my wrist.

"You knew, didn't you?" Niall's voice came from a place close to my head.

After what we had shared I could not lie. "Yes."

He pulled me against his bare chest and held my head against him. He tasted of gunpowder and ash.

"Holy God, Nuala. Do you know what you have done?"

"I could not go against him, Niall. He is my husband."

"My archers murdered your mother and your sons. Will you blame me for that as well?"

I struggled for air but still he held me. His words were bitter. "Why did you risk it, Nuala? After last night, do you really believe I would have harmed your children?"

Somewhere his harsh voice floated over my head and powerful arms held me in a grip of steel, but all I felt was pain and rage, a rage so intense and sweeping that nothing of me was left inside my brain, not even questions. I knew that Rory would never consciously harm his children, but he had exposed them to risk and, in so doing, their lives were forfeited.

Or perhaps it had nothing to do with Rory. Perhaps it was all my fault. Perhaps my wee lads were taken from me because I had broken the sacrament of marriage. Better to have sent them to England or to Niall. At least they would be alive. My hurt was too deep for tears. I could neither speak nor respond. 'Twas all for naught. If Rory had prevailed, Niall would not be here in my bed.

His mouth touched my ear. "Stay with me, Nuala," he whispered. "Bear my sons. The church is finished in Ireland. Submit to Elizabeth, divorce Rory and marry me."

I could not believe what I heard. "I betrayed you, Niall. I sent my children to their father. I knew Rory would attack this morning."

"What of last night? Was your desire false? Did your body lie?"

I pulled away and sat up, knowing that his eyes must have adjusted to the darkness as mine had. I no longer cared. There was nothing of me that his eyes had not already seen nor his mouth tasted. "I would have refused you if Rory's message had not come," I told him. "I feel nothing for you."

Even through the darkness I could see that his eyes

were black with rage, and I was afraid. Niall Garv was an Irish chieftain and to anger him was beyond foolishness.

He reached out to pull me beneath him. His hands gripped my wrists and the weight of his body held me prisoner. "I care little for your feelings, Nuala. You will share my bed and I will replace the sons you lost. Then we shall see if your Rory still wants you."

I was dry and lifeless when he entered me that night and for all the nights thereafter. I had only to think of my husband and the wee lads we had lost and my body refused to respond.

One morning, weeks later, in the early hours after Niall had left my bed, I smelled charred wood. Believing it to be the kitchen fires, I slept again. When I woke my chamber was filled with smoke. Throwing on my oldest gown, I ran down the hall and up the stairs to the nursery. The heat had blistered the whitewashed walls. Gushes of blackened smoke surrounded me, filling my lungs. I swayed and leaned against the wall.

Someone called my name. I tried to speak and coughed instead. Niall Garv, his face black with soot, came through the smoke and lifted me in his arms.

"The children," I gasped. "Please, help me."

He hesitated, searched my face, looked up the smoking stairs and lowered me to the ground. "I'll find them and meet you outside," he said, pushing me back. "Go now. Quickly."

I fought for breath. Precious seconds passed. Smoke seared my lungs as I followed Niall to the third-story landing. There was a loud explosion and the door to the hall went up in flames. A huge wall of fire consumed the floor, just missing Niall as he fell back, curling his body into a ball and rolling down the stairs to where I stood, frozen with horror. Unbelievably, he stood and pulled me behind him.

"You can thank your husband for this as well, Nuala," he shouted, his voice raw from smoke. "Rory's army surrounds us. The fire is his doing."

"But the babies and Kathleen," I cried. "What of them?"

"Dead," Niall said flatly, maintaining his pace, pulling me along. "Burned to death in their beds."

My mind could absorb no more. I heard Niall's words with a curious detachment. We were in the courtyard now, and it seemed as if the entire world were ablaze. The gates were nearly gone. In another moment Rory's soldiers would ride through the opening.

Niall caught at the bridle of a nearby horse and swung into the saddle, pulling me with him. He took my face between his hands and kissed me fiercely.

At the same moment, Rory rode through the flame-choked September sunlight to see his wife in the desperate, passionate embrace of his enemy.

16

Belfast, 1994

Since the cease-fire, British tanks no longer routinely patrolled the Falls Road. Michael strolled casually down the dimly lit streets to his mother's house and walked in without knocking. He heard voices from the kitchen and followed the sound, stopping at the doorway to take in the scene before him. Connor and Davie sat at the table eating soup and fries smothered in brown sauce while Annie stood at the stove stirring something that smelled delicious. "Is there room for one more?" he asked.

Three heads turned in his direction. His brothers, hardened by life on the run, acknowledged his presence with a mere lift of their eyebrows. Annie's lips paled and she dropped her ladle into the soup. Collecting herself, she hurried to pull down the window shades before holding out her arms to her son. Michael walked unashamedly into them, finding the same comfort he had as a toddler with skinned knees and a bloody nose.

Annie held onto him for several minutes without speaking. Finally she dropped her arms, wiped her

eyes with her apron and shook her head. "Thank
y've got some meat on your bones. Y're a lovely ~~sight~~,
Mick, much better than the last time I saw you. Sit
down and have some supper with y'r brothers."

Connor grabbed his brother's hand and squeezed
while Davie slapped him on the back. Annie filled his
teacup and set a hot bowl of soup on the table.
Hanging his jacket on the back of his chair, Michael
sat down and applied himself to his meal.

"What's happened, Mick?" Connor asked quietly.

Michael swallowed and wiped his mouth with a
linen napkin. "There's a safe house in Sligo. I'll hole
up there until a trial date is set. If I'm allowed a jury,
I'll go back to the Maze."

Annie gasped. "Why would y' go there?"

"Life on the run isn't living, Ma. That's all over for
me. If Meghann believes I have a case, I don't mind
the risk."

Davie interrupted. "What if the Brits want a Diplock Court?"

Michael looked across the table at his younger
brother. "Then I'm done for," he said softly.

Annie's hand flew to her mouth. "God help us.
Have y' found out anythin' yet?"

"Not yet, Ma."

Connor Devlin stood and carried his plate to the
sink. "It's clear enough t' me," he said bitterly. "The
Brits want an excuse t' keep us away from the negotiations. Look at the newspapers. We're executioners
again. No one wants to deal with terrorists."

Michael shrugged.

Connor swore under his breath and looked guiltily
at his mother. "Sorry, Ma. Why aren't the Provisionals saying anythin', Michael? I don't like it. I don't
like it at all."

"Will we be able to reach you?" Davie was always
practical.

Michael held the soup in his mouth, savoring the last

delicious mouthful. No one made soup like his mother. Reluctantly, he swallowed. "I'll be back in prison as soon as it's out that Meghann's defending me."

Annie's eyes widened. "Don't y' know, Mick? Meggie's left her firm after sellin' out to Mr. Thorndike. She's here in Belfast until after the trial."

Michael's lips twisted into a derisive grin. "It appears that my days of freedom are over."

Folding his arms against his chest, Connor leaned against the counter. "I'd see Liam first, if I were you. Y' won't be much good at findin' answers in the Maze." He hesitated. "Do y' trust her that much, Mick?"

Did he trust her that much? The question hung in the air, demanding that he face it. Michael wasn't rational when it came to Meggie. He never had been. Now, his life depended on her. She might be unable to save him, but not for a minute did he believe she would betray him. "Aye. I trust her that much."

Annie released the breath she had been holding. "Thank God. I was afraid—" She looked at the expression on Michael's face and stopped. "Never mind," she said hastily.

Michael stood, reached for his jacket and bent to kiss his mother's cheek. "Don't worry, Ma. I'll keep in touch."

Annie nodded and turned back to the stove, refusing to watch him leave. The Falls were much safer since the cease-fire. But that didn't mean the house of a man wanted for murder wasn't under surveillance. "Mother of Jesus," she prayed. "Keep my son safe and let Meghann come quickly."

Michael stopped at the door, reached out with both arms and wrapped his brothers against his chest in a crushing embrace. "Tell Meggie anything y' can find out," he said huskily, "and don't let anyone, not even Liam or anyone else, know where I'll be. Don't even tell them y' saw me."

Connor frowned and would have spoken, but Davie

had already nodded in agreement. "Aye, Mick. We'll say nothin' to anyone, not even to Andrew himself."

Meghann rubbed the frown from her forehead, pushed aside the deposition copies she had committed to memory and stared blankly out the window of her hotel suite. Five witnesses stated that on March 18, Michael had been seated at a table near the back of the room and that he'd disappeared shortly before Killingsworth's speech. Yet the guest list from the Europa Hotel did not include his name. The claim ticket he swore was in his pocket had disappeared at the interrogation center, and the number he remembered as his own belonged to a man named Peter Fitch. The list had been entered as part of the Crown's evidence.

She stood and massaged her temples while pacing back and forth across the carpeted floor. Relief eluded her. Collapsing on the low couch, she tucked her legs beneath her and played devil's advocate with herself.

Why was it necessary to position Michael as a man without a ticket? The answer came immediately. *To portray him as an intruder in the legal political process. Why would a Protestant glassmaker from the Shankill Road, a conservative Tory, pay five hundred pounds to hear a Labour candidate speak?* This one wasn't so easy. *Because he wanted to see and hear the man who would most likely be England's next prime minister?* Possibly, but not likely. Five hundred pounds was a healthy sum, enough to take a glassmaker's family on a two-week holiday to Donegal. Politics to the working-class Shankill Protestants had never meant more than food on the table.

Something didn't fit. The hotel guest list was a forgery, of course, and not a very good one. Even an untrained eye could see that the printing on Peter Fitch's newly entered name was slightly different. Meghann had visited the man earlier in the day. He was a cretin, an uneducated brute with bad teeth who had never traveled two miles outside the Shankill. Meghann was sure he'd been bribed. She would need to discredit him immediately.

All the other evidence was circumstantial. Other than Michael's connection with the IRA, there was nothing to convict him. She should have felt optimistic, but the legacy of Catholic persecution in the Six Counties was strong. British law was sound, but representatives of the Crown did not always strictly adhere to the law in Northern Ireland.

There must be someone who had seen Michael and remembered. Someone who could place him at the same moment that James Killingsworth lost his life helping his daughter into a taxi. Meghann had spoken with nearly everyone who had been in the audience. No one on the list could be sure of Michael's whereabouts with absolute certainty. That left the usual crowd of onlookers and the press. *Who, among Protestant Belfast and the British Broadcasting Company was brave enough to come forward and clear an official of the Sinn Fein council when even their own members remained silent?* That one had no answer. *But where was the motive?*

Meghann abandoned each new idea as quickly as it came until there was one she couldn't discard. It was not uncommon for the Ulster SAS to recruit insiders for information. Communities in the Six Counties were small and tightly knit. Sinn Fein and the IRA could not be infiltrated by outsiders. Men and women who became informers were among their own, usually lured by fear and more money than they would normally see in a lifetime.

A young man would be kidnapped by the RUC, the life of a family member threatened, and then he would be dropped off where his neighbors could clearly see that he had been consorting with the enemy. Shortly after, some secret spot would be hit, and word would leak out that the young man had supplied the information. He would have no choice but to turn to his enemies.

Instinctively, Meghann knew her case was much more than a random killing. Given the current direction of politics, neither Michael nor James Killingsworth had been a threat to any of the major forces shaping the future of Northern Ireland. That left only one far-fetched possibility. Michael had been set up as a scapegoat for political maneuvering. Someone important wanted to change the direction of British politics and destroy all hope of a united Ireland. Perhaps money was involved. That kind of money could change a man's life, make him forget his lofty ideals.

The *why* of such a convoluted objective no longer mattered. That would come later. If her hunch was correct, there must be something she could do. But what?

Turning off the lamp, she made her way into the luxurious bedroom, picked up the phone and pressed zero. Housekeeping answered immediately. "Can I help y', Miss McCarthy?" asked a voice, vowel-flat and softly accommodating, the brogue of West Belfast.

Unconsciously, Meghann slipped into the familiar cadence. "If it's not too much trouble, you can wake me at nine. I've an appointment in the Falls."

"No trouble at all, dear," the voice replied. "Get some rest now."

Grateful for the comforting thickness of the down comforter, Meghann snuggled into its luxurious warmth. Her last conscious thought was that, at this very moment, reporters were assembling in the downstairs lobby. This time she would tell them everything.

At eleven o'clock the following morning, Meghann arrived on Annie Devlin's doorstep. She carried a kidskin briefcase and wore a designer suit of forest green tweed. The pleated skirt ended above her knees, and the jacket, nipped in at the waist and tailored to perfection, was both feminine and professional.

A news crew stood on the pavement filming her arrival, but Meghann appeared oblivious to the attention. She flashed them a brilliant smile, tucked an errant curl behind her ear and knocked on the door of the refurbished brick house.

Annie was no stranger to Meghann's charm. Hiding her amusement, she motioned the younger woman inside, closed the door against the invasive cameras and hugged her fiercely. "We heard the news this mornin'," she said, her voice thick with emotion. "John Hume was on the telly. He's talking about a jury trial for Michael if he'll come in on his own. However did you manage it, Meggie?"

Meghann squeezed her godmother's shoulders and stepped back. "He's still only talking. He'll have to do more than that before I believe him." Annie's forehead wrinkled and Meghann laughed. "Never mind. Just remember to be very kind to the press. Answer their questions. Tell them about Michael and what he was like as a child. Be sure they know about his writing and his academic credentials. Personalize him as much as possible, and never, ever mention the IRA. If anyone asks, tell them you know nothing about such nonsense. Always repeat that Michael is a good boy who wants nothing more than to come home. Can you do that, Annie?"

Annie nodded. "Aye. It's the truth, except for the IRA part. I knew that he was one of them. Mother Mary, how could he not be? I prayed every day that he would change his mind. Michael is brilliant. He had choices, something the others didn't have. Never underestimate the power of prayer, Meggie. It was prayer that finally made Michael come t' his senses and leave that violent nonsense behind."

Meghann sat down on a chair. A strange ringing sounded in her ears. She couldn't have heard correctly. "What are you saying, Annie? I thought Michael was the leader of the Falls Road Brigade for West Belfast."

Annie's blue eyes widened. "Michael is an elected member of the Sinn Fein political council. He hasn't been active in the IRA for years, not since he argued for a cease-fire and decommissioning in exchange for a seat at the peace talks."

"Sinn Fein is legal."

"Aye."

All at once a very large piece of the puzzle fell into place. The Irish Republican Army wasn't turning on one of their own. Michael was a dissenter, worse than a dissenter. He was a talented writer, an inspirational orator who had defected from the ranks. Discrediting him would be of great benefit to them. But why had he allowed her to believe he was still connected? There were too many missing pieces to make any sense of it. "Where is he, Annie?" Meghann asked.

Annie Devlin's face went blank. "He asked us not t' tell you, for your own protection."

"Can you get a message to him?"

"Aye."

"Tell him I need to see him." Meghann hesitated and chewed the inside of her lip before continuing. "Tell him I need to arrange a meeting with Andrew Maguire, off the record."

"It will be very dangerous for you, Meggie, especially if no one knows y're goin'. It may be dangerous for Michael, too."

"I wouldn't ask if it wasn't important." She patted the older woman's lined hand. "Why don't we let Michael decide if it's too dangerous?"

Annie snorted. "Y're talking about a boy who grew up on these very streets. When did danger ever stop him?"

Meghann flushed and looked away. When she spoke her voice was so low that Annie cupped her hand behind her ear and leaned forward. "He may not mind for himself, but this time he's not alone. Michael would never put me in danger."

She felt her godmother's eyes on her face and knew that Annie was assessing her statement. Not much escaped Annie Devlin's piercing blue gaze.

"Y' trust him that much, do you?" Unconsciously, Annie repeated the question Connor had put to Michael just two days before.

Meghann lifted her head and looked directly at the woman who had raised her. This time her voice was confident, her words clear and strong. "I trust him with my life, Annie. I always have."

Satisfied that everything was going in the right direction, Annie reached over and touched Meghann's clenched hands. "Keep me company while I make us a pot of tea. Such talk is a wee bit tiring. How do y' do it, Meggie, and still stand up at the end of the day?"

Meghann followed Annie into the kitchen and sniffed the air. She had never felt more energized. "I'm used to it. Um, something smells delicious."

Annie beamed. "Soda bread was always y'r favorite. Did y' think I'd forgotten?"

Annie never forgot anything, not a birthday, not a First Communion, not a favorite color. Make the slightest wish in her presence and it was stamped indelibly on her brain, resurfacing at some future date, wrapped in colored foil under the Christmas tree, beside a plate at Easter dinner, or under a pillow on Saint Stephen's Day.

Horrified at the mist appearing before her eyes, Meghann turned away, pretending to search for the teacups.

"They're in the same place they always were," Annie said gently, "and there's no shame in a tear now and then. Emotions keep us all humble."

"Tell that to your son," Meghann mumbled under her breath.

Annie's eyes twinkled as she set out the napkins. "I believe I'll leave that to you. And remember that I'm not deaf yet."

Meghann unlocked the door of her hotel room and stepped inside. Immediately she sensed it, the sweet unmistakable smell of recently burned carbon. Someone had been in her room. Maybe he was still here. *Breathe, Meggie, breathe,* whispered a memory from Cupar Street. Meghann breathed, gathered her nerve and fumbled for the light switch.

"Don't turn it on," said a voice she would have known anywhere.

Relief weakened her. She sagged against the wall. "For heaven's sake, Michael," she gasped. "You might have given me some warning."

He stepped out of the shadows and waited for her eyes to adjust to the darkness. "There wasn't time. Why do y' want to see Maguire?"

She ignored his question. "Why did you allow me to believe you were still part of the IRA?"

Michael shrugged, walked across the room to the couch and sat down. "Once an IRA man always an IRA man. That's all that matters t' the British and the RUC."

Her voice was soft, like music. "What made you change your mind, Mick? Why aren't you one of them any longer?"

Something flickered in his eyes. "It isn't important, Meggie."

"It is to me."

"Would my reasons make a difference t' you?"

She thought for a minute. Michael was no longer a soldier in the Irish Republican Army. Somehow, some way, he had come to the conclusion of all reasonable men, that murder could not be justified, not even in the name of freedom. Would there be anything that wasn't worth that end result, any reason at all that would make her draw back in horror, leave this room, this country, this man, and take up her sane and comfortable life in London? "No," she said quietly. "The only thing that matters to me is that you are no longer connected."

He kept his eyes on her face, wondering how much to believe. After all, she was the girl who'd left him without a word. She smiled and his heart swelled. She was also the woman who'd come back without conditions. "Frankie McLeish was killed the morning of his daughter's baptism," he told her.

"I know. I'm so sorry, Michael. I read about it in the paper."

Michael's mouth twisted into a bitter grimace. "He was seen comin' out of the RUC station. They didn't even bother t' check it out before they targeted him as an informer. Turns out he was a community advocate for peace. The Kashmir neighborhood is mixed, and the people there have done well together mostly because of Frankie. All he wanted was a contribution for the rummage sale. That's why he had two hundred quid in his pocket. I tried t' convince them. I thought I had until he turned up dead on the steps of Saint Stephen's, his wife holdin' the baby and his family all around." He looked up, pain and rage reflected in his eyes. "Can you imagine it, Meggie? A boy you loved like a brother gunned down on the steps of his church, by mistake?"

She shook her head, her eyes wide and unblinking in an effort to keep the tears at bay.

"I kept wonderin' how many other mistakes we'd made and how many more we'd make. That did it for me."

Meghann crossed the room and sat down beside him, deliberately pushing aside her reaction to his nearness. "It explains why you're suddenly expendable."

"I'd thought of that, but ten years is a long time. Why would they wait so long to be rid of me?"

"Perhaps because they never had reason before."

Michael frowned. "I don't understand."

Meghann leaned forward, elbows on her knees, hands clasped. "Until very recently a peace settlement has never been seriously considered. Suddenly it's a real possibility. But Britain stalls, first to pander to the loyalists, second to wait out the elections. Fourteen months go by. Tired of waiting, the IRA breaks the cease-fire, hoping to frighten the parties involved into coming back to the table, thereby moving the process forward."

"Why James Killingsworth, and why me?"

"This is only speculation, of course, but it's possible that someone wants to discredit you. By claiming you are not connected and that you acted on your own, two goals are accomplished: Sinn Fein is painted in a positive light and an eloquent critic who was one of their own is eliminated. As for choosing Killingsworth for a victim, who in all of Britain had more press coverage? Of course, there's another possibility."

"What's that?"

"Perhaps not everyone wants peace, and Killingsworth was a serious threat. Your part could have been played by anyone who was at the Europa Hotel that day."

She watched him as she spoke, hoping to gauge his emotions from his eyes and the expression on his face. To her disappointment, he kept himself carefully neutral, veiling all thoughts from her probing gaze. "This can't be a surprise, Michael. Surely you knew that someone set you up."

He nodded. "Aye. But I hoped it would take a bit longer for you to come to the same conclusion."

"Why?"

He reached for her hand. Keeping his eyes fixed on hers, he lifted her palm to his lips and kissed the warm center before answering. "Because now you'll insist on something dangerous like interviewing Andrew Maguire, and there won't be anything I can do t' stop you." Bending his head, he kissed her palm again and then turned her hand over and leisurely kissed each finger before drawing her into the circle of his arms.

Meghann released her breath and closed her eyes, giving herself up to the erotic pressure of his mouth on her skin. For a few insecure moments she had thought Michael intended to behave as if their relationship was nothing more than that of any client with his attorney, as if their last two days in Donegal had never been. She had prepared herself to go through the motions, to pretend there was nothing between them if that was the way he wanted it. But the moment he reached for her and their eyes locked, Meghann knew she couldn't have managed it. She would have promised him anything, groveled if necessary, just to have him touch her again. Silently she blessed him for removing the possibility of that humiliation.

"Christ, Meghann, I've missed you," he whispered against her hair. "Tell me y' feel the same."

She nodded, burrowing her face into his shoulder, afraid to speak and disturb the magic.

He lifted her chin and found her mouth. Desperation and the limits of time heightened their exchange, and too soon he forced himself to pull away, removing his hands from beneath the smooth skin of her jumper. "I wasn't planning t' do that," he admitted shakily.

Meghann went completely still. "Why not?"

"It isn't fair, not after what I came here to ask."

"Are you suggesting that I'll do whatever you ask because of a few kisses?"

"Of course not."

"No?" She stared at him, noticing the rising color under his skin.

Lord, she was quick. Exasperated, Michael came out with it all at once. "I don't want y' anywhere near Andrew Maguire."

"I need him, Michael."

"He won't crack. You can't really believe that a

man who's held his position for fifteen years will tell you anything."

"He doesn't have to. It's his reaction I want."

Michael shook his head. "It won't work. Andrew has dealt with this before. He already knows what you'll ask him."

"I hope so. That strategy usually works best."

"What are y' talking about?"

Meghann shook out her hair and straightened her shoulders. "I'm a barrister, Michael, and a very good one. Trust me on this."

"You, I trust. I wish I could say the same for him."

She slipped her hand under his. "Arrange the meeting. He can't hurt me. I promise."

Michael was so preoccupied that he almost didn't see the army barricade set up on the corner of his mother's street. By the time he did it was too late to turn back. Holding his breath, he kept his head down, slowed his pace and walked right past them.

"Hey, you there. Stop and turn around."

Michael cursed under his breath and turned. There were three of them, and they were too close for him to make a run for it.

The short one lifted his flashlight. "Why, it's Devlin again. I'll be damned if I'm going to run his papers through another time. Don't you ever stay home, Devlin?"

Michael took his cue and pretended to be Connor. "Y' know how it is, lads. A pint tastes that much better in good company."

"Go along with you, bloody Taig. You're making our job that much harder. Don't come through again or I'll take you in."

Michael couldn't resist. "And what might the charges be?"

The soldier thought a minute, then grinned. "Suspicious activity."

Michael turned and continued walking until he reached his mother's porch. There, he lifted his hand in a mock salute to the soldiers and opened the door.

"For pity's sake, Mick." Annie hurried over to lock the door behind him. "Y' can't just walk down the street pretendin' you're John Major. I nearly took my last breath when I heard them shoutin' at you."

"It wasn't me they were shoutin' at, Ma. It was Connor."

"What nonsense are y' talking, lad? Connor's asleep in his bed."

"I'll need to wake him. Someone must take a message to Andrew Maguire. He'll know who to trust."

Annie's brow wrinkled. "Y' must be slippin', Michael, if y' couldn't talk her out of it."

Michael grinned and Annie's heart leaped. It was there again, the old brightness that drew everyone into the circle of his charm.

"Meghann's tough, Ma. I don't think anyone could talk her out of something she wanted to do."

"No one ever could," his mother agreed. *"Except you,"* she added quietly before climbing the stairs to wake Connor.

Meghann shivered and moved closer to Michael. The night was bitterly cold, unusual for late summer. A heavy fog hung uneasily over the brick buildings and high above, shrouded in mist, streetlights glowed, changing the color of the fog from gunmetal gray to a dull yellow-white. Fifteen years ago Meghann had known the streets of West Belfast as well as she knew the songs in her mother's music books. Now, everything had changed.

Tidy brick-terraced buildings had replaced the rowhouse tenements where she had grown to maturity. Hearth fires had given way to central heating, and indoor plumbing provided every family with its own bath and toilet. No longer did boarded-up dwellings with broken windows hide Irish political prisoners, and the dark entries that back in the seventies had served many a lad fleeing from English bullets were now sealed and whitewashed.

The standard of living had improved tremendously for residents of West Belfast, but it frightened Meghann to see how similar and characterless each residence had become. O'Connor's pub no longer bordered Springfield Road's Peace Line. McMahon's convenience store had given way to a gravel parking lot used primarily as a storage site for British tanks.

There was little time for reflection. Michael moved through the backstreets at a murderous pace. He seemed unusually preoccupied and in no mood for conversation. She refused to delve too deeply into the reason for the tension lines creasing his forehead, but she knew intuitively that the stiff angle of his right arm and the way he kept his hand concealed inside his pocket did not bode well for the meeting ahead.

He made an immediate left, leading them down the stairs of a neat brick building, where he knocked three times and waited without speaking. Minutes passed. Finally someone opened the door.

Michael reached out to pull Meghann against him. His breath tickled her ear. "Stay behind me," he ordered, waiting until she nodded before releasing her.

She followed him down the stairs into a well-lit sitting room. At the back of the room, behind a large desk was Andrew Maguire, Belfast Brigade's Officer Commanding and the man believed by many to be the warhawk of the Provisional Irish Republican Army.

Two burly men in denim trousers and black ski jackets stood by his side. One stepped forward, frisked Michael and pulled the gun from his pocket before moving back to his original position.

Maguire never blinked. Meghann's heart pounded. She had never seen Andrew Maguire. For as long as she could remember he had been a legend in the streets of Belfast, and yet his fit body and thick blond hair made him look much younger than his forty-five years.

Few in the movement commanded as much respect as Andrew Maguire. He had never been convicted of a crime, and for the last twelve years his canny intelligence had kept him out of the interrogation center, something few IRA men could claim. Among the Falls Road nationalists his reputation for fairness assumed heroic proportions. The mere mention of his name engendered more reverence than a papal visit.

Michael had explained it to her. Within the small Catholic population of Belfast, the IRA's leadership came from a close-knit clan of approximately forty active volunteers and twice as many supporters. Blood relationships and family ties were strong. Leaders came from within the political wing of Sinn Fein and other individual IRA men. The structure of the Brigade began with the Officer Commanding. Below him was the Belfast Brigade command, approximately ten experienced men with two or three elected Sinn Fein officials. Then came the command staff responsible for supplying all weapons, the engineering staff for constructing bombs, the finance department for raising funds and the internal security unit for routing informers. These were small, fluid groupings of two to three men, more like the branches of a family than a true military structure. Everyone knew everyone else. Families frequently intermarried. To penetrate the security of the IRA extended family in Belfast was virtually impossible.

Andrew Maguire personified the Irish republican struggle. He, more than anyone else, had kept the movement together for more than twenty-five years. Maguire appeared to be what every IRA man aspired to be. His dress was casual, consisting of tweed jackets and denim trousers. No one had ever seen him wear a tie. He accepted no special favors, standing in the queue at the infirmary and walking his children to church. It was reported that he didn't drink, smoke or cheat on his wife. He attended Mass every Sunday and spoke ill of no one but the British. If Andrew Maguire said something, every Irish Catholic in Belfast believed it. He had been Michael's mentor. He was also a complete fraud.

Meghann took the initiative. Without approaching the IRA leader or extending herself in any way, she greeted him from where she stood. "Good evening, Mr. Maguire. I'm Meghann McCarthy, Michael's attorney."

Cold gray eyes flicked over her, assessing her accent, the color of her hair and the deceptively simple but expensive navy wool coat and low-heeled shoes. There was no doubt that she despised him. His mouth twisted into a contemptuous smirk. "How does a high-powered London barrister become interested in the case of a former IRA activist?"

"I'm sure you already know the answer to that," she replied. "In fact you probably know everything about me including the fact that I was born and raised in the Falls."

Michael slouched by the door, looking relaxed. He returned Andrew's thoughtful gaze with a level, unblinking stare.

"How are y', Michael?"

He shrugged. "I've been better."

Meghann cut in. "I'd like to ask you some questions, Mr. Maguire."

The blond man nodded. "For obvious reasons I don't give interviews. But for Michael's sake, I'll make an exception."

"Very well, then." Meghann approached the desk and sat down in a chair. "Shall we begin?"

Andrew raised his light eyebrows and looked at Michael, who remained silent. "I'm at y'r disposal, Miss McCarthy, or shall I call y' Lady Sutton?"

"Don't call me anything, Mr. Maguire. This isn't a social visit. We won't be meeting again. Please tell me what your position is regarding the murder of James Killingsworth."

"Surely y' already know the answer to that."

"No, actually, I don't."

For the first time since their arrival, Andrew Maguire appeared impatient. "My position is the official one. The IRA has no knowledge or information regardin' the murder."

"Michael was in the audience at the Europa Hotel at your request. Why wasn't his name on the guest list?"

Maguire shrugged. "I assume he used another name or he attended without an invitation. We don't usually advertise our whereabouts."

Meghann folded her hands in her lap and looked directly at Maguire. "Who do you think is responsible for the murder of James Killingsworth?"

His features assumed an impassive expression. "Mr. Killingsworth is responsible, as is the British presence in Ireland. There will be no more political murders when people like you realize that y' have no future in Ireland."

"I'm Irish, Mr. Maguire," she reminded him. "My parents died in the Cupar Street burnings. I have no reason to apologize for my presence here. As for your answer to my question, I can only say that you are incredibly naive for a man in your position. There most certainly will be political murders. In fact there will be a bloodbath such as this country hasn't seen since the Easter Rising. I only hope you're prepared for it." She stood. "I believe I've enough information for now. Thank you for your time."

She didn't like him. He could sense it. It was more than his IRA affiliation. It was something deeper, something personal. In response to a subtle inclination of his head, the two men flanking him moved from behind the desk to take their positions on either side of Meghann. "Turnabout is fair play, Miss McCarthy. There are some questions I'd like t' ask you."

"Another time." She started toward the door, but

the men stepped closer, blocking her way. "I beg your pardon," she said to the expressionless faces. The men didn't move. Meghann turned back to Maguire. "Do you have any idea who I am?"

Andrew Maguire stood and leaned over his desk, resting on his hands. "A Catholic girl from Belfast who made good among enemies. But this isn't England, Meghann. It's Belfast. And in West Belfast, I am the law."

"Not quite, Andrew," Michael said steadily. His voice, deadly and cold as ice, cut through the tension in the room. In his hands, aimed straight at Andrew Maguire's heart, was a nine-millimeter handgun, an identical copy of the one sitting on Maguire's desk. "Call off your guards, put your hands over your head and turn around."

"Don't be an arse, Devlin. Y'r no killer."

"What do y' think, Meghann? The man knows I'm not a killer. Should we call him in as a character witness?"

"Let's go, Michael," she stammered.

"You're right, Andrew," Michael continued. "I'm no killer, but I've kneecapped a man or two in my time."

The man on Maguire's right lunged toward the gun on the desk. Meghann heard a muffled crack. The man cried out and fell against the desk, clutching his knee. Blood gushed from the artery. No one moved. Meghann looked at the spurting red stream coming from the hole in the man's leg and her legs buckled. She would have fallen if an iron hand hadn't closed around her arm.

"Don't faint now, Meggie," Michael ordered, pulling her behind him. "We've got t' get out of here first."

"Not just yet, Devlin." In those few seconds when Michael's attention had been distracted by the whiteness of Meghann's face, Andrew Maguire had reached into the drawer of his desk and pulled out a long-barreled handgun with a checkered handle, calling card of the Irish Republican Army. He leveled it at Michael's head.

"Y' were never unreasonable, although we didn't always see eye t' eye. Because we've come through a great deal together I won't lie t' you now. We had nothing t' do with Killingsworth's murder, but the Brits won't believe it. They want one of us t' pay, and you were there when it happened. I won't say that it doesn't tie ends up nicely for us, because it does. Consider it your sacrifice for Irish freedom. You'll be a martyr, Mick, unless this pretty Irish colleen can produce the real killer."

"Kill me now, you bloody son of a bitch. Do y' think I don't know what this is about? Y' don't want peace. What would happen t' the powerful Andrew Maguire if Irishmen were no longer shootin' at each other?" Michael sounded nothing like himself. The man in the ski jacket continued to bleed on the floor. He appeared to be unconscious. Meghann watched in horror as Andrew's fingers closed around the trigger.

"No," she cried out. "My God, please, don't!" She closed her eyes, praying for a miracle, waiting for the muffled crack and the sound of Michael's body dropping to the ground. But neither came.

Weak with relief, she opened her eyes and witnessed an unexplainable phenomenon. The lights had dimmed. Andrew's gun was no longer pointing at Michael, and standing between the two of them was a woman dressed in white, speaking in the low tones of the language Meghann had first learned at her mother's knee. She barely had time to notice the coppery color of the woman's hair before absolute darkness settled in.

Across the room, Andrew cursed. A gun discharged and the acrid unmistakable stench of gunpowder filled the room. Meghann dropped to the floor. Close to her head, someone breathed. A hand closed over her arm and Michael whispered, "Hold on."

Meghann reached out, found the leather of his belt and clung to it while he dragged her across the room to the end of the carpet. She felt stone steps beneath her knees. Releasing her hold, she scrambled to her feet. The smell of roses was overwhelming. Instinctively, she knew which way to go. Fumbling for Michael's hand, she took the initiative and followed the floral scent, leading him through the twisted maze of quiet streets at a pace that burned her lungs until her breath would no longer come.

The distance back was traveled in much less time than it had taken to arrive. Strangely enough, there were no English troops at the Falls Road barricade. They crossed without arousing attention. Neither one spoke. A thick mist cocooned them in a foggy chrysalis. Meghann's senses were unusually sharp. Occasionally, when she leaned forward, she caught the fragrance of dried rose petals. She wanted to speak, to ask if Michael had seen the apparition in white. But something held her back.

All at once the fog lifted. Bewildered, Meghann stopped and turned to Michael. He stared at her oddly. "Why are you looking at me like that?" she stammered.

"Like what?"

"As if I were some strange creature you had never seen before."

He shook his head. "Sometimes I try t' imagine what your life was like after y' left the Falls."

She laughed uncertainly. "What has that got to do with anything?"

Michael searched her face. "One minute you're so pale I thought I'd have t' carry you all the way and the next you're leadin' us out of that death trap as if the devil himself was at our heels."

"I didn't lead us anywhere," she said flatly.

He frowned. "Of course, y' did. How do y' think we got here?"

Meghann opened her mouth to speak and then closed it again. The woman was nowhere to be seen. Michael would have told her if he'd seen her, and if he hadn't he would never believe her. She shrugged. "I'm not sure. Call it intuition."

He nodded slowly. "Perhaps. Your instincts are very good, Meghann."

She considered lying and rejected the notion. Neither would she tell him about the woman who had led them to safety. Settling on a partial truth, she said, "I grew up in the Falls, Michael. If that doesn't teach self-preservation, nothing will."

The set of her jaw told him he would learn nothing more tonight. Wrapping his arm around her, he held her closely against his side. "Y' need some rest, Meggie. I'll leave y' at your hotel."

"Where will you go?" she asked.

He smiled grimly. "I'll turn myself in. Thanks to you I've been allowed a jury trial. I'll be all right."

Meghann rested her head against his shoulder and bit her lip. "I won't let them hurt you. I promise."

He smiled against her hair. Despite her profession she was an innocent. "I've no choice, Meggie. I've got to go back. We've always known that." Brushing his lips against her forehead, he pulled away too quickly. "I'll see y' on visitors' day."

She smiled. "Along with every Devlin in the Six Counties."

"Don't pout," he teased. "If y' do your job, you'll have plenty of time with me later."

"You have no idea how the thought reassures me."

Michael grinned. "Y' aren't prone t' flattering a man, are you, Meg?"

She considered his question, remembering the elegance of her London town house and the three country seats she had inherited upon David's death. For fifteen years Meghann had grown accustomed to the taste of aged wine, the softness of cashmere against her skin, the scent of expensive perfume, the dull glow of gold at her neck and wrists, the company of people who had never known what it was to be hunted, trampled and spat upon.

Michael would never know how much she had given up to defend him. His world was one of secret meetings, abandoned houses, plastic bullets and the constant fear of treachery. He knew nothing of elegance or comfort or the never-ending surge of relief after one's bankbook was tallied to find that the principle had never been touched. Michael was not materialistic. He had the ideology of a true socialist, taking only what he needed and nothing more. She had grown up in semipoverty, just as he had. Why were her needs so much more complicated than his?

Meghann ran her tongue over dry lips and looked up. In the darkness, under the white light of the street-lamp, he stood before her, tall and capable, his face leeched of all color except black, stark white and shades of gray. Black hair fell across his forehead. Black brows were etched against white skin. Gray shadows filled in the hollows beneath jutting cheek-bones, and around the black pupils of his eyes the dramatic blue had become clear shards of gray. His jaw was set, his eyes narrowed. He seemed harder somehow, and filled with purpose, nothing at all like the man she had lived with in Donegal.

This man was a street fighter, a rebel, a former member of an illegal underground organization. He really didn't need her at all. Win or lose, Michael Devlin would never hang from the end of a rope. If the verdict did not turn out in his favor, someone from that world into which he was tied would spirit him over the walls and far away until the name of Michael Devlin was all but forgotten in the streets of Belfast.

All at once the horror of it consumed her. She had found him again and she didn't want to lose him. But where was her place in the life he had chosen? Where did an anarchist fit into the world of an English barrister? The widow of Lord David Sutton could not marry a man who had admitted to being a member of a terrorist organization. Dampness seeped through the wool of her coat. She shivered. Neither one had spoken for several minutes.

"Cold?" Michael asked, breaking the silence.

She nodded.

He held out his arms and despite everything she knew she walked into them. His heart beat evenly, reassuringly, against her chest. "It isn't that I don't know how to flatter a man," she explained, "but with you, I never think of it. You don't seem to need your ego polished. It's one of the things I most admire about you."

Amusement colored his voice. "Oh, but I do need it, Meggie. Can y' imagine how I felt all those years ago when y' left my house and took your own flat? Except for a few brief months I never knew where I stood with you."

Meghann lifted her head and stared at him. "You're joking."

"No."

She settled back against his chest and forced the confession from her lips. "From the time I was ten years old, I adored you."

"Y' ran away the first time I kissed you and wouldn't speak t' me for days," he reminded her.

Color rose in Meghann's cheeks. "The girls at school were obsessed with sex. The nuns knew it and told us that kissing the way we had was a dreadful sin." She laughed shakily. "I was such a child, Michael, and so very sure you would think I was fast."

His breath was warm against her cheek. "All I could think about was how young y' were and how very much I wanted t' kiss you again. I fell in love with you, Meggie. I've never wanted anyone else."

Meghann's heart lifted. The air felt like spring. "Have you any idea what a fourteen-year-old girl would give to hear that? Why didn't you tell me?"

"You ran away. I knew you weren't ready."

"I'm not running now," she said just before his mouth stopped her breath.

Later, Meghann couldn't recall how they managed the walk to the garage in Donegall Square where her car was parked, nor could she tell anyone how they avoided the roadblocks set up at random intervals throughout the city. Michael knew a backstreet route to the hotel. Meghann distracted the man at the desk by asking for her messages while Michael walked up the utility stairs and slipped into her room.

She took the elevator. Pressing her ear against the door, she heard the sound of water running. Reassured, she opened the door, bolted it behind her, slipped off her shoes and curled up on the bed. Minutes later Michael came out of the bathroom with a comb in his hand and a towel around his waist. He held up the comb. "Do y' mind?"

Suppressing a smile, she shook her head. He had kissed her senseless, used her toothbrush, touched every inch of her body in ways she had never dreamed possible and still, he asked permission to use her comb.

Meghann disappeared into the bathroom. It was one of those times for a direct appeal. "Please, God," she prayed, "don't let him fall asleep before I'm finished." Surely that wasn't too much of a request, not nearly in the same league as *let the jury declare him innocent* or *make the IRA and the British government forget all about him.*

The room was dark when she'd finished with the bathroom. Feeling very vulnerable, she groped along the wall until she found the empty side of the bed and climbed in. Her heartbeat was deafening. Forcing herself to relax, she lay quietly, listening to Michael's breathing. It was slow and relaxed, the kind that can't be forced or staged, the deep even breathing of sleep.

Disappointment swept through her and the ache growing in her chest was painful. Tears leaked from beneath her closed eyelids and ran down the sides of her cheeks. She turned over and faced the wall. Still restless, she turned once more.

A strong arm wrapped around her, pulling her back against a warm chest. "Meghann," Michael's fingers stroked her wet cheek, "lie still."

She sniffled.

He sat up. "Are y' crying, lass?"

Meghann shook her head and buried her face in her pillow.

He switched on the lamp. "You're crying," he said incredulously. "Whatever is the matter with you?"

Meghann rolled over, the last of her tears dried by the blazing temper leaping within her. "You are either joking or the most insensitive man in the entire world."

He frowned.

"For pity's sake, Michael." She waved her hand to encompass the entirety of the room. "We're here in my hotel room, on what may be the last time we ever see each other without bars between us, and you have no idea why I'm crying?"

Michael ran his hand through his shower-damp hair and sighed impatiently. He would never get this right. He never got anything right when it came to her. Moonlight filtered through the opening in the curtains. He studied her critically, hoping to find a flaw that would make him indifferent.

She was lovely, lovelier even than she had been as a girl. Tonight she had shown uncommon loyalty and courage. Physically she was everything he wanted in a woman, and she cared deeply for him. He knew that. If anything, she cared too much, but that was hardly a liability. A man looked a lifetime for a woman like Meghann.

He rested his hand on the dip of her waist. "Don't make me play games. I know less than nothing about the mind of a woman. Tell me what y' want."

She pushed back her hair, and when she spoke her voice was unsteady, as if forming the words took great effort. "I want you, Michael, and damn you for making me ask."

He stared at her. She was Lady Meghann Sutton, wealthy, educated, beautiful, and she actually believed he didn't want her. This time, he knew what to do. Slowly, inexorably, he lowered his head to her mouth.

Meghann was unprepared for the assault on her senses. She swam in whorls of heat and need and longing, muscles tensed, nerves hungry, pulse leaping toward a flame that had simmered too long and too deep to burn through in a single night. And so, when his mouth opened over her breast, she was ready as if it were the first time and when his hands moved against her skin and his arms tightened yet again around her waist, she wrapped her legs around him, inviting the intrusion of hard, heated flesh, urging him again and again to fill her, forgetting the aching soreness, the morning to come and all the terrifying nights and days ahead.

He left in the morning, once again making no promises. Meghann watched him go and when he turned back she smiled bravely. Later, after her hurt was under control, she checked to be sure the *Do Not Disturb* sign was still on the door, crawled beneath the sheets on Michael's side of the bed, inhaled his scent and slept for sixteen hours.

18

***

Tirconnaill, 1597

I blamed Rory for the loss of my bairns. Perhaps I was unfair. Certainly Niall was the greater player in their untimely and tragic deaths. But in those first days when my sleep was haunted by their screams, I hated everyone even remotely connected to bringing about the end of their short lives, including myself.

For weeks Rory waited for me to recover, treating me with tenderness, mindful of my pain, solicitous of my need for privacy, to no avail. But I could not respond. Staring out over the battlements of Dun Na Ghal toward the Irish sea, I stood for hours without moving or speaking. I, once so quick to laugh, thought of my dead children and the laughter dried up within me. Such a loss was too great to be endured by a mortal woman. Even the blessed Virgin had lost only one child. I was only five and twenty and I had lost nine.

Rory found me leaning against the turret wall, staring at the sea. I had no desire to speak with him. A fierce wind pressed me against the stone and mortar. Not until he was close enough to touch me did I turn to him. There was no light of welcome in my eyes. A wiser man would have refrained from speaking, but Rory O'Donnell would not be remembered for his wisdom. As always, he blurted out what was first in his head.

"I miss you, Nuala."

I frowned, wishing him away. "But I am here."

"Only in the flesh. Your spirit is elsewhere." He lifted my chin and looked into my eyes. "Could it be that you had no wish to be rescued, my love? Is it my cousin you pine for? Because if it is so——"

"How dare you!" I lashed out. "How dare you presume that what you see in me has anything to do with a man."

"I am glad of it," he replied, "for I shall not let you go, not now, not ever."

I pulled a strand of hair away from my mouth. "Are you so arrogant that you imagine me the same as you? I lost my children, Rory. Nine children I bore and every one dead, some directly and others less so, but all because of you." I lost my anger and slumped against the wall.

His mouth was grim. "I miss them too, Nuala."

I said nothing.

"You are my wife. I could demand your favors."

"It has never been like that between you and me, Rory, but do what you will. I care little enough what happens to me."

He sighed. "I would not lose what was, and what I still hope will be, between us."

I did not bother to hide the condemnation in my eyes.

"Damn it, Nuala. What is a man to do when he learns that his wife is a prisoner, his children held hostage? Once I called Niall Garv my friend. You told me to beware of him. I was wrong. I played the fool, secure in my strength, never dreaming that he would betray me despite his yearning for my wife."

He'd known all along and yet he heeded not my warning. "You convict yourself out of your own mouth."

"Yes, I knew he wanted you. I knew from the beginning, but I thought it long settled. You chose me over Niall and despite all that passed between us, I never believed you regretted your choice, not until now."

"Why now?"

"A man does not risk his honor or his life for mere wanting. Nor does he fight his way through searing, smoke-filled rooms in an attempt to carry her children to safety. A man does not linger within the shadow of an enemy sword just to hold a woman against his heart, to kiss her lips one last time, unless he loves her deeply."

"Niall Garv's feelings are his own. They are not shared by me."

"I'm relieved to hear it. Niall stole what was mine. For that alone his days on earth were numbered. It is you who worry me, Nuala. Despite your words, you do not appear to have been ill-used by Niall Garv O'Donnell."

It was past time to speak. He would know soon enough anyway. "You will not like it, Rory."

"Undoubtedly," he replied, "but as you say, some things are better spoken."

The sun slipped farther into the sea outlining his head in a halo of light. I could not look at him. Instead I walked to the guardrail and rested my head in my arms.

"Nuala," he said gently, "war is not kind to women and children. Whatever he did to you, you are not to blame."

He moved to my side and spread his hand across the nape of my neck. " 'Tis over, love," he murmured. "After this, we'll not speak of it again."

"We must, Rory. When you hear what happened, you will understand why it is not over."

He pulled me back against his chest. My words came slowly, haltingly, from a place deep within me. "He came soon after you left Dun Na Ghal, surprising everyone, even the watch you left to guard us. For a long time he was very kind, especially to the children. We spoke of peaceful things, you, me, his hopes and fears. Days came and went and then weeks and months. Soon I forgot that he was an invader in my castle. He became a close companion."

I pressed my cheek against Rory's chest. His arms tightened to hold me closer and I nearly burst from the pain I knew he would feel. When a man has loved a woman, slept and wakened beside her, borne children with her and buried them, heard her fears and shared his own, the hurt is the same as if it happened to both.

He kissed my forehead. "Go on, Nuala."

My voice was muffled against his chest. "I missed you, Rory, through all the years of our marriage, more than you will ever know. You said I was strong. You praised me for my care of Tirconnaill. I didn't want to disappoint you, but it seems I needed you more than even I realized." I lifted my head and stepped out of his arms. "I was a child when we married. When Niall came to Dun Na Ghal, I was ripe for a man's gallantries. He courted me as you never did. Nay, he worshiped me and I was weak with longing for a man. But I would never have touched him, until the day your messenger came for our boys. I thought to save the children."

He would have spoken, but I lifted my hand to silence him.

"My weakness for him passed before I ever shared his bed. Know that at least." I felt the heat in my cheeks. "He came to me after the archers killed them.

He cursed me for my betrayal. I told him what we had shared was merely lust and that I could never love him. He hated me for it. For weeks he came to my bed, forcing himself upon me. I did not want him. I did not want him the night our sons died. But before, when I was lonely and I missed you so dreadfully, I thought of him and for that I will be forever punished."

He no longer looked at me but stared blindly at the ocean. My stomach burned. "Speak to me, Rory. Tell me what is in your heart."

"Rape I understand," he said, his voice low and shaking. "It is not uncommon for a castle to surrender and one lord's lady to become another's. But desire, Nuala. I never believed you would desire another over me."

"You were not there," I reminded him. "I desired no one over you."

His fists clenched. "Do you think I wish to be away from you and from Tirconnaill? We are at war, Nuala, our people in servitude, our religion persecuted, our lands forfeit to the English bitch who calls herself a woman. I left you to fight for what is ours, for us and for children, for a man's right to stand up and declare himself a man. Holy God, have you forgotten what we endured? I will kill Niall for making you want him. Perhaps I'll kill you as well."

I laughed bitterly. "Oh, Rory. You could never kill me." I voiced the fear on the edge of my mind. "Will you put me away?"

"If you wish it." His voice cracked.

"I do not wish it," I said firmly. "Do you?"

He straightened to his full height. "We shall speak of this again, Nuala. Now, I must think."

I dropped my hand. It was not the answer I wanted, but I refused to beg. "You must know something else as well, Rory," I said. "I am breeding. Come spring, I will give birth to Niall Garv's child. I love you. I will always love you, but if you cannot find it in your heart to forgive me, tell me now."

He cursed and I wished for the pain of a clean sword thrust, a broken bone, even a festering wound, anything but this living nightmare.

"Will you go to him?" was all he said.

I shook my head. "I go to Tyrone."

"What of the child? Will you give him to his father?"

"Aye."

His pain gave way to a murderous rage. His hands reached for my shoulders. His thumbs searched out the pulse points on the sides of my throat. I felt my lifeblood through his fingers. "Damn you, Nuala. Damn you to hell. Through it all, the prison years, the war years, the years your father demanded I chase his enemies across Ireland, did you believe I was never tempted?"

I kept my eyes on his face.

"I *was* tempted, Nuala. I was tempted and I burned, but never once was I unfaithful to you."

My tears spilled over. I felt the warm wetness run under his thumbs. He released me suddenly and walked away without speaking. Later, when I looked into his chamber, I found him sprawled on the bed, unconscious, two empty drams of whiskey by his side.

The seasons seemed to stop, so slow was the progression from fall to winter, winter to spring. Rory was gone for weeks at a time and when he was home, he did not seek my company. We never did speak of the year Niall Garv held me hostage, nor would we. I should have gone to my father in Tyrone but I had no wish to leave Dun Na Ghal. For eleven years I had called it home.

Here, the seasons of my life were marked by love,

birth, death and loneliness. It was here, in the cavern-
ous O'Donnell bedchamber, that Rory and I learned
to love. Here my childhood ended. Here I became first
a wife, then a woman, then a mother. Here my
children were born, took a single brief taste of what it
was to be born O'Donnell, to stand upon the rich
green of Ireland beneath the skies of Tirconnaill,
before they were buried beneath the soil where the
spirits of their ancestors walked.

Dun Na Ghal was my home, even more so than
Rory's. His claim was a hereditary one, mine was
earned. It was I who made it a home, a place of refuge,
a beacon for all of Tirconnaill. It was I who stayed
while Rory fed his hatred by waging war against an
undefeatable foe. It was I who held my children as
they gasped their final breaths and I who watched the
soil thrown over their small coffins until the ground
was smooth and flat again.

It is said that through every Irish family runs the
bloodlines of the Picts, the first people to inhabit our
island. They worshiped the seasons, the sun and
moon and, most of all, Mother Earth, the life bringer.
A wife took her husband into her mother's hearth. A
child inherited through his mother, and his closest
male relative was his mother's brother. All posses-
sions belonged to the woman, and the tribe was ruled
by the decisions of a healer who had "the sight," a
woman who carried the memories of her people. How
had they become so wise, these ancient ones, and
where had we, their descendants, lost our vision?

And so I wondered as I walked the ramparts of Dun
Na Ghal, waiting for my child to be born. This time
the bairn did not sit well with me. The retching lasted
for months. My back ached and I bled whenever I
stood. The physician ordered me to my chamber, and
there I stayed until a rainy morning in June, when my
labor began.

Nine times I had given birth, but I did not remember that the pains had ever before seemed so fierce. I desperately wanted my mother and nearly cried out for her until I remembered that she was dead. For hours, my body stretched and the bands around my stomach hardened and pulled taut, but still the child would not come. Poor wee one. Perhaps he knew already that there would be no welcome awaiting him.

A day and a night passed and then another day. I faded in and out, weak from pain and blood loss. From across the room I heard voices, first Rory's and then the physician's. Their words had no meaning. Time stopped. I was lost, aware of nothing but the stench of blood, the pull of flesh, the terrible weight that settled on my lower spine, pinching my nerves until I prayed for death.

Once I recognized Rory's face. I would have called out to him until I remembered why I could not. The physician's hands pressed down on my stomach. The child moved, shifting still lower, increasing my agony, dragging me into a state of hysteria. I screamed and screamed until the walls moved closer, shutting out everything except the hideous echo of my own voice.

I could no longer lift my eyelids. The pain receded and everything went black. A different pain woke me. I knew it well. The burning between my legs and the cramping of my stomach were symptoms typical of birthing. But where was my bairn? Fear gave me strength. I struggled to sit up.

A cool, dry hand rested briefly against my forehead. "Gently, my lady. You must sleep and regain your strength."

I recognized the physician's voice. "What of the bairn?" I asked through cracked lips.

"A healthy wee lad with a head of black hair. The wet nurse has him."

Relieved, I leaned back against the pillow. A son with black hair. How odd. Rory's bairns were always fair. "I want to see him," I whispered.

The physician soothed me. "Of course. I shall speak to the woman now."

I closed my eyes and waited, hungry for the sight of my child. The door opened and the nurse entered, bearing a blanketed bundle in her arms. I reached out for my son and settled him in the crook of my arm. Pulling aside the blanket, I stared down at the tiny face, so pure and new, and gasped. All hopes I'd cherished of raising him here at Dun Na Ghal were shattered.

No one with eyes would mistake this child for Rory's. He was the image of Niall Garv, from the whorl of black hair on the crown of his head to the squared-off chin and beautifully shaped hands. I smiled through my tears. He was a son to be proud of, a son I could never claim because his father was not my husband.

Were I a milkmaid or a tavern wench or even the mistress of a nobleman, a bastard child would be tolerated. But I was Nuala O'Donnell, Rory's wife, countess of Tirconnaill. Such a breach was unpardonable.

Cradling him against me, I kissed his downy head. No matter who his father was or what he had done, this child, born of my body, belonged to me. He was smaller than my other sons had been, as was Niall compared to Rory's great height. But his hand clutching my finger was strong and the dark eyes, wide awake and staring into mine, were focused and alert. He was beautiful, with a dark, archangel symmetry of feature and I loved him desperately.

The door opened and the physician stepped inside my room. He watched, smiling faintly, as I nestled the babe into my arms and leaned against the pillow. "Are you comfortable, my lady?" he asked.

"Very." I was annoyed that he had interrupted me. "Is something wrong?" I asked in the frosty, nononsense tone that meant I wanted the truth quickly.

He hesitated. "I thought it best to speak to your husband first."

"Yes?" The man was truly beset. What could Rory have said to make him so agitated?

"You have come to childbed ten times, my lady. Perhaps," he stopped and fiddled with the lace at his sleeve, "perhaps 'tis time for you to thank God for the son you have and try no more."

The man was shockingly presumptuous. Bracing myself on my elbow, I sat up. "Surely that is a matter for my husband and me to decide."

"You will be choosing death."

I felt the color leave my cheeks. "What are you saying?"

He came closer to the bed. "My lady, I beg of you. Do not attempt to bear more children lest the one who lies beside you be left without his mother."

At last I understood the full intent of his words. To even consider such a possibility was unthinkable. Rory would be childless. There would be no heir for Tirconnaill. A thousand years of unbroken O'Donnell succession would end because of me. No more fair-haired sons and daughters to laugh and tumble in the courtyard, bringing a smile to their father's lips. Horror filled my soul. No more long winter nights curled close to my husband's side while his hands and lips rekindled the magic that flamed between us, stronger, richer and bolder as the years passed. No more soft laughter and intimate conversation after the first rush of desire had been satisfied. No more rides through summer sunlight into shadowed glens where I would listen, barefoot, as Rory played his lute and together we searched for faerie toadstools.

He would put me away. I knew him as surely as I knew myself. I was his wife and he loved me. But he would not disobey the physician and risk my life. He would never seek to annul our marriage or demand that I leave Tirconnaill. He would find another woman to warm his bed and bear his sons. He would apply to Rome for a dispensation to legitimize his heirs, a common practice for a peer.

I clenched my fists and something inside me hardened. There was no hope. That fool of a physician had already told him. I would not stay and watch Rory love another woman. I would leave Tirconnaill when my son was weaned.

Courage gave me dignity. I lifted my chin. "You may dismiss the wet nurse," I said to the physician. "I shall feed my son alone."

The man bowed. "As you wish, my lady. Shall I send in your husband?"

"Is he here?"

"Aye."

"For how long?"

"Throughout the birth, my lady. We were afraid for your life."

I looked for my hand mirror and found it on the side table. "Pray, give me my brush and mirror, sir, and engage my husband in conversation for a time."

"Aye, lass," the physician replied. "Perhaps I should send for your maid."

"No." I shook my head emphatically. "Take the child with you. I need only a moment."

A glance told me all I needed to know. I looked dreadful, as if someone had taken a rolling pin to my head. My hair was matted and tangled like a wild woman's, and the shadows beneath my eyes were giant purple bruises against the paleness of my skin.

Never before had I considered my appearance after a birthing. Rory had been grateful for every babe I'd given him. He demanded nothing more. This time would be different.

When he entered the room, my hair lay smooth and shining against the bedclothes and I had pinched the color back into my cheeks. Rory appeared agitated, as if he had never before entered a woman's chamber.

"Welcome, my lord," I said steadily.

He took my hand and sat down beside me on the bed. "Are you well, Nuala?"

"Aye."

"The birth was brutal. I heard your cries." He lifted my hand to his lips. "My God, Nuala, I almost lost you."

My heart lifted. Perhaps the physician hadn't told him everything.

His jaw was hard under my caress. It had been so very long. "I will soon be well again, Rory. There is nothing to fear."

"Until the next time. The man's words ring true, my love. You must never give birth again."

I swallowed to keep the tears back and watched him play with my fingers. "You have no heir," I reminded him.

"Keeping you alive is more important to me than having an heir."

I knew my husband. He was a man of appetite and would take a woman to warm his bed and to heal his soul. I could do no more than bite my lip and turn away from the concern in his eyes.

19

Belfast, 1994

Recognition came slowly, comfortably, awakened
from a long sleep where bits of reality focus into
consciousness one piece at a time so as not to jar the
delicate psyche of its subject. Because of the way it
came Meghann couldn't pinpoint the exact moment
when she first knew the identity of the woman she had
seen at significant moments of her life. One morning
she woke up and just knew.

Looking back, she wondered why she hadn't seen
the resemblance before, in the red-haired child with
bare feet, in the woman who had known her name on
the beach at Donegal, in the faceless stranger who led
her out of danger through the streets of Belfast.

She closed her eyes and rubbed the oval at her
throat, savoring the delicate edges and the feel of
warm metal between her fingers. Nuala's form materialized before her. Red hair, dimmed slightly with age
but still gloriously long and thick, framed a face as
lovely as the likeness of the Virgin Mary burned
immortally into the glass panels of Westminster Cathedral.

Meghann sat up on the edge of the bed and opened her eyes. Nuala disappeared. She closed them again and her image reappeared. "Why can't I see you in the light?" Meghann whispered.

"I'm not comfortable there," replied a soft, strangely accented voice.

Meghann knew that voice. She'd heard it in the burned-out skeleton of what was once her home on Cupar Street. She'd heard it in Donegal and again last night when the lights went out in Andrew Maguire's meeting room. She wanted to hear it again. "Tell me your name."

"Nuala O'Donnell."

"Why are you here?"

The woman sighed impatiently. "I expected more of you, Meghann McCarthy. I'm here to help you and that impossible young man who keeps you awake at night."

"Will you disappear when I open my eyes?"

There was a slight hesitation before Nuala spoke. "The light is difficult for me."

"Once before I saw you in the light. It was early morning and you were playing a melody."

"And you were fleeing from the English."

"How did you know?"

"You asked if there was another way into Donegal. Everyone who asks that is looking for a way around the checkpoints."

"In Donegal you were standing in the light," Meghann remembered.

"Aye, but the light in the west is soft and fey. It does no damage to the aged."

Meghann kept her eyes closed. "I'll dim the lights."

Again, Nuala sighed. "That won't be necessary. Open your eyes. I won't go away."

Meghann opened her eyes. Nuala stood near the curtains, her white gown blending with the white around her, enveloped like a cloud. She was small, almost frail-looking, with light, compassion-filled eyes.

"I know you," Meghann's voice cracked. "I've always known you."

Nuala nodded. "Aye. I've been with you, child, many times."

"You've been following me all my life."

"Aye, and I've shared mine with you."

Meghann rubbed her temples. "I don't understand."

"Perhaps not now. But if you think for a bit you'll find that you have an unusual understanding of the events that occurred in those last days when Ireland belonged to the Irish. An understanding you could never have learned from any present-day source because there simply isn't one."

"Why do I know this?"

Nuala moved closer. "I've allowed you the knowledge, Meghann. I've re-created it all in your mind so that you would see what I did and follow my example."

"But your life was dreadful," Meghann burst out. "You lost your husband, your children and, according to what I've read, your land. What could I possibly learn from a woman who lived in the sixteenth century?"

Nuala drew herself up to her full height. "I did not lose my husband, you foolish girl. 'Tis true, the land was lost, but I saved our lives, that and a great deal of gold that did much to soften our banishment. As for my children," she crossed herself, "they are in a better place. But know this, Meghann McCarthy. I did not lose them all."

"What does all this have to do with me?"

"You are of my race, Meghann. You are a descendant of Irish chieftains. My blood flows through your body. Ireland needs you as she once needed me. After five hundred years of English dominion there is a chance for freedom to prevail. You must take up the standard, Meghann. Show the world what it has never seen."

Meghann watched as Nuala fingered the pages of a book on the nightstand. It was a volume of poetry authored by Michael Devlin. "What is it that I'm supposed to do?" she asked softly.

"Save this rebel, this Irish warrior," Nuala continued in her low, firm voice. "When this voice speaks of what it means to be Irish, the world will listen."

Caught up in the moment, Meghann thrilled to her words. She would save Michael and he would write passionate, heart-breaking words, words that would open the eyes of the Western world and shock it into condemning the British presence in Northern Ireland. In her mind she could see it happen.

Just as suddenly her enthusiasm disappeared. Wearily, she pushed her hair away from her forehead and lifted red-rimmed eyes to Nuala's face. Meghann blinked. Nothing changed. She blinked again and rubbed her eyes. Had sleep deprivation blurred her mind to the point where she could no longer define where her subconscious ended and reality began? Was this an absurd nightmare, or was she really having a conversation with a woman who claimed to be her ancestor, a woman, history said, who had died four hundred years before?

Somehow Meghann's mind had twisted into itself, losing its direction. Her waking hours were filled with concern, divided between worry over Michael's safety and planning his defense. Sleep took her back nearly half a millennium to a world where a woman battled multiple enemies, invaders, nature's cruelty and, most insidious of all, a man she had no wish to come up against.

"How do you suggest I perform such a miracle?" Meghann asked the white-robed apparition.

Nuala tapped her bottom lip with her forefinger.

"Elizabeth was a formidable opponent. She was also very English."

Meghann laughed. "Really?"

"Aye." Nuala nodded, completely ignoring Meghann's sarcasm. "She was a strong ruler, but a ruthless one. It was her weakness, that and her vanity. She was Henry's daughter and she displayed many of his qualities. But she couldn't bear to have anyone think she was less than feminine. Public humiliation was unthinkable. She would do anything to avoid it."

Meghann stopped listening. *Public humiliation.* The flicker of an idea grew in her mind. It meant something. Blood pulsed in her temples. Her lethargy was gone. On the coffee table, the screen saver of her portable computer flashed green, then blue, then green again. She slid her feet into fleece-lined slippers and walked to the sitting room couch. Tucking her legs beneath her, she rested the computer on her knees, moved her mouse to the Internet connection and typed in her password. She bypassed her mail, world news and the chat rooms, moved to the American media bulletin boards and began to type.

One hour later her in-box contained forty messages. She answered them all. Two hours later the number two hundred flashed in the lower left corner of her screen. Again she answered, this time to names familiar to every household throughout the world with a television set.

It was nearly dawn before she finished. Meghann closed down the computer, stretched and smiled, satisfied with her night's work. There would be no Diplock Court for Michael Devlin, not after the reactions of the American press corps. The prosecution would be forced to fight fairly.

She looked around. Nuala was gone. Or maybe she had never been here at all. Meghann shivered and rubbed her arms. Of course she hadn't. Nuala, the

Nuala who materialized when Meghann needed her, spoke to her and guided her through the power of suggestion, was a figment of her imagination, most likely summoned because Meghann was spending too much time alone.

Light crept through the lined draperies. She stood and walked into the bedroom, every bone-weary movement protesting her sleepless night. Meghann stared at the bed. For some reason, shutting herself off in the mindless cocoon of darkness and the vivid images that came with it did not appeal to her. She picked up the telephone and dialed Annie's number, smiling when her familiar voice answered.

"Annie? It's Meghann. I've good news."

"Then you'd better come down. I'll fix us a bite of breakfast."

Thirty minutes later Meghann hailed a loyalist taxi with its identifying red poppy in the window to take her to the Ormeau Road. There she flagged down a black nationalist taxi the size of a hearse for the mile-and-a-half trek to the Devlin house.

True to her word, Annie moved about the kitchen preparing her usual Irish breakfast of oats, eggs, bacon, potatoes and wheat bread. No one in Ireland considered their cholesterol intake. Life was too hard and too short to worry about heart disease.

Meghann sat down at the small table in the kitchen. The larger dining room was rarely used except on holidays. Years ago when she had first come to live with the Devlins, meals were served in three shifts to accommodate a large family with a small kitchen. Annie was up long before dawn cooking hot food for her brood. Meghann looked at the table, which was set for two. "Isn't anyone home today?" she asked. It was impossible to imagine Annie Devlin without a child attached to her hip or clinging to her leg.

"Only yourself," Annie answered, ladling the steaming oatmeal into bowls. "Add a wee pinch of salt, Meggie darlin'. Don't wait for me. Oats are best at their hottest."

Meghann stared at the array of food before her and swallowed. Had she ever eaten such stupendous amounts of food? "I can't do justice to all this, Annie. London forever cured me of large meals. My stomach can't possibly manage it."

Annie surveyed her figure critically. "You are a narrow bit of a thing. A larger appetite would round out y'r angles."

"I'm healthy. That's all that matters."

"I suppose," Annie remarked doubtfully, "although I wonder if you could carry children at that weight."

Meghann laughed. After years of living alone, it was comforting to have someone worry about her. "I'm a thirty-five-year-old widow, Annie. It isn't likely that I'll have children." She saw the frown gathering on Annie's brow and continued hastily, "Don't you want to hear my news?"

"Of course. I was just waitin' until y' were ready t' tell it."

"Last night I e-mailed every news correspondent who wrote an article about the Troubles.

Annie's forehead wrinkled. "I don't understand."

"It means publicity in the American press." Meghann forced herself to curb her excitement and speak coherently. "Don't you see? No government in its right mind would offer a biased jury to a world-renowned political prisoner. Britain would make the front pages of every large newspaper in the world."

Annie thought about it. The prospect of a condemned England cheered her. "Y're clever, Meggie. I knew that long before I asked you t' help Michael." She sipped her tea, leaving the cooling oats untouched. "He wasn't happy about it, you know. But I convinced him it was the right thing to do."

Meghann pleated the layers of napkin protecting

her lap. "Why do you think he didn't want me to come?"

Widening her eyes innocently, Annie pretended to ignore the color staining Meghann's cheeks. "It isn't that he thought you weren't competent," she said. "We've known for a long time how successful you'd become."

"Then, why?"

Annie shrugged, picked up a fork and stirred the eggs around on her plate. "I'm not sure really. Something about the two of you parting in a bad way."

The corners of Meghann's mouth turned up. "It wasn't such a bad way, really. He wanted to marry me and I refused because of his politics. I couldn't imagine living that kind of life."

Annie sighed. "No, I suppose y' couldn't, not after what y' saw at such a tender age. Most of us learn such news through a phone call or a knock on the door, days after the deed is done. It must have been a dreadful shock for such a small girl, the sight of all that death and the night that followed."

Meghann thought back to those terrifying hours after finding her parents lying in the destruction of Cupar Street. Some of the horror had diminished, leaving memories of a different sort. A woman dressed in white offering comfort, a boy leading a small girl to safely through burning streets, his body warm and solid, pressing her into the ancient stone floor of the monastery, a priest, the first of his kind to climb down from the fence and take a stand, a family who had offered an orphan their home. She swallowed and breathed deeply. "The pain lasted a very long time, but it's over now."

"Have y' come t' terms with the past, Meggie?"

Meghann nodded. "Aye. These recent months have opened my eyes. Running away from Belfast did no good at all."

Annie ran her finger across the fragile edge of her

cup. "I wouldn't say it was entirely for nothing. Where would my son be now if y' were someone other than y' are?"

Meghann reached across the table and covered the older woman's hand with her own. "Oh, Annie. Would Michael be who he is if I had stayed?"

"No one determines another's fate, Meggie. Even God says we have free will. Michael made his choices just as you did. Never blame y'rself. We're all very glad to have y' home. Now, tell me what t' do."

The windows were open. Lace curtains, Annie's favorite, caught the breeze and billowed like ladies' panniers, those absurd wide-hipped petticoats fashionable centuries before. Dust, caught in the light of a milk-colored sun, filtered in through the screens. Except for the measured ticking of the clock, the silence was absolute. Meghann rested her finger against her lips and listened. Where were the street noises, the bantering voices exchanging gossip over a shared fence, lads playing at hurling, shouting cheerful vulgarities when a ball missed its goal? Where were the prams crowded with babbling, rosy-cheeked children, the drone of a telly, a baby's cry, the bark of a dog, the slurred conversational hum of men who'd stayed too long in the pubs?

Something was wrong. Instincts acquired from those long-ago years in the Falls kicked in. Meghann resumed their dialogue, her voice higher and breathier than before, her words nothing like the ones she had planned to share. Deliberately, she reached over and gave Annie's hand a warning squeeze. "Don't do anything. Leave it all to me. Would you like to walk to the market before I go?"

Annie stood, instantly alerted. "That's kind of you, Meggie. I'll find my jumper and we'll give it a go."

Meghann relaxed, rested her chin on her hand and casually inspected the back entrance. How much had they heard, and when would they make an appearance? She heard Annie's footsteps on the floor above.

Without warning, the screen door opened and a man wearing a balaclava stepped inside and leveled a firearm at her chest. Meghann froze. She heard her breath, loud and rasping in the silent room.

"Easy now," a voice behind her spoke. "There's no need t' upset yourself. We won't hurt you."

Meghann's ear was exceptional. She'd heard that voice before. "What are you doing here?" she managed, keeping her eyes on the man holding the gun.

"Do y' know who I am, Miss McCarthy?" he asked.

"Yes."

"Good girl. Lies accomplish nothing."

Upstairs, the toilet flushed. Meghann wet her lips. "What do you want?"

"Information."

She laughed shakily and some of her fear dissipated. "That's what I want."

"Suppose we share what we know?"

"That's a lovely idea, but it won't work."

"Why not?"

Annie's footsteps sounded on the stairs. The masked man had changed position. His gun was pointed at a spot over Meghann's head, the exact spot where Annie would have a straight view of her kitchen.

Meghann turned around and looked into Andrew Maguire's pale eyes. "Because a man who sells out a friend can't be trusted."

His skin reddened.

"Jesus, Mary and Joseph!" Annie's outraged voice filled the room. "What are y' doin' in my kitchen with a gun, Andrew Maguire? I won't have weapons in my house." She looked at his dirt-stained clothing and wrinkled her nose. "Y' look like something washed up from the sewer. Take y'r man outside and clean him up."

Maguire nodded politely. "How are y' feeling this morning, Mrs. Devlin?"

"I'll feel much better when you and your friend have seen the better part of a bar of soap."

"We were just leaving," Andrew assured her. "Please go back upstairs, Mrs. Devlin. I need to speak privately with Meghann."

Annie opened her mouth to protest, but Meghann cut her off before she could speak. "It's all right, Annie. Do as he says. I'll be up in a minute."

Maguire watched Annie leave the room before shifting to meet Meghann's gaze. "They'll settle on a lesser charge if y' pull out of Michael's defense and allow Miles French to become lead counsel."

Shock, followed by a quick surge of triumph, momentarily robbed Meghann of speech. They were afraid of her. But why? There must be something else, some small piece of evidence she had missed.

Years in the courtroom helped her cultivate just the right expression, a combination of self-control and polite disinterest. "I don't think so," she said softly.

"Let Michael be the judge of that."

Meghann stiffened and her facade slipped. "Apparently you don't know Michael as well as you think you do."

Maguire nodded to the masked man and backed away toward the door leading outside. "Discuss it with Michael. He'll see that it's best for all of us. I'll be in touch."

Meghann waited a full five minutes until the neighborhood sounds normalized before calling for Annie to come down the stairs.

"Lord, Meggie." Annie joined Meghann in the sitting room. "I thought the worst."

Drawing her knees up to her chin, Meghann chewed her thumbnail and thought out loud. "They're offering Michael a lesser charge if I leave his defense to Miles French."

"Would Michael have to plead guilty?" asked Annie.

"Aye."

Annie sat down on a straight-backed chair and frowned. "How would Andrew come by that bit of information?"

Meghann froze. Of course. That was it, the missing piece. Andrew Maguire was IRA. He had no authority to make promises for the British government. Either he was lying or— Dear God!

Her hand flew to her lips. Why hadn't she thought of it before? Because the idea was preposterous. Another thought occurred to her, icing the blood in her veins. If she hadn't had the foresight to involve the press, what would her own life be worth after such an idea had been handed to her?

"What are you thinking, Meggie?"

Annie's face looked like death. Shaking off her ominous thoughts, Meghann smiled, stood and walked over to where her godmother sat. Kneeling at her feet, she took Annie's work-worn hand in her own. "I don't know whether Andrew Maguire has any authority. But it doesn't matter. In the eyes of the world's newspapers, Michael must be separated from all IRA association. It is the press who will try him publicly and decide his guilt or innocence. Believe me, Annie. If they decide Michael is innocent, the British government will fall into line."

20

❦

Nuala, Tirconnaill, 1598

"I wish to keep him with me."

Rory's face hardened. "It isn't possible."

"Please, Rory," I begged, twisting the costly velvet of my gown between my hands. "He's but a babe, barely weaned. Wait until he's old enough to be fostered."

Rory stood and walked to the fire. We were in his private chambers, where I had not been invited for over a year. I saw only his back and the rigid lines of his body. He meant to refuse me. I could feel it.

"I know what you want, Nuala," he said, his voice gone low and cold. "You would keep the child at Dun Na Ghal and force me to recognize him as my own." He turned and fixed upon me a look such as I had never seen from Rory. "Hear me now. It will not happen. Niall Garv's son will never have Dun Na Ghal."

I wished to wound him as he had wounded me. Lifting my head, I met his gaze and flung the words at him. "No man with Irish blood will ever have Dun Na

Ghal. Before Niall's son is grown the English will have conquered all that is left of Ireland."

"If you are as sure as you say, then why——" He stopped and frowned.

I knew what he asked. Only a man would ask such a question. Defeated, I sat down on a low stool. "Because he is my son," I said, "the only child I will ever have. I cannot live without him."

His laugh held more bitterness than humor. "You are a woman of remarkable resources, my love. You will live. You always do." He turned away again. "Prepare yourself. I have sent for Niall."

I gasped. "How could you? It is I who should have told him."

Rory words dripped with sarcasm. "When were you planning this confession?"

My cheeks burned, but I refused to look away.

He crossed the room and stood before me, lifting my chin to meet his accusing gaze. His mouth twisted. "Just as I thought. A man has a right to his son, Nuala."

"More than likely Niall has a dozen bastard sons while I have only one."

"Niall has no sons or daughters."

"How can you possibly know that?"

"He is my cousin. His seed was never spilled lightly."

I could not prevent the blush stealing across my chest and cheeks. Rory saw it immediately, and his words spewed bitterness. "What was it like for you, Nuala? Did Niall please you? Did you think of me when you spread your legs for him?"

If he had asked in good faith, I would have answered him differently. But his words were laced with contempt.

"I've already told you," I said coldly. "Once, I wanted him, and although my desire soon passed, I cannot change what was."

269

If ever Rory would strike me, it would be now, at this moment. I watched him struggle with his emotions, watched the anger rise within him, war with his pride and fade from his eyes. Once again he was in control, the chief of Dun Na Ghal.

"Niall will come for the child after he returns from London." He forced me to look directly at him. "You may go with him if you wish. I would not keep you against your will."

My reply froze on my tongue. I was close to collapsing. Wetting my lips, I opened my mouth to speak. Nothing came out. I tried again. "You are generous, my lord. I will think on it."

He nodded and looked pointedly at the door. We had nothing left to say. He wanted me away from him, out of his sight. I could not leave fast enough.

From my place on the battlements I watched him come. Without mail and only a bonnet covering his head, he rode at the head of a small company of men, his face hidden behind a metal plate. We had spent only a brief time together, yet I knew him immediately. Few men rode as he did, his body at one with the animal beneath him, his hands loose on the reins.

I swallowed. The time was near. It seemed as if my entire life was spent bidding farewell to yet another one of my children.

My mount was saddled. I rode out, alone with the boy. Rory would not interfere. He had pledged his word on it.

Too soon, I reached the slope of the hill that marked the halfway point between Dun Na Ghal and the ridge where Niall waited, still on horseback. I saw him remove his bonnet. He handed it to the man behind him and rode toward me, alone. My mouth tasted like ash. I could scarcely breathe. My arms must have tightened because the baby whimpered in his sleep. I kissed his downy head and breathed in the delicious scent of him. "Holy Mother of God, please help me through this," I prayed, closing my eyes against the inevitable.

"Hello, Nuala."

Slowly, I lifted my eyelids and stared at the man who had been my lover. His coppery hawk's face was very brown, and his eyes were narrowed against the sun. Framing his face was the shining hair that once, in a moment of madness, I had yearned to touch. The words I had practiced refused to come. Speechless, I could only stare.

"Have you nothing to say to me, Nuala?"

Mutely, I shook my head. He urged his mount closer and gently removed the child from my arms. For a long moment he looked at the lad we had made together. Then he looked up and smiled. My breath caught. He was pleased, more than pleased. He was wildly happy. Without warning, he leaned over, with the babe still between us, drew me close and kissed me soundly.

I pulled away, mentally cursing the fairness of my skin for its tendency to color. "Don't do that," I snapped.

He grinned. "It's lovely to hear your voice, Nuala. I was afraid you wouldn't speak to me."

Niall always caught me at a disadvantage. He was too charming and much too handsome for a woman whose husband no longer shared her bed. I looked away.

His voice changed. "You will speak to me, won't you? I have forgiven you for not telling me of the child."

"There is nothing to say. This day fills you with joy. 'Tis not the same for me."

His words were pitiless. "You should thank the Virgin Mother and all the saints that I want my son. Not every man would under the circumstances."

I lifted my head and looked at him. "I also want my son."

The warmth left his face, deepening the hollows. "Spare me your blame. Rory does not want him at Dun Na Ghal. The tone of his missive was clear."

Suddenly I was furious. "This is all your fault. If you hadn't come, my children would be alive. You raped me and left me with child and now you would take him from me."

His voice was cold as stone. "Your memory is clouded. It was not rape. I asked you to come with me. I wanted you. I've always wanted you. I waited and waited until my head throbbed and I thought of nothing but the ache in my groin. Still I waited, until the night you appeared before me, half-naked, with loose hair and painted lips. You wanted me as well. You would have wanted me still if Rory hadn't ordered the burning of Dun Na Ghal."

"That isn't true," I whispered.

"Aye, it is so, whether or not you will voice it."

I stared at him accusingly. "You are cruel, Niall Garv O'Donnell. Why did I never see it before this?"

Without answering he changed the subject. "News from Dun Na Ghal reaches even beyond the pale."

"What are you saying?"

"I know that the chief of Dun Na Ghal no longer shares his wife's bed."

I blushed furiously. "That is no concern of yours."

He hesitated and studied my face as if the words he would say were unpleasant to him. Finally he spoke. "Everything about you concerns me. Rory will not wait forever for a woman, not even if the woman is his wife."

"How can you know such a thing?"

"Our world is a small one."

I shook my head. "Rory will not put me away. I know him better than you."

A cool wind rose from the east, rustling the marsh

grass. Niall's stallion danced beneath him. He shifted the baby to his other arm to better control his mount. When the horse was quiet again, he resumed our conversation. "No woman knows a man better than one of his own blood."

Niall had voiced my own suspicions. Tears burned beneath my eyelids. Blinking, I forced them back. "Perhaps 'tis your own mind you speak of and 'tis you who would not be faithful to your wife."

He whitened under his tan and his face was very stern. "I do not lie with harlots. You, of all women, should know that." His mouth gentled. "I would give my life for you, Nuala. My intent was to open your eyes, nothing more. Rory said he would not hold you if you wished to leave him. Come with me. I offer you a life with honor. Be a mother to our son and the ones that will surely follow."

Nothing had changed. I loved Rory no less nor Niall more. But it was heaven to hear that I was wanted. The voices within urged me to accept him. After all, there was nothing for me at Dun Na Ghal. No husband, no children, not ever.

Then I realized what Niall could not have guessed. My mind battled with the demons of my conscience. I glanced at his face. His skin was drawn tightly across the high bones of his cheeks. He waited for my answer. I must give it. Despite what he had done to me, Niall had fathered my son and he loved me. For that alone he deserved the truth. "I can bear no more children," I whispered. "The lad is my last child. I would risk it but Rory will not."

"Nor should he," replied Niall. "My God, Nuala, I am sorry."

No longer able to speak, I merely nodded and would have turned away but Niall reached out and held my reins. "You haven't answered me, my love. Will you come home with me and be my wife?"

The man was addled. "Did you not hear me?"

"It changes nothing."

"I can give you no more children. You should wed a woman who can bring you heirs."

He nodded at the bairn in his arms. "I have an heir. I need a wife."

For that single moment I loved him. But I knew it would pass just as I knew that I could not take advantage of his kindness. He deserved a woman who would not measure him against Rory O'Donnell. I covered his hand with mine. "May God bless you, Niall Garv. Take our son and raise him well. Tell him that I shall always love him. Send him to me when he is grown."

He straightened and withdrew his hand, cradling the babe against his chest. "Are you sure, Nuala?"

"Aye."

"It will not be easy for you at Dun Na Ghal."

"No."

"If I thought he would be safe, I would leave the lad with you."

"Please don't." I could bear no more of his sympathy. Pulling on the reins, I turned toward Dun Na Ghal.

His voice carried on the wind. "I'll wait, Nuala. I'll wait forever."

I rode through the open gates at full speed, pulling tightly on the reins as I neared the banquet hall entrance. Perhaps what Niall told me was true. Perhaps, even now, Rory was with a woman. Sliding from the saddle, I threw the reins to the stable boy and hurried inside.

The hall was quiet and very dark, steeped in the shadows of late afternoon. I could hear my heart pound as I climbed the stairs. Rory's chamber was my destination. But as I climbed, my courage left me as my imagination grew. His door would be bolted. Should I knock and reveal myself, or should I wait until they came out together?

Pride rose within me and my steps slowed. I would accomplish nothing by playing the wounded victim. If Rory wanted a castle wench, he would take her. Accusations would accomplish nothing except raise in the woman a sense of false importance. No. I was Nuala O'Donnell, descendant of kings, countess of Dun Na Ghal. I would keep my position and let Rory believe I knew of his sin and it troubled me not at all. Of course, there might be no sin at all. Rory had never been unfaithful to me. He had told me so himself, and of the all things he did well, lying was not one of them.

21

Meghann entered the roundabout, flipped on her left turn signal and exited from the far left lane toward the N63 at Balyclare. County Roscommon and Clonalis House, principal residence of Denis and Georgiana O'Conor, lay ahead. Although Georgiana had invited her often, it was the first time Meghann had ever visited the remote seat of the ancient O'Conor chiefs.

Georgiana Reddington had been the first Protestant with whom Meghann had ever carried on a conversation. They had met years before at Queen's University while searching the boards for their exam results. Scores had been posted since morning, but Meghann's shift at O'Malley's Tea Shop began at 7 A.M. It was after five before she wiped down the last counter, locked the door and caught the coach to the Gothic buildings that were Belfast's proudest landmarks.

Behind the pointed wrought-iron gates, blue papers boldly marked with the black ink of matriculation or failure were visible through the glass display cases mounted on the walls. The courtyard was empty except for a slim blond in black jeans and a blue, too-large pullover.

Meghann recognized her immediately. Lady Georgiana Reddington was the only daughter of Nigel Reddington, duke of Somerset, and his ex-wife, American film star Hilary Wade. Before enrolling at Queen's, Georgiana spent summers with her mother amid the glitz of Beverly Hills, California, and the remainder of the year in the rolling hills of Somerset, her father's estate in England.

For the past several years her Nordic good looks had been a common sight in the tabloids, beginning with her break from convention when she attended the opening at Ascot on the arm of a married Brazilian soccer player. From the soccer player she had moved on to the lead singer of a rock band recently paroled after serving time for a heroin conviction. Her newest conquest was the owner of a controversial pornography magazine for which she had posed as a centerfold, tripling the magazine's circulation. Her mother's amusement angered her even more than her father's fury, which had resulted in her banishment to Queen's.

Meghann didn't buy the tabloids, but the magazine rack was located at the market stand where she bought her groceries. The celebrity status of a fellow classmate was too tempting to ignore. Openly, Meghann shook her head at such an obvious bid for attention, but secretly she admired the girl. Georgiana Reddington was a rebel and she wasn't afraid of public disapproval. She was also extremely intelligent. The scores posted behind the protective glass reflected the girl's honors standing.

Generally Meghann's reserve with strangers reflected itself in cool politeness, which was why she never quite knew what made her volunteer her unsolicited comment. "I wonder what y' could have done if you'd come t' class now and then."

The blond girl turned her cropped head in Meghann's direction and stared. "Do you disapprove of me, Miss McCarthy?"

Meghann looked startled. "Not at all. How do y' know my name?"

The girl shrugged carelessly, pulled out a roll of peppermints from the pocket of her jeans and offered one to Meghann. "Everyone knows you."

Meghann took the mint and transferred it to the zippered compartment of her handbag. The girl looked amused. "You didn't have to take it if you didn't want it."

"I want it," Meghann replied, "but I may want it even more later."

"You're very careful, aren't you? I mean, that's why you're at the top of the list."

"Am I?" Meghann turned away from Georgiana's probing gaze and looked for her student number. It was on top, just as she'd expected it to be. "How did y' know it was mine?"

"The same way you knew mine. We've got the same number except for the last digit. I'm competing with you."

At that, Meghann laughed. "It's a poor sort of competition you're offering. You never attend class, you don't participate in study groups, and there are zeros next to your last three themes. I'd have to be an idiot t' come in after you."

Georgiana lifted one darkened eyebrow and motioned toward the posted scores. "A great many did."

Meghann sighed. "Yes, they did. Perhaps I have more at stake."

"What *do* you have at stake, Meghann McCarthy?"

Somehow Meghann knew that the question wasn't a formality, a well-brought-up girl passing time until she could leave her present company. There was something desperate about this pale-skinned blond with the dreadful haircut and garish lipstick, something desperate and sad. Under her speculative gaze the girl flushed. It was that, and the unexpected trembling of her mouth, that caused Meghann to make a decision completely out of character. "Have y' had tea, Lady Reddington?"

"Call me Georgiana. No, I haven't."

"Will y' join me?"

"With pleasure. I'm stuck in student lodging. Shall we go to your flat?"

Meghann swallowed. Her flat on the outskirts of Queen's was a poor setting for a girl whose father was a duke. She was about to refuse when she looked once more into the red-rimmed blue eyes. What she saw made her change her mind.

Straightening her shoulders, Meghann linked her arm through Georgiana's and took a deep breath. "I'm sure it isn't what you're used to but I can't afford any more."

"You'd be surprised at what I'm used to," the girl said wryly, allowing herself to be pulled along. "Lead on, Meghann. I'm starved."

Rain drummed on the roof, fogging the windows and drowning the newly planted seeds in the flower garden outside Meghann's flat. But inside the small sitting room the air was warm, the tea milky-sweet, the day-old biscuits crisp and the conversation satisfying.

From that day on an unusual friendship was forged, a friendship based on little more than a shared setting and an appreciation of opposites. Meghann's protective reserve melted before the blond girl's greater need, and Georgiana, raised in England and liberal America, had no patience for the prejudice of the Northern Ireland problem. She simply refused to allow Meghann to dwell on it.

Although never mentioned, an unspoken agreement existed between the two that prevented them from extending their relationship beyond the confines of university life. Never once did Meghann set foot on the massive estate in the south of England that was Georgiana's home. Nor was Georgiana invited into Annie's spice-scented kitchen with its plastic-framed pictures of the Virgin Mary, although the entrance to the Falls was only a ten-minute ride to the west of the university.

Both respected the sanctity of the other's right to live and behave as she wished until May 5, 1981, when the Irish political prisoner, Bobby Sands, died from starvation in Long Kesh prison camp.

Meghann never knew Bobby Sands. He wasn't from Belfast and he'd already been in prison for more than eight years before he died. Sinn Fein stood him for their MP and he won by more than two thousand votes, a slim majority but more than Margaret Thatcher's lead when she ran for prime minister. To protest the loss of political status, Bobby Sands began a hunger strike that led to the death of thirteen men and brought the Irish problem to the doorsteps of the world.

For Meghann, intent on removing herself from the torturous inequity of life in Northern Ireland, the hunger strike was one more stake in the bleeding heart of a population that would forever live in the throes of war. For Georgiana, it was the first real cause of her life, and she embroiled herself completely, so completely that had it not been for Meghann, and Meghann's careful nature that her friend so deplored, it would have cost the young Englishwoman much more than the money that appeared regularly every quarter in her bank account.

Driving through the haunting beauty of Roscommon, the county that had inspired so many Irish laments, Meghann knew that Georgiana would not have forgotten the circumstances of her debt. The fear that kept her knuckles white and her foot pressed to the pedal around hairpin turns and country roads

crowded with sheep had everything to do with whether Georgiana was finally prepared to pay.

Clonalis House was everything the guidebooks
promised it would be. Located just outside of Castlerea at the end of a long, winding, tree-studded drive, it
stood, a three-storied Georgian structure covered in
lichen, sentinel to a distant age. A tour bus sat in the
gravel carpark, testimony to the historical significance
of the O'Conor home. Meghann swung her compact
into the lot near the bus, collected her bag and walked
up the stone steps.

The door was ajar. Stepping into the wood-lined
entry, she waited for her eyes to adjust to the typical
dimness of a country manor house. No one was
about. A Louis XVI couch done up in a floral pattern
stood behind a cherry hunter's table, its center dominated by a priceless Waterford vase filled with Queen
Anne's lace, fuchsia, wild mustard, foxglove and
rhododendron, flora that grew wild along the roads of
Ireland. Beside an ornamental mahogany screen
carved in an Oriental style stood a sideboard covered
with neatly stacked leaflets advertising the sights of
Roscommon. Elegantly faded Persian carpets covered
the oak floorboards, and a magnificent mantel clock
announced that it was past four o'clock. Hanging on a
side wall, reflecting it all, was a beveled mirror in an
intricately carved and gilded frame. Voices came from
the hallway, faint at first and then growing stronger.

Meghann sat on the couch and waited. A slim
young woman with Irish skin and clear blue eyes led a
group of men and women wearing anoraks and cameras into the entry, where she thanked them for
booking their tour of Clonalis House and pointed
them toward the tearoom. Then she turned to Meghann. "May I help you?" she asked politely.

"I'm here to see Georgiana O'Conor," Meghann
explained. "She's expecting me."

"I'll tell her you've arrived," the woman said, disappearing through the hallway once again.

Meghann hadn't long to wait before Georgiana, beautiful and serenely confident, welcomed her warmly. "I hope you intend to stay the weekend," she said, leading Meghann into a meticulously restored drawing room. "I told Denis to cut short his golfing plans and hurry home. I'm dying to have him meet you."

Meghann stared at her friend in admiration. It was true that she hadn't seen Georgiana in years, but she would never have imagined that anyone could change so completely. Gone was the unevenly cropped hair, the bitten-down fingernails, the blood-red lipstick and the jittery laugh that, more than anything else, had reflected insecurity. The new Georgiana sported a shoulder-length bob, a cashmere pullover and tailored slacks. Her dark eyes were artfully made up, and her lips were outlined in a flesh tone a shade darker than her skin. She radiated such contentment that Meghann's heart sank. How could she bring up the past and destroy what Georgiana had achieved?

"You'll love Denis," Georgiana continued. "I've told him all about you." She waved Meghann into a chair across from her own and pulled the bell rope. "Do you like it?" she asked, waving her arms to encompass the room. "This house isn't all that old actually, only a little over a hundred years or so, but we've so many artifacts that it seems much older. Denis says we're sleeping with ghosts. Of course, he doesn't mind a bit. He grew up here."

The young tour guide entered the room with a tray of tea and pastries. "Set it here, Lucy," Georgiana said, scooting to the edge of her chair. "You're welcome to join us if you like."

"Thanks all the same," the girl said, placing the tea tray on the card table beside Georgiana, "but I'm in a rush to get back to Dublin. If you don't need anything else, I'll be leaving now."

Georgiana laughed. "Run along then. I can remember when Dublin was more to my liking than a quiet place like Castlerea." She turned to Meghann. "Do you still take your tea with milk and sugar?"

"Yes, thank you." Meghann accepted the cup and saucer.

"I was sorry to hear about your husband, Meghann. My father said David Sutton was a fine man."

Meghann sipped her tea. "Yes, he was." She changed the subject. "How did you meet your husband?"

Georgiana's eyes danced. "In a pub."

"You're joking."

"I was tipsy. No, I was more than tipsy. I was sloshed. It was quite humiliating really, but it's the truth. It was after—," she hesitated. "Well, you know. I was about to leave when I fell flat on my face. The next thing I remember was waking up in a strange man's bed with all my clothes on. I don't know which shocked me more, finding myself in bed with a strange man or finding myself in bed with a stranger with all my clothes on. He was deliciously handsome, even though I didn't notice it at first. It took a while, but he was patient, and by the time I knew that I couldn't live without him, he asked me to marry him." She looked up and the laugh lines deepened around her mouth. "Father hates him, which is a point in Denis's favor, don't you think?"

Meghann frowned. "Why would your father hate him?"

"Because Denis is Irish Catholic, of course." She waved away her father's disapproval. "Don't worry. We're not entirely estranged. That ended after the children were born. The duke of Somerset couldn't very well resist his own grandchildren."

Meghann looked down at her teacup. "No, I don't imagine that he could."

Georgiana sighed. "You look as if you've the weight of the world on your shoulders, Meghann. Would you like to talk about it?"

Shaking her head, Meghann set down her cup. "I've come on a fool's errand. Let's not talk about it. You said you had a baby. Boy or girl?"

"Two girls and a boy, and they're not babies anymore. Sarah, the youngest, is visiting her aunt in Dublin." She probed gently. "Is it about this case you've taken up?"

Meghann looked directly at her friend. "Yes, it is."

"You were wondering if I could help."

Meghann nodded. "Yes," she said again. "But now I see that it's impossible."

"Why?"

Meghann looked around at the elegant Victorian drawing room, at the Sheffield furnishings, the pink and gold Minton china, the original carpet woven in identical shades of pink and gold, the velvet upholstery and the stern faces of generations of O'Conors staring down at her. "Don't ask, Georgie. Seeing you here, like this, makes me realize how foolish it was to think you could do anything. I'm sorry I bothered you."

"I want to know, Meghann. I want to know what it is about Michael Devlin that made you accept a ten-year-old invitation to visit my home when nothing I said or did would make you come earlier."

Meghann twisted the delicately edged lace napkin in her lap. "Michael Devlin is the boy I grew up with. He's the reason I left the Falls."

"Oh, Meggie." Georgiana laughed softly. "You would never have stayed in the Falls. Don't give him that much credit."

"It's not credit I'm giving him," Meghann said quickly. "Besides, you don't understand. The Falls isn't like the Shankill. It's a real community, with professional people living right alongside everyone else. If you're Catholic that's where you live in Belfast. It's the only place that's safe."

Georgiana's dark eyes never left her face. "You don't have to tell me about the Falls, Meghann."

Meghann felt the red wash across her face. "No, I don't suppose I do."

"You were filling me in on Michael Devlin."

"He's been set up. He didn't do it."

"Are you sure?"

"Yes."

Georgiana left her tea untouched. "Who is responsible?"

Meghann sighed with relief and sank back into the comfortable chair cushions. She should have known that Georgiana would believe her. "I don't know for sure. At first I thought Paisley's group and then the IRA. But now I think there's more to it." In clear, concise terms, leaving nothing out, Meghann explained how she had reached her conclusion.

Georgiana sat with her back straight, never once interrupting. When Meghann had finished, she stood and walked over to the window. The heavy drapes had been pulled aside, and an enormous window reflected a postcard view of well-kept lawns, huge trees and pristine gardens, the ancient seat of the O'Conor Dons, kings of Ireland and Connaught. She was silent for a long time. At last she spoke. "Do you know how long the O'Conors have lived here, Meghann?"

"Fifteen hundred years or thereabouts."

Georgiana nodded without turning around. "I should have known what your answer would be. You always did pay attention to your history. You're right, of course. The O'Conors are the oldest family in all of Europe. Denis can trace his ancestors back to the first century, back to King Conor of *Emain Macha*. For fifteen hundred years an O'Conor chief has left his mark on Irish history."

She pointed toward a portrait on the wall. "That's Denis O'Conor. He would be the man to interest you, Meghann. In a historic case, he won a portion of his lands back after his father lost them fighting against William of Orange. Next to him is Owen O'Conor, who became the first Catholic member of Parliament in Roscommon after Catholic Emancipation. He was succeeded by his son and grandson." She nodded toward the portrait of a stern-looking man with fine blue eyes. "That was Charles Owen O'Conor, founder of the Gaelic League. He was responsible for having the Irish language included in the school curriculum."

She turned around, a slim figure outlined against the drapes, centuries of aristocratic breeding evident in her regal carriage. "Do you have any idea what it is that you are asking of me?"

Meghann stood and walked across the room to stand before the girl who once had been in love with Andrew Maguire, leader of the Belfast Brigade of the Irish Republican Army, the girl who had thrown gasoline bombs at British tanks. "Before your speech I wasn't about to ask you to risk everything you've achieved since our Belfast days. But you've convinced me otherwise, Georgiana. You're an O'Conor by marriage. Your children carry the O'Conor bloodline. Through every adversity possible, through death and famine and destruction and penal laws, the O'Conors have been true to Ireland and to their faith. Can you do any less?"

"Ireland isn't in question, nor is Catholicism. The IRA are terrorists. You've as much as admitted that Michael was one of them. Why should I do anything to help him?"

Meghann whitened, and then her eyes blazed with angry golden sparks. "How dare you criticize Michael after what you were and what you've done."

Georgiana flinched. "I suppose I deserve that."

"Without your help, a man will go to prison for the rest of his life for a crime he didn't commit."

"I have children and neighbors and a life that I love."

"Does your husband know about Belfast?"

"Of course he does, but I'm sure he wouldn't wish it spread about the golf club."

"The Georgiana Reddington I knew would never let an innocent man suffer," Meghann said slowly.

"The Georgiana Reddington you knew was a desperate fool," Georgiana shot back.

Meghann knew when an argument was lost. She had spent too long at the Old Bailey to continue hammering when there was no longer the possibility of winning. Georgiana refused to open old wounds. Not that Meghann blamed her, or at least she wouldn't have if her client had been anyone but Michael. She rubbed shaking hands against the nubby tweed of her skirt. "I understand. I'm sorry to have troubled you. Under the circumstances I think I should leave. Give my regards to your husband."

"Meghann." The desperate plea stopped Meghann at the door. "Don't leave. I'll speak to Denis. Perhaps there's another way."

Meghann sighed. She was in no position to refuse any possibility of help, no matter how small the crumb. Besides, Belfast was two hours away and the house really was lovely. "Thank you, Georgiana. If you really want me and you're sure it's no trouble, I'd love to stay the night."

Georgiana relaxed. "Come along. I'll show you to your room. You can rest if you like or we can take a walk before dinner."

Meghann sat on the green satin settee by the window and looked around her room for the night. During her marriage she had become accustomed to the size and splendor of aristocratic country homes, but this one affected her differently. The lemony wallpaper with its flecks of green, the cherry dressing table and matching desk, the massive four-poster bed and the bathroom with its clawed tub and wing-back chair, twice the size of her own master bedroom in London, were lovely but not unusual enough to create the sense of timelessness that now held her in its grip.

Through the window she saw horses, their noses deep in pasture grass. Golden calves lay beside the cleanest milk cows Meghann had ever seen, and down the gravel road, behind a copse of cypress trees in the middle of a muted wood, lay the ruin of the first O'Conor castle, the one that Dermot O'Conor had surrendered to Rory O'Donnell in 1599. How odd that she'd known that. The date had jumped into her mind as easily as if she recited it every day of her life.

Meghann's eyelids felt heavy. The peat burned cozily in the grate, burning off the room's chill. Pulling the afghan around her, she leaned back against the pillows and closed her eyes. Her hand moved to the oval at her throat. Behind her lids the flames grew, rising above the mesh screen, throwing an arc of light against the south wall. Shadows danced along the frieze, twisting into figures, first narrow, then wide, then reshaping again until they assumed human form.

Her fingers played with the locket. It was almost over now, her sojourn into Nuala's life. She'd studied the documents, especially the dates. Nuala had died shortly after the battle of Kinsale.

Meghann wanted to resist, to prolong the finale for as long as possible. There were no happy endings for this story. For some inexplicable reason, Meghann had come to depend on Nuala. There was comfort in their shared conversation and the occasional glimpses into her mind. Once it ended, would the ties between them be broken? Would she ever see Nuala again?

For the first time, here in the antique splendor of

Georgiana's country home, Meghann admitted to herself that she was terrified, terrified of losing her case, terrified of losing Nuala, her one ally, and most of all, terrified of permanently losing Michael.

Andrew Maguire's reputation in his community was second to none. It was his only claim to the power he wielded more thoroughly than any elected official. Without Georgiana to expose his true character, his testimony would be accepted as gospel and there was every likelihood that Michael would spend the rest of his life in prison with no possibility of parole.

22

Nuala, Tirconnaill, 1599

Despite our differences, I was the countess of Tirconnaill and my loyalties had not changed. When Elizabeth of England sent Robert Devereux, earl of Essex, and his army of sixteen thousand men against the Catholic earls of Ulster, I gathered the strength of my resources to divert them.

It went against all that Rory believed not to meet them in fair combat, but I tried to make him see it was the only way we could win. I urged him to allow Essex to take castle after castle without a fight, leaving his soldiers behind to guard his holdings. Fool that he was, Essex decimated his army, leaving too few men to hold the castles he'd claimed and too few to fight the battle he faced against the O'Neill and his allies. Marching farther and farther into the rain-wet mists of the north country, with only a fraction of the army he'd started with, Essex had no choice but to accept our conditions. The O'Neill was as canny an old fox as any Irishman ever born, and I had inherited some of his gift for strategy.

I was not bothered by stories of Irish cowardice. I

was the daughter of a fighter and had learned my lessons well. Knowing when to draw back and when to strike gave Rory many a victory. The Irish wars were wars of the frontier and the forest. The Englishman relied on the fort or castle he had erected against the wilderness. The Gael relied on the forest, his defense the wilderness. If a castle was taken by the British in three days, an Irish army would camp beneath it for weeks, destroy the caravan of provisions sent to fortify the men inside and wait until hunger drove them out. Castles fell without a single shot. The Irish war was a defensive one. We simply waited the enemy out.

Only once did Rory ignore my advice and wage the war of the aggressor. It was in Connaught, that terrible desolate land where Cromwell had driven what was left of the population of Northern Ireland after he'd ordered old men, woman and children to be thrown to their deaths off the bridge of Enniskillen. Richard Bingham, Elizabeth's lieutenant, held our people in a yolk of oppressive tyranny. It was the only time in two years that I asked to meet with my husband privately.

He came to me in the late afternoon when the mists came up from the boglands, swallowing the trees in lengthening circles of silver-gray smoke. The last vestiges of winter light poured through the large window I had ordered installed in the book-lined room. I sat at the desk, accounts forgotten, fingers stained with ink, staring out at what was left of the day. The familiar ache that I was to forever associate with Rory came over me. My throat moved in an effort to swallow. At that moment I would have handed my kingdom over to Essex to regain what we had lost.

I turned to look at him, and the full force of his gaze moved over me. "You came quickly, Rory. I thank you."

"Your message sounded urgent."

"Aye." I picked up a letter from my desk. "You are accused of the murder of George Bingham. Essex demands your immediate surrender."

"Aye."

I rose to stand before him "Is that all you have to say?"

"Essex is a coward. I'd not expected him to demand my surrender."

"What did you expect, Rory? You put to death every man between fifteen and sixty, sparing none unless they spoke Irish. You burned Longford and returned it to O'Farrell. You returned with the spoils of the Protestants. Not a single settler, farmer or Englishman living outside the protection of the forts remains alive. When a man leads an army on a rampage of death and destruction, should he expect no more than a slap on the wrist?"

I was coldly, bitterly angry. Rory tried to defend himself. He looked away and mumbled, " 'Twas all for Connaught."

"Connaught was years ago. You have destroyed everything that I've worked for, all my efforts of the last decade. While your war was fought for the purpose of keeping your lands and those of the Ulster chieftains, Elizabeth dallied with you. She danced between you and the warhawks in Parliament, satisfying their demand for Irish land. Do you actually believe that she will countenance this one? Holy God, Rory, you have sentenced us to death."

"That I can live with. I am a Celt, raised on the tales of King Conor and Brian Boru. Death holds no fear for me."

Standing before him, my back unyielding as Irish steel, I spoke the words that needed to be said. My words were low and calm and filled with unmistakable contempt. "You might have thought of the rest of us. We have no such desire to die before our rightful time. 'Tis a poor chieftain who cares nothing for those who depend on him."

Without knowing it I'd turned the subject, giving him the lead he wanted. Connaught was forgotten.

"Do you still depend on me, Nuala?"

I rubbed my arms. "Like it or not, I must." It had been so long since we'd spoken of what stood between us. Had he really consigned Niall Garv to the past?

"My heart aches for you, my love," he said. "I am nothing without you."

"'Tis a cold love you offer, husband. If you would have the truth, I would rather be in your bed than in your heart."

"I would have it both ways, Nuala."

I looked at him curiously. "Is that true, Rory? Have you forgotten Niall?"

He reached for my hands and drew my slight body against the length of his. Like warm butter, I molded against him, shaping myself to his contours with the familiarity of experience. Although I fought it, my body shuddered with wanting.

"Niall is in the past, Nuala," he murmured. "I have not forgotten, as you do not forget the bairn that is yours and his. But we must go on, and I would have it be together."

My arms circled my waist for a brief moment before I pulled away and voiced the suspicion that never left my heart. "I would have us be husband and wife again, Rory, but I will not share you."

He frowned. "What are you saying? There is no one else, Nuala. You share me with no one."

"Truly, Rory. Will everything be as it was in the beginning?"

I saw his face and knew that I had misunderstood.

"I cannot bed you, Nuala. To lose you would be to lose myself. I will not risk your life."

I turned away. "This is not living, Rory."

Meghann woke slowly, regretfully, with a feeling of urgency she wasn't yet prepared to meet. A persistent, twentieth-century sound invaded her dream, and despite all efforts it wouldn't go away. Groggily, she forced herself to wake and listen. Someone was knocking at the door.

"Meghann, are you all right?" Georgiana's voice sounded worried.

"I'm grand, Georgie, really I am." She sat up and swung her legs to the floor. It was becoming harder and harder to pull herself out of whatever was happening to her. Sometimes she was so very tired and everything appeared to be in such a jumbled mess that it was easier to stay in that other place, in another time, viewing another woman's life. It was absurd, of course. Involuntarily her hand reached for the locket, but she forced it back down to her side. There was no other woman, just her own very fertile imagination. "Wait a minute," she called out. "I'm coming."

Georgiana, slim and splendid in a turquoise skirt and lime sweater, stared reproachfully at her from the hallway. "I thought you'd passed out or something. I don't remember that you ever slept like that."

Meghann ran her hands through her hair. "It's been a long time since I've had a full eight hours. My mattress is marvelous. Do I have time for a wash before dinner?"

"Of course. I only came up to tell you that Denis is home. We'd like you to join us in the drawing room when you're ready."

Meghann stared at her friend's elegant clothing. "I didn't bring anything as fancy as your outfit. I hope I don't embarrass you."

Georgiana shook her head. How could someone like Meghann be so unaware of her appeal? "You could wear burlap and no one would notice anyone else."

Meghann looked surprised. "What is that supposed to mean?"

"It means that whatever you wear always looks wonderful. Do hurry, Meggie. Everyone is dying to meet you."

Georgiana's husband was handsome, witty, charming and, despite his Irish name and heritage, very much the English gentleman. Meghann's heart sank. Her judgment of character was usually quite accurate. Denis O'Conor wasn't a man to encourage his wife's excesses. Which was why she was completely taken aback when, after pouring her a glass of excellent sherry, he came right to the point. "Georgiana tells me you've taken counsel for Michael Devlin."

"That's right."

"Does he have a chance?"

Meghann sipped her sherry. No one would have known that her hands felt like ice and her heart hammered in her chest. "It depends."

"On—?"

"On what, precisely, you mean by *a chance.*"

Denis O'Conor laughed, and Meghann decided that it would be possible, after all, to like him.

"I've never met Mr. Devlin," he said, meeting her gaze steadily, "but I've read his work and I support his views. He's a nationalist but not a fanatic. I don't believe for a moment that he's a terrorist."

Meghann released her breath. "You're quite right, Denis. Michael isn't a terrorist, but I would be very interested in knowing how you came to that conclusion."

He took a moment to answer. "I've heard him speak. He approved of the cease-fire and argued for decommissioning. In fact, he's directly responsible for my voting pattern in the last two elections."

Meghann didn't realize she was shaking until some of her sherry splashed on her wrist. Denis O'Conor with his gray English eyes, his BBC English, his long, aristocratic fingers and his fifteen-hundred-year-old pedigree actually believed that he was a liberal. She wet her lips and said what she had driven from Belfast for. "Michael has a chance, but it would be a much better one with Georgiana's support. Is that possible?"

Denis O'Conor looked across the room to where his wife sat on the Georgian sofa. Their eyes met and held. Meghann held her breath, at first uncomfortable and then envious of the intimacy of their exchange. Finally Denis spoke. "The decision, of course, is her own. Whatever Georgiana does, I will support her."

Meghann watched as Georgiana bit her lip and downed a healthy swallow of her gin and tonic. Without meeting Meghann's eyes, she smiled bracingly at her husband. "Well, that's that, I suppose. The children will be down shortly. Shall we move to the dining room?"

All at once Meghann had no appetite. Denis stood over her chair and held out his arm. "Shall we?" he asked pleasantly.

Meghann stood. "I'm looking forward to it," she lied. "Isn't Clonalis on the tour of 'hidden Ireland'?"

"It is," he said. "Georgiana put us there. Without her recipes, her knowledge of O'Conor history and her ability to manage the hundreds of guests who traipse through here every year, I wouldn't even consider it."

"She's changed a great deal." As soon as they were out, Meghann wished the words back.

"Yes, she has," he said noncommittally.

Dinner was superb. Salmon mousse, spring lamb with rosemary, fresh garden vegetables and crème brûlée were served in succession, with enough time between courses to appreciate each one. Georgiana's children were pleasant, well-informed, confident and respectful. Meghann envied her.

Not that she wanted Denis O'Conor for herself even if he had been available. He was attractive enough, although a bit soft. Those who were generous would even call him handsome. But Meghann had already married a man whom she considered attractive and never once had he come close to inspiring the kind of bone-weakening lust that she now knew could exist between a man and a woman. Only one man had ever done that for her. That man had blazing blue eyes, sharp-cheeked Celtic bones and a way of speaking that sounded like music. No one would ever call him soft. Meghann might envy Georgiana her circumstances, but she wouldn't exchange places with her.

"Would you care to have a go-round at a game of chess after dinner, Meghann?" Denis asked politely.

"Oh, please, Denis," Georgiana begged. "I haven't seen Meghann in years. Enlist one of the children."

Two pairs of identical brown eyes looked up from their plates. "Do we have to, Mum?" Barbara O'Conor appealed to her mother. "The Ellis boys just returned from Dublin and we've plans for the evening."

Georgiana raised her eyebrows at her husband. "Denis?"

He sighed and nodded at his children. "Run along. I won't keep you from your friends tonight."

Without the two young people, so remarkably like their English mother, the room felt bereft of energy. Meghann wasn't the only one who felt it. Within moments Georgiana stood. "There's a lovely fire in the library. Let's have our coffee in there."

Meghann noticed the familiar smell of turf as soon as she stepped into the book-lined room. She inhaled deeply. The bogs of Roscommon produced the richest peat in the world, and the sweet, earthy odor of its singular turf distinguished the boglands of Ireland from those of its Scottish and Welsh neighbors.

Meghann looked around appreciatively. Among the treasures of Clonalis House was its library. Historically the O'Conors produced readers, with each generation adding to the inventory. Their library boasted over five thousand manuscripts, making it the finest private library in all of Ireland. An unusual rolltop desk faced the long, draped windows, and Georgian couches and chairs were tastefully arranged around the fireplace. Georgiana sat beside the tea service and ushered Meghann to a seat across from her.

"I won't keep you waiting, Meggie," she said matter-of-factly, her hands folded in her lap. "I don't think I can help you. I'll think about it but I won't promise anything and, quite frankly, my answer will probably be no. I won't put you off. I'll need a few days, perhaps a week. I know you're disappointed in me and I'm sorry. But when this is over, you and Michael will go off somewhere together and I'll be left with my life and my reputation in pieces. I hope you can appreciate my position even if you don't agree with it."

Meghann reached across Georgiana's tightly clasped hands and poured her own tea. Without adding milk or sugar, she stirred the dark liquid absently. "Of course, I understand," she said softly. "I didn't really expect you to agree." She sat silently for a long moment, tea forgotten, her mind somewhere else. Finally she remembered where she was. "Please consider this before you decide, Georgiana. Your life may be in pieces, and I don't mean to minimize that at all. But you'll have a life. Michael won't." Dry-eyed she looked across the table at her friend. "And neither will I."

Georgiana stared at the heartbreaking vulnerability so evident in Meghann's face and wondered, not for the first time, what it was about this woman that made everyone draw breath and take a second look. Meghann McCarthy was very lovely, very Irish and very reserved in her emotions. It wasn't like Meghann to fall apart over a man. Once, long ago, Georgiana had known what it was to love like that. Her lip trembled. "Oh Meggie," she whispered. "I wish it hadn't gone as far as that with you."

"I never had a choice," Meghann replied simply. "There is no one else like him."

"I've seen his pictures in the paper. He's very attractive."

Meghann waved the comment aside. "It's much more than that. When Michael walks into a room, everyone else disappears. There's a brightness about him. He draws people in with nothing more than his sheer presence." She shrugged self-consciously. "It isn't something I can explain. I don't even understand it."

"You don't have to explain, Meghann." Georgiana bit her lip and looked away. "I understand it completely."

Meghann nodded. "I thought you would," she said quietly. "That's why I came to you."

The next morning Georgiana braved the cold to stand on the steps and watch Meghann pull out of the gravel carpark. Looking back out of her rearview mirror Meghann noticed that she stood by the coronation stone of the O'Conor kings, the stone that had seen fifteen hundred years of O'Conor history. Georgiana had become absorbed in that history, so much so that it had become her own. The twenty years she had spent without Denis O'Conor, the years her personality and character were shaped, had faded and blown away like so many dried leaves before the October winds. Meghann held out little hope of help from Georgiana.

Belfast, 1995

Meghann walked across Donegall Square into the Linen Hall Library, named for the workhouses that once thronged the streets of Belfast's industrial district, and climbed the stairs to the reading room. As usual it was filled with men and newspapers. A familiar surge of annoyance flared in her chest, quelling the smile she would have sent the young man who looked up from the opposite table. Didn't the women of Belfast ever read? Did it ever occur to them, or to the men so fond of their newspapers and libraries, that a woman might care to take time from her domestic responsibilities to occasionally improve her mind?

The woman at the reference desk smiled. "Good morning again, Miss McCarthy. Have you found something else for me to look up?"

"Yes, please." Meghann flipped the pages of her notebook until she found the scribbles she'd penned last night. "I need a copy of *The Annals of the Four Masters* and Tadhg O'Cianain's Gaelic description of *The Flight of the Earls.*"

"That may take a while."

"There's no rush. I'll reserve a private room and take a pot of tea while I wait."

Three hours later, after the library had emptied and filled again, Meghann found what she was looking for, an exact accounting of the events leading to the Battle of Kinsale.

23

❦

Nuala, Tirconnaill

By the end of that year of our Lord, fifteen hundred and ninety-nine, Elizabeth's sixteen thousand men had scattered to the four winds and Essex was in disfavor with the queen.

All of which bought us time. Elizabeth was furious, but she would not give up. With Essex gone she would send another, this one more versed in military strategy and less awed by stories of Irish devils with flashing swords and flying steeds. This time it would be a man less moved by emotion and unlikely to ride into London in the middle of a snowstorm and surprise Her Majesty in her private chambers.

My stomach turned to imagine such a scene, for Essex was ten years my junior and Elizabeth was old enough to be my grandmother.

My father sent Rory to Spain to once again appeal to Philip for help. The loss of his three armadas and the treatment of the Spanish survivors by the O'Flahertys of Galway four years before did not bode well for my husband's journey. A thousand men died in those waters off the western coast of Ireland and too many on shore after surviving the shipwreck. Because of a blood feud Liam O'Flaherty of the isles aided the storm-tossed Spaniards while Cormack O'Flaherty of Galway butchered their comrades as they struggled to shore. It would be a cool reception that Rory would receive from His Most Catholic Majesty, Philip of Spain.

He was absent those next years far more often than he was home, each task he undertook more dangerous than the one before. Perhaps he wished for a swift end to assuage the coldness that had grown like a frozen lake between us.

He loved me still. I knew it as surely as I knew the reflection of my own face in the rivers of the Eske. But his was a man's love and by its nature a selfish one.

He would give his life for me, for he was a warrior and the blood of Ireland's high kings ran through his veins. To draw sword and stand at the head of a silent army waiting for the moment of attack, to thrust cold steel into yielding flesh, to feel the burn of the dirk, the spurt of hot blood, to stand barefoot on grass slippery with enemy blood, this was second nature to him.

What he would not do was allow a woman to rule him. It was a man's world, and he said that a man who was soft did not live to enjoy the fruits of his labor. Perhaps he was right. Weaned before he could walk, he'd know from the beginning that his role was to command. His rewards were greater than those of most men, but the burdens were greater still. I was strong, but still a woman. I knew little of the path where he was pledged to walk.

Meghann sighed and looked up from the yellowed pages. She fingered her mother's brooch. "How arrogant he must have been, how difficult to live with, how incredible."

"He was all of that and more," said a voice in old Irish.

Meghann blinked her eyes. Across the table, as comfortably ensconced as if she came to the Linen Library's reading room every day, sat Nuala O'Donnell. For some reason it seemed perfectly natural to see her sitting there.

"He was hot-tempered, blunt to the point of rudeness, wildly jealous—"

"And wonderful," Meghann finished for her.

Nuala's expression softened. "Aye, he was wonderful."

"You loved him very much."

"So much that I felt my heart would stop with the weight of holding my love for Rory O'Donnell."

Meghann slipped a bookmark between the pages to hold her place. "Tell me about him, in your own words."

Nuala shook her head. "Isn't that what I've been doing, all this time, showing you our lives and the measure of the man he was?"

Meghann opened the book again and held it out to Nuala. "Would you like to read what is written about him?"

"I can't read English. 'Tis a harsh, unnatural language with little poetry to it. You read it to me."

Meghann cleared her throat.

His exploits would be forever immortalized in the secret brown script of the monks. Centuries after his death men would read the beautifully crafted words surrounded by colorful borders and detailed pictures drawn in red, gold, cerulean blue and forest green. They would marvel at the greatness of such a man, exclaim over his daring, celebrate his strength, create legends that would survive in Irish myth until the end of time. Aye, Rory O'Donnell, Chief of Tirconnaill, would be remembered but few would envy his lot.

They worshipped him like a god, forgetting that he

was only a man, bigger and brighter than most but still a man, until someone came along and reminded them in a most final and irrevocable fashion.

Rory was successful in Spain. Philip promised fifteen hundred Spanish troops for the siege against Elizabeth. United with the O'Neill's army of two thousand and Rory's two thousand again, Ireland should have won the day.

Meghann looked up. "Do you agree?"

Nuala nodded. "He describes him well. But there is more, so much more." Slowly, haltingly, in a voice of pure anguish, she described what O'Cianain only imagined.

"Fate transpired against us. It was the worst September of my memory. Rain swept across Ireland, hurling great waves against the shorelines. Wind bent the tree trunks until the forests lay flat against green hillsides, pressed into subservient postures as if in obedience to a mighty master. Wooden huts were leveled, and families without shelter scurried to safety inside the stone walls of Dun Na Ghal Castle. Lightning lashed the turrets and thunder drowned the voices in the Great Hall to terrified whispers. Those with Viking bloodlines spoke of the Hammer of Thor striking vengeance against his Christian defectors.

"Rory wore a pattern in the floorboards with his pacing. I knew his worry and shared it. We had much to lose. If the second Spanish Armada met the fate of its predecessor, all of Ireland and our way of life as we knew it hung in the balance. The look of strain on his face made him appear much older than his years.

"The Spanish were to have landed in Ulster, but Irish currents carried them far south to the southern coast of Ireland and the town of Kinsale. They marched into the city only to be surrounded by English troops under a commander by the name of William Mountjoy. There, without fresh supplies, they starved for nearly one hundred days.

"Rory and my father gravely underestimated Lord Mountjoy. I, who had known him from my brief stay in London, did not. He appeared to be indecisive and mild-mannered in temperament, but this deceptively meek facade concealed a keen instinct and a cool wisdom not often seen in the person of a soldier. For many years Elizabeth had suffered fools in the men she had chosen to lead her Irish wars. William Mountjoy was not a fool despite his headaches, his superstitious wearing of three waistcoats and his despicable habit of inhaling tobacco smoke to ward off disease.

"My husband was not a cruel man, and the thought of allies come to aid his cause eating sewer rats did not sit well. He prevailed upon my father and the O'Neills, the MacDonnells of Dunluce, the O'Driscolls of Baltimore, the O'Sullivans of Beare and several other chiefs to engage the English troops at Kinsale.

"I could imagine no other end than disaster. Kinsale was hundreds of miles to the south. Even in good weather an army of six thousand would take weeks to march the distance. It was December and bitterly cold. Snow muffled the mountains in blankets of white. Food and water would be scarce, and there would be no crops to sustain the marchers. They would meet Mountjoy's rested army weak, footsore and exhausted.

"To make matters worse, the Irish were now on the defensive. For reasons unknown my father, after digging trenches, building sconces and having the thickets plashed, withdrew his troops from Mowry Pass, leaving it wide open for the English to march through and erect a fort. It was the O'Neill's most strategic error in nine years of fighting.

"Rory was beside himself, and when Niall Garv rode into Derry offering his services to the English in exchange for the right to be called the O'Donnell, his hatred rose to heights I had never before seen. Over the years I had seen Rory work himself into a rage more times than I could count. His bellowing voice and fist-pounding anger were common enough inside the walls of Dun Na Ghal. But this was different.

"This time Rory was not at all loud. Indeed, he was so still that I grew uncomfortable watching him. His eyes chilled to narrow chips of blue ice, and the white line around his lips appeared permanently hewn into the chiseled flesh. He would not volunteer his thoughts and I, who shared more than a little responsibility for kindling the flame of his hatred, dared not ask him.

"Niall's outrageous presumption spurred Rory to action sooner than he had intended. Leading an army of five hundred men, with one thousand more to follow, he left Tirconnaill to rescue the Spanish at Kinsale."

"What about you?" Meghann interrupted. "Were you at Kinsale with him?"

Nuala shook her head. "I remained at Dun Na Ghal. Is there anything else in that book that concerns me?"

A smile played at the corner of Meghann's lips. "I think this will interest you. It's written in Irish in your husband's own words." She handed the book to Nuala, who stared at the words, squinted and handed it back. "Perhaps those are Rory's words, but they are not written in the Irish I know. Read it to me, please."

Meghann took the book and read.

The night was clear and the men who rode with me complained of bitter cold. But my purpose was strong, and the rage that festered within me boiled my blood until I felt only a pleasant tingling in my veins. Niall Garv was my target. Tonight he would know the taste of O'Donnell steel through his ribs. For years I'd restrained myself, controlling my anger, believing that his betrayal was only important if I regarded it so. But once again I was reminded of what every man learns sooner or later. A predator will not retreat with a mere taste of power. He will take more and still more until there is nothing left. I would have been better served to have stopped Niall in the beginning after he had taken my wife and my castle.

My heart pounded with anticipation and my hand reached for the handle of my dirk. Already, I felt better. Niall Dhu, prepare yourself. You will die like the English dog you've become.

The trees thinned into a clearing. I signaled to the men behind me. Soundlessly, they stopped in perfect formation. Like King Conor's warriors of the Red Branch, they were knights of the finest order. Without speaking, I dismounted and walked through the clearing into the thickest part of the forest. The men would wait in position until dawn.

There was no moon, but I did not falter. For nearly two leagues I walked until I smelled the smoke of turf fires. Niall's tent would be in the center, the O'Donnell standard posted at the entrance. Untying the dirk, I slipped it between my teeth and dropped to the ground. The remaining distance would be traveled on elbows and knees. It was after midnight. No one was about. Even the watch, a whiskerless lad, nodded at his post. My mood was light. I did not relish taking the lives of schoolboys.

Smeared with bog juice, I crawled to Niall's tent. Lifting the standard out of the ground, I let it drop. I drew aside the flap and took the dirk from my mouth.

It was too easy. Niall proved to be an unsuspecting mark. Within seconds my blade had creased the skin of his throat, leaving a thin scarlet line. Skill alone made a line so red and yet so thin that the blood did not spill over.

To his credit, Niall did not flinch. Neither did he beg. "Do it now," he rasped against the silver steel binding his throat.

I climbed on top of him, pinning him to the ground with my weight. "In good time. First I would have you suffer a bit."

"'Tis not a warrior's way, Rory."

I nearly killed him then. "How dare you speak of a warrior's way. Is it a warrior's way to make war on women and children?"

"Agnes and the children were a mistake."

Pressing the point of the dirk at the base of his throat, I asked, "What of Nuala? Was she also a mistake?"

Niall could barely speak. "Nuala was mine first. It had nothing to do with you."

"Nuala is my wife."

The blood flowed freely now. Speech was no longer possible. His mouth opened, shut and opened again. I released the pressure of the blade.

He gasped, breathed deeply and spoke. "Kill me and raise my son. 'Tis the law. Is that what you wish for, Rory, to watch Nuala mother the lad she bore me?"

The truth was always hardest to bear. I stared down at my cousin's sharply hewn features, struggling to match the quickness of his mind. Like Nuala, Niall was swift to understand and unusually articulate of speech. I knew the law. Blood bonds of Ireland's high kings handed down from the Hills of Tara were unbreakable. Niall was my cousin, son of my father's brother. Only the death of the lad would release me from fostering Niall's son. Much as I relished the thought, I could not murder Nuala's child. She had already lost too much, but neither would I take him into my home. Niall Garv must be spared.

Slowly I withdrew the knife from his throat. The only sign that he had feared for his life was the brief, nearly imperceptible flickering of his eyes. Before he could move, I lifted the handle of the dirk and brought it down against his temple. I watched his mouth slacken and his skin grow purple before I backed out of the tent.

The blow had been intentionally hard. He would not wake for several hours, enough for me to reach safety. Meanwhile, tomorrow was Christmas Eve, and William Mountjoy waited at Kinsale with an army of three thousand.

Meghann closed the book and looked up at Nuala. Her eyes were unnaturally bright. "There was great goodness in Rory. Thank you, my dear. I knew nothing of this."

Meghann nodded. "I envy you."

Nuala's eyes grew round with astonishment. "Rory would never have done for you, lass. The man you've chosen is much more suited to your temperament."

"How can you possibly know such a thing?"

"I know this." Her image was blurry now and her words a mere whisper. "For Michael Devlin there will never be anyone but you."

She was gone, and with her went the light and the warmth in the room. Meghann looked at her watch. It was late, and Annie had invited her for dinner.

24

After it was over and all was lost, Rory said that Macha's curse of the silver mist was on the Irish army that day. How else could their defeat be explained? They had twice the men, the support of all around them and a knowledge of the glens and boglands that no Englishman would ever have. Still, in less than three hours, they lost the day and with their defeat the course of Irish history would be forever changed.

They had marched south to find Don Juan de Aguila and the Spanish troops imprisoned behind the walls of Kinsale. Mountjoy's army, camped outside the walls, had ravaged the countryside to prevent provisions from being smuggled in to the starving Spanish. Without the Spanish troops the Irish were outnumbered, forcing the O'Neill to return to his old tactics of surrounding the enemy and starving them until they surrendered.

It was very nearly successful. Reports told of horrendous losses, of wasted men and lingering illness. But on Christmas Eve, pleas from the Spanish imprisoned in Kinsale could no longer be ignored.

The night was violently stormy. Lightning flashed from Irish spearheads, and in the darkness the English saw the lighting of their fires. Mountjoy was ready. He launched a furious calvary attack on the Irish infantry, knocking the men off balance and scattering them to the four winds.

From Rory's position at the head of his mounted troops, he could hear the cries of battle. Leading the charge, he followed the sounds of shouting men and clashing blades. His sword slew many that day, but in the end it was all for naught. The Irish could not regroup quickly enough and for the first time my father, the great battle tactician, exposed his troops in the open with fatal consequences.

His men were not suited to fighting in the snow-covered fields. They had camped at Coolcarron on the low ground while Mountjoy's troops had the advantage of a camp at Ardmartin. The Irish had to cross the low ridge and break through the English lines at Camphill or Ardmartin to reach the Spaniards. Our men had been trained to ambush and retreat, melting into the forests like the shadowy ghosts of our legends. The English mowed them down like cattle.

Rory's command became separated from the rest, and by the time they came around, Irish bodies littered the snow and the Bandon River ran red with the blood of Ireland's best. He tried to rally as many men as possible to continue the fight, but there were few left to obey. Many a family name disappeared that day, never to recover. The magnitude of such a loss had never before been experienced in Irish history.

In less than three hours the battle was over. The Spanish surrendered and the Irish retreated north with those who had survived.

It was the passing of an era, the end of Irish Catholic supremacy in Ireland, and it was to have consequences more far-reaching than any other event in our history.

JEANETTE BAKER

The Franciscans recorded it in *The Annals of the Four Masters* far more poignantly than I ever could:

Manifest was the displeasure of God. . . . Immense and countless was the loss in that place; for the prowess and valour, prosperity and affluence, nobleness and chivalry, dignity and renown, bravery and protection, devotion and pure religion, of the Island, were lost in this engagement.

The battle was an even greater disaster for Spain than the loss of her Armada in 1588. With France paralyzed by a religious civil war, Kinsale turned the tide in favor of England. Philip was forced to make his peace with his archenemy. But first the subjugation of Ulster was executed.

For nearly a year after Kinsale, Rory and my father, with a few loyal men, held out in Glenconkeyne and then in the woodlands of Fermanagh. Meanwhile, Mountjoy destroyed our castle at Dungannon and the ancient coronation sight of the O'Neills at Tullahogue.

I cannot speak of that time without a coldness surrounding my heart. The ancient circle of stones where the High Kings of Ulster took up the sceptre, walked three times around the stone and placed a gold-cased slipper into the footprint of every O'Neill king who had ever been crowned, came to us a thousand years before Saint Patrick set foot upon our shores. The coronation stone was said to be a living thing. Only when it cried out in the voice of Macha, goddess of Ulster, would a man be recognized as the O'Neill. It had happened so with my father and with his before him and so on in an unbroken line of succession so far back into the mists of time that only Cia'ran, the oldest of our bards, could recite the entirety of our lineage without reading the scrolls.

After Kinsale it was over, the stones scattered, the posts burned, the legacy of our people destroyed. I came to believe during those trying years when my husband was on the run, before my father surrendered to Mountjoy at Mellifont Abbey in Drogheda, that life is more a question of character than a series of incidents and there is little we can do but learn to bear what we must. And so I did.

My burdens were light compared to the peasants of Ulster. Mountjoy concentrated on burning fields and seizing cattle until the famine was so widespread there was no relief in sight. I did what I could for our own tenants until there was nothing left in the larder of Dun Na Ghal. It was then that I saw a spectacle so horrible that to this very day I can see the details vividly in my nightmares.

While returning from Newry on a futile quest to learn of my husband's whereabouts, we came upon a village of women and children so thin they resembled living skeletons. They looked upon us strangely, and I was relieved when they were behind us. We made our way down an embankment and were ready to camp when I noticed a multitude of decaying bodies with mouths stained green. Before I could question my guard, he had reined in his mount to block my path. His breathing was labored and his face deathly pale.

"Please, my lady. Do not pass this way. 'Tis a sight unfit for human eyes."

"You've seen it."

"Aye, and I wish to God I hadn't."

"Move aside, knave," I commanded him. "We are on O'Neill land. Who better to see what takes place here."

Reluctantly he pulled back his horse and I looked upon a travesty that surely transgressed every law of God or man be he Protestant or Catholic. Three small children, the oldest no more than six or seven years, sat beside a dying ash-white fire. Before the fire were the remains of half a woman. Her head, torso and arms were whole, although black with death, but her legs were missing and below her waist, her belly and hips looked as if they had been torn apart. In the midst of the fire lay the charred remains of her entrails.

At first I did not understand and then when I did, I would have given much of my share of heaven that I did not. The children, desperate in their starvation, were eating their dead mother's body. Holy Mother of Jesus. I should have prayed. I should have fallen to my knees for the children, for myself, for Ireland, that her people should be reduced to such atrocity. But I could do no more than slide from my mount, lift my skirts and run behind a thick oak, where my stomach revolted and I heaved up every bit of food I'd taken in since morning.

My escorts indulged in no such weakness, but they were kind enough to ignore mine. I, who had cleaned out maggot-infested wounds, seared flesh and ordered plague-ridden bodies burned, could not touch these hell-damned children. I ordered that they be fed and put up behind three of the men but Siobhan, my maid, advised against it.

"There are a thousand more just like these, my lady. 'Tis no service that you do them. The men will talk and no woman will take them. Leave them food. We will find a priest in the next village. He will know what to do."

To my shame, her words brought me great relief. I did not want these children behind the walls of Dun Na Ghal. I did not want these children nor any like them in all of Tirconnaill. "Have you ever seen the like, Siobhan?" I asked, watching her rub the gray from her lips.

"Nay, my lady. But the travelers brought word of women who lured the cowherds from the pastures." Her voice dropped to a whisper. "They killed them, cut them up and cooked them in their soup kettles."

Once again the gagging feeling clutched at my throat and I turned away. What had our grasping power wars done to our people? Did Elizabeth in the opulent comfort of her palace think of the motherless bairns of Ireland? Did Mountjoy or my father or Rory? Did I? Holy God, perhaps we were past prayer. Perhaps we were all damned.

Tirconnaill, 1605

"Connor Maguire, you are a fool." Rory's words, as always, were inflammatory. He would have said more, but the slight pursing of my lips warned him to keep silent.

"Mountjoy's treaty with the O'Neill is still good despite Elizabeth's death," I said. "Surely, there is no need for flight."

Maguire slammed his fist down on the table. "Those who fought against us are uneasy, Nuala. They feel slighted and stir King James against us. Your father keeps his lands and strengthens his control over his tenants and subchieftains. But his good fortune cannot last. Fermanagh has been portioned among two hundred freeholders, leaving me with half the land that was mine. Niall Garv holds the lands above Lifford, the jewel of Tirconnaill. Even now there is talk of granting Inishowen to Sir Cahil O'Doherty. Will you watch while Protestants encroach upon us until there is nothing left?"

Again I answered his impassioned speech with a single reasonable question. "Have you proof of this, Connor?"

"My lands are gone. Is that not proof enough?"

"Perhaps." I spoke gently. Connor Maguire was not a man to offend. "There is also the possibility that it is our company you wish for on your journey to Spain. I am not certain that a military career in the service of Philip of Spain is in Rory's best interests." I smiled at him. "'Tis nothing which must be solved tonight. Come, Connor. Sup with us. At last there is enough for everyone."

Rory was not deceived by my diversionary tactics. We would speak of Connor's visit later. He had given me food for thought.

I came to him later that evening, wrapped in wool against the chill of an early autumn. "What would you have us do, Rory?"

He grinned and shook his head. "In many ways you are predictable, my love. You decide what we shall do and pretend that the idea came from me."

"That isn't true," I protested.

He sighed. "What are your thoughts on the matter, Nuala?"

"We are greatly beholden to Spain, and I cannot believe that Philip will reign for long." I twisted the fringe of my shawl. "We have gold in Rome and we owe no one there. Rome would be a better home for us."

Dismay showed on his face. I hurried on, not allowing him to speak until I finished. "I know the pain it must bring you to leave Ireland, Rory. But since we were born we have known how it would be. Three hundred years ago, when the first Red Hugh O'Donnell acknowledged Henry of England to be his overlord, the Irish chieftains were doomed. You have done more than any man in Catholic Europe to hold this land. But you are not God. 'Tis time to give up the fight and live a life that does not include bloodshed." I fixed my eyes on his face, forcing him to meet my gaze. "Do you ever sleep without a sword by your bed or a dirk beneath your pillow? When have you closed your eyes for an entire night? 'Tis time, Rory. I fear that if we do not go now there will be no life for us at all."

He knew that everything I said was true, but he did not answer immediately. It seemed a long time before he stood and rested his hands upon my shoulders, testing the small bones beneath his large hands. "What of you, Nuala? It has been many years since we have lived together as man and wife. Will you come with me to Rome or will you stay in Ireland?"

The golden light of the candle danced in the blue of his eyes. "Have you been faithful to me, Rory?"

"I have loved only one woman, Nuala, and she stands before me now."

I sighed. "'Tis not precisely what I asked you."

"It is to me."

"Then why—" my voice broke.

He folded me into his arms. "Don't cry, beloved," he whispered into my hair. "When you told me of Niall I felt as if my heart had been torn from my body. But I never stopped loving you."

My voice was muffled against his shirt. "I am no longer your wife."

His arms tightened around me. "You will always be my wife. Having you beside me, even when you are angry and willful, is better than not having you at all. You are everything to me, Nuala."

I lifted my head, my eyes burning from the tears I would not release. "I will not go to Rome with you, Rory, unless we go as man and wife in every sense of the word. It is more my choice than it is yours."

"Aye, love." Gently he put me from him. "You are still very beautiful, Nuala. I understand your reasoning, and you must understand mine. Without you I will never leave Ireland."

"Then we will stay."

"So be it," he said. "There is nothing I would not give you, Nuala, nothing except this."

I did not weep. I never wept. Instead, my lip curled contemptuously and I pulled the wool shawl close around my shoulders. "You are a fool, Rory. No woman on earth would choose the life of a clam over the dance of the firefly."

The night we left for Rome, Rory burned Dun Na Ghal Castle to the ground. I watched the rushes catch fire, sending the shooting flames across the wooden floors to the tapestry-lined walls. I had set great store by my Flemish tapestries. Greedy flames licked at the costly thread before gobbling them completely. The fire leaped to the roof. Walls, weak from fire, collapsed, while chairs, tables, footstools, bedstands, mattresses, portraits, everything that was mine, fell down around me.

It seemed that not even the loss of his children caused Rory more pain than losing this place where centuries of O'Donnells had walked, slept, mated and given birth. To be forever known as the last O'Donnell chief, the one who had lost Dun Na Ghal, shamed him sorely. Only the Norman tower remained standing when he rowed the boat across the Eske to where the vessel that was to carry us to Rome waited. We had lost it all. Never had we needed each other more.

Years ago when I left Tyrone for the wind-hammered beaches of Dun Na Ghal, I left behind the trappings of childhood. The earl of Tirconnaill wanted a woman of courage, a woman of O'Neill blood descended from the High Kings of Tara, a woman who would instill honor and wisdom in the warrior sons she would bear him.

From that first moment when he lifted his head, I stared in wonder at the sun-dark skin and flashing smile, at the strong neck rising from his saffron shirt, the blue flame vivid in his eyes, the shoulder-length fall of moon-bleached hair, and my mouth went dry. I vowed to have him, no matter the price. And the price had been more than dear.

Rarely, during those sorrow-filled years, had I succumbed to tears. Not on all the dreadful nights when Rory left to fight with my father or when Niall Garv O'Donnell captured Dun Na Ghal Castle, not on Midsummer's Eve when the priest prayed over the last two of the nine wee bairns I had borne to Rory and buried them beneath the salt-laced soil of the tower cemetery, nor when my lord and love, fearing for my life, said there must be no more children.

I was Nuala O'Donnell, countess of Tirconnaill, daughter and granddaughter of chiefs, descended from

Brian Boru, Lion of Ireland, greatest of Tara's High Kings. If I no longer served my husband in all things, I knew he needed me still, and I had prepared well. There was gold waiting in Rome, O'Donnell gold, and land as well. The O'Donnells would live on, but not here, not in this faerie land where every stone, every plot of soil, every silver lough carried its tale of Irish blood.

It was over, eight hundred years of O'Donnell history, eight centuries of Catholic dominion, lost to the bold sweep of a woman's quill, a woman who had never borne a child or taken a man inside her body, a bastard queen, spawn of a lecherous Tudor king and a greedy woman who rotted in the fields behind the Tower of London.

I stared straight ahead, seeing much more of the kingdom of Tirconnaill than the mists allowed. Fog hung thick as smoke, shrouding trees, stables, thatched roofs and castle turrets in a suffocating blanket of dreary gray. The only sound breaking the hushed stillness was the steady slap of ship's oars parting the waters of the River Eske in uniform precision, irrefutable evidence that with every groan of the mast all that was familiar and beloved slipped farther and farther away.

I narrowed my eyes, straining to catch a final glimpse of *Mainistir Dhun na nGall,* the monastery below the castle on the left bank of the Eske where a century ago another O'Donnell chieftain had conceived the idea of *The Annals of the Four Masters.* Unable to contain his excitement, this warrior king, known for his wisdom, his generosity and his tolerance for spirits, commissioned Michael O'Leary, a Franciscan friar, to write the story of Eire. After nearly five years, forty centuries of Irish history, documented in painstaking detail, was scripted for all to see. Rory's story was there, and mine too.

Behind the monastery, flames licked at the mist, burning through the gray, leaving a sickening bile-colored glow. A desperate gutteral sound escaped my throat. How could I leave it, my home, my childrens' graves, the glorious memories of sun-steeped afternoons and those early years when Rory and I had loved with one mind and body? A strange burning rose beneath my eyelids. I fought against it. My vision blurred, and tears, harsh and long overdue, welled up in my eyes and spilled down my cheeks.

Without warning, strong arms pinned my cloak to my sides. Instinctively, I rested my head against my husband's shoulder, waiting for the feel of his lips against my throat. I shivered, allowing the familiar heat to claim me. If only I could have this for a while longer, until I was old and the fire within me had ebbed. I leaned into him, fitting my body to his.

He cursed and pulled away, breathing harshly. "By God, Nuala. Why do you torment me this way?"

I smiled bitterly. He wanted me still. At least there was that. Drawing a deep breath I faced him. He was thin, his skin dark and tight across the high bones of his cheeks. The hollows beneath were deeply shadowed, and the lines around his startling blue eyes spoke of worry and sleepless nights.

I lifted my chin. His suffering was no greater than mine. Five and thirty years was not old enough for a woman's life to be torn from her. I nodded in the direction of the castle from which we had come. "Why did you burn it?"

He turned to look at the leaping flames. His answer was bitter, defeated. "I want no English dog to claim my keep."

When I did not speak, he turned to go. "My lord." I hesitated. How many times had I made my request only to have him reject it? He stood tall and straight, his eyes once again on my face. "My lord," I began again, "I ask your leave to go with my brother to France."

"Why?"

"I am not well."

Fear replaced the wariness in his eyes. He reached for me, but I backed away and leaned against the railing.

I shook my head. "Nay, 'tis not what you think. My body serves me well. 'Tis my soul that sickens. I am no longer a wife, Rory. You have put me away without a child to comfort me."

The accusation was unfair. Even I knew it.

"I gave you nine bairns, Nuala. Even the church can expect no more of us."

Simply, brutally, I meant to hurt him. "They died."

He nodded. "Aye. No one is to blame. 'Tis sometimes the way."

He was very much to blame, as was every Irish lord who refused submission to Elizabeth. But I would not win him back by reminding him of what he already knew. "You have no heirs," I said instead.

He refused to meet my eyes. "I have lost Tirconnaill. I have no need of heirs."

"Liar."

Furious, he looked up. "I know your mind, Nuala. But it will never be. I will not risk your life. You heard the physician. Another child will kill you."

I looked down into the calm waters of the bay, counting the ripples from our wake. "I've heard of herbs—"

He refused to listen. "Nay. Holy church condemns it. I'll not have your death on my hands."

"The choice should be mine."

"Nuala! By the blood of Christ. This world holds nothing for me without you."

"I want a child, Rory. Every woman wants a child."

His hands tightened around the railing. "I need you. We will make our lives in Rome. I am the earl of Tirconnaill, a fighter, not a courtier."

I knew how hard it was for him to beg. I would have stopped him, but he went on as if in opening his heart he must empty it. "If you will not stay for me, Nuala, stay for our people. The Romans will think us barbarians without you."

Could this man I loved more than my own life be such a fool? "I am the daughter of Irish barbarians, Rory O'Donnell, no different from you. Your words are not what a woman would hear."

His hands reached out to hold me. For a long moment he looked at me, saying nothing. What did he see, this man who knew my face better than he knew his own? Did he see me as I was, or did he remember the girl of years ago, the child bride with her laughing, berry-stained mouth, her thin, high-bridged nose and the carven, sharp-cheeked beauty of small bones under lightly freckled skin? Once, long ago, he claimed that the Madonna herself could not have been more lovely. What, now, did he see in the woman he'd wagered a kingdom for?

He spoke slowly, haltingly. "If it is words you need, Nuala, hear them now. Even before I saw you, I loved you. Tirconnaill was your bride price. After the betrayal of Chichester and Maguire, when I alone stood by your father, he asked my pardon for demanding my lineage. But know this. I would do no differently were he to ask again."

There was more that needed saying, but I did not expect to hear it. Still, he spoke on.

"Do you know why I left you untouched for more than a year after our wedding?"

"You said I was too young for bedding and too small for bairns."

He smiled. "Nay, love. That was pride, not truth. I feared that you would find me wanting, that I was not man enough for the daughter of *Aedh Ruadh* O'Neill. Not until you demanded that I leave off my wenching and make you a wife did I come to you. It was past time. I burned for wanting you but still I was afraid. You welcomed me and that night I learned what it was to love." His voice was hoarse and earnest. "Do not ask to leave me."

Unchecked, the tears streamed down my face. I, Nuala, who never cried, turned away. "I want to feel our bodies joined in the act of love, Rory. I want a child. A woman is nothing without a child."

Smothering an expletive, he released me. "Have mercy, Nuala. I love you. You are my wife, and I will have no hand in your murder."

I grew weary of words. There was nothing left to say. I stood my ground, a slight, small-boned woman against the Lion of Ireland. "I will not bargain, Rory. You know my mind."

I saw the rage unleash within him as if my words had been the key that unlocked the floodgates. "Do you threaten me, my lady?"

I refused to answer, refused to look away.

Reaching behind my head, he threaded his fingers through my hair. Under the flickering torchlight, I saw his eyes glitter with something dark and terrifying, something that had no place in the life we shared. I tried to move back, but he would not allow it. He twisted my hair around his fingers so that my head was held immobile.

"How much of this do you think I can take? Or is that your game, to wear me down until I break from the coldness you show me?"

I said nothing. He cursed again, using words he had never before spoken in my presence. I had pushed him too far, and for the first time in my life I was afraid of my husband.

"You win, Nuala. We shall play the game your way. If you want this, you shall have it." He pulled me roughly against him. Lowering his head, he teased my mouth with the tip of his tongue.

I closed my eyes, waiting for his anger to dissipate, willing the husband I knew to return to me. His mouth was warm on my throat and his free hand roamed my body, settling on my breasts.

He lifted me into his arms, taking me down the darkness of a long hall and through the low-hung cabin door, where he dropped me on the bed and began shedding his clothes. A single candle burned on the mantel. I could barely make out his outline. I pulled off my dress and shoes and was struggling with my laces when he joined me in the bed. Without speaking, he tore the knots of my undergarments and threw them on the floor. Then he turned to me. "I ask you one last time, Nuala. I am no saint and will not turn back. Are you willing, knowing what the end will be?"

I trembled with anticipation and fear. This was my husband and yet he was not as I remembered. It had been years since we shared a bed. I had borne ten children and my body was no longer firm and supple. I had no wish to be compared to the woman I once was and found wanting. Still, I could not change the past. It was this or nothing. Resting my lips on his chest, I spoke against his skin. "I am willing, my lord, if you are."

A harsh, wordless sound rose up from his throat. I touched his cheek. It was wet. Shocked, I sat up and peered at him through the darkness. Only once before had I witnessed my husband's tears. "There is no need to weep, my love."

"Don't do this, Nuala," he whispered. "Don't make me do this."

With soothing hands, I stroked his brow, drying his cheeks with my hair. "Hush," I murmured. My hands moved slowly, coaxingly, down his body. "We were made for this. There is no other way for us."

His hands were still as skilled, his mouth as firm and tender as I remembered. He was immediately and powerfully erect and when he came inside me and our passion rose together, I knew that it was right and that Rory knew it too. Nothing mattered but this. Ireland would survive. Rory would survive and, when my time was at hand, there would be no regrets, for I would be with him always.

Belfast, 1995

Meghann looked at her watch impatiently and rolled down the window of her automobile. The prison swarmed with visitors and she'd waited for nearly thirty minutes in the queue to enter the gates. Armed RUC and British soldiers stood at the checkpoints screening all visitors as if each one had an explosive strapped to his shoe. It was nearly marching season in the north, that time of tension when Protestants celebrated the victory of William of Orange by marching through the streets of heavily populated Catholic areas, banging their drums and singing "God Save the Queen," proclaiming their God-given right to control the territory.

After the Protestants marched, the Catholics rioted. Burned-out lorries and hijacked cars blocked every major motorway, and swarms of pierced and tattooed young people who cared nothing about nationalism, except as an excuse to vandalize the premises of hard-working families, prowled the deserted streets. It was always the same, this dreadful two weeks in July. The RUC forced the marches through and then brought out the batons to beat the inevitable looters.

She inched her car forward. A pleasant, round-faced young man with the bright yellow vest of the RUC poked his head in the window. "What is your business here, Miss?"

"Counsel for a prisoner."

"May I see your papers, please."

Meghann handed over her documents. The man perused each one carefully before allowing her to pass. She parked and locked the car. Hitching her briefcase over her shoulder, Meghann walked through the security detection device, submitted to the tentative frisking by a woman guard and was ushered into a room with a table, two chairs and reinforced glass panels. Outside, three more guards stood at attention.

A man with a thick neck and meaty hands led Michael into the room, pushed him down into one of the chairs and uncuffed him. Meghann sat down across from Michael and waited until the guard left the room before speaking. "Are you all right? You look too thin and terribly pale."

He grinned, leaned across the table and bussed her cheek. "That's what you said last week. Nothing ever changes in here, except perhaps a wee bit more excitement due to the season. What about yourself?"

She hesitated. The latest development wasn't good. She wanted to look at him first, to gauge his reactions, to satisfy herself that he still thought the decision to return and face his trial had been the right one. Meghann knew that if she hadn't been involved, Michael might have taken another road. Escaped prisoners with new identities were living out their lives quite comfortably overseas and in the Republic. There were times, like this one, when she wished she had advised him differently.

Meghann opened her briefcase and pulled out a manilla file, avoiding his probing gaze. "There's a situation we've got to sort out, Mick. Do you know Danny O'Rourke and Patrick Feeney?"

He nodded. "Aye. They're intelligence, not insiders but close enough."

"They were arrested three weeks ago. Since then they've confessed to furnishing information that led to the Killingsworth murder." Meghann paused and drew a deep breath.

Michael's eyes narrowed. "What is it that you aren't telling me?"

"They claim that Killingsworth was too important a

target to be taken out by anyone other than an experienced man, someone implicitly trusted by everyone at the top levels of the organization." She raised her eyes to his face. "They've named you, Michael."

He was quiet for a long time. "Poor blokes," he said at last. "I wonder what was done to them."

"Your trial is scheduled for Thursday. Bruises wouldn't heal by then. More likely they were promised immunity."

"I could use a smoke."

Meghann pulled out two packs of American filtered cigarettes and a book of matches from her briefcase and pushed them across the table. "These will shorten your life, you know."

He struck a match, brought it to the end of his cigarette and inhaled deeply before lifting mocking blue eyes to her face. "Pardon me if that's the least of my concerns at the moment. In case it hasn't occurred t' you yet, Meggie, love, I'm as good as dished."

"That's not true," she said defensively, standing up to pace the floor and rub her arms. "I've enough evidence to discredit the glassmaker, and I'll discredit Feeney and O'Rourke as well."

Michael watched her cross the tiny room, stop briefly at the window, turn and go back the way she came. Her hands were clasped tightly together and her knuckles showed white beneath her skin. She was wound tight as a spring. He ached to touch her, but the three peelers posted outside the windows discouraged him. Instead he spoke softly. "Something is troubling you, Meghann. What is it?"

She stopped, sank into the chair across from him and dropped her head into her hands. "I think I've made a dreadful mistake, Michael, and there isn't anything I can do about it."

He waited patiently until she had composed herself.

"Andrew Maguire is on the list of the prosecution's witnesses."

"We already knew that. What difference does it make now?"

She lifted her head and stared at him. "It wouldn't make any difference to a judge. Andrew has no more nor less credibility than you do. Even though he has no convictions, he's IRA. Everyone knows that. The SAS have been trying to arrest him for years."

"I still don't understand the problem."

"You will be tried by a jury, Michael, not a judge. Andrew Maguire's standing in the community is beyond question. There isn't a Catholic family in the Falls who doesn't believe he stands next to God."

Michael reached for Meghann, saw the guard frown and start for the door, and pulled back. "Damn peelers," he swore bitterly. "They're inhuman."

Meghann tried to laugh and failed miserably.

Under the table his hand closed around hers. "There's no need for you t' worry yourself like this. You've been away from Belfast for a long time, Meghann. 'Tis highly unlikely the jury will be made up of residents from the Falls. The way I see it, Andrew has no more credibility than I do."

"They'll try to fill the jury with Catholics."

Michael shrugged. "I've a few friends in West Belfast, myself."

Meghann stared at him. "Aren't you concerned at all?"

He laughed and her heart lifted. Dear God, how she loved this man.

He brought the cigarette to his lips and blew out a ring of smoke. "I've been here before. What puzzles me is how you can do this."

"What do you mean?"

He released her hand and leaned back in his chair. His words were measured and thoughtful, without the slightest hint of censure. "How can a Catholic girl from the Falls administer British justice for her livelihood?"

"It's the best we've got," she said simply.

His eyebrows lifted.

"It's true. Not that it's always administered properly or by impartial people," she amended hastily, "but when it is, it works better than anything else."

Michael's face was impassive. "We'll see if British law applies to Catholics from Belfast."

Suddenly Meghann was embarrassed. Michael was on trial and his attitude was better than hers, his attorney. "Do you have a suit?" she asked, changing the subject.

Michael was startled. "Yes."

"You'll need it for the trial." She straightened, assuming her professional role once again. "We'll be meeting every day until then. I want you to do exactly what I tell you without exception."

"All right."

"The Crown will present its case and call witnesses first. I will cross-examine them. I want you to remain seated at all times and make no comments, no matter what is said."

Michael nodded.

"Do not react to anything. Do not smile, frown, laugh, grimace. Keep your face as blank as possible unless I instruct you to do otherwise. This is extremely crucial, Michael. You must promise me that you'll cooperate."

"I will."

Meghann nodded. "Answer only what is asked of you. Do not explain or elaborate unless you are told to do so. Do not speak quickly. Take as long as you need to formulate an answer, and if you're confused, request clarification. Confusion on the part of the accused is lethal. You must be sure of your answers."

"Anything else?"

Meghann shook her head. There was no need to warn Michael about the tone of his responses. His voice was beautiful, deep, perfectly pitched, rich in quality and wonderful to hear. It was his strongest weapon, that and his physical appeal. Meghann made a mental note to select as many women jurors as possible.

She looked at her watch. "It's time," she said softly. One more thing. "Do you know a man named O'Shea?"

He shook his head. "The name doesn't ring a bell. Why?"

"He's on the prosecution's witness list. I'll have Miles check him out. Your mother says to give you her love. I'll be back tomorrow and we'll begin preparing."

"Look at me, Meghann."

She did and quickly looked away. "This isn't a good idea."

"What isn't?"

"We've both got to concentrate. I won't be of any use to you if we forget what's most important."

"And what would that be?"

"Right now? Securing your release."

"And later?"

She looked at him again and what she saw in his face terrified her. What if she couldn't save him? "Prepare yourself, Michael," she said. "God help us both. I have no idea how this will turn out. Prepare yourself for every possible outcome."

He smiled, a brief turning of his mouth. "There's no trick to that, Meggie. I've lived my whole life that way."

25

Thursday dawned bright and clear, a beautiful July typical of the North of Ireland. Leaving her porridge untouched, Meghann looked across the table at Annie Devlin. The older woman said little and under her eyes were etched the dark circles of sleepless nights. Meghann ached with pity. How many times had Annie been through this? How many children had been tried and sentenced by the Crown?

Annie Devlin was descended from the nationalist aristocracy of West Belfast. Her family had flown the republican flag during the dry years of the thirties, forties and fifties. She had grown up on tales of Daniel O'Connor and Charles Parnell. Nothing had occurred in her life and her children's that she hadn't anticipated. But she was old now and, of all of her children, Michael was her pride and joy. She'd had different hopes for Michael.

Meghann reached across the table and covered the work-worn hand with her own. "I'm sorry, Annie. I wish I could offer you some guarantees."

"Aye." Annie sighed. "I was thinkin' that the good

Lord is hard on mothers, especially the mothers of sons."

Meghann's eyes watered. Horrified by her unprofessional behavior, she pressed her fingers against her eyes and stood. "I'm not really hungry," she said. "Do you mind if we leave early?"

"You go on, Meghann. Davie and Connor will be here soon, and Bernadette said she'd bring the car. I'll see y' there."

Meghann nodded, kissed Annie and picked up her briefcase. There was nothing more to say. Assurances were out of the question. The evidence on both sides was just short of circumstantial. Everything depended on the jury.

The moment she stepped outside she could feel the tension. The air itself quivered with rage and fear and a heightened sense of expectation. Voices were muted. Women who normally took their babies outside for a morning walk stayed inside, the prams empty. Even the dogs were silent. Teenagers hurried back and forth with odd pieces of wood and twisted metal, hubcaps and rubber, tires, bottles filled with suspicious-looking liquid, old toys, bicycles, clothing, any fuel they could get their hands on. The bonfires protesting the Orange marches would be especially big tonight. Tomorrow was the twelfth of July, a national holiday in the North. Springfield Road, where the Peace Line ran between the Falls and the Shankill, would be a line of glowing fires, some as high as twenty feet.

Her stomach knotted. There would be violence and British tanks on the streets today. Someone's child, brother, sister, mother or father would be injured or killed, just as they had been last year and the year before that and every other July 12 that she could remember.

Pressing the remote to unlock her car, she climbed in and pulled down the rearview mirror to check her lipstick. Something in its reflection caught her attention. Her appearance forgotten, she turned to the block wall at the end of the street. In bold red letters, each one six feet high, were the words, *Free Michael Devlin*. Meghann turned the key and swung the car around, making her way down the road. She turned left toward Mackie's factory and saw it again, this time in black. By the time she'd passed the Springfield and Ormeau Roads, she'd seen at least six different references to Michael's internment. Apparently he did have friends in the Falls.

Meghann pulled out onto Lisburn Street and chafed at the delay. Small parades of Orangemen in bowler hats and orange sashes marched down the street to the beating of drums and the cheering of spectators waving the Union Jack. In Belfast during the weeks leading up to the twelfth, the parades were small and less controversial. The Orangemen marched through strictly Protestant areas. Tomorrow the route would change, drinking would be excessive and the mood would be ugly as the marchers wound their way through the Catholic neighborhoods of the Falls, Andersonstown and Portadown, streets whose curbs and flagpoles were painted green, red and orange, the color of the republican tricolor, streets that were now inhabited by Catholic families.

The drums, the cheering and the thick Belfast accents grated on her ears. Where was it written that such a flaunting display of one-upmanship should be tolerated by a downtrodden community? Why didn't the British government with their policy of neutrality stop this nonsense that resulted in more and more anger and sectarian killing every year?

A police officer wearing the yellow vest of the RUC knocked on her window. Meghann pushed the automatic button and it rolled down.

"Sorry, Miss, but you'll have to go around. The parade's coming this way."

"I'm due at the Crumlin Road courthouse in fifteen minutes. This is the only way"

"You'll have to park and walk. This is the parade route."

Anger, long-repressed and lying dormant, flared to life in Meghann's chest. "This isn't a holiday. I don't give a damn about the parade. Clear the way and let me pass."

There was something in her eyes that made the young RUC officer think twice about refusing her request. Lifting his whistle to his lips, he blew three loud, long blasts, clearing a path among the crowd of spectators blocking her way.

Meghann inched her way through, ignoring the ugly murmur swelling through the mass of people. Hands pressed against her windows. Faces peered in at her. She'd nearly made it to the courthouse when she heard a shout through the tinted glass. "It's Devlin's lawyer, the bitch who's defendin' the Taig murderer."

A wall of bodies pressed close to the car. Thick fingers found their way to the edge of the glass where she'd left the passenger window rolled down nearly an inch. Meghann felt the car rock. At the same time she slammed her palm against the lock and pressed her foot down hard on the accelerator. The car leaped forward, separating the crowd. She heard a howl of pain, more cursing, and then she was through.

Moments later, in the Crumlin Road carpark she rested her forehead against her arm. Her fingers ached from their grip on the steering wheel and perspiration beaded her forehead. The metallic taste of fear coated her tongue, and every word of her opening statement had faded from her mind. They hated her as much as they hated Michael, maybe even more because she was the vehicle through which he might escape his sentence.

Nearly twenty minutes passed before her heart stopped its erratic pounding. After another ten she felt composed enough to cross the carpark, settle the barrister's wig on her head, shrug into her robes and enter the courtroom.

Miles French was seated at the table beside Michael. When he caught sight of her he released his breath audibly.

Michael, heartbreakingly handsome in a dark suit, watched her cross the room. He winked, took another look at her face and frowned. Meghan smiled shakily and slid into her chair.

"Is everything all right?" he asked softly.

"I'm grand, Michael," she assured him, "just grand. How long have you been here?"

"They brought me in early this morning." He grinned. "I expect no one wanted to start a riot."

"Is there a chance of that happening?"

Michael studied her face for a moment before answering. She looked as if she were under an enormous strain. The hollows of her cheeks were more pronounced than they'd been a week ago, and shadows marked the skin under her eyes like giant purple bruises. "Are y' worried?"

"Did you cross the parade route this morning?"

"Aye."

"Then you saw the lettering."

He nodded. "I told you I had friends in the Falls."

"It won't help you, Michael," she said desperately. "They'll only make an example of you. Somehow, you've got to convince these people to do nothing at all."

He lifted one eyebrow incredulously. "How shall I do that, Meggie? At the moment I'm a guest of the Crown."

"There must be some way you communicate. I'm quite sure nothing goes on in that prison without everyone on the streets knowing about it."

Michael leaned back in his chair and sighed. "Let's just manage today, shall we? You look as if y' could use a long holiday. Either that or one of those Irish coffees you've acquired a taste for."

Meghann leaned forward. Fierce hazel eyes locked with blue. "You must promise me, Michael. You must promise me that you will not allow your trial to become an excuse for killing."

He met her gaze steadily. She looked away first. "You've lost touch, Meghann," he said. "Otherwise y' wouldn't even suggest such a thing."

Before she could defend herself, the courtroom clerk stood and asked everyone to rise in anticipation of the entrance of His Honorable Lord Justice, Charles Flewelling. Flewelling walked into the room, adjusted his robes and sat down. Lifting his gavel, he brought it down hard. Jury selection had begun.

Two days later, Meghann looked down at her list of jurors. The sick feeling in her stomach had escalated to a severe ache. She'd used up all of her exceptions, and only three of the jurors were even remotely sympathetic to the nationalist cause. Two more were working-class Protestants from the Shankill. She'd tried everything she knew to expose their bias, but she hadn't been able to shake them from their neutral positions. There was a dentist from Lisburn, a teacher from the Malone Road and the wife of an investment banker. The remaining four were middle-class, professional Catholics living near the university. Meghann hadn't been able to discern their politics, but she had the distinct feeling they wouldn't be sympathetic to a bloke with an IRA blot on his past.

She closed her portfolio and rose. They were the best she could do. There was no way around it. "The defense is satisfied, my lord," she said crisply.

The judge turned to the prosecution. "Is the jury satisfactory, Mr. Cook?"

The chief prosecutor stood. "Quite satisfactory, my lord."

Justice Flewelling lifted his gavel and let it fall. "The jury stands. Jurors will remain on notice until requested to appear. Prosecution will begin their arguments at the voir dire hearing tomorrow. Court is recessed."

Michael leaned over and spoke into Meghann's ear. "What's happening?"

"A voir dire is a trial within a trial," she explained. "The judge will decide whether certain evidence is admissible. It could last a few days or several months as witnesses are questioned and cross-examined."

He smiled grimly. "In other words, a Diplock Court."

"In a manner of speaking," she admitted. "However, I believe it's our best chance."

The bailiff approached. Meghann held up her hand. "I need a moment more, please."

He hesitated. She flashed him a brilliant smile and he retreated to a position near the door.

"Precedent has already been set," she continued in her low, clear voice. "Paddy O'Meara's conviction was overturned completely because a portion of the evidence gathered against him was the result of duress. We're fortunate that this judge was the very man who overturned the evidence. He's a fair man, Michael. It won't be easy, but there's certainly a chance."

Light from the ceiling lamps caught the tiny flecks of white in his irises, turning them to blue ice. "If everyone tells the truth," he said softly.

She nodded. "If everyone tells the truth."

Meghann arrived at precisely quarter past eight the following morning, one hour before Michael's hearing was scheduled to begin. It was a practice she had acquired years ago primarily to settle her nerves and plan her presentation. Meghann understood the power of a first impression. Because this was a high court she was able to walk about freely with access to both the jury and the witness box.

She arranged her notes, pen and paper neatly on the dark wood table and looked around, measuring the distance from where she sat to the back of the courtroom. She stood and measured off the paces to the jury box, the witness stand, the table and back to the jury box. The room was empty, small by the Old Bailey standards. With more luck than she could hope to expect, an opening argument wouldn't be necessary. Most lawyers wouldn't bother preparing one until the hearing was settled. But Meghann was different.

Beneath her pragmatic exterior, hidden behind the polished sophistication of an English barrister's cloak and wig, lurked a soul formed by generations of Irish superstition. Her logic was simple Murphy's Law. To forego preparing an opening argument would be an act of confidence bordering on pride. Meghann, a child of St. Mary's Hall, had learned her lessons well. Pride was a sin and it came before a terrible fall. To prepare an argument and not use it was preferable to needing it and not having it. A bit of practice never hurt either.

Deliberately, she pitched her voice at a level that would reach the back yet not overpower the jurors in the front, and recited her opening argument. "Your Honor, my worthy colleagues, ladies and gentlemen of the jury. We are not here in this courtroom today to judge a man for the sins of his past. After all, who among us has not reproached himself for acts committed in the foolishness of youth? Would that we could call back those days of impetuous behavior, of reckless irresponsibility, of apologies not made and consciences not cleared."

She walked over to the jury box. "But, ladies and gentlemen of the jury, we cannot. Was Michael Devlin an ardent nationalist? Yes. How could he not be? Raised in the streets of West Belfast, what young man is not fed tales of revolution? Who, whether he is nationalist or loyalist, is not tempted by stories of heroism? Coupled with unpleasant choices such as immigration or unemployment, the young men of working-class Belfast are seduced into behavior not normally considered by children of other neighborhoods. This trial is not about a young man's mistakes. This trial is not about retribution."

She took a deep breath and walked back to the table where Michael would be seated. "Michael Devlin has long since realized the depravity and pointlessness of violence as a solution to the troubles of Northern Ireland. This trial, ladies and gentlemen, is not about Michael Devlin. This trial is about murder, the murder of a man respected by everyone in the nationalist community, a man considered by Michael Devlin and the Catholic population of the Six Counties to be the answer to the troubles in Northern Ireland. The evidence presented here will prove that Michael Devlin not only did not murder James Killingsworth but that his hopes for peace were dashed by the unfortunate demise of a man he admired greatly."

She stood for a moment, visualizing the jury, allowing the silence to expand, the words to sink in. Then she sat down and looked at the agenda for the morning. There would be no drama for the hearing. The judge was experienced, a man known for his ability to ignore histrionics and sift through the facts until he came to the clean, uncomplicated core of the issue. Meghann knew Charles Flewelling by reputation although she had never met him. He was a man who could not be influenced. She laced her fingers together. This case could very likely be the most difficult she had ever taken on.

Six hours later, Meghann watched the worst piece of theater she had ever witnessed and wondered why she had ever chosen the law as a profession. Torpedo-shaped bomb casings, sharp metal cuttings, nails and bolts littered the judge's dais. He lifted cynical eyes to the prosecution. "What is the purpose of this rubbish, Mr. Cook?"

The prosecutor pulled a Browning automatic from a bag and introduced it as evidence. "This, your lordship, is a gun recovered in the Republic. It is the gun that was used to kill Mr. Killingsworth and injure his daughter. This gun is the personal property of Michael Devlin."

A slender blond woman rose from her seat in the courtroom. Tears streamed down her face as she stumbled into the aisle and out the door. Meghann recognized her immediately. She was Pamela Killingsworth, the widow of the murder victim.

The judge leaned forward, his expression a mixture of contempt and rage. "Take this away immediately. I will not have such theatrics in my courtroom, do you understand, Mr. Cook?"

The prosecutor's face flamed with embarrassment. He obeyed the command instantly. "Yes, your lordship."

Meghann sighed with relief. There would be no cross-examination on this issue. She stood. "Your lordship, I call Michael Devlin to the witness box."

The tension was thick in the silent courtroom as Michael strode to the box. The bailiff swore him in. Meghann waited until he had settled into his seat and fixed his eyes on the judge as she had instructed him. "Mr. Devlin, please tell this court everything that happened to you at Castlereagh Interrogation center."

He detailed everything, in a voice as rich and smooth as French cream. Rarely had such a precise account of horror been told with such lyrical beauty. By the time he'd finished, more than a few in the public gallery had resorted to their handkerchiefs.

Meghann was not one of them. Deliberately, she kept her eyes on Michael's face until he'd finished. "Thank you, Mr. Devlin," she said before taking her seat.

Mr. Cook rose and buttoned his jacket. "You said that the police recorded your interrogation, Mr. Devlin?"

Michael's eyes never flickered. "That's correct."

The prosecutor looked smug. "But there are no electrical outlets in any of the cells, Mr. Devlin. Were the recorders battery operated?"

"No."

"On what power were the machines run, Mr. Devlin?"

"On electrical power."

Cook appealed to the judge. "I submit that Mr. Devlin is lying. There are no power outlets in the cells of Castlereagh. He has lied about his internment, he has lied about his interrogation and he has lied about his involvement in the murder of James Killingsworth."

The judge looked at Meghann. "Would you care to cross-examine, Miss McCarthy?"

Meghann flipped to the back of her portfolio and pulled out a grid. "I would like to submit a photo of the barracks at Castlereagh, your lordship. Every cell has two electrical points."

After a startled silence, the courtroom buzzed with conversation. "Enough." Charles Flewelling pounded his gavel. "Shame on you, Mr. Cook, for not giving this issue your personal attention."

Mr. Cook was nearly purple. "May I ask for a recess, your lordship?"

"You may not. Bring your next witness."

"I call Mr. Patrick O'Shea to the stand."

The bearded man with the massive shoulders and the bewildered expression looked faintly familiar, but

341

Meghann couldn't place him. She frowned and glanced at Michael. His face was unnaturally pale. "What is it?" she asked.

Michael leaned over and whispered into her ear. "Did you know about him?"

"His name is on the witness list. You said you didn't recognize the name."

"I didn't. But I do recognize him."

Frustrated, Meghann watched as the man was sworn in. His was a face that was easy to read and Meghann saw that he was not pleased with his position. He took a long time to settle comfortably. The prosecution approached the box. "State your name, age and place of birth."

"Patrick O'Shea, thirty-two, Donegal, Ireland."

Cook pointed to Michael. "Do you recognize that man?"

O'Shea narrowed his eyes and stared at Michael. "Aye."

"How do you know him?"

"Him and his wife was stayin' in Donegal for their holiday."

"When was that?"

"Spring it was, over a year ago, the twenty-second of April."

"How can you be sure of the exact date? After all, it was more than a year ago."

"My wife went int' labor that very night. After four girls, we had a son."

Cook handed the judge a piece of paper. "Let the evidence show that last spring Michael Devlin escaped from Long Kesh Prison and remained at large for nearly six weeks."

Meghann froze. Mr. Cook's next question came as if from a long distance. "Did he give you his name?"

The man shook his head. "Seems t' me he told it, but I don't remember."

"Do you remember his wife?"

Again the man nodded.

"Please speak up, sir, for the recorder."

"Aye." He pointed at Meghann. "She's right there beside him."

Mr. Cook placed another piece of paper before the judge. "Let the record show that the witness has pointed out Meghann McCarthy, counsel for the defendant, and that for the period of time between April 27 and May 23, Miss McCarthy was on extended holiday from her office."

Behind her, someone gasped. Miles French leaped to his feet. "Objection, your lordship. Miss McCarthy is not on trial here."

"Overruled."

"Permission to cross-examine?"

"You may do so, Mr. French."

Deliberately, Meghann willed her features into an expression of cool control. Somewhere deep within her, her blood pumped and her organs functioned normally while her mind recorded the unbelievable words spoken by the prosecutor. Beneath the soles of her shoes, the floor was hard and cold. Minutes passed. She concentrated on Miles French's next question.

He squared his shoulders. "Mr. O'Shea, are you absolutely certain that the woman you saw in Donegal was the woman you see before you? And if so," he continued before the man could respond, "will you tell the court what it is that is so distinctive about Miss McCarthy that you remember her after more than a year has passed? May I remind you that you are under oath, Mr. O'Shea, and that the penalties for perjury are severe."

O'Shea stared hard at Meghann. "Her hair is darker and she's thinner, but otherwise—"

"You've made an outrageous accusation, Mr. O'Shea, and now you tell the court that the woman's coloring and build are not even the same?"

The prosecutor leaped to his feet. "Objection, my lord. A woman's hair color may vary."

French waved his objection aside. "Yes, yes, Mr. Cook. Hair color may change, eye color may change, weight may change. Next we will hear that Miss McCarthy and this unknown woman were not even the same height."

"That will be all, Mr. French," broke in the judge. "Miss McCarthy, I am prepared to recess this court until tomorrow morning. Is that acceptable?"

"Quite acceptable, your lordship," Meghann replied crisply.

"Very well. Court is recessed until tomorrow at half past nine."

26

She smiled tenderly at the slight form huddled beneath the blankets. Even in the deep restorative sleep Nuala had forced upon her, Meghann clutched the locket as if it were a lifeline. And why not? It had never failed her before. It would not fail her now. Nuala would see to it. This young woman, born with a nature so serene, so capable of loving, who had already suffered such irreparable wounding, would suffer no more.

Nuala was determined that this time Meghann would find happiness. Otherwise, why would she have been called through the hazy portals of time to offer the guidance of the spirit world, guidance offered to a select few?

Placing her hand on Meghann's forehead, Nuala concentrated, sending the energy from her brain down through her arm and the tips of her fingers, setting in motion thoughts that would lead to a satisfactory conclusion to this muddle.

Meghann breathed more easily now, and there was a slight curve to the corners of her mouth. Nuala nodded and stepped back. Unconsciously she rubbed away the strange feeling beneath her eyelids and then stopped in amazement. She was Nuala O'Donnell of Tirconnaill and she was very near to weeping.

Michael looked across the visitor's table at his mother and smiled bracingly. "Don't look like that, Ma. It will come about."

Annie fidgeted with her handkerchief. "What about Meggie?"

"Mr. French handled it well. Meggie won't be harmed."

"Will it be enough, do y' think?"

Michael nodded. "Meghann's firm, Thorndike and Sutton, trained her well."

Alerted by the change in his voice, Annie tightened the grip on her purse. Why had he emphasized the name *Thorndike and Sutton?* She knew the name of Meggie's firm. Carefully she listened as Michael continued his conversation. Was there anything important that she was missing?

Suddenly he reached out and gripped her by the arms. Startled, she allowed him to pull her halfway across the table where he kissed her full on the mouth. Annie nearly gagged as he forced a small wad of paper past her lips with his tongue.

She maneuvered the wad into the side of her cheek and wiped her mouth. "I'll be leavin' now, Mick," she whispered.

He nodded. "Good-bye, Ma."

Annie emptied her pockets and submitted to the pat-down without comment. A woman guard rifled through her purse and handed it back to her. Without a word to anyone, she climbed on the bus, yawned with her hand over her mouth and stared out the window. Only after she was safely inside her own home with the bathroom door shut did she unfold the ball of paper, slip on her glasses and read the tiny print.

Breathing deeply, she shredded the note into pieces and dropped it into the toilet where she watched it flush away. Then she walked into the sitting room and called Connor at the *An Phoblacht* news office, amazed at the normalcy of her words and the cleverness of her excuse. "I'm not feelin' well, Connor. Will you stop by the grocer and bring home some soup?" She had never bought canned soup in her life. Connor would know something was up.

He was home before she could change her dress. Quickly, she relayed Michael's message, leaving nothing out. Connor listened to his mother, whistled softly and walked out the door to carry out his brother's plan.

The courtroom was filled to capacity. Charles Flewelling walked to his chair with a menacing scowl. Meghann busied herself with the papers before her, avoiding his eye. She knew the prosecution had scored valuable points yesterday, but for some reason it seemed less threatening in the light of a new morning. She planned to move forward as if nothing had happened, performing her role with such cool professionalism that the idea of Meghann McCarthy aiding an escaped prisoner was unthinkable.

The bailiff stood. "Court is in session," he announced.

Over the rim of his glasses, the judge looked pointedly at Meghann. "Is the defense prepared to begin?"

"Yes, my lord," Meghann said.

Miles French interrupted smoothly. "My lord, after yesterday's testimony, the defense would like to call a new witness, Mr. Cecil Thorndike, to the stand."

"So added, Mr. French."

Beside her Michael tensed. Meghann's eyes widened as the door opened and Cecil took his position in the witness box. The words of the oath and Cecil's response floated past her ears. What was he doing here, and why had Miles called him without consulting her?

"Please state your name, your position and your relationship with Meghann McCarthy."

"Cecil Thorndike, partner in the law firm Thorndike and Sutton. Lady Sutton was a colleague and partner at Thorndike and Sutton."

"How long have you known her?"

"Nearly ten years."

"Describe your perceptions of Lady Sutton, Mr. Thorndike."

Cecil cleared his throat and looked directly at Meghann. His cheeks were very pink. "Meghann is a barrister of excellent repute, conscientious, competent and devoted to her clients."

Miles changed the subject. "Do you recall the evening of April 22, Mr. Thorndike?"

"I do."

Meghann closed her eyes. Cecil wouldn't lie. What in bloody hell was Miles doing to her? Under the table, Michael's hand found hers and squeezed briefly.

"Tell the court what you remember, Mr. Thorndike."

"Meghann had been feeling unwell for several days," Cecil began. "I was concerned and dropped around to check on her." The clipped Oxford English sounded so legitimate. No one would ever believe that the scenes he called up were fabrications. "She told me she was thinking of leaving Thorndike and Sutton. Naturally, I was shocked. I argued with her quite strongly before leaving."

"Why do you remember the specific date, Mr. Thorndike?"

Cecil looked incredulous. "Never, in the history of the firm, has a partner chosen to leave Thorndike and Sutton. It is a date I am not likely to forget, Mr. French."

"Thank you, Mr. Thorndike." Miles sat down.

Meghann schooled her expression into one of polite interest. Every muscle ached and her eyes burned with the effort. Cecil Thorndike, an uninspiring barrister with only a modicum of intelligence, had saved her at great risk to himself. Cecil, a man she had silently ridiculed, had made the journey from London, most likely against his father's wishes, to defend her in a terrible lie. How would he hold up against the prosecution? Meghann looked down at her hands and prayed.

"I have no questions for the witness."

She looked up in surprise. Mr. Cook sounded reluctant, as if he hadn't meant to say what he had. He was staring at Cecil, a bewildered expression on his face. All at once Meghann understood. Despite his credentials and his blue suit, Ian Cook was working-class Irish. Cecil, in his expensive double-breasted suit, tailored shirt and immaculate shoes, was English aristocracy. It didn't matter that Cook was twice the lawyer, with a brain that if pitted against Cecil's in another courtroom would leave it gasping in the dust. Cook was shanty Irish and Cecil was a gentleman. That was enough to give one man credibility and the other an inferiority complex.

"You may step down, Mr. Thorndike," said the judge.

"Thank you, my lord."

Beside her, Meghann heard Michael release his breath. She watched as he turned, found his mother in the second row and smiled.

The hearing was nearly over. The prosecution entered the name of one more witness, Andrew Maguire, the hero of Catholic Belfast. Charles Flewelling would not be susceptible to the IRA leader's charm but if Maguire's story was in direct contradiction to Michael's, Meghann knew Flewelling would have no recourse but to take the case to trial. Unless she could prove Maguire had ulterior motives, his word would stand over Michael's.

Mr. Cook rose. "I would like to call Andrew Maguire to the witness box."

Maguire, in a brown suit that exposed too much wrist, took the stand to be sworn in.

"State your name, address and occupation, please."

"Andrew Maguire, 63 Kashmir Place, Belfast. I'm a barman at Keneally's pub."

"Do you know the defendant?"

"I do."

"In what capacity?"

"We met twenty years ago at—" He broke off, his sentence unfinished.

Meghann heard the squeaking hinges that signaled the opening of the courtroom door. She would not have looked around but for Maguire's reaction. He was unable to continue. The color drained from his face, leaving it leeched and doughy.

Confused, Meghann turned. Framed in the doorway, making no move to take a seat, was Georgiana Reddington. She was dressed in the tight bell-bottomed jeans and leather jacket that had been her statement twenty years before. Her eyes, fixed on Andrew Maguire's face, held no warmth. She stood there for a full minute absorbing the curious stares from the crowded room.

Meghann turned back to Andrew. His color was still bad but his control had returned. "Michael Devlin and I grew up in the Falls. The community is a small one. Everyone knows everyone else."

"Was your relationship distinguished by anything else?" Mr. Cook asked.

"We are both nationalists and members of Sinn Fein."

Mr. Cook was clearly frustrated. "Is there another organization of which Mr. Devlin is a member?"

A hush filled the room. Andrew looked at Michael. Their glances met and locked. Meghann sucked in her breath and laced her fingers together. Somewhere behind her a clock ticked, one minute, two.

"Would you like the question repeated, Mr. Maguire?"

"No." The word was expelled in a rush of breath. "I am unaware of any other organization to which Michael Devlin belongs."

Ian Cook was furious. "You are under oath, Mr. Maguire. I will rephrase. Is Michael Devlin a member of an illegal organization?"

"None that I am aware of."

The prosecutor hovered over his witness. "Did you not tell me in your own words that Michael Devlin was a member of the Irish Republican Army?"

Meghann stood. "Objection, my lord. Counsel is badgering the witness. After all, Mr. Maguire is a witness *for* the prosecution."

Flewelling's eyebrows rose. "Quite right. Objection sustained. Rephrase the question, Mr. Cook."

Ian Cook was breathing heavily. "No, thank you, my lord. I have no further questions."

Meghann turned once again to look at the door. Georgiana was gone.

The judge interrupted. "Will the defense cross-examine?"

"No, my lord," Meghann answered. "The defense rests."

"You are excused, Mr. Maguire."

Flewelling rose. "Court is adjourned until tomorrow morning. All parties will report back here at nine o'clock for my decision."

Michael's brow wrinkled as he watched Meghann

slide her notes into her briefcase. "Who was that woman?"

"What woman?" she asked innocently.

"The blond who castrated Maguire on the witness stand."

Meghann sighed. "It's a long story, Michael. Tomorrow, when this is over I'll explain it all to you." She frowned. "Did you have anything to do with bringing Cecil here?"

He grinned. "Tomorrow we'll both have a story or two to tell. Are you up t' it?"

She laughed, liked the way it made her feel, and laughed again. "I can't think of anything I'd rather do than listen to you tell a story."

He leaned over and whispered into her ear. "Given enough time, I could come up with something even better."

If the courtroom were empty and Miles French not less than two feet away staring curiously at the two of them, she would have wrapped her arms around his waist and buried her face in his shoulder. Instead she mumbled under her breath. "I'm sure you could."

"Where did you get the woman?" Miles asked as they walked together to the carpark.

Meghann told him. She had nothing to lose. "Andrew Maguire was going to lie. I used Georgiana O'Conor to blackmail him into telling the truth."

Miles stared at her incredulously. "That's all? Surely there's more to it than that."

Meghann pressed the button on the remote, unlocked her car and threw her briefcase into the back. Folding her arms across her chest, she leaned against the door and surveyed the man before her. "I don't know what you did, Miles, but I must warn you. Don't ever take a risk like the one you took with Cecil Thornkike again. You'll lose your reputation and your career."

He looked down at his shoes. "If I were you I'd worry about my own career."

Meghann's eyes narrowed. "Why don't you tell me what's really going on."

Miles met her accusing glare. "You don't want to know."

"Let me guess," she said quietly. "Michael was set up by the British government. The same British government who publicly refuses to consort with terrorists has one hand in the IRA's pocket. How else could Andrew Maguire have offered Michael a lesser sentence if I dropped out of his defense and allowed you to take over as lead counsel?"

She was bitterly, coldly angry. Sunlight reflected off the sideview mirror, bathing her face in a golden glow. Miles wondered why he'd never noticed that hint of green behind the whiskey-gold of her eyes. Suddenly, she looked very Irish. "Let it go, Meghann," he said softly.

"Who did it, Miles? Who decided that James Killingsworth was too liberal to be prime minister of England? Who decided that he was a threat to the status quo in Northern Ireland and that an innocent man should go down for his murder? Tell me, Miles. It had to be someone powerful enough to make the rules."

"Don't do this, Meghann. You'll only endanger yourself."

She could hardly bear to look at him, but she had to know. "It didn't turn out the way you expected, did it? Will you be slapped on the wrist because you didn't know about Georgiana and because Cecil turned out to be decent?"

Miles rubbed the sole of his right shoe over the pavement. "You're a very intelligent woman, Meghann, but you're only half right. I'm not your villain. I was told from the beginning how this case was supposed to turn out. It was all arranged. That's all I knew. I believed Michael was guilty. I would have gone along with the plan until I realized they were out to get you too. You surprised everyone by stepping in and taking over the defense. Because you couldn't be controlled, they wanted to do much more than discredit you. They wanted to charge you with aiding an escaped convict. I couldn't go along with that and still live with myself. Michael knew what was happening long before I did. He sent for Thorndike, counting on the man's devotion to you."

She stared at him for a long moment, noting the flush staining his face and the way his eyes met hers, steadily, honestly. He had a conscience but she couldn't like him, not after what he tried to do to Michael. "It appears I owe you an apology," she said stiffly, "and a thank you."

"It isn't necessary." He hesitated.

"Go on."

"I think you should consider leaving England. There won't be much for you here anymore."

Her face was very still and she looked somewhere over his shoulder. "Perhaps you're right. Good-bye, Miles."

He watched her drive away. Something about the way she said good-bye alerted his instincts. Meghann McCarthy was brilliant in the courtroom and out, one of those rare attorneys who went the extra mile and verified every piece of information that came across her desk. It would be a shame if she gave up the law for good. His thoughts flew back to the courtroom and the way the two of them had looked at each other before Michael was taken back to his cell. Miles shrugged. It was late. If he hurried, Finchley's pub would still be serving bar meals.

The house she'd rented was a narrow Georgian structure located on a tree-lined street at the end of

Lisburn Road. It wasn't as elegant as her London flat, but it was charming and comfortable. Meghann felt more at home in Belfast than she ever had in London.

She poured boiling water into the teapot, arranged a plate of cheese and crackers, a pitcher of milk, sugar and a cup and saucer on the tray and carried it into the sitting room. A bay window overlooked the park. Meghann set the tray on a side table and curled up in the window seat. Slowly, her hand inched up to the locket at her throat. She resisted, reaching for her tea instead. "After all," she said to herself, "I can't rely on you forever. It's nearly over. I won't need you anymore."

"That's true."

Meghann jerked, nearly upsetting her tea. "You can't be here. I'm wide awake and I never touched the locket."

Nuala sat down on the floor and clasped her knees. She looked very tired. "The locket won't help you anymore, Meghann. My time here is over, my purpose served. Michael will go free. 'Tis up to the two of you to decide how the rest of your lives will turn out."

She sat silently, absorbed in her own thoughts. Meghann, filled with questions, did not interrupt. Finally Nuala shook herself and asked, "What is it that you're always drinking?"

Meghann looked down in surprise. "Why, it's tea. Don't tell me you've never had it."

"No, never. Describe it to me."

Meghann lifted it to her lips and sipped slowly. How did one describe tea? "It's hot," she began, "but not too hot. I've added sugar and milk to make it sweet and ease the bitterness. It has an herbal flavor and it's quite comforting."

Nuala nodded. "You've done well. It sounds wonderful."

Meghann set down her cup. "Will I see the end of your story?"

"Aye. But first I must prepare you. We've grown close, you and I. Not every story has a happy ending."

"Will you tell me why you came to me?"

"You already know why. I came to help you save Michael Devlin."

Meghann shook her head. "Martyrs have died in the name of Irish freedom for centuries. Why did you choose Michael to save?"

Nuala's eyes misted over and she looked somewhere beyond Meghann to another time. "On our way to Rome, Rory and I made a child, a daughter. When she was grown, Rory sent her back to Ireland to wed the McCarthy Reagh of Kilbrittain. Niall's son also grew. Generations passed. Bloodlines mixed." She sighed and focused the power of her green gaze on Meghann. "I never knew either of my children, but I know you and I know Michael, children of my children's children. You have brought me great pleasure and even greater pride. I thank you for that."

Meghann could barely see through her tears. Without thinking, she reached for Nuala's hand. When she touched human flesh, she stared in surprise.

Nuala smiled. "It happens sometimes."

"I want to see the rest of your story, Nuala. May I see it now, please?"

"My story is finished, love, but I'll tell you a bit of Rory's. His lasted longer than mine. Will that do?"

Meghann nodded and watched the expressions flicker across Nuala's face.

Her name was Chiara and her every feature and limb was the image of me, from the brilliant green of her eyes to the flame-red fall of her hair. Rory didn't want to love her. I think he was afraid of loving anyone again and that was his reason for remaining distant. But from the beginning she stalked him, throwing herself into his arms, running across the marbled floors of the palace I had worked so hard to make beautiful before my time in this mortal world was finished, leaving him alone with the flame-lit child created in my own image.

It was very hard in those early years watching my husband reject the child he should have adored. Then came the day he wished to be alone to ride the boundaries of his estate, a dry land that made those of Irish descent dream of silver lakes and pelting rain.

Chiara would have none of it. She was barely three, a red-haired tyrant with every servant in the palace under her thumb. She stamped her foot, spat out hurtful words and threw herself on the ground at his feet, sobbing as if her heart would break.

Rory watched until her tears must have smote his heart, for he picked her up and set her in the saddle before him. To her credit she did not once complain on that silent ride. During those hours he came to know something of this child we made together.

The O'Neill came once to Rome, took one look at his granddaughter and crossed himself. "'Tis the spirit of Nuala, Rory," he said. "Can you not see it in her? Look at her hands, her face, the way she speaks. God help you. You must send her to Ireland for a husband. This land where the sun weakens the mind and muscle does not spawn men strong enough to tame the woman she will become."

I think it was then, at that very moment, that Rory realized the gift he had been given. This child of light and laughter was as close to me as anyone would ever be.

And so he and Chiara became inseparable. Her mind was sharp and her heart a warm and forgiving one. He would tell her of me and of the children we had lost. One day he even told her of the half-brother he had forced me to give up.

Her small chin quivered. He saw the tears in his

daughter's eyes and was ashamed. But she crawled into his lap, rested her head upon his shoulder and forgave him.

She was nineteen when he sent her to Ireland to her grandsire, the O'Neill of Tyrone. It was another year still before she became the bride of the McCarthy Reagh. It was a love match, she assured him, and Rory was content. For he knew that of all people, Chiara, like her mother, was a woman meant for loving.

Crumlin Courthouse, Belfast, 1995

The public gallery was filled to capacity. The judge arrived in his long black coat. "All rise," the bailiff said.

Meghann stood automatically and sat down again. She was very anxious for this to be over.

Justice Flewelling did not mince words. "This trial was a travesty, a waste of this court's valuable time. Not only is the evidence linking Michael Devlin with the murder of James Killingsworth sketchy at best, but it was scurrilously obtained. I am not satisfied that Mr. Devlin was not assaulted, and the Crown has failed to exclude the possibility that the assault was inhuman and degrading. I repeat what Lord Lowry, the Lord Chief Justice, observed in *Regina versus Hetherington:* 'Our criminal law demands that not only the evidence but the means of obtaining it be above suspicion.' Mr. Devlin, you are free to go, and this court apologizes for your inconvenience."

Michael looked at Meghann in disbelief. She was not so reticent. Throwing her arms around his neck, she kissed him full on the mouth. "I love you," she said before stepping back to allow his family to surround him.

27

Hilyard, Maine, six months later

Michael dusted the snow from his shoulders, opened
the door, stepped inside and wiped his feet. He hung
up his jacket and walked toward the warmth and
tempting smells coming from the kitchen. The blond
wood floors gleamed with wax and care. Frost rimmed
the windows, and the scent of lemon mingled with
onion, pot roast, cinnamon and sage. Engulfed in an
enormous apron, Meghann stood at the stove stirring
with the same concentration she gave to her studies.

"Smells delicious," he said.

She smiled and turned to see him framed in the
doorway. "It's pot roast on top of the stove instead of
inside. How was it today?"

"It was grand, Meggie. I like teaching. Every one of
the boys has a fine mind."

She smiled doubtfully.

"What's wrong?"

"It's just that they seem hard to handle." She wiped
her hands on her apron, lowered the flame and
crossed the floor to where Michael stood. Slipping her
arms around his neck, she pressed her lips against his

cheek for a quick kiss. "I don't understand why you want to teach hoodlums when there are students out there who really want to be in school."

He measured her waist with his hands, taking pleasure in the added inches. "They're not hoodlums, love, just boys who've lost their direction. Besides, we need the income, especially now. Have you been out today?"

"I have. Winter is beautiful here," she admitted.

"The loveliest place outside the Glens of Antrim."

"I'm afraid for you."

He found her mouth and kissed her lingeringly. "Don't be. I grew up in Belfast, remember? The only difference between them and me is a purpose."

She sighed and rested against him. "I wish the hours weren't so long."

"I thought you needed the time to study."

Meghann shrugged and pulled away. "Help me set the table."

He removed two plates from the cupboard. "At lunch I stopped in at the library to read the *Belfast Telegram*. The IRA has admitted to the murder of James Killingsworth."

Meghann frowned. "I suppose the truth would be too much to expect. What will happen to everyone who believes their motives are pure?"

"Someday it will end, the killing will stop, and then the real work will begin. A way of life has grown up around the Troubles. Peace will only be the first step."

She sighed. "We're a long way from home, Michael. There's nothing in the local paper at all."

"Aye. Meanwhile, I like it here, Meggie. There's something to be said for water that comes from the tap at just the right temperature."

"What a wonderful reason to emigrate from all you love and know," she teased.

"Americans are a friendly sort, especially to the Irish."

Meghann carried the salad bowl to the table, wondering, not for the first time, how Michael could be so unaware of his personal appeal. She was profoundly grateful that he had taken a position at a boys' correctional facility instead of a girls'.

After the food was dished out and they had taken their places, she resumed their conversation. "I'm not so interested in studying law anymore. There really isn't much point. I won't be practicing for a long time."

"That's up to you," Michael said reasonably. "Is something bothering you, Meggie?"

She shook her head, avoiding his eyes.

Michael looked at her, a worried frown forming on his forehead. When they finished eating, he cleared their plates, walked back to the table and held out his hand. She took it and followed him into their cozy family room. He pulled her down into his lap and she curled around him, fitting herself to his relaxed length with the ease of familiarity.

"You never told me about the woman who scared Andrew Maguire into silence," he said after he'd kissed and caressed her into a contented doze.

"Yes, I did," she murmured.

"Not completely. Only her name and her relationship with Andrew."

Meghann hesitated. "I don't know if I should tell you everything. Maybe Georgiana wouldn't want me to."

"Keep her confidence, love. It isn't important."

"On the other hand, she doesn't keep anything from her husband."

Michael waited for Meghann to finish arguing with herself. It didn't take long.

"I told you they were lovers," she began. "What I didn't tell you was that Andrew was married when Georgiana got pregnant. She told him and he insisted on an abortion. He didn't have any money, and she'd gone through her allowance for the year." Meghann swallowed and rubbed her rounded stomach, uncomfortable with the role she'd played in the drama. "I gave her the money from my supplement and went with her to have it done. From then on Andrew avoided her completely. It broke Georgiana's heart."

"The bastard." A white line had formed around Michael's lips. He splayed his hands protectively over the bulge of her stomach. "Saint Andrew of Belfast. I imagine he couldn't very well allow his image t' be spoiled, not even if it meant murderin' one of his own. No wonder he was terrified when she showed up in the courtroom. Poor lass."

"She's happy now, Michael, really. She has a lovely family."

The tight look disappeared from Michael's face. "Now will y' tell me what's bothering you?"

Meghann twisted her hands nervously. "Do you really like it here away from your home and family?"

"My family is here."

"What about Ireland?" she burst out. "Can you turn your back on it the way we have and watch what's happening from thousands of miles away? Don't you miss it, Michael, the talk in the pubs, the people you grew up with, Davie and Connor and Bernadette and Annie?"

"It sounds as if *you* miss it."

She shook her head. "I'm the one who lived in England for eighteen years. I'm asking you the same questions you once asked me."

"Why?"

"I don't want you to resent me for making you turn your back on Ireland."

Michael reached out and played with a wisp of auburn hair that curled below the lobe of her ear. "I haven't turned my back on Ireland, Meghann. I'm reevaluating, that's all. A child does that sometimes, makes a man reevaluate his priorities. I want t' be a good parent, and revolutionaries don't make good parents. Y' haven't forced me into anything." He grinned. "If I remember correctly I had to convince you that it was time t' have a baby."

"You aren't disappointed that she's a girl?"

"Lord, Meggie, what makes you think that?"

She shrugged. "Men always want sons."

"Not this one." He rested his hand on her stomach. "I grew up with seven brothers and a sister. Bernadette was always my favorite until you came along."

Meghann released her breath. "Promise me you'll tell me if you ever want to go home."

"I promise." He tilted her chin up, forcing her to look at him. "Is there anything else?"

"You won't believe me."

Under his hand he felt the child flutter. Meghann's eyes glowed gold like liquid sherry in her lightly freckled face and her hair was now the deep russet of her youth. His golden girl had given him a life he'd only dreamed of. "Trust me," he said gently.

"I miss—" She hesitated.

"Yes?"

"I miss . . . my mother."

He frowned, perplexed. Meghann had never mentioned her mother, not in all the years since her death.

"I suppose that's natural with the baby coming."

"She's not my mother exactly—"

He waited and still she didn't speak. "Meghann, unless you explain yourself I can't help you."

She struggled to find the right words to explain. "All my life I've had someone with me. Ever since Cupar Street. She's taken care of me. I saw her in my dreams and sometimes even when I was awake. I felt her, but I didn't know who she was until just recently, during your time in prison and your hearing. She saved us, Michael. She told me what to do. But now she's gone and I miss her. I feel orphaned all over again."

A log snapped in the fireplace. The room was sinfully warm and Meghann felt delicious in his lap. He tightened his arms. His head slipped to her shoulder

"You don't believe me."

The glow disappeared and his head snapped to its original position. "I didn't say that."

"You didn't say anything."

He sighed. Pregnant women were highly emotional. He would tread carefully. "Who am I not to believe you, Meghann? The Irish are a superstitious people. Our entire history is based on legend and myth. I can't say that what you believe isn't true."

"Her name was Nuala O'Donnell. We talked about her in Donegal. Remember?"

He did, vaguely. "Aye."

"She's my ancestor and yours, too. Remember the night we left Victoria Hospital? I told you that Nuala O'Donnell had given me a way around the checkpoints and you told me she'd died hundreds of years ago and that there was no longer a Tirconnaill."

Now he did remember and the Celtic part of him, the part that had given him his love of literature and his gift for language, sat up and took notice. "Why has she left you?"

"Her story ended. She died and you were saved. I think she believes that I don't need her anymore."

"Do you?"

"Perhaps not," Meghann confessed.

"'Tis the natural way of things," he said gently, "to have your parents pass on." Again he rubbed her stomach. "Soon we'll be parents ourselves. I wonder if I'm old enough."

Meghann laughed. "I should hope so. If you aren't now, you won't ever be. Besides, it's too late."

"I wouldn't take it back for all the world, Meg, my love. If someone had told me three years ago that we'd be here, together, like this, I'd never have believed him." He brushed the hair back from her temple and kissed the spot reverently. "You gave up everything to start fresh with a wayward lad like myself. Not many are so lucky." He grinned. "Come now. Cheer up. I even have a name for the lass."

"What is it?"

"Chiara. 'Tis an old family name. Do y' like it?"

Meghann looked into the brilliant blue of her husband's eyes. "I love it," she said. "It's the most beautiful name in the world."

He bent his head and breathed in the scent of her hair. Later, when the time was right, when she was curled around him in that enormous American bed, he'd tell her about the book contract, a book about the streets of Ireland where they'd grown up, a book unlike any other he'd written. He'd tell her about the way the words came to him more easily than they ever had and about what never would have been if she hadn't walked back into his life, demanding that he accept what she had to offer, making him fall in love with her all over again.

Author's Note

Northern Ireland is a country of soft rain, gray mist, turbulent clouds and long winter nights. This cold and sometimes bleak setting is home to the wittiest, warmest, most hospitable population on earth. Ask an Irishman for directions or the time of day and you'll be sharing afternoon tea and some *craic* in front of a cozy turf fire. Ask for parking change and he'll dig into his pocket to find what you need or he'll walk to the nearest news agent or off-license to make sure you find the way. Ask a waitress for her opinion on a menu item and she'll sit down beside you while you eat to be sure you're pleased or else she'll take the food away and bring back something else, no charge, of course.

Poverty, revolution, emigration, famine and subjugation have molded the Irish into people of great character, great loyalty and great tenacity. For centuries the native Irish have fought, starved, died and buried their children, refusing to give up their religion, their culture, their language and their principles.

Unlike the Scots and the Welsh, who also have a history of English resistance, only the Irish fought on into the present century to win their independence, their own republic, a complete separation from the British state with the exception of the Six Counties of Northern Ireland, a partition formed in 1921 to satisfy a small minority of the population who wished to remain British.

Ulster, the ancient name of the original nine counties of Northern Ireland, was the last Catholic enclave to surrender to Elizabeth Tudor in 1607. It is in Ulster where Irish history and Irish legend come together. Emain Macha, Deirdre of the Sorrows, King Conor, The Warriors of the Red Branch, Cuchulain, Red Hugh O'Neill and Red Hugh O'Donnell are not only heroes of Ireland, they are heroes of Ulster.

I have taken tremendous liberties with Irish history. Nuala O'Donnell was not one person, but several people. There was a Nuala O'Donnell married to the first Red Hugh O'Donnell who commissioned the writing of *The Annals of the Four Masters* in the fourteenth century. She was an O'Brien. Another Nuala, married to Niall Garv O'Donnell, sailed for Rome with Red Hugh O'Neill and his family after his exile.

The Rory O'Donnell of my story was really Red Hugh O'Donnell, and he was bound by friendship and marriage to his father-in-law, the O'Neill featured in *Irish Lady*. He died in Spain, probably of food poisoning, after the Battle of Kinsale. Rory O'Donnell was a distant cousin who played a less significant role in the fight against English invasion.

Red Hugh O'Neill, known as the Great O'Neill, was a thorn in Elizabeth Tudor's side for decades. She lived to see him defeated but never subdued.

Bernadette Devlin, a Catholic from mid-Ulster, was the youngest MP in the history of Westminster. Her relationship to the Devlin family in my story is pure fiction. Meghann McCarthy and Michael Devlin do not exist outside of this book.

AUTHOR'S NOTE

Internment, the holding of suspected terrorists without trial in Northern Ireland, no longer exists. It was used in 1922, 1939, 1956 and 1971–75. The hunger strikes of the early eighties, resulting in the deaths of thirteen prisoners, including Bobby Sands, gave political prisoners privileges denied to those convicted of other crimes. Among these were the right to wear their own clothing, the right to freely associate with each other at all hours and exemptions from all types of penal labor.

Diplock Courts and torture as a means of securing confessions from suspected terrorists were exposed by Amnesty International in 1978. Ninety percent of all Diplock convictions were found to be the result of confessions signed under such conditions.

The conflict in Northern Ireland is not, nor has it ever been, a religious war. It began as a power struggle between Catholic Spain and Protestant England over dominion of Europe. In a country of huge unemployment, insufficient housing and a population whose average citizen is under twenty-five years of age, it is still a power struggle between those who wish to keep what they have and those who would like to share a limited amount of resources and wealth.

Ireland was England's first colony, and Northern Ireland may very well be her last. But there is no doubt in the hearts and minds of those who strive for self-determination that one day it will all be "sorted out" and everyone, Catholic and Protestant, will be the better for it.

Glossary

craic   conversation, fun

the Falls   Catholic Area of Belfast

Fenian   derogatory name for an Irish person, from the Fenian nationalists of the nineteenth century

Long Kesh (The Maze)   British prison where political prisoners are housed

marching season   weeks surrounding July 12; parade season commemorating the Battle of the Boyne, King William's victory over Catholic King James; a time of tension and violence in the North

Orange Order   founded in 1795 to preserve Protestant supremacy and links with Britain; no Catholics or those with Catholic relatives may be members

peelers   police

RUC (Royal Ulster Constabulary)   Six County Police Force

GLOSSARY

SAS (Special Air Services)   elite undercover unit of British Army trained to shoot to kill

screws   prison guards

the Shankill   Protestant area of Belfast

Sinn Fein   nationalist political party

Taig   derogatory name for a nationalist

UDA   Protestant paramilitary organization